20/4/22
9/9/22

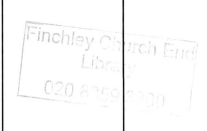
Please return/renew this item by the
last date shown to avoid a charge.
Books may also be renewed by phone
and Internet. May not be renewed if
required by another reader.
www.libraries.barnet.gov.uk

LONDON BOROUGH

ALSO BY LEIGH RUSSELL

BOOKS PUBLISHED BY BLOODHOUND BOOKS

The Adulterer's Wife

≈

Suspicion

≈

Rachel's Story

For Michael

'There is no greater sorrow than to recall happiness in times of misery.'
— **Dante Alighieri**

'The history of the world is inexplicable without Jewish history.'
— **Sir Simon Schama**

A NOTE TO READERS

From pogroms ordered by Ivan the Terrible, to the pivotal Battle of Lepanto, and the witch craze that spread throughout Europe in the wake of the Spanish Inquisition, all the events that form the backdrop to Abigail's story are historically accurate.

With the exception of Jacob Mantino, Henriette d'Encausse and Marco Antonio Giustiniani, the named residents of the ghettoes are fictitious. Almost all other named characters existed, from the Popes of Rome and the Dukes of Venice, known as Doges, to Prince Joseph Nasi and the courtesan Veronica Franco. They have been extensively researched and are portrayed as accurately as possible.

1

The year 5322, corresponding to the Christian year 1562

One afternoon my mother came rushing into our home, a rare smile lighting up her face. She nodded at my father before turning to me.

'Come with me, Abigail,' she said. 'Put on your shawl and your best smile.' She looked me up and down and sighed. 'Stand up straight, and wipe the dust from your shoes.'

'Where are we going?'

She paused for a second before announcing that we were going to see Jehudit.

'Does Abigail not possess a clean gown?' my father wheezed, as he heaved himself from his chair.

My threadbare skirt bore stains from the forest floor where I foraged for food with my little sisters. Some days we were fortunate and filled our pockets with nuts, but sometimes we returned with only a few withered berries, or a handful of fallen acorns which our mother would soak in water.

'Sit down at once, Saul,' my mother cried out, seeing my father on his feet. 'You are too sick to walk all the way there.'

'I am coming with you,' he replied with unaccustomed firmness. 'A visit to the matchmaker is too important to be left to women.'

My mother spat on a rag and wiped my face roughly. Ignoring my protests, she rubbed my cheeks until they felt sore. 'Good,' she said. 'You look less pasty now.'

By the time we set off, my initial burst of excitement had given way to trepidation. Of all the girls of my age in the ghetto, I alone was not yet matched, although my face was pleasing enough, and my body, though slender, was sturdy. Raised to walk in the path of righteousness, I would be a virtuous wife. Marriage was a blessing for which I had prayed dutifully, but now the time had arrived, fear threatened to overwhelm me. I was not ready to leave my home, austere though it was, and the thought of being separated from my parents and my little sisters filled me with unspeakable sorrow.

As I followed my parents along narrow shady streets of the ghetto, I thought about the other girls in our community who were of marriageable age. None of us had been surprised when Jael was the first of our class to be betrothed, since her father was a physician with the means to support the family of a scholar. As soon as she bled, Jael would accompany her mother to the ritual baths before standing under the wedding canopy beside the youngest son of the Rabbi, who was destined to follow his father's calling.

Rizpah was another of my friends who had been betrothed from an early age. She was a good-natured girl with a plain face; everyone knew that her father had given a generous dowry to his daughter's bridegroom, the son of a physician from Krakow.

My friends were happy with their future husbands, but I

scarcely dared to hope for an agreeable match. Since my father had fallen sick, he had been unable to sit long at his cobbler's bench, and we survived on the charity of our congregation. Although my friends assured me I was good-looking, no man had ever shown the slightest interest in me when I went to the synagogue each day to study. My beauty, it seemed, pleased only my girlfriends. My virtue, on the other hand, was irreproachable. I studied every morning, and attended synagogue three times a day, sitting upstairs with the other women while the Rabbi conducted prayers downstairs, with the men.

As we approached the matchmaker's lodgings my heart pounded in my chest, not with eager anticipation but with fear. Like my friends, I wished for a husband who was not only well off and a learned scholar, but also young and handsome. Realistically, such an outcome was unlikely for me. A man able to take a mendicant's daughter for a wife must himself be prosperous, yet such a man would hardly choose to marry a pauper; even a man of means will seek to augment his own fortune.

In addition to my faith that my virtue could not go unrewarded, I knew that my mother and father cared about me. They would never agree to a match against my wishes. Yet despite my trust in my parents, and my determination to obey them, I approached Jehudit's door with foreboding. Whatever happened, I vowed to do my best to embrace my fate, confident that Hashem would not choose a path of suffering for me.

My mother knocked at the door, which was opened by the matchmaker, an ancient crone with a hunched back and black hairs sprouting on her upper lip. Jael had once told me Jehudit had buried five husbands, but I was sceptical, since it was well known that the matchmaker had no children.

'If she was barren, why did her husbands not divorce her?' I asked.

'They could not,' Jael replied, lowering her voice confidentially. 'Jehudit has magic powers. She knows how to enchant a man so he can never leave his wife. She's going to share her secret with me when I am married.'

Her expression earnest, she exhorted me not to breathe a word of what she had told me to anyone else.

'Is her magic forbidden?' I asked.

'Probably, but even if it is allowed, my parents will be furious if they discover I have promised the old woman a gold ring in exchange for her instruction.'

It was hard to believe five men had been willing to marry Jehudit, when it had been difficult for me to find even one. Grinning and rubbing her hands together, the old woman ushered us into a room that smelt of musk and spices. Jehudit lowered herself onto a stool with a faint groan, and gestured at a wooden bench.

'Sit,' she wheezed, placing her gnarled hands on her knees. 'Saul, the chair.'

My father sat on one of two chairs, while I took my place beside my mother on a rickety wooden bench which rocked every time one of us shifted. I kept as still as possible, afraid my mother would complain if I fidgeted. Jehudit studied me in silence for a moment, nodding her ancient head and making a curious sucking sound through her teeth. Without a word, she struggled to her feet and came over to me. Reaching out with her claw like hands, she pinched my cheeks. Not until I squealed in protest did she desist.

'I have found a young man for you,' she declared, as she shuffled back to her stool.

I glanced at my mother, who was staring at her feet, twisting her hands in her lap. Although she had never said that she would miss me, I realised this must be painful for her too. Resolving to be cheerful for my mother's sake, I smiled at Jehudit, forcing my eyes not to dwell wistfully on a pitcher of wine that was giving off a rich and piquant aroma.

'Tell me about my future husband,' I begged her. 'Is he a scholar?'

'Oh yes,' the old woman replied promptly. 'He is a scholar, to be sure. And he is an upright man, Hashem be praised.' She drew in a breath before continuing in a wheedling tone of voice. 'It was not easy to find a husband for you, my child, but Hashem has answered my prayers.'

She broke off as her front door slammed shut, followed by the sound of heavy footsteps. Keeping my eyes modestly lowered, I saw a pair of large feet encased in boots of fine leather, and felt a tremor of consternation in the presence of a stranger. Raising my eyes, I glanced at my prospective father-in-law. He had a bald head, a bushy moustache and beard, and a large dark mole on the right side of his nose. Older yet more vigorous than my father, he seemed gruff and belligerent. I cringed at the prospect of living under his roof after my marriage to his son, but that was inevitable. Certainly my husband could not sleep in my parents' one room, with my sisters.

Jehudit plied the stranger with sweetened wine while she praised my virtue. I kept my eyes lowered and wondered about the man whose bed I was to share. Hopefully my husband did not resemble his father. Perhaps my bridegroom was a scholar, too dedicated to his studies to drag himself away from the holy books to meet his future bride. My studious nature was well known, and it made sense that our teacher would have recommended me for such a match. Perhaps the Rabbi himself had suggested the union. That was a pleasing thought. I loved to study, and had often fantasised about becoming a scribe.

Women were forbidden to participate in such work, but my husband might permit me to study at his side, learning to write the prayers for myself. Comforting though my musings were, the woman in me would have preferred to see my future husband in the flesh before our betrothal, but one look at my mother's hopeful expression dispelled my selfish desire.

My father held his head upright, his narrow shoulders flung back, as he gazed at the stranger with a kind of desperate pride.

'We are a poor family but–' my father began.

Jehudit silenced my father with a commanding gesture before refilling the stranger's goblet. My mother fixed her eyes on me, mutely pleading with me to please my prospective father-in-law. The stranger glanced at me for only a moment before barking at me to stand up. I obeyed, keeping my eyes modestly lowered. He must have given a sign of some sort, because my father spoke again.

'Jehudit has advised you of our misfortune,' he muttered. 'My infirmity prevents me from working, and I have five daughters to feed and clothe.'

'I do what little I can, watching loaves in the communal bakery,' my mother added in a low voice.

'We are reduced to accepting charity from the communal funds,' my father murmured, stooping once more under the weight of his humiliation. 'So you understand there can be no dowry.'

'Abigail is a righteous and submissive girl, and she will make an excellent wife.' Jehudit barely paused to draw breath. 'She can cook and sew and she has raised four younger sisters. She is diligent and virtuous, and you can see for yourself how beautiful she is.'

My face grew hot at her extravagant praise.

'I have brought you a young virgin raised with four sisters. She is a true innocent who knows nothing of men. Her father, as you can see, is a sick man. You must bear in mind that what you see now is not her true beauty. She has been brought up in penury. Her parents cannot afford to feed her. They have five daughters all living on the charity of the community. Many a time Abigail has selflessly gone without supper to ensure there was enough food to sustain her younger sisters. But with a prosperous husband like yourself, she will blossom into a magnificent young woman such as most men can only dream of possessing. With a little feeding she will soon grow plump, for all that she is barely more than skin and bones now.'

'And she will eat so much that my prosperity will be frittered away,' the bald man replied in a rumbling voice.

'How much can a young girl eat?' Jehudit replied quickly. 'Abigail is renowned for her frugality. She makes and mends–'

'I will feed her, and that is all,' my prospective father-in-law interrupted her. 'There will be no hangers-on in this match. Her sisters may starve for all I care. I am here for a wife, not a whole family. Her relations will get no special charity from me.'

'That is a reasonable request,' Jehudit said, with a fawning smile.

'It is not a request, you imbecile,' the stranger replied.

The man's speech shocked me, but Jehudit did not appear to be troubled by his boorish manners. My sisters and I had been taught to be polite at all times and, in spite of our impoverished circumstances, we had been brought up to appreciate the blessing of giving to others.

'However poor we may be, there is always someone whose need is greater than ours,' my mother used to tell us. 'Hashem remembers our good deeds.'

Jehudit's eyes flicked towards me and she pressed her lips together, as though warning me to remain silent. 'You need only to pay me before you leave, and the girl is promised to you,' she gabbled, turning back to the bald man.

'Very well,' he replied, 'I will pay you half of your exorbitant fee, witch.'

I trembled to hear him call Jehudit a witch. Admittedly she lived alone, and women were condemned as witches for less than that, but Jehudit was a widow who attended the synagogue regularly and she was respected in the community. My parents would not have brought me to the house of a witch, of that I was sure. All the same, I glanced uneasily at the old woman, and wondered by whose favour she had lived so long. Jael had told me about Jehudit's magic powers. Perhaps they were a gift from the devil.

'Let us hope for her sake the girl proves worth the money,' the man said, stirring in his seat and drawing a pouch from his shirt.

He dropped a few silver coins into Jehudit's outstretched palm, and held out his goblet to be refilled.

'So, it is concluded.' Jehudit turned to my father. 'Praise be to Hashem, you have a wonderful match for your eldest daughter, a prosperous groom and a generous one.'

'Please,' I piped up, and all four of them turned to stare at me, as though surprised at the sound of my voice. 'When will I meet my future husband?'

Mumbling under her breath, Jehudit scowled at my prospective father-in-law with a calculating look in her eyes, while her gnarled fingers clutched at the pocket in her skirts where she had slipped the silver coins. My mother looked as though she might burst into tears, and my father glared furiously at me. No one uttered a word, yet still the truth eluded me.

Suddenly the bald man laughed, a raucous sound that did not soften the coldness in his eyes. 'An innocent indeed,' he spluttered, draining his goblet and wiping his lips on his sleeve. 'And a simpleton.' He spat on the floor. 'She will suit me well.'

My parents exchanged a glance, clearly relieved that the stranger had not been angered by my words, and Jehudit relaxed her grip on her pocket, satisfied at the conclusion of her transaction. But I was dumb with horror. The man who had been discussing me as though I were a fowl he might purchase and fatten for his table, was my future husband.

2

Overnight our household became cheerful. Only once did I dare to raise my concerns with my mother.

'What would happen to me if I never married?' I asked her.

She glared at me and I sensed, rather than saw, her fear. 'You would end up living alone, surviving on roots and berries from the forest, and the charity of the community. Your father and I have long prayed for a better future for you, my child, and our prayers have been answered. You will be a blessing to us in our old age. Hashem has given you a husband who can afford a physician for your father. Praise be to Hashem, the Most Holy, for his mercy and goodness.'

Considering my future husband had unreservedly refused to support my family, I was afraid my mother's optimism was misplaced, but I could not bring myself to disappoint her. So preparations were made for the wedding, which was to take place as soon as possible. The day before the ceremony the fire in our lodgings was lit for cooking, making it unbearably warm in our two rooms. The sun beat down on the closely packed buildings in our street, until the air itself seemed too listless to move. Even leaving the door open made no difference. Heedless of the heat, my mother bustled about, fashioning pie crust out of ground oats, to which she added acorns that my sisters and I had gathered in the forest, while I chopped goose skin to bake inside the pies.

When we were not busy preparing food for the wedding guests, my mother and I stitched dresses for my little sisters, while they chattered eagerly. My fingers flew over the fabric, and I concentrated all my attention on making the stitching as neat as possible. I had always enjoyed sewing, and it was a relief to think about something other than my future husband.

'If only you had been a son,' my mother said, as she admired my handiwork with a shake of her head.

It was not the first time she had lamented the fact that I was a daughter. A son could have assisted my ailing father in making and mending shoes. As a girl I was not considered strong enough for the work and besides, my mother was convinced that no man would want to marry a cobbler's assistant.

'It will ruin your hands, and you will look old while you are yet too young to bear children,' she said when I offered to help my father at his trade.

Unaware of my misgivings, my younger sisters were wildly excited about the wedding.

'I'm going to have a new dress, aren't I, mama?' Keturah exclaimed, whirling around in our cramped room. 'And we're going to have music and marzipan and we'll dance and dance and dance.'

'Yes, child,' my mother replied, 'you shall have a new Sabbath dress for Abigail's wedding. We cannot afford marzipan, but your father has ordered a special sweetmeat for our guests.'

'And we can eat it, can't we?' Keturah pleaded.

'Yes, we will all share in Abigail's good fortune.'

My mother did not often have cause to smile. As for Keturah, she was too young to understand that her new dress would be a cast-off from a neighbouring family.

'And can I have ribbons in my hair?' she asked. 'Long ribbons, all different colours?'

She swung her head making her hair sway behind her. My mother laughed, but my father chastised my sister for her vanity.

'Leave her be, Saul,' my mother said. 'She is still a child.'

'She is nearly nine,' he replied. 'In a few years she will be a bride herself. It is time she began to think about growing up.'

'A girl cannot grow up by thinking about it,' I muttered under my breath.

'Come and help me, Abigail,' my mother said. 'The vegetables for the soup won't prepare themselves. And wipe that sullen look off your face,' she added under her breath as I joined her. 'This is a time to be joyful. Hashem has blessed you with a fine husband.'

My sister was irrepressible. 'But I can have ribbons in my hair, can't I, Mother?' she said hopping from one foot to the other and jumping up and down. 'Father didn't say I couldn't have ribbons, did he? Can they be yellow and pink?'

My thirteenth year was half over. Outwardly I was a woman, yet inside I felt like a frightened child. The following day I would be married to a man who had terrified me on the one occasion we had met. He had visited me in nightmares ever since, until I was afraid he might be a dybbuk, a malevolent spirit, sent to haunt me in my sleep.

My father lay down to sleep and my mother looked up from stirring the broth. 'Abigail,' she scolded me impatiently, 'you must look cheerful tomorrow. You are marrying a prosperous man.'

'Were you cheerful when you married my father?'

She smiled fondly at some private memory. 'It was the happiest day of my life.'

'My father was not a prosperous man when you married him, but a poor cobbler. Would you have preferred a rich husband you could not care for? Would such a man have made you cheerful?'

'Enough of your nonsense,' my mother snapped. 'You must learn to be grateful for the good fortune Hashem has granted you in sending you a prosperous husband.'

'If I hear my future husband referred to as prosperous one more time, I shall refuse to marry him!' I cried out in a fury of disappointment at her refusal to listen to me. 'What is the benefit in my husband being prosperous if he is prepared to see my parents and sisters starve before he will spend even a small part of his fortune to feed them? Mother, those were not the words of a righteous man.'

'Be patient, my child,' she said. 'As his wife, you will be able to soften his heart. Did Hashem not soften Pharaoh's heart in Egypt? Put your trust in Hashem and for all our sakes, look cheerful at your wedding.'

'How can I rejoice, knowing I am to marry a man who is selfish and avaricious, and–'

'Enough!' my mother cried out. Soup splashed my gown as she slammed her ladle down in the pot, her cheeks flushing with choler. Agitated, she glanced over at my father, but he had not stirred.

'You will never repeat such brazen sentiments in your father's presence,' she hissed. 'Jehudit has found you a husband. We will speak no more of this, and tomorrow you will stand under the wedding canopy with the man to whom you are promised, and you will be content.'

'A rich husband is not necessarily a good one,' I muttered.

'I said enough!'

My father opened his eyes. 'What is the matter, Rebeka?'

'Your daughter is as nervous on the eve of her wedding as I was the day before we were married, my dear,' my mother replied, forcing a smile. She resumed stirring the soup, and I was silent.

'Reuven ben Yitzhak will look after you,' my father assured me. 'You will never go to bed hungry again, my child.'

But he turned to face the wall and did not look at me as he spoke. He must have known, as I did, that there is a hunger that goes beyond our physical needs.

The following morning I rose early to prepare myself. After visiting the ritual bath, I dressed in a gown borrowed from a neighbour.

'You look beautiful,' my mother said, standing back to admire me, with tears in her eyes.

Clean and well dressed for perhaps the first time in my life, I scowled. 'But it's not my gown, is it?' I replied unkindly. 'And this should not be my wedding.'

As we walked to the synagogue, I tried not to think about leaving my home to live with a stranger. At least I would not starve, and I trusted Hashem would give me strength to endure the adversity with which He had chosen to afflict me. The synagogue was packed when I was led around my husband seven times while the Rabbi recited the seven blessings. I saw my husband's face indistinctly through my veil, and prayed Hashem would forgive me for my wicked thoughts: I wished there was a different man standing beneath the canopy with me, a young man who would be kind to me and my family.

When the Rabbi spoke solemnly of the blessing of the love between a man and a woman, I trembled. For his part, my groom went through the entire ceremony with every appearance of grim stoicism. He did not once glance at me, but kept his eyes fixed straight ahead. Several times he yawned, as though he found the ceremony tiresome. It was demeaning to think that the identity of his bride scarcely mattered to him.

Hashem sent no miracle to release me. Unless Hashem relented and moved my husband to divorce me, I would be tied to Reuven ben Yitzhak for the rest of my life. Quietly I stood at my husband's side with a smile fixed on my face. We were a married couple joined together in the sight of the congregation and, more importantly, in the sight of Hashem, yet we were strangers who had not yet exchanged a single kind word. Possibly we never would. The rest of the day passed in a haze as I struggled to control my tears, determined not to shame my parents.

The wedding supper was lavish, but I could not swallow a morsel of soft goose flesh cured in salt or chopped carp seasoned with sugar and pepper, or any of the other delicacies that Reuven had provided. My parents had been as generous as their scanty purse allowed. My mother had scurried off to the communal oven very early that morning to bake large meat pies for the wedding guests. Her pie crusts were the best I had ever tasted, yet I overheard Reuven complain that they were more pie than meat, and her pastry tasted of mouldy acorns. Noticing my chagrin, my mother shook her head, and whispered to me to ignore him.

'All men are louts when they drink too much wine,' she muttered uneasily.

Gazing around the assembled company, I did not hear anyone else insulting my mother's hospitality. Besides, it was well known that our Rabbi was partial to the sweet kosher wine we drank on the Sabbath. He had been intoxicated at more than one celebration, yet he was never discourteous, however riotous he became. I felt a wave of self-pity as I sat, a smile plastered on my face, trapped in marriage to a man who belittled my mother's efforts in front of the whole congregation.

'There is nothing but gristle and rotten acorns in this pie,' my husband roared in his stentorian voice. 'This does not bode well for my marriage. I hope my wife's cooking is better than her mother's.'

I quaked at his words.

'Stop bellyaching, Reuven,' my Uncle Abraham called out.

My uncle's back was bowed as though his head was too heavy for his neck, and his eyes were lifeless, like those of a man who had suffered great sorrow. Nevertheless he was tall and broad-shouldered, and gave the impression that he would not tolerate trouble. I was grateful for his intervention.

'With a belly as large as Reuven's, he'll have an ache big enough for ten men,' a neighbour replied with a chuckle.

Only one man did not join in the laughter. The watching congregation fell silent as he rose to his feet and raised a massive fist in the air, his broad face ruddy with choler.

'I've thrashed better men than you!' he shouted, his voice slurred.

'It was a joke,' the other man protested. 'Just a joke.'

'I don't see anyone laughing,' my husband bellowed.

'Lighten up, Reuven,' my uncle urged him, taking him by the arm. 'Come, man, it's your wedding. Is that not cause enough to celebrate? Relax, enjoy yourself. You have a beautiful young bride, barely thirteen.'

There was a faint murmur among the women. It was not unusual for girls to marry as young as twelve, but I was slim and some of them probably judged my body was not yet ready for the marriage bed. I had heard them muttering that Jehudit had been too eager to offer a match for me, and my father had been too quick to accept.

When no one could eat any more, my mother handed round thin slabs of dough that had been placed between hot iron moulds, which she explained was a new delicacy called waffles.

'Eat, eat,' she urged the guests, beaming. 'This is my daughter's wedding day. Her father had the baker make them specially. These waffles are very fashionable in France.'

'Nothing more than flour and water, insufficiently sweetened with honey,' my new husband grunted.

He spat a mouthful of dough onto the table, and dismissed the confection with a wave of his hand. Keen to flaunt his wealth in front of the congregation, if not in private, my new husband provided a gigantic cake made of sugar, ground almonds, spices and flour.

'Such extravagance! You could have asked him for a wedding gift,' my mother muttered to my father.

'Be silent and eat,' my father replied, although he was probably thinking the same.

The wedding feast concluded with a dish of macaroni fried with honey, butter, cream cheese and cinnamon. Gazing around the table at my family looking so happy, I felt a spasm of remorse for having begrudged them this moment of joy. But I was paying a high price for their fleeting happiness.

Before the prayers after food, my father rose to his feet and raised his glass. 'I wish you many happy years together, and may you be worthy of so righteous a wife.'

'I will do my duty,' my husband replied, thrusting his hand up my skirt and pinching my thigh until I yelped in pain. 'I know how to lie with a woman. Let no man say otherwise.'

My father sat down abruptly.

As she rearranged my skirt when I stood up, my mother whispered to me, 'Jehudit tells me your husband is shy with women. She said things will be better once Hashem has blessed you with children.'

I turned away to hide my bitterness, wondering what kind of life my children would endure, the issue of a loveless match. 'He does not care for me,' I murmured.

'Why would he marry you, if you don't please him? There was an agreement.'

'Made by my father.'

'But your husband could have refused, as could you.'

'Refused to obey my father? You think so? When we have no food on the table?'

'My child, when did you become so sour? I don't understand you.'

I turned away from her, unsure whether I understood myself.

3

Everyone else seemed to be enjoying the festivities, and I did my best to appear cheerful for fear of upsetting a husband who barely even glanced at me. Every time I looked at him, he had a glass of wine in his huge hand, and it was not long before his face grew hot and flushed with drink. The music grew ever more riotous, and I saw him beat time on the table, although he never smiled. A taborer tapped out a rapid tattoo on his drum while a piper played a lively melody and fiddlers vied to play ever louder and more wildly. Guests who did not join in the dancing tapped their feet and smiled as others whirled around.

A wedding was a joyous affair in our community. In a life filled with pain and drudgery, overshadowed by the fear of our enemies, we seized on any opportunity to celebrate. Unmarried young people, segregated for the wedding feast, danced together modestly, holding kerchiefs to prevent any risk of physical contact. Girls dressed in their Sabbath finery cavorted self-consciously, their eyes flitting around the room to see who was watching, while a circle of young men danced vigorously to the fiddler's tunes, stamping their feet and racing around faster and faster in increasingly wild circles.

Stoically I watched entertainments that had amused me at my friends' nuptials: tumblers contorting their bodies, jugglers performing deft feats, and dancers who spun and crouched and kicked while balancing bottles on their heads. Only my little sisters' joy on the occasion of my wedding made me smile, and for a few moments I forgot my own tribulations, witnessing their merriment.

Jehudit hobbled over to me to offer her congratulations. 'Your groom may seem cantankerous,' she hissed, sitting down beside me, 'but be comforted. You are married to a man capable of great passion. He was devoted to his first wife, and will cleave to you, I have no doubt of it.'

'What about his second wife?' I asked.

The old woman patted my hand, her fingers hard and stringy, like the chicken feet my mother boiled to make broth for my father to give him strength. Mumbling a blessing, she clambered to her feet and shuffled away, leaving me alone in a room full of people celebrating my wedding.

All too soon, the party drew to a close. Too nervous to eat, I had barely tasted a morsel all day. Now I was hungry, yet I dared not complain. Despite his own foul temper, I was certain my husband would not tolerate ill humour in his bride. My head felt light with hunger, which exacerbated my misery. Picking up my light bundle of clothes, I followed my husband in silence from the synagogue across the central square of the ghetto and along unfamiliar streets. My status as a new bride troubled me; not only was I intimidated by my husband's ill humour, but I had no idea what was expected of me on our wedding night. The prospect of lying beside his gross sweaty body, stinking of ale, made me feel nauseous. My mother had made little attempt to prepare me for sharing my bed with a stranger.

'It's like sliding a finger into a glove,' Jael had told me, giggling.

'Or like slipping your leg into your hose,' Rizpah added, nudging Jael and sniggering.

Thanking my friends, I had turned away to hide my bewilderment.

'Your place is to obey your husband,' had been my mother's only advice. 'You don't need to know anything else. Your husband will do the rest. Has he not buried two wives before you, and did they not both bear him children?'

'Children who all died,' I said.

'That is beside the point. Your husband knows what to do to give you children. Your duty is to submit. That is the will of Hashem, and may your union be blessed with many children to tend you in your old age, as you will care for me.'

It was not clear to me why Hashem in his great loving kindness and compassion had chosen a man nearly thirty years older than me to be my husband. Doing my best to ignore my pangs of hunger, I followed my husband along dark streets until we were nearly at the far wall of the ghetto. For a few moments I panicked, fearing that he would lead me right out of the ghetto. I had never set foot in the streets beyond the walls, leaving the safety of the ghetto only through a concealed gap in the wall that led directly into the forest, where my sisters and I foraged for food.

Reuven did not take me out through the gate, but to a low wooden hut on the outskirts of the ghetto. The dwelling was even smaller than my parents' lodging, just one room with a small bed and a fireplace. A single chair stood at a dirty table.

'We do not have guests,' my husband growled. 'Your family are not welcome here.' He grabbed a besom from the corner of the room and thrust it at me. 'Clean up this mess. Hashem did not create us to live like animals.'

Even if you are one, I thought, with a flash of anger.

It was hardly my fault the hovel was dirty. Perhaps hunger loosened my tongue, but the injustice of the situation felt intolerable. 'I am in my wedding gown,' I protested. 'Surely sweeping the floor can wait until tomorrow, Reuven?'

I smiled at him, in imitation of my friend Jael's winsome manners. My attempt to cajole him failed miserably. He raised his hand and slapped my face. 'Don't ever let me hear my name on your lips again.'

Too shocked to remonstrate, I took the besom from him and began to sweep. Turning his back on me, my husband relieved himself on a heap of soiled rushes in the corner of the room. In my parents' house, we had used a bucket which we emptied daily and I had never visited a house where the residents pissed on the floor. Although I did my best to control my distress, tears slid down my cheeks.

'Cease that blubbing,' my husband growled.

I bit my lip until the salty tang of blood filled my mouth, and prayed to Hashem to give me strength to endure the affliction He had sent me.

'What the hell is wrong with you?' Reuven snarled. A trickle of saliva dribbled from the edge of his slack lips to disappear among the bristles on his chin. I lowered my gaze and stared at the soiled rushes.

'Nothing's wrong, nothing at all,' I stammered, struggling to conceal my distress.

My husband grunted and pulled off his shirt. The sight of his burly arms and barrel chest filled me with dread.

'I am content,' I heard myself lie. 'What would you have me do?'

As he took a step towards me, I noticed a shred of meat lodged between his front teeth, and smelled his breath, heavy with a foul odour of grease and onions and wine.

'What are you pulling that face for?' he demanded as I took an involuntary step away from him. His broad face flushed with anger, and he clenched his huge fists. Before I realised what was happening, he flattened his hand and swiped at me a second time. The slap beside my ear was so loud, the noise startled me even more than the pain of the impact. As I staggered backwards, he lunged at me and grabbed me by the throat, gripping me so strongly I feared he intended to suffocate me. It flashed across my mind that he had already buried two wives.

As I struggled to breathe, he shoved me roughly, causing me to stumble, striking my shoulder on the wall as I fell to my knees. Ignoring my weeping, he hoisted me up bodily and threw me on the hard bed. His rough fingers fumbled as he pulled at my gown. Caught beneath me, my skirt did not lift up easily over my trembling legs. Frustrated, he clawed at it, ripping the fabric all the way down the front. I wept for my torn gown, and the raw pain between my legs where it felt as though my flesh was burning inside my body. At last he let out a curious grunt and rolled off me, pushing me to the floor. A few moments later he was snoring and I was able to release my pent-up terror in silent weeping.

All that night I lay awake, trembling, fearful that he would awake and repeat his assault on my body, but the wine had quietened his humours and he slept until dawn. Hashem who sees our most hidden desires, forgive me for my prayers that night. I prayed my husband would never wake. I wondered how my mother bore the torment of the marriage bed. Yet I had watched her lovingly tend to my father throughout his sickness.

'Leave off your fussing,' he would say. 'Far better for you if I die and you are free to take another husband, a man who can take care of you as you deserve.'

His words had distressed my mother. 'I want no husband but you,' she would insist, with tears streaming down her cheeks.

'Do not say such things to me, my husband. With Hashem's help, you will recover from this sickness, so let us not speak of your dying again. I pray that Hashem will write you in the Book of Life for many years to come. How would I live without you?'

My friend, Jael, had recently stood under the wedding canopy beside the Rabbi's youngest son. When we met in the synagogue she beamed when she spoke of her husband who, according to her, was the kindest, bravest, and most learned man in all the world. She had always been one to exaggerate, yet I truly believed she was satisfied with her husband. It did not seem possible that every other married woman had joined a conspiracy of silence about their wedding nights, vowing never to reveal the horror of the marriage bed to single girls. It had to be my own misfortune that Hashem had chosen a difficult path in life for me with a man who enjoyed seeing me suffer.

I had done nothing to deserve such torment. The Holy Book of Exodus taught us that Hashem punished children for their father's sins: 'For I the Lord your God am a jealous God, visiting the iniquity of the fathers upon the sons to the third and fourth generation of those that hate me, and showing mercy to thousands of those that love Me and keep My commandments.' My father was a righteous man who had surely never committed a sinful act in his life, but he had been struck down with sickness. I wondered if the clue to our plight lay in the words: 'The third and fourth generation.' Perhaps my father's father, or his father before him, had transgressed, and my own misery was part of my own father's punishment. His sickness was of the body. My own affliction was hidden, but no less painful to endure. Only prayers could help me now.

On the morning after our wedding night, my husband ordered me to rise. Every time I moved, the pain between my legs pierced me as if the blade of a dagger was stabbing me below my belly, but I was too frightened to disobey his command. Painfully I clambered to my feet. Looking down, I was shocked to see that my legs were soiled and stained with blood.

'You must summon a physician,' I stammered, seeing how badly he had injured me.

'Why?' he replied, barely glancing at me as I cowered in the corner, clasping my shawl around me to hide my nakedness. 'Are you sick of me already?'

'No, husband, but can you not see that I am bleeding?' I opened my shawl a little to show him the trail of dried blood running down the inside of my leg.

He shook his head and yanked the linen off the bed. Rolling it up, he turned to me.

'Did your mother teach you nothing? Is it possible you are such an ignorant fool? Do you not know it is the will of Hashem that a woman bleeds the first time she lies with a man? How else is he to know she is pure? I will take this to a friend of mine who will clean it for us, since my wife is clearly too grand to dirty her fingers on such a task.'

'I can do it, my husband,' I answered humbly.

If he would let me go out and wash our linen, I might meet my mother, or my sisters, down by the river. Seeing them would make me feel less isolated in my new situation, although I had no intention of ever confessing my wretchedness to them. To my dismay, my husband walked around the bed and snatched my shawl from me, leaving me to cover my nakedness with my hands. Adding it to the bundle he was holding, he left the house without another word. My relief at his departure was soon followed by despair. Sobbing, I pulled on my drab everyday gown and sank to the floor, alone and hungry. I longed to run home to my parents, but that path was closed to me.

My husband knew that without my yellow shawl I could not leave our hut. Even within the confines of our ghetto, Jewish women were forbidden to set foot in the street without the badge of their identity. Were I to be apprehended walking around without my shawl, a fine would be imposed. If it was not paid, I might face prison. I had no money of my own and now that I had a husband with the means to take responsibility for me, the ghetto funds would not be available to help me, as they were for the poor of the congregation. I was not confident my husband would be willing to pay the fine and, even if he did, I suspected he would make me suffer for my transgression afterwards. All I could do was remain in the house until my husband returned my shawl.

After some time, I recovered sufficiently to raise myself from the floor. Seated at the table, I drew some threads from my old gown and attempted to repair my wedding gown, but a task that could have been accomplished in a few hours with a needle and a decent length of thread proved impossible without them. The day passed. Hunger gnawed at my guts so that I was even pleased to see my husband again. He looked well fed, and stank of vomit.

'I am hungry,' I stammered, too ravenous to fear his violence.

He drew a hunk of bread from his shirt and handed it to me without a word.

After a few weeks my anger faded into a dull despair, and I stopped fantasising about walking out of the house and trusting in Hashem to protect me, not only from the law, but also from the monster I had married. Eventually I persuaded my husband to bring me a needle and some thread, by which time I had become effectively inured to my captivity. But my wedding gown suggested to me a way I could at least visit my mother. If she saw how I was suffering, she might allow me to return to her.

'I need to return this to my mother,' I told my husband, holding up my mended wedding gown. 'She borrowed it from a neighbour, who will want it back.'

'You can give it to your mother at the synagogue,' he replied shortly.

Biting my lip to conceal my excitement, I stammered that I would need my shawl.

'You will have a shawl,' he said. True to his word, the next evening my husband returned home with a yellow shawl and a grey gown.

'I have never worn a new gown before,' I said, thanking my husband for the clothes.

It was raining lightly and the garments were damp.

'You may light a fire and hang them up to dry,' he told me, not unkindly. 'Soon we will go to the synagogue together.' He paused, examining me closely. 'There has been talk that you are never seen. Look glad, wife, that the prying gossips may see that all is well with you.'

'Yes, my husband.'

It was less than a month since my wedding, but I felt as though years had passed since I had seen my family. Pulling on the gown and placing the yellow shawl over my head and shoulders, I resolved to say nothing against my husband for fear it might be repeated in his hearing. The fabric was soft and smelled fresh, but the gown was several sizes too large for me and hung loosely on my body. After carefully wrapping my shawl around my arms so that my sleeves did not slip easily up my arms and reveal my bruises, I scurried along the darkening streets of the ghetto, behind my husband. Before we entered the synagogue he assured me that he would be waiting for me at the foot of the stairs at the conclusion of the service. On his lips, the words sounded like a threat.

4

My mother shifted along the bench and threw me a shrewish glance as I took my place beside her, clutching my shawl around my arms. She looked even paler than I remembered, as though all the colour had been bleached from her face. Leaning towards me until our heads touched, she whispered under her breath so my sisters would not hear.

'Why don't you visit us? Are you ashamed of your mother and father, now you have a prosperous husband? We hoped you would share your provisions with us, but we have not received so much as a crumb fallen from your table.'

My throat seemed to close up and I shook my head helplessly. It seemed there could be no way to appease her without betraying the truth about my husband, who barely allowed me enough food to keep myself alive, and forbade me to leave the hovel where we lived.

'Have you forgotten us? Are we to be strangers, my child?' My mother's indignation was clear in her blazing eyes, although her voice was quiet. 'I don't even know where you live.'

'Better you don't,' I murmured.

'Is your husband kind to you?' she asked in a gentler tone, grasping my hand in her skinny one and gazing earnestly at me.

Somehow she had penetrated my mask of composure and glimpsed the truth.

'He is good to me,' I lied, blinking back my tears.

My mother's eyes narrowed in suspicion, but before she could reply the Rabbi began the evening service. Only when we stood up to honour the Holy Scrolls did I realise that she was still holding my hand. I glanced at her, but her eyes were closed. The synagogue was the only place where she could ever relax, confident that the worshippers downstairs would notice if my father felt faint or dizzy. Gently I disentangled my fingers from her clasp but she did not stir. She seemed oblivious to my movement, and I realised she was asleep standing upright. When we sat down her eyelids flickered and she sank onto her seat with a faint sigh, but she did not wake up.

Focusing my attention on the communal prayers, I added a few of my own, hoping that Hashem might hear me more clearly in the house of prayer. Like most of the congregation, I recited the regular prayers from memory, prompted by the Rabbi. Some of the older men in the congregation clutched Soncino prayer books from Salonika, while wealthier men had books that had been printed more recently in the Republic of Venice. I had never held a book in my hands, and I snatched furtive glances at them, filled with awe and longing.

Soothed by the repetition of familiar prayers, gradually my resentment at the injustice of my mother's accusation faded. Observing her pallor and her gaunt features, I could only guess at the desperation that had driven her to agree to my marriage. Certainly my parents must have welcomed having one fewer daughter to feed, and if their own dire circumstances had compelled them to wilfully close their eyes to the truth, surely they deserved my pity not my hatred. As the service went on, I realised that their foreknowledge or ignorance of my husband's character made no difference to me now. Whatever had gone before, I was tied to him and had no choice but to endure my fate. Reciting the communal prayers I knew that my trust in Hashem must remain steadfast. He would protect me, my rock and my shield.

All at once, the Rabbi's chanting was interrupted by an unexpected clamour. Raising the curtain that hung behind the metal lattice shielding the women's gallery from view, I craned my neck and peered down into the prayer hall. Other women were doing the same. Below us, a bedraggled man was limping towards the bimah, the dais on which the Rabbi stood at his lectern. The stranger was pale, and his clothes were filthy and torn. It was not unusual for vagrants to visit our ghetto, along with respectable merchants and other travellers from Russian Principalities to the north and east, Lithuania in the west, and Belarus in the south. What was shocking on this occasion was that the stranger interrupted our worship. Without a word of explanation, he began to lament and beat his chest, rending his shirt as a sign of bereavement.

The Rabbi cast a stern look around the congregation before speaking gently to the newcomer. 'What is it that troubles you, my friend? You may speak freely. You are welcome here, and Hashem will bless us for comforting you in your sorrow. But first, let us conclude our service.'

He turned away from the man to resume the ritual prayers.

'I have travelled for many days to seek refuge here in the ghetto,' the stranger cried out in a wild voice, dashing tears from his eyes. 'I no longer know what day it is or how long has passed since I left my home.' His voice rose in a wail. 'I have no home.'

A faint sigh rippled along the row of listening women. We all knew how the stranger's story would end, before he had even begun his account.

'Be silent for the Rabbi,' the stout baker scolded him.

Other voices were quick to join in, reprimanding the stranger for the disturbance. I could not see all the men who were calling out to the vagrant to hold his tongue. My father might have been one of them, but his seat was below the women's gallery and hidden from me.

The Rabbi turned and raised his hand and the discontented murmuring petered out. 'What is your name and where are you from?' he asked the stranger.

'Rabbi, what about our prayers?' the butcher demanded.

The Rabbi responded mildly, 'Are we not commanded to show compassion to our fellow man? Do you pray to walk in the paths of righteousness only to ignore another man's suffering?'

He turned back to the stranger who fell to his knees, weeping.

'Do not kneel before me, but tell us what has happened,' the Rabbi said.

'Rabbi,' he replied, clambering to his feet, 'my name is Ya'akov ben Mordecai and I come from the village of Cekenai in the Duchy of Lithuania. My grandparents settled in our village nearly seventy years ago, along with others escaping persecution in Spain. Many moved north to the town of Lvov, but a few families remained in Cekenai. Until a week ago there were barely thirty of us living quietly there in four houses. We were no threat to anyone. Every week we took vegetables and eggs to the market in Lvov, and so we lived peaceably off the land, paying our rent and saying our prayers.'

Ya'akov paused, and tears dribbled down his unshaven cheeks. He was shivering, although it was not cold in the synagogue. Someone ran forward and placed a cloak around his shoulders, and he resumed his tale.

'A gang of ruffians burst into our house one evening, while we were eating our Sabbath meal. Our assailants were not from

Cekenai, but came from the town. They invaded our homes wielding cudgels, axes, knives, and all manner of crude weapons. Caught unawares, we were unable to defend ourselves from these brutes. They ransacked our homes, spat on us and called us "dirty Jews", took what loot they could find, clubbed and beat us and left us for dead. My wife and children were struck down in front of my eyes. They left me for dead, lying unconscious in a pool of blood. In the morning, I came to and crawled from my house. The few who had managed to flee from the onslaught returned, and we sent to Lvov for help in burying our dead.' He paused to control his shaking voice. 'The looters desecrated the house we used as a synagogue.' He raised his face to the Rabbi, his question wrung from quivering lips. 'What sin had we committed? We lived quietly and served Hashem. My wife was a virtuous woman. Why does He give strength to the wicked, and punish the righteous?'

'You must stay here with us, Ya'akov,' the Rabbi said kindly. 'Pray with us for the souls of your dear departed, may they rest in peace, and then you will come home with me, eat at my table and sleep under my roof. You were wise to come here. We are safe in the ghetto, my friend.'

'We thought we were safe in Cekenai,' Ya'akov replied bitterly.

5

After the service, the men congregated in the prayer hall to talk amongst themselves, while the women gathered in an anteroom at the top of the stairs to exchange news and gossip, before going down to the street to accompany their menfolk home. Ignoring my husband's command to join him by the entrance to the synagogue at the conclusion of prayers, I lingered with the other women, enjoying the comfort of their presence in the small chamber at the top of the stairs. For a few moments, at least, I could forget my own troubles and pretend that I was still a young girl living safely with my parents, full of naive hopes for my future.

That evening the women's talk was of Ya'akov ben Mordecai and the massacre at Cekenai.

'They were fools to live in such a small community,' Jael said. 'How could they hope to defend themselves? They should have joined us here in the ghetto. There are enough men here to repel our enemies if they attack us.'

'We are safe behind the ghetto walls,' her mother said.

'Hashem will protect us,' Naarah added. Everyone listened to her because she was the Rabbi's wife, although her words were often foolish.

'They stayed because they were few in number and thought no one would notice them,' my mother answered Jael's question. 'That's why they chose not to follow their neighbours to the town. Sometimes it is best to keep your head down and avoid attention.'

She glanced at me and I shivered, wondering how much she had guessed about my husband.

'And look how that worked out for the families in Cekenai,' Jael muttered, rolling her eyes. 'Women and children murdered.'

'How can anyone hope to hide from the Muscovite Tsar Ivan the Terrible? He has armies of soldiers roaming the countryside,' Rizpah said.

An old woman made a spitting sound to ward off the evil eye.

'There are no enemy armies roaming through the Duchy of Lithuania,' my mother said, glancing anxiously at my younger sisters who were listening to the discussion. 'This was an attack by random thugs. We all heard what Ya'akov ben Mordecai said. He witnessed the attack himself, and he said it was a gang of ruffians from the town, not the soldiers of Ivan the Terrible.' She too made a spitting sound to ward off the evil eye.

'You say "random" as though this was an isolated incident,' a neighbour replied. 'But we hear of attacks on Jewish communities throughout the Russian Principalities, and they are not unheard of in the Duchy of Lithuania.'

'They are becoming more frequent,' Naarah said. 'It is all the fault of Ivan the Terrible and his army of Streltsies.'

'You cannot demonise one individual,' someone else protested. 'He is hardly the first Jew hater.'

'But he is a powerful ruler,' Naarah replied, 'and he is cruel and violent.'

'It is certainly true that men can be cruel,' I said.

A few of the women turned to me, perhaps surprised by the sharpness in my voice.

'Look at what happened in Cekenai,' I added quickly, lowering my eyes in confusion.

When I looked up, I avoided my mother's gaze, afraid she had seen through my pretence that my marriage was fine. My parents did not deserve to suffer the shame of my failure to please my husband. Meanwhile, the women continued talking, oblivious of my discomfort.

'Naarah is right: Ivan of Moscow is Tsar of all Russia, and his power is greater than we can imagine,' Rizpah's mother said. 'Hashem preserve us, if this Muscovite Tsar decides to destroy our ghetto in Polotensk; no power on earth can stop him.'

'Only the power of Hashem, which is greater than the strength of any man,' the Rabbi's wife corrected her.

Rizpah's mother grunted. 'Of course, Naarah, of course. I am talking about the power of men.'

'How can a man knowingly cause such suffering?' Rizpah asked.

'Ivan the Terrible was Grand Prince at the age of three,' her mother replied. 'And he became the first Tsar of all Russia when he was sixteen. What can such a man know of the troubles and suffering of ordinary men?'

'Yet he is a man like other men,' I said.

'No,' Rizpah's mother replied gravely. 'That is just my point, Abigail. The Tsar is not like other men. He has no personal experience of trouble.'

'I think you are wrong about that,' my mother said. 'I have heard he started to lose his sanity after his first wife died.' My mother spoke to everyone but she was looking straight at me and I trembled, wondering what rumours she had heard about my own husband.

'Well, be that as it may, the Tsar is a wicked man,' Rizpah's mother said. 'He killed his son and his daughter-in-law, when she was carrying his own unborn grandson, to prevent any challenge to his power. If he can do that to his own family, he would not hesitate to slaughter us all if it pleased him.'

'Hashem save us all,' Jael muttered, turning pale.

'None of this has anything to do with Ya'akov's story,' my mother said. 'And we have no reason to suppose the Russian Tsar will turn his attention to our peaceful ghetto. He is too busy fighting his great wars with the Polish-Lithuanian Commonwealth. He is not interested in a few Jews living quietly beside the River Dvina, going about our business. All this fuss and anxiety over a stray gang of thugs who looted Cekenai to line their own pockets.' She smiled reassuringly at my little sisters. 'There is nothing to fear here. We are safe behind the walls of the ghetto.'

'Ya'akov travelled a long way to get here,' Rizpah said. 'It must be at least a week's walk from Lvov.'

'He has lost his home,' Naarah replied. 'Where else was he to go?'

There were many other places where he could have sought refuge. The Jewish congregation in the town of Lvov would have taken him in, for a start, yet the other women nodded in agreement as though Naarah's words were wise.

'Was there nowhere closer to his home for him to go?' my sister, Keturah, asked.

'He came here because he knew he would be safe in the ghetto,' Jael said, her customary complacency seemingly restored.

'He needed to be with people he can trust,' my mother added. 'It's understandable a man would wish to put a certain distance between himself and a scene of such horror.'

Rizpah sighed. 'It's difficult to believe such things can happen.'

'Yet it's hardly an isolated incident,' the Rabbi's wife insisted.

'Naarah is right. Look what happened in Spain,' Rizpah's mother agreed.

'What is still happening in Spain,' someone added.

'You don't need to look so far from home,' Naarah said. 'The Inquisition in Spain is not alone in hating Jews. Everyone fears and despises us.'

'Why?' my youngest sister, Hannah, asked.

'Because we are different,' my mother said.

'They fear us because we are educated, and can read,' Naarah explained.

'Why don't we stop learning to read then?' my sister asked, and everyone smiled.

'We cannot combat hatred with ignorance,' I told her gently.

'If we do not read the words of the living God, we are no better than animals in the field,' Naarah said.

The town of Polotensk lay at the confluence of two rivers in the Duchy of Lithuania. The land was fertile and transportation was on hand along the two rivers. Many Russian rulers had attempted to conquer the town and finally Ivan the Moscovite had succeeded. So far he had overlooked our ghetto, and we kept our heads down, praying to be left alone. In that we were no different to the residents of Cekenai.

'Everyone knows that anti-Semitism is on the increase throughout the Catholic world,' Jael's mother said. 'We cannot shut our eyes to what is happening beyond our walls. Now that the Moscovites have conquered the town, we are more vulnerable than ever. Let us pray to Hashem our ghetto does not turn out to be a trap rather than a sanctuary. If the Russians attack us inside the ghetto, they need only to block our gates and there will be no escape for us.'

'Mother, don't be ridiculous,' Jael replied. 'What are you suggesting? Do you want us all to run off and live in the forest like wild beasts? Or arm ourselves with knives and sticks against the army of Ivan the Terrible?'

The talk about violence worried me, but I could not linger long. Muttering that my husband would be waiting for me, I took my leave. My mother followed me to the top of the stairs where she reached out to straighten my shawl. With an involuntary cry I drew back from her touch, afraid she would uncover my bruises. Her tired eyes widened in confusion and her mouth gaped open. Without a word of explanation, I spun round and scurried down the stairs, praying to Hashem to forgive me for turning my back on my mother in her perplexity. But the sight of my bare arms, blackened with bruises, would have hurt her more than my apparent coldness towards her.

To my relief, my husband did not chastise me for loitering upstairs with the other women, but led me away from the synagogue without a word. To anyone observing us, we could have been a contented married couple, making our way home in companionable silence. Instead of going to our dark hovel on the outskirts of the ghetto, he led me to a house which was close to the synagogue. Opening the door, he ushered me inside with an impatient gesture. I gazed around in wonder at a living room with a brick hearth and chimney, a woven rug on the floor, and space for two large wooden seats as well as a table and six upright chairs. Two internal doors led from the living area.

'This is my house,' he announced flatly. 'My sister is coming to stay. You will shake out the rug and make the bedroom ready for her.' He pointed at one of the doors leading off the living room.

'There is more than one bedroom?' I asked, making no attempt to hide my astonishment. 'Why do we not live here all the time?'

My husband glared at me. 'You ask too many questions. Do as you are told and make the house ready to receive a guest. You will find linen for the beds in the bureau.'

He pointed at a beautifully carved wooden trunk standing against the wall. Tears sprang to my eyes as I studied the craftsmanship. My parents lived in one room along with my four sisters, while this large house was standing empty, but I held my peace, thankful that for once my husband had not raised his hand against me. After giving me my instructions, he went out and returned home late, staggering and stinking of ale. He must have visited a tavern, perhaps beyond the ghetto walls, but I dared not question him. He went into the largest of the bedrooms and fell onto the bed without pausing to remove his boots. Within seconds he was snoring.

Grateful for the respite, I lay on the bed in the other room, and whispered my nightly prayer to Hashem that he would take my husband in the night. I fell asleep considering the implications of my husband's property. With my husband dead, I would take possession not only of the small hut where we lived, but of the large house as well. My parents would move into the house with me, and have their own room to sleep in, while my sisters and I shared the second bedroom, and we would have a separate living room, with a proper hearth, where my mother could bake her own bread. We would rent out the smaller of my two properties, and would be able to afford a physician to cure my father of his lingering sickness.

But first my husband had to die.

6

M y sister-in-law, Orpah, was a short, thin woman with a pointed nose and beady black eyes. Jerky in her movements, she reminded me of a little bird, pecking at scraps. Were it not for her delicate features, she could have been a boy, with her flat chest and straight hips. Although her face was wrinkled, her movements were lithe. Her hair might have given an indication of her years, but she kept it hidden beneath a scarf wrapped tightly around her narrow head, and it was impossible to judge her age. She smiled kindly at me when she arrived, and embraced me warmly.

'I hope you are happy with Reuven,' she said when my husband had gone out and we were able to talk freely.

We were sitting at the table where I was preparing vegetables for our Sabbath meal.

'My husband is a stern man,' I replied evasively, keeping my head lowered over the carrots.

She must have seen unshed tears in my eyes because she lowered her voice, although we were alone. 'Do not cry before him,' she said. 'Trust in Hashem.'

'I do trust in Hashem, but your brother shows me no kindness,' I said, wiping my eyes on my sleeve.

Orpah reached out to lay her hand on my arm. 'He has not always been this way,' she told me. 'Can you find it in your heart to pity him?'

'He shows no pity towards me, only bitterness.' I knew my question was rash, but I had to know the truth. 'What did his other wives die of?'

'Reuven was very young when he took his first wife,' she replied. 'My poor brother. He was devoted to her, with the kind of passion that can consume a man. As soon as I saw them together, I knew that she had captivated his soul. A man risks everything if he loves a woman more than he loves his creator.'

'Only the love of Hashem lasts from everlasting to everlasting,' I agreed.

'His devotion was understandable because Zipporah was a beautiful creature, graceful and full of joy.' She heaved a sigh. 'She bore him only one child before Hashem took her from him.'

'How did she die?'

Orpah shook her head. 'Poor Zipporah was too frail for this life. She was so young. After the birth of her child she never rose again from her bed. She was still a child herself. For three days she lay unconscious before Hashem took her. My brother was inconsolable. The baby was puny and died soon after her mother, and my brother has been a broken man ever since. He railed against his fate, pleading with Hashem to take him too, but we come from strong stock. I outlived two husbands before I grew too old to bear children.' She paused and lowered her voice. 'In an excess of grief, my brother threw himself into the Vistula one day, but a fisherman saw his desperate plight; he pulled more than a fish from the river that day. After that, my brother bowed to the will of Hashem and accepted his burden of grief.'

'It is the will of Hashem to decide whose name is written in the Book of Life,' I said. 'But he married again. Tell me, what happened to his second wife?'

Orpah drew in a deep breath. 'She died in terrible circumstances, and I think that second loss finally turned his wits. For some men the tribulation Hashem sends us proves too hard to bear.'

My sister-in-law's words sounded dangerously like a criticism of our maker, but I let that pass, eager to satisfy my curiosity about my husband. 'How did his second wife die?'

'She was set upon by a thief and beaten to death. Reuven had gone out to the synagogue, leaving her at home in bed with a fever. He returned home to find his door open and his wife lying in bed, covered in bruises and dying as he reached her side.'

I was too shocked to speak.

'He summoned the best physician he could find, but it was too late to save her. After that he left Krakow, a disappointed man, and travelled through Warsaw and Vilna and finally settled here in Polotensk where I pray you will bring him some comfort in a life that has been blighted by tragedy. Have pity on him, Abigail, and may you comfort him in his grief and lead him back to the path of righteousness so that he may once again give thanks for the love of Hashem.'

I nodded, muttering that I would do my best. Her words had agitated me. When I was able to speak calmly, I enquired whether his second wife's violent assailant had been apprehended.

Orpah shook her head. 'By the time Reuven returned from the synagogue, his wife's attacker was long gone.'

Hearing her answer I said nothing, stunned that my

parents had married me to a man I now suspected had slain his second wife in anger. In the absence of any proof of his guilt, he had escaped punishment on this earth by leaving Krakow, but wherever he went there would be no hiding from Hashem who sees into our darkest and most carefully hidden secrets.

After that, I took great care to avoid provoking my husband's wrath. Like the Jews of the ghetto, I was afraid of attack, but my fear was personal. Where other wives yearned for a son, I prayed fervently to Hashem not to bring any child into our violent household. If I proved barren, there was a chance my husband would divorce me, releasing me from my nightly terror. My prayers to Hashem grew ever more frantic, but He sent no sign that He had heard me. It seemed that I would have to continue to suffer. There were even times when I feared the Lord had forsaken me.

Orpah stayed with us for ten days. After our initial exchange, we had no further opportunity to talk in private. Only once did I attempt to engage her in conversation again.

'Tell me, Orpah,' I said, 'what is it like where you live? I have never spoken to anyone who lives outside our ghetto walls before.'

'I live in a ghetto much like this,' she began.

'Enough of this chatter,' Reuven interrupted his sister. 'You are talking to my wife, Orpah. There is no need to fill her head with your idle nonsense.'

After that I spoke little but sat listening to our guest exhorting my husband to look more cheerful and take comfort in his new wife. They spoke in my presence as though I was not there while I sat some way off, mending torn linen.

'She is a righteous and a virtuous girl,' Orpah said. 'The poor creature rarely smiles. See to it that you bring some happiness into her life, brother.'

'I do my duty by her,' he replied sullenly. 'You would do well to keep your nose out of my affairs, sister.'

'A good husband does more than his duty,' Orpah replied sharply. 'May Hashem move you to be kind to her.'

Reuven shrugged. 'No amount of wishing can change us from who we are. Hashem forges our nature in suffering and affliction, and we must submit, however heavy the yoke.'

After Orpah left us, we stayed in the large house. For a few weeks, my husband was too drunk to go near me at night, and I used the occasion of my next bleeding as an excuse to sleep in the guest room. My husband muttered about my being unclean, and I scurried away, relieved at his ready acquiescence. The second bedroom became mine, but sometimes my husband summoned me to his bed and I had to obey, terrified of conceiving a child. As the weeks turned into months, my feelings towards my husband hardened into a cold hard hatred, and my fear of giving him a daughter grew. He was not fit to share his home with a young girl.

In desperation I went to see the midwife while my husband was away from the house one day. Skulking in shadows I stole along narrow alleyways between the houses of the ghetto, avoiding busier streets where tailors and cobblers, apothecaries and bakers, hawked their wares. If my husband saw me abroad on the street, he would punish me for leaving the house without his permission, but I reached the midwife's lodgings without any hindrance. By the time she opened her door to me, I was trembling too much to speak.

Hagar was a hefty ruddy-faced woman with strong arms and no imagination. I envied her phlegmatic attitude to life and death without which she would probably have found her work unbearable. She was not much older than me and had learned her trade from her own mother who had worked as a midwife until her death a year or so before my visit. When I had expressed my condolences, Hagar had answered me with a shrug of her broad shoulders.

'Hashem writes us in the Book of Life and takes us away according to His will,' she had replied with dispassionate certainty.

'How can I help you?' she asked, glancing curiously at my belly, which did not look swollen.

'Can I come in?'

She stood back to let me enter and ushered me to take a seat in her neat living room. A row of bloodstained rags and linens were drying by her fireplace although the fire was not lit, and the room stank of rotting meat. Hagar nodded encouragingly at me.

'How can I help you?' she repeated. When I hesitated, she leaned forward in her chair. 'Let me tell you then, since you are bashful. You have not bled for a few weeks and you wish to know if you are with child?'

I shook my head. 'No, it's not that.'

She frowned. 'What then?'

'I need your help, but first you must give me your word, as you love and fear Hashem, that you will never tell a living soul about my request.'

She nodded slowly and I could see she was intrigued.

'I want you to make sure I never have a daughter.'

That seemed to me a shocking request, but Hagar greeted it with her usual slow smile. 'Everyone wants a son to say the prayers of mourning after they are gone.'

'No,' I said. 'That's not it.' I frowned at the enormity of my next request. 'I want you to give me something to stop me conceiving. I don't want a baby at all, male or female.'

Hagar looked startled and half rose from her chair. 'You wish to be barren? That is a sinful thought, Abigail. You know your husband will abandon you.'

I nodded. She must have seen the flicker of hope in my eyes because she said, 'A wife must do her duty, however painful. We are commanded to multiply.'

'So you will not help me?'

'You know I cannot.'

'Very well.' I stood up. 'Remember your promise to me, as you hope for redemption on the day when all men will be called on to answer for their sins.'

'I can be discreet,' she replied.

'Then be so for me, or may my life lie heavy on your conscience.'

Hagar watched me leave with a faintly troubled look on her broad face.

I had one more visit to pay before going home. Once again I slipped in and out of narrow alleyways, avoiding the busier streets where I might be seen. Even with my shawl pulled low over my brows and wound around the lower part of my face, I was afraid of being recognised, but I made my way to Jehudit's lodgings without being seen. The matchmaker looked surprised to see me on her doorstep.

'Jehudit, are you alone?' I asked her.

She nodded. 'Do you come to speak for your sister?' she asked, looking around for my parents.

'No, this is not about my sister. I have come here to speak of a matter that concerns me alone. Please, let me come in. I need to speak to you in private.'

She led me to her sitting room and gestured to the chair on which my father had sat when I had first set eyes on my husband. It seemed like a long time ago. The matchmaker watched me warily as I sat down.

'How are you, Abigail?' she asked with fake cheerfulness when we were both seated.

'Jehudit, promise me–' I faltered.

'What is it, child?'

'I want you to promise me you will never arrange another match for Reuven after my death.'

Before I could find words to explain that no other girl should ever be made to suffer my torment, Jehudit's mouth stretched in a toothless grin. 'Such loyalty,' she lisped, 'such devotion. Did I not promise your mother he would be a good match for you? May you enjoy many years of happiness with your beloved husband before you need contemplate such morbid thoughts.'

Stammering my thanks, I rose to my feet. The old woman was an inveterate gossip; it was not safe for me to be more explicit about my marriage. If anything, I had made the situation worse. If I died before my husband, the matchmaker would no doubt assure Reuven's next victim that he was a husband who inspired deep love. I hurried home, my shawl damp with tears, my soul wracked with guilt at what I had just done, unwittingly encouraging another young innocent to suffer the torments of my husband's bed after my death.

7

Lost in misery, I barely registered an outcry nearby. Avoiding the main thoroughfare, I hurried to reach home before my husband discovered my absence. As I stole along a deserted passageway, several men ran past the end of the alley. More people followed, this time women and children as well as men, all fleeing in panic, their shouts and screams accompanied by the sound of distant gunfire. The ghetto was under attack. Numb with fear, I pressed myself against the wall, hoping to escape attention, but I could not remain there indefinitely while soldiers rampaged through the streets of the ghetto, no doubt raping and pillaging in the slaughter. On shaking legs, I turned and ran towards my parents' house. Behind me in the alley came the sound of footsteps pursuing me. I ran faster and might have escaped had I not tripped on a flagstone and fallen headlong. As I lay trembling on the ground, a voice called my name softly.

'Abigail? Abigail? Is that you?'

Peering up through the shadows I saw my Uncle Abraham leaning over me. He stood back to give me room to clamber to my feet. All the while we could hear a violent commotion nearby.

'Uncle, what is happening? Is it the Russian soldiers?'

'Hush,' he replied. 'Follow me and, for the love of Hashem, do not make a sound.'

The light was beginning to fade as we stole away from the centre of the ghetto.

'Somehow we have to find a way to climb over the wall without being seen,' my uncle whispered to me, as we crept along hidden alleys.

'Wouldn't it be safer to escape through the hole?'

My uncle stopped abruptly. 'What hole?'

I explained how my sisters and I used to sneak through a gap in the wall when we were sent to the forest to scavenge for nuts and berries. It saved us having to go out through the gate and walk all the way round the outside of the ghetto to reach the forest. We had never told anyone about our shortcut for fear adults would block it up.

'Thanks be to Hashem,' he replied in a whisper, while the hubbub continued not far away: shouting and screaming, running footsteps and the clash of metal. 'Would you be able to find this gap in the wall now?'

I nodded. 'Of course, but first we must find my parents and my sisters,' I said. 'We cannot leave without them.'

'There is no time. It is already too late for them, and it will be too late for us if we don't hurry. Listen, my child, one of the beadles of the town is a friend of mine, even though he is not a Jew. He risked his life to warn me the Muscovites had gathered by the gate and were about to launch an attack.' In his agitation he let out a curious sound that could have been a sob. 'I had less than a minute to save myself. There was no time to warn anyone else. We need to get out of the ghetto right now. There is not a moment to lose. Hashem has shown you the way. As you value your life, do not lose this opportunity to save yourself. The alternative is certain death.'

Stumbling in the fading light, we made our way to the breach in the wall. Concealed behind a gnarled tree trunk, the gap was difficult to spot from inside the ghetto, and equally well hidden from outside, where it was masked by thick shrubs and weeds. It was a gap that only children might discover by climbing the ancient tree growing just inside the wall.

My uncle gazed at the opening in consternation. 'I doubt I can squeeze through that,' he muttered. 'You are slender, Abigail. You go first. Once you are through the wall, run to the forest and hide. And make sure no one sees you.'

'Uncle, you must come with me.'

For answer he shoved me roughly towards the wall. 'Go now! There is not a moment to lose!'

My legs shook as I pushed myself through the gap to the other side of the wall. As soon as I was through, I crouched in the bushes to watch as my uncle forced himself into the hole after me. For a moment it looked as though he would pass right through, but then he stopped squirming, apparently stuck, half in and half out of the ghetto. Had the situation not been so horrific, he would have looked comical. His face turned red with the effort of pushing his bulk into the gap, until his eyes bulged in their sockets. After a moment, his hand appeared above his head, and I saw he was clutching a pouch.

'Here,' he whispered, 'take this and save yourself.'

When I shook my head, he threw the pouch. It landed at my feet with a faint thud.

'Take it,' he called softly, 'and go. Even now the Streltsy are running wild in the ghetto, rounding everyone up. So go, go! They will be here any minute now. Run and hide in the forest and stay there until you are sure they have gone. Remember, if they find you, they will kill you. Save yourself, my child.'

'But my mother? My father? My sisters?' I stammered. 'We have to go back for them.'

'Abigail, please, you must understand,' he replied in a hollow voice. 'It's too late. They're all dead. Everyone's dead. If you don't get away, right now, you'll be killed too. The Muscovites have come here to massacre us all.'

Other than Ya'akov of Cekenai, I had never seen a grown man cry.

Snatching up my uncle's pouch, I turned and raced for the cover of the trees. Behind me the tumult grew louder, with men yelling and women shrieking in terror. I had barely reached the edge of the forest when a crowd of men, women and children came into view running around the perimeter of the ghetto wall. Flinging myself down on the ground, I lay there, quivering. The threadbare fabric of my gown offered scant protection from the brambles and brittle grasses that scratched at my skin, but I dared not stir.

At first, in all the panic and pandemonium, it was difficult to see what the inhabitants of the ghetto were running from, but after a moment, a horde of soldiers in red coats and black hats appeared in pursuit. I saw the grinning faces of the front runners, as their long pikes prodded stragglers fleeing from the ghetto. Other soldiers brandished axes, while yet more carried muskets on their shoulders. From time to time one of them would shoot up in the air and the bolting Jews would cry out in alarm and put on a spurt as they sprinted past my hiding place. But they could not outrun the soldiers.

Women ran with children in their arms, while men carried the elderly and lame. In all the shouting and confusion, the soldiers drove their victims inexorably towards the river. A few moments later the screaming and yelling was accompanied by shouts and cheers and loud splashing, and I realised the Muscovites were driving my friends and neighbours into the Dvina.

Hauling myself cautiously through the scrub, I dragged

myself on my belly in the direction of the river. Pressing a hand over my mouth to stifle my whimpering, I watched musketeers shooting at the heads of swimmers whenever they appeared above the surface of the water, cheering when they hit a target. My family, my friends and neighbours, men, women and children, were being slaughtered in front of my eyes. Transfixed with shock, I could not tear my eyes away. Feverishly I repeated the prayer for the souls of the dead, but it was hard to believe Hashem was listening, when no bolt of lightning fell from the heavens to strike down the murdering Streltsy. Ya'akov of Cekenai had survived the attack on his village only to drown in the waters of the Dvina.

A couple of the Streltsy strode past, close to my hiding place. 'What if the cockroaches can swim?' one of them asked.

For answer, his companion raised his musket, shot into the air and bent quickly to reload his weapon. Volleys of shots echoed from the river. As the two Muscovites strode on towards the water, laughing at their sport, I inched away slowly, making no sound. If the soldiers spotted me, I would be shot, or driven into the river to drown. I slithered along the forest floor, serpent like, until the tumult faded to a distant hum, and the gunshots grew muffled. Hidden from the enemy, I lay in the dirt, weeping for the dead and the dying. In all, it had taken the musketeers less than an hour to wipe out the entire population of our thriving ghetto. As night fell, I clambered to my feet and staggered through the forest, away from Polotensk and the only life I had ever known.

8

_____

S tumbling through the trees, I was too stunned to believe the horror I had witnessed. In a moment, my little sisters would come running up to show me the berries and nuts they had gathered.

'You have done well,' I would say to them. 'Now come, let's go home.'

But Ya'akov of Cekenai's words rang in my ears, 'I have no home... I have no home...' The room where I had grown up, the hovel where I had lived with my husband, our beloved synagogue, all might yet be standing, but the inhabitants of the ghetto had vanished beneath the fast-flowing waters of the Dvina. Worse than dead, their bodies would not receive the blessing of a burial in sanctified ground. Until the Day of Judgement, when all men are called to account, their spirits would be condemned to wander restlessly, seeking in vain for peace.

After a while, I gave up trying to keep moving. There was nowhere for me to go. Overwhelmed with grief, I fell on the ground and waited for death to take me too. I do not know how long I lay there, before I felt a hand slapped suddenly across my mouth, preventing me from crying out.

'Abigail, do not be afraid,' a voice whispered in my ear. 'I saw you creeping away through the trees, but it was a job to find you. I have been searching for hours.'

He moved his hand away and I turned and looked up at my uncle.

'Are you living?' I asked in wonder.

He gave a strained smile. 'As living as you are,' he replied. 'Come, we must leave this cursed place before the Streltsy find us, or the sickness of the dead invades our humours.' As he was speaking, he wedged his flagon in his belt.

'But how did you get away?' I asked, sitting up. Without thinking, I began picking leaves and twigs from my hair and clothes. Brambles had torn at my skirt and scratched my legs, and my knees and elbows were grazed, but I had otherwise suffered no harm from crawling on the forest floor. I had received far more painful injuries at my husband's hand.

'Only by wriggling free of my doublet,' my uncle replied with a grimace. 'It was a very tight squeeze but I finally succeeded in pushing myself through the wall. The skin is painfully scraped on my belly and my back, and for a long time I lay in the grass and weeds beneath the bushes, shocked, and fearful of discovery. But the Streltsy did not find me and eventually I crawled to the edge of the forest and Hashem guided me here.' Solemnly he added, 'We are the only survivors of the ghetto, Abigail. Everyone else drowned in the Dvina. All gone.'

We sat there for a long time, weeping silently, and then we recited the prayers for the dead, hoping that Hashem would hear us and look with mercy on the souls of the dead of Polotensk. It felt strange, praying to a God who had turned from us.

'Uncle,' I ventured hesitantly.

'What is it, my child?'

'How can we pray to Hashem after all that has happened? So many innocent souls...'

My uncle sighed. 'What else can we do?' he asked. 'What is left to us but prayer?'

I nodded. Like my uncle's, my faith was rooted too deeply in my soul to be shrugged off. 'What of the bodies?' I asked.

My uncle shook his head and did not reply. At last we clambered to our feet and set off.

'Where are we going, Uncle?'

'I'm not sure, but somewhere far away from here.'

'How will we know where to go?'

'Hashem will guide our footsteps. He will protect us.'

I wondered why Hashem would take care of us, when all the other members of our congregation had perished, but I did not have the strength to challenge my uncle. It was fortunate that I had spent so much of my childhood foraging for food in the forest, because I knew where to look for nuts and berries, and could distinguish edible moss and insects from the poisonous varieties. Away from the bustle of human life, the only sounds we heard were the faint whispering of a breeze in the branches high above us, and the occasional trilling of a bird. Comforted by our trust in Hashem, and the company we had in each other, we managed to keep going until we reached a track in the forest.

The familiar forest of my childhood grew strange, as the trees I had foraged among became thicker and more densely packed the further we moved from Polotensk and the river. We were well hidden by the closely packed trees, but the terrain was difficult to travel, and my uncle tired easily.

'It's this that slows me down,' he grumbled, patting his large belly. 'Too much fried goose skin,' he added wistfully.

Grunting at the effort, he wrenched an overhanging bough

from a tree, and used it to support him as he walked. Several times I stumbled from exhaustion but we had to continue on our way. After a while we came across a stream, where my uncle filled his empty wine flagon. He forced me to drink the brackish water.

'Come on,' he urged me. 'We will die if we do not keep moving.'

He had always been kind to me, and I was glad he had survived the onslaught of the Streltsy. As for the rest of my family who had drowned in the river, I pushed them from my thoughts, as though my memories had been shut inside a locked chest. One day I might learn to acknowledge what had taken place and mourn for the people I had loved, but not yet. The pain of my loss was still too raw to bear. Even the death of my husband could not comfort me, although I had prayed for it every day of my tormented marriage. But mainly we were preoccupied with the effort of surviving. In the depths of the forest the coins in my uncle's purse were of no use to us. We could not purchase food from the trees that surrounded us in all directions, nor could we bribe the birds we heard high above us in the branches to fly low enough for us to capture them. We followed the path, constantly looking around for other travellers, and listening for horses or footsteps or the sound of voices approaching, fearful of being assaulted and robbed.

So we limped on living a kind of half life, traumatised and starving. Pressing forward on aching legs we travelled deep into the forest, far from our broken home. Left alone, I would have succumbed to exhaustion, but my uncle was with me, guiding my feet and encouraging me to keep going along the overgrown path through the forest.

'Hashem did not save us from the Streltsy only to surrender our lives out of weakness of spirit,' he said. 'We bear a heavy responsibility, to bear witness to the truth. No one else remains to remember the names of the dead of Polotensk. It is our task to recite the memorial prayers for them, just as we hope one day to be remembered, if it pleases Hashem.'

One day, we gathered a store of berries and paused to rest beside a welcome trickle of water. Refreshed, I withdrew behind a tangle of bushes to relieve myself. Scarcely had I finished when a voice cried out nearby, followed by a thump and the sound of several blows accompanied by much yelling. Crouching low to remain hidden from view, I crept forward to see what had disturbed the gentle rustling of the forest. Peering around the bushes, I saw a scruffy man squatting on the ground, calmly examining the contents of my food pouch. Nearby, my uncle was lying on his back, wrestling with a second man who had pinned him to the ground. The stranger raised one hand in the air and the blade of a dagger glinted in a shaft of sunlight.

A fury possessed me, sweeping aside my terror, and I leapt to my feet, ignoring the pain in my legs. My spirits were seized by a demon, and pent-up rage against all the cruelty I had suffered lent me power. Darting forward, I snatched up the stout stick that had served my uncle as a crutch, and swung it at his assailant's head. My arms quivered at the impact, and a loud whack echoed in my ears. Caught off guard, the stranger was thrown sideways, leaving my uncle writhing on the ground, moaning. Almost at once the thief was on his feet, staggering dizzily towards the trees. Panting, I raised my cudgel and struck him again. He pitched forward and fell to the ground. As his fingers scrabbled frantically at the earth, I raised my stick and bludgeoned him about the head until he lay still, his matted hair bloody from my onslaught.

His accomplice meanwhile had risen to his feet and was glaring at me, clutching my pouch in both hands. For an instant his eyes darted to my weapon but instead of leaping to wrench it from my grasp, he lunged forward and grabbed my uncle's pouch, which was stuffed with berries we had painstakingly gathered on our journey through the forest. Crazed with terror, I took a step towards him, screeching and brandishing my club. He let out a yelp of alarm and fled, crying out to his false god to protect him from evil spirits. Horrified, I gripped my bloody cudgel, only dimly aware of my uncle clambering unsteadily to his feet.

'I didn't mean to–' I stammered, dropping the foul stick and breaking down in tears.

My uncle interrupted me. 'You saved my life, Abigail, thanks be to Hashem. I never would have believed you capable of–' He broke off, unable to complete his sentence. 'There were two of them,' he muttered at last. 'Thanks be to Hashem for giving you strength to defend us. And now let us leave this accursed place.'

'I thought he was going to kill you,' I sobbed. 'Are you injured?'

He shook his head and gathered up a few scattered nuts and berries that had fallen from our food pouches. We walked away without another word, leaving the victim of my frenzied attack where he had fallen beside the deserted track.

We travelled on through the forest without seeing another living soul, and my uncle's flesh seemed to fall away in front of my eyes. Where once he had been portly, he now looked frail and I feared his strength would give out. And all the while I was tormented by guilt. I could not understand why Hashem, in His great loving kindness, had allowed me to murder a stranger. Worse than the death of a thief, hundreds of innocent souls had been slaughtered in the massacre at Polotensk. Human life was a sacred gift from Hashem, who loved every one of us, yet He allowed such atrocities to be committed. How could the one true God be so capricious in the love He showed His creatures?

Eventually I came to understand the reason for my doubts lay in my own capacity for evil. Despite my righteous

58

upbringing, I had proved as evil as the Streltsy. To begin with, I had done nothing to help my own family, but had fled at the first sign of danger, leaving them all to be slain. Intent on saving my own life, I had made no attempt to rescue my sisters, or any of the other children living in the ghetto. When I closed my eyes, I again saw infants being tossed into the Dvina, like so many bundles of garbage. The images plagued my waking thoughts and tormented my dreams. Yet Hashem had allowed me to leave Polotensk and save my uncle's life. It made no sense. Admittedly life in the forest was hard, and many nights we could not sleep for hunger gnawing at us like rats tearing at our guts, but we were alive. I did not understand why. The deaths of so many people I had known lay heavy on my conscience; I should have drowned with them.

At last we reached the town of Vilna, where we had relations who welcomed us into their home and commiserated with us in our grief.

It was poor comfort to sleep in a bed, and pray with a congregation again, when my mind was consumed by grief and guilt. The congregation clothed us and offered us a home. Unable to swallow a morsel of the food they offered us, I could barely acknowledge their hospitality.

My uncle chided me for my ingratitude. 'Hashem has saved us to bear witness to the destruction at Polotensk. Are the names of our loved ones to be forgotten in the prayers of the living?'

Gradually I accepted the comforts of life and began to enjoy the baked fish and fried goose skin we were served, while my spirits were consoled through prayer. But it was never long before my guilty secret disturbed my repose. After a few weeks of rest, my uncle insisted he travel on, spreading the news of the massacre in Polotensk.

'We cannot settle here as though nothing has happened,' he insisted, declining his cousin's invitation to stay. 'We must tell the world what went on, in memory of our dearly loved family and friends who perished at the hands of the Muscovites. And we must warn every Jewish community to be wary of becoming complacent. What happened in our ghetto could happen anywhere. It could happen here, my friend.'

Guilt drove me to accompany my uncle. I had survived the massacre, and Hashem had surely made me the instrument that saved my uncle, so that we could tell the story of Polotensk. So we travelled on for nearly three years, visiting Jewish communities in Bialystok, Warsaw, Krakow, Budapest, Zagreb and Split, and I was amazed to discover so many Jews living so spread out across the world. Wherever we went we were fed and given shelter and charity to help us in our travels.

'These Jews are so fragmented, yet they recite the same prayers. We should all gather and live together in one place,' I said. 'That way we would be able to defend ourselves against attack. Surely there is safety for many where few are vulnerable to stronger enemies.'

'And how would our people defend themselves? By fighting wars with other territories as the Christians and the Muslims do?' my uncle replied. 'Is that how you would propose to save many lives?'

'It might not be the best idea,' I conceded sullenly, 'but what happens now is hardly a happy state of affairs for us, is it?'

'The world has never been a happy place for Jews to live in,' he replied. 'We are hounded from place to place, and hated wherever we go.'

'That is exactly my point,' I said. 'We should find our own place, where we will not be hated, because the land will be our own.'

'A foolish dream,' he told me. 'You know as well as I do that will never happen. Now come, it is time we were on our way.'

9
_____

My first view of the sea stopped my breath. Truly the power of Hashem was without end when He could create so vast an ocean as the one that now stretched out before us. I had read about seas in the Bible, enjoying the drama of the story where Moses divided the waters to allow the Jewish people to walk on dry land, but to my mind, a sea was like the wide River Dvina, a stretch of water that a boat could cross in an hour with strong arms on the oars. This sea was very different to the river I knew.

Standing beside my uncle at the water's edge, I observed the busy harbour, where huge galleys and galleasses lay at anchor alongside small rowing vessels and long barges lying low in the water, while men scurried around, loading and unloading cargo and shouting to each other in foreign tongues. A man with skin as black as burnt wood hurried past carrying a bale of silken fabric blue as the ocean, his head swathed in a red turban, and a curved scimitar at his hip. Behind him came a pale man with hair like straw and eyes the colour of the morning sky, carrying a small chest. I wondered what it contained, pearls perhaps, or rubies, or exotic spices from the East. Every sight was a revelation to me. Truly I had come a long way from the ghetto in Polotensk to see these wonders. Yet I would have given it all up to return to my family and friends in the ghetto. All but one.

A weather-beaten sailor with scaly skin and bulging eyes told us that we were in Split, an outpost of the Most Serene Republic of Venice. By paying the sailor handsomely for his help, my uncle secured us a passage on a merchant ship bound for Venice. With a strong wind behind us, and a full complement of slaves at the oars, we set sail. My excitement at being on board a ship was short lived because the motion of the waves made me violently sick. It seemed that Hashem had resolved to punish me, even as I fled from the land of my sin. But like my husband who had fled Krakow for Polotensk, I could not leave my guilt behind me.

As we left the harbour, the crew of the galley recited a prayer to their various gods to preserve us from the Uskoks of Senj.

'Who are the Uskoks of Senj?' my uncle asked.

One of the sailors told us that although the authorities of the Republic of Venice laid claim to the waters of the Adriatic, calling it the Gulf of Venice, a name could not protect merchant ships and their cargo from Uskok pirates who roamed the seas. Venetian merchant ships provided them with rich pickings. We could only hope the sailors' prayers would be heeded, and we would be safe from marauding pirates.

After a day, my sickness abated. Gazing out over the endless ocean, I began to enjoy the fresh sea breeze. But the merchants on board and the crew were nervous. Our merchant vessel was a prize for any brigand who saw her riding low in the water, laden with a cargo of spices and silks. My uncle had disappeared below decks to pray and I fell into conversation with a fellow passenger on the ship. She told me her name was Domitilla, and she was travelling to Venice to seek work. She had dark eyes, and an abundance of black hair that she wore piled on top of her head. Several strands had come loose and hung in curly disarray over her slender shoulders and down her back.

'There are many wealthy patricians living in Venice,' she told me. 'I am hopeful of finding honest employment in one of their households.'

Her own family had been struck by famine following a long drought in their region. First her parents, and then her husband, had died, and she had left her village to seek a better life in the city of Venice. When I told Domitilla I was sorry she had lost her husband, she turned away from me and spat over the rail.

'He was no loss,' she said, tossing her head.

'Nor was mine,' I replied, with a strange feeling of release.

This was the first time I had admitted to anyone that I was glad my husband was dead. To say the words out loud was like a kind of confession and as we sailed away from Split, and all that lay beyond, I felt as though I was leaving my former life behind me, with all its misery and suffering, and sailing to a new world.

For the first time since my ill-fated wedding day I began to feel cheerful, but on our second day at sea, our lookout spotted a fleet of light vessels gaining on us from a distance. The sight terrified the boldest in our company. The crew did their best to outrun the pirates, bending their backs to the oars and tautening the sails, but even with a strong wind behind us it was hopeless. Our heavy merchant ship was no match for the pirates who skimmed lightly across the waves. We were an easy target for their swift craft, and were soon surrounded by half a dozen small braceras.

The Uskoks are masters of the seas they plunder. Domitilla told me they burn fires in a mountain cave to raise storms at sea that no vessel but their own can survive, and once they have a merchant ship in their sights, there can be no escape.

'Having raided the open seas, their swift braceras vanish into the swamps where heavy Venetian and Turkish merchant and naval ships can't pursue them. They are as slippery as eels,' she said, 'and as ferocious as tigers. We will be lucky to survive their assault.'

Near us a merchant bit his lip and rested his hand on the pommel of his sword, while the crew ran around seizing cutlasses and muskets, preparing to defend the ship and its cargo. Having caught up with us, the brigands boarded our vessel, brandishing a fearsome array of weapons: muskets, pistols, axes, swords, cutlasses and daggers. In bright red hats and short waistcoats, mouths stretched wide with barbaric cries and eyes glaring like wild beasts, they were a terrifying sight as they swarmed aboard. Our crew made a feeble attempt to resist while the savage pirates slashed at the air and discharged random shots, killing and wounding a few of our crew who fell to the deck, screaming in agony.

In all the clamour of clashing weapons and shrieking, I flung myself down on the deck to avoid the swinging blades and flying shots, and prayed that I would not be trampled to death. I cannot describe the horrors of that day, with men and boys writhing in death throes, their limbs shattered, their torn flesh streaming with blood. In the noise and confusion of pirates bellowing, the thunder of musket shots, and screams of the injured, I thought we would all be killed. In spite of my grief, and heavy burden of guilt that plagued me, I did not want to die and prayed to Hashem to save me.

The brigands' leader, a man they addressed as harambasa, was called Ulfo. Although short, he was easy to identify as their commander, from his wide bonnet and silk brocade coat, and his proud bearing as he strode around the deck slashing at the air with his cutlass, yelling encouragement at his savage followers. Like many of his men, his head was shaven, apart from a single lock of hair, and he had no beard but wore a long curling moustache. The barbarians' bloodlust was roused, but

Hashem empowered Ulfo with control over his ravening horde, or we would all have been slaughtered. At last Ulfo wearied of the killing. He had only ever been interested in our cargo, and he castigated our ship as clumsy and weather-beaten, and dismissed our sailors as feeble. It was true, our galley was battered by many journeys, and her crew were too weak to resist the brigands, but our valuable cargo remained intact. The pirates set to, lugging chests of perfumes and spices up from the hold, along with bales of raw silks and cloth-of-gold, and loading them into their braceras.

By now several of our crew had been injured or killed yet Ulfo proclaimed himself merciful. Hashem defend us from such mercy! Having seized our cargo, Ulfo called off his barbarians, and addressed the trembling captain of our ship, who had survived the battle with a wound to his leg. The captain fell to his knees on the bloody deck and raised his hands, begging for his life.

'On your feet, pig!' the harambasa yelled.

The captain stood up, his legs shaking, his stockings drenched with blood.

'I am not going to throw you overboard,' Ulfo said, gazing at our captain from beneath lowered eyelids. As the captain stammered out his thanks, the harambasa continued, 'I am going to let you walk off your ship like a man.'

Issuing instructions for his followers to lay a plank of wood over the side, Ulfo ordered the captain to climb onto it. 'Now walk!' he commanded. 'And we will spare your ship with all its crew and passengers.'

The poor captain limped hesitantly along the plank which shuddered every time a wave beat violently against the side of the ship. Before long he toppled headlong into the sea, letting out a desperate shriek before the waves swallowed him up. Within minutes the pirates had gone, their victorious cheers carried to us on the wind as they sailed away with their plunder.

To my relief I saw my uncle, looking pale and staring around the deck anxiously. As I hurried to join him, his worried face broke into a smile.

'Uncle,' I cried out. 'Tell me you are unhurt.'

'My only pain was fearing I had lost you, Abigail,' he replied. 'Hashem has saved us both again, so that we may continue to spread word about the massacre and ask more Jews to pray for the souls of the departed.'

10

The surviving crew set about restoring order on board the ship. At first they worked in wretched silence, throwing bodies over the side with barely a prayer, and sweeping blood and gore and remnants of shattered limbs from the deck.

Domitilla went below to offer her assistance to the surgeon. Having seen my fill of agony and death, I could not face witnessing his grisly ministrations. But while it was possible to ignore the sight of his butchery, there was no escape from the sounds of his hacking and cauterising. The screams of the injured could be heard all over the ship. Trembling, I stood on deck, staring out over the endless ocean, wondering if we would ever see land again.

I might have succumbed to my melancholic humour had a sailor not thrust a bucket and mop at me, gesturing at me to help sweep bloody muck from the deck. The physical exertion, combined with the satisfaction of feeling useful, restored my humours to their natural balance. For the first time since the massacre in Polotensk, I was thankful that I had escaped when so many others had perished.

Gazing over the side of the ship, we saw a city of astonishing beauty rising out of the waves. Two monumental stone pillars dominated the harbour. One supported a winged lion, which we learned was the emblem of the Most Serene Republic of Venice, while the other bore a statue of Saint Theodore, patron saint of the republic. Spear in hand, the statue stood with one foot on a lowly stone monster.

'The Venetians believe their stone lion and saint protect the city from the sea,' a sailor explained. 'Who can say they are not right in their belief?'

Of course the Venetians were misguided in seeking salvation from graven images when only the one God, Hashem, has the power to save and protect, but I refrained from explaining this, in case the sailor believed in his tales and took offence. There followed a great deal of shouting, while men strode backwards and forwards along the deck, yelling at one another in a language I did not understand. Eventually we climbed down a rough rope ladder into a small boat that rocked precariously on the waves.

'Sit down, lady,' a sailor yelled out.

It was the first time anyone had called me a lady. I hoped this courtesy boded well for my stay in Venice, and felt a stirring of hope for the future. An oarsman rowed us swiftly to shore, negotiating a passage between the light galleys and heavy galleasses lying at anchor in the harbour. As we stepped off the boat, I breathed a prayer of thanksgiving to Hashem for bringing us safely back to dry land. We were standing at the edge of a spacious square on one side of which stretched the lagoon, where our vessel lay at anchor. The other three sides were bordered by lofty palaces, exquisitely decorated, more beautiful than any building I had ever seen before, with their elegant colonnades, magnificent domes and splendid statuary. It was hard to believe men were capable of constructing such beauty. Surely the designers had been guided by divine inspiration.

A trumpet sang out, persistent as a baby's cry. A host of clamouring voices rang around the square, which was packed with people on a sunny afternoon: noblemen dressed in velvet and brocade, ladies in beribboned silk gowns, their hair piled high on their heads in elaborate swirls, swarthy men from distant lands with turbans wound around their heads, uniformed guards outside the main palace, pedlars selling their wares, gulls screeching, and a musician strumming a lute while his partner blew out a shrill melody on a flute. A woman in extravagant finery walked towards me, her hair the colour of grain. The stomacher on her bodice glittered with bright ribbons, but as she drew near, I saw that her skirts were threadbare and beneath her thick paint she was old, the expression in her eyes as hungry as the beggars who loitered in the piazza.

A noisy rabble in slashed breeches and cloaks marched by in a blaze of scarlet and blue, while around them traders hawked their goods, overhead gulls shrieked, and in a corner of the piazza another band of musicians struck up a lively tune. The cacophony of sounds swelled and ebbed, like waves on the sea. A peasant woman with a squawking chicken scurried by; a courtesan rustled her silken skirts; a dark-skinned man strolled across the piazza carrying a tethered ape on his shoulder; a group of foreign mercenaries in slashed doublets strode past, their swords swinging at their sides.

My uncle made his way along the waterfront, and I followed him. Down by the water's edge, tucked away at the end of the quay, we spotted a couple of boys splashing in the lagoon. A man was standing by the waterfront, calling out instructions to them. One of the boys in the water was clutching a floating wooden board, which was attached to a rope the man was holding. From behind I could see only that his thick dark hair fell to his broad shoulders. Telling me to wait further back, my uncle took a handful of soldi from his pouch and offered the coins to the swimming master.

'Keep your head up, Lorenzo!' the man was shouting. 'Strongly, Elia, strongly! Longer strokes, you lazy scoundrel! Don't forget to breathe!'

Below him in the water, the two boys paddled furiously up and down, causing a great spray. Without turning his head, the man called out to my uncle. 'Who are you and what do you want with me?'

My uncle was facing away from me, and I did not hear his reply.

'My name is Galeazzo Bonaro,' the man replied, 'and I am the best swimming master in the Republic.' He tightened his grip on the rope as he spoke, without turning his shaggy head around. My uncle spoke again.

'You are in luck,' the swimming teacher answered, glancing at my uncle over his shoulder. 'One of these boys is a Hebrew, like you.' He turned back to the boys in the water. 'Elia! Get out! There is a job for you here. A chance for you to earn a few soldi.'

I saw my uncle hand a coin to the swimming master as one of the boys clambered out of the water, and quickly pulled on rough breeches and a doublet. His wet hair was plastered to his head, but I could see it was thick and dark, matching his eyes. His movements were swift and supple, and in no time he was dressed and shod, and ready to offer us his service.

'The gentleman here is asking for a guide to show him the way to the Jewish ghetto,' the swimming master said.

'Will you take us there?' my uncle asked the boy. 'I'll pay you for your trouble.'

'Oh, it's no trouble,' the boy replied, gazing at my uncle with a ready smile.

'Imbecile,' the swimming teacher said, cuffing the boy on the ear, 'he would have paid you more if he thought he was taking you out of your way.'

'It is a blessing to help others,' the boy replied, shrugging off the reprimand. He nodded at my uncle. 'I'm going back to the ghetto anyway.'

'We interrupted your swimming lesson,' my uncle said.

'Oh, that doesn't matter,' the boy replied cheerfully. 'I don't really need lessons any more. My grandmother wanted me to learn, in case I ever fall in the water, but I'm a really strong swimmer now.' He glanced at the sky. 'If I'd stayed in the water much longer, I would have been late, so you've done me a favour. I get in trouble when I'm late.'

'Late for prayers?' my uncle asked.

'Yes, that as well,' the boy replied with a grin. 'My father would be cross if I missed prayers again. But I meant I'd be in trouble if I got back after the curfew. You know they lock the gate of the ghetto at night? The walls are high and impossible to climb,' he added with a hint of regret in his voice.

'What if an army attacks you during the night?' I asked, remembering what had happened in Polotensk. 'You would be trapped in the ghetto with no means of escape.'

'Oh, we're quite safe from invading armies here,' the boy replied cheerfully. 'Venetian ships control the sea, and the city is unassailable by land.'

'Why does the ghetto have need of a curfew then?' I asked.

'It keeps us Jews safe from thieves and ruffians. Now, come on, or we'll be late,' he added, glancing at the sky which was beginning to glow red over the wide lagoon.

11

The boy led us down streets that ran beside busy waterways, where narrow gondolas jostled against barges and small rowing boats. The River Dvina had been busy with cargo vessels, but I had never seen so many small craft packed together on so many criss-crossing canals. At some intersections the boats were packed tightly against one another. Everywhere boatmen were yelling at one another, in greeting or in frustration at being jammed together unable to move. We hurried to keep up with our guide as he scurried along. Wherever we walked, elegant buildings surrounded us, shrouded by a mist that rose from the water carrying a stench of damp and mould that pervaded everything. Within minutes my clothes stank of the pestilential water.

'Do we always have to walk beside water?' I asked.

The boy shook his head at the question. 'You'll get used to it. There's no getting away from water in Venice.'

As we crossed a bridge I glanced around and began to glimpse what he meant. The entire city appeared to have been constructed on land reclaimed from the sea. We saw no horses or carts or donkeys wherever we went, only narrow walkways and water teeming with small boats. We passed by a stinking fish market and the boy abruptly turned away from the water. A guard standing beside a large open gate nodded at our escort.

'Gate's closing soon, my lad,' the guard called out. 'Are your visitors planning to stay the night?'

'Sure they'll stay,' the boy replied. 'They've only just arrived. Come on, this way.'

He beckoned us to follow him through a covered tunnel and along a narrow street hemmed in by very tall blocks that looked as though they had been so awkwardly put together they might collapse at the slightest impact. Rags and garments hung outside open windows, fluttering in the foul air; the street stank of fish, cured meat, excrement and the ubiquitous stench of stagnant water and mildew. We had reached the ghetto.

'We'd better go straight to the synagogue, because evening prayers will be starting soon,' the boy said, glancing towards the sinking sun. 'The Rabbi never minds if we're late. He's too kind to scold anyone. He believes in teaching us by example, and is always mild and gentle. But there are certain members of our congregation who frown on latecomers and are likely to clout you if you walk in after the Rabbi has started.' He sighed, as though he had received this treatment on more than one occasion. 'Come on, it's this way.'

We passed some shopfronts within the ghetto, all closed for the Sabbath. Above them and around them tall buildings rose as high as the splendid palaces of the aristocrats of the city, but the architecture of the ghetto was far from grand. On the contrary, buildings here were wedged together, one on top of another, dilapidated and devoid of charm. Our guide led us over a wooden bridge and the narrow twisting streets opened out into a broad piazza where a single tree grew, spreading its leafy branches towards the darkening sky. People were streaming through a door in a corner of the square. Apart from the line of people entering, there was nothing to distinguish the building from the neighbouring properties.

A few of the congregation gave us curious glances as we joined the queue of people, but they were clearly used to visitors and no one challenged us. Inside, I followed the women up a stone staircase to the gallery upstairs, while my uncle entered the men's prayer hall with our young guide.

Through the curtain I heard the Rabbi welcome my uncle with the courtesy due to a visitor.

'What is your name, and where are you from?' another voice questioned him more directly.

I peered beneath the curtain and saw my uncle standing in front of the bimah, looking up at the Rabbi. Some of the men were hidden beneath the women's gallery, but those I could see were all looking at my uncle with solemn attention.

'My name,' he replied heavily, 'is Abraham ben Tedeschi. But you will wish you had never listened to my story.'

'You may speak freely here, Abraham ben Tedeschi,' the Rabbi said.

'I come from the ghetto of Polotensk in the Grand Duchy of Lithuania, where we were once a thriving community.' My uncle heaved a sigh that could be heard upstairs, and his shoulders shook. 'All but two of the Jews who lived there are dead. Only I and my niece escaped. We are spreading the news, that our neighbours may be remembered in the prayers of communities more fortunate than ours.'

'What happened in Polotensk, Abraham ben Tedeschi?' the Rabbi asked gently. 'Tell us that we may share your suffering and lighten your burden of grief with our communal prayers.'

The grim expressions on the faces of the women around me assured me that everyone in the synagogue already knew what my uncle was going to say. They had heard the story repeated too many times before. Only the setting changed with each retelling. On the periphery of my vision I saw several of the women turn their heads to give me sympathetic glances, but I fixed my eyes on my uncle, listening to his words and mourning inwardly. Had I been shown any kindness, I would not have been able to control my grief.

'Jews first settled in Polotensk over a hundred years ago,' my uncle said. 'And more came when the Jews were expelled from Spain. The land around Polotensk is fertile and trade is brisk along the Dvina River that runs by the town, so the region drew the attention of the Russian Tsars. Many times they attacked the town, and many times those barbarians were repelled, thanks be to Hashem. But in the end the Muscovite Ivan the Terrible captured Polotensk.' He paused and passed his hand over his eyes. 'The Streltsy, soldiers of the Muscovite, drove the congregation of three thousand devout Jews into the river. Those who were able to keep their heads above water were shot by the watching Streltsy, who laughed and cheered as they hit... men, women, children...' He paused for a moment, overcome with emotion. 'My niece and I managed to escape and fled to the forest. We have been travelling ever since, spreading the news of the massacre at Polotensk. We are here to tell our story, that the righteous may be remembered for a blessing in your prayers.'

He stood in front of the Rabbi in silence, while tears coursed down his rugged cheeks.

'We will forget our own concerns for now,' the Rabbi said, gazing around his congregation. 'Our hopes and fears will be as nothing as we recite prayers for those who perished in the massacre of Polotensk. Let every man here recite the prayer of mourning for the good souls of Polotensk this night. In His loving mercy may Hashem forgive them their sins and write their souls in the book of everlasting life.' He turned back to my uncle. 'We mourn with you. Your loss is our loss. Those who perished in the massacre at Polotensk are as dear to us this night as our own brothers and sisters. Abraham ben Tedeschi, you are welcome here in the ghetto of Venice. And now, let us pray for the dear souls of the departed.'

At the conclusion of prayers, while men gathered in the prayer hall to discuss their affairs, the women gathered in a chamber at the top of the stairs to talk together. They formed a line and embraced me in turn, and wept with me. A few of them muttered their own words of comfort, but most recognised there was nothing to say beyond the customary greeting to mourners. At last, a stout woman of around thirty stepped forward. Holding me by my arms, she studied my tear-stained face before introducing herself as the widow Hadassah.

'I lost my dear husband and my daughter to the fever last year,' she said, her ruddy features contorting briefly at the memory. 'My lodgings are spacious enough to accommodate another person comfortably enough. You must stay with me tonight. I have not yet adapted to cooking for one, and have far too much supper for myself alone, so you can rest assured you will be well fed.' She drew back and gazed at me again. 'You look as if you could do with a few good meals inside you before you leave us. No,' she added, when I shook my head uncertainly, 'I will not accept a refusal.'

Her forthright and practical attitude was more heartening than the other women's tears. Much as I appreciated their sympathy, the prospect of a decent meal and a comfortable bed for the night was far more pleasing.

'You are very kind, but I need to ask my uncle before I accept your hospitality. He might have made other arrangements for me. But I do thank you for your kindness and will accept your invitation willingly, if he does not object.'

'He'd better agree,' she grinned. 'Or I'll be eating tsimmes all week.'

I could not help returning her smile. 'Much as I love cooked carrots – and I've no doubt yours are really sweet and tasty – I don't think I'll be able to eat a week's worth of tsimmes in one night.'

'Then you must stay for a week.'

My uncle was content for me to go home with Hadassah. He had arranged for us both to stay with the Rabbi, but the Rabbi seemed keen for me to accept Hadassah's offer. I accompanied her to her lodgings close to the Agudi Bridge that led from the Campo del Ghetto Nuovo piazza towards the gate of the ghetto. She chattered cheerfully on the way, doing her best to distract me from my troubles. Doubtless the Rabbi had perceived her need to distract herself from her own misery as well. Her kindness in welcoming me to her home was a blessing for us both.

'I promise you will enjoy my sweet carrots,' she told me as we walked side by side through the streets of the ghetto, cool after the heat of the day. 'I cook them in lashings of goose fat, flavoured with honey and sugar and plenty of cinnamon. You do like cinnamon, don't you?'

I assured her that I did.

'And did you know that golden carrot wheels are a symbol of good luck? We all need some good fortune in our lives, and I suspect the two of us need such mazel more than many. But Hashem be praised we are alive and in good health, and will one day be reunited with the souls of the departed, may they rest in peace.'

A narrow bed along one wall of the living room doubled as a seat during the day, and Hadassah slept in a small separate bedroom. It was enough space for two women to share comfortably, and what the apartment lacked in size, it made up for in warmth and comfort. The floor was clean, as though it had been swept that day, and bunches of dried herbs hung around the room, in a vain attempt to mask the damp stench of the ghetto. We sat on stools at the scrubbed wooden table where Hadassah served me a bowl of sweet carrots.

'Was I wrong to praise my tsimmes?' she demanded.

I shook my head, my mouth full of deliciously flavoured carrots. When I finished, she filled my bowl with a steaming bean and barley stew that had been simmering on the fire since the previous day.

'Eat, eat,' she urged me, when I put down my spoon.

'I cannot manage another mouthful,' I protested. 'I haven't eaten so much in years.'

'Tomorrow we will have cured goose meat with our tsimmes,' she told me. 'And now, I will clear away the dishes and leave you alone to sleep.'

When Hadassah had retired for the night, I lay down on the bed in the living room and closed my eyes, my stomach full for the first time in many months. I had barely had a chance to say goodbye to my uncle, and it felt strange to be abandoned to the care of a stranger, however kind she was. Confident that my uncle was being well looked after by the Rabbi, I fell into a deep sleep, hoping my uncle would decide to stay in Venice.

12

The following morning my uncle spoke to me after prayers at the synagogue to tell me he was leaving on his journey to spread the word far and wide about the massacre at Polotensk, both to enlist more people to remember our dead in their prayers, and to warn other Jews against becoming complacent. It was a familiar speech. I had heard him recite it many times on our way to Venice. All at once, a wave of lethargy crept over me, as though my humours had been exhausted by travelling. Without considering my words, I asked if he would mind my staying in Venice when he left.

If he was taken aback, he recovered himself quickly. 'Of course you may stay,' he replied. 'You are young and should settle somewhere. You still have your whole life ahead of you, and it's understandable you would want to find a home and make a future for yourself.' He smiled and spoke more forcefully. 'Yes, my child, remain here in Venice, if you feel at home here. It is as good a place as any, and you will be safe here.' He paused, at a loss of what else to say to me.

Neither of us mentioned his warning that nowhere was safe for Jews.

'Will you stay here with me in Venice?' I asked. 'You said yourself, it's as good a place as any, and a man has to live somewhere.'

He shook his head sadly. 'My path lies elsewhere,' he replied. 'You are young, Abigail, but there is nothing left for me but memories of happier times. I will not find another home on this earth.'

'Please stay here with me,' I begged him. 'Uncle, you are the only family I have. We can find lodgings together and–'

But even as I spoke, I knew what his answer would be.

'When will I see you again?' I asked, desolate at the thought of his leaving me.

He shook his head. 'Only Hashem knows what the future holds.'

'But you will come back, won't you?' I said, struggling to restrain my tears. 'You will always have a home with me, my uncle.'

Only when he held out his arms to me and we embraced did I remember that I had no home of my own, and could offer him hospitality in name only.

'May Hashem guard you and keep you safe until I return,' he murmured. 'Do not fret. You have suffered enough in your short life. Stay here, Abigail, and find what happiness you can.'

I had known my uncle all my life, and I wept as he turned and walked away from me. He did not look back. Perhaps he was afraid that he would not be able to leave if he saw me in tears.

Once again Hadassah comforted me with her phlegmatic humour. 'Well, he's gone and there's no point in crying about it,' she said. 'He has his path in life and you have yours, and if you have any sense you will not spend the rest of the day moping. If you don't cheer up I might regret inviting you here to share my lodgings.'

She smiled kindly at me, but her words made me think. The

last thing I wanted was to be a burden to my new friend. Until now, my life had been controlled by other people: my parents, my husband, and my uncle. For the very first time, it was up to me alone to decide how I was going to live. Above all, I wanted to be strong and independent. Other women managed it, and I would take my inspiration from them.

'Work?' Hadassah repeated, when I expressed my intention to earn a living.

'Yes. You surely do not think I expect you to feed and house me indefinitely without offering you any money for rent or food?'

'You are welcome to stay under my roof for as long as you please. I will be glad of the company.'

I shook my head, recalling the lesson my parents had taught me. 'It is not good for a person to live like a leech on the efforts of others. Blessed are those who give.'

'But what do you propose to do?' she replied. 'You have no money to start a business, and no skills to put to use. Seriously, Abigail, your company will be enough of a gift, if you are willing to fill my lonely evenings with your companionship.'

Once I had been the wife of a prosperous man, but everything he owned had been taken by the Streltsy, leaving me destitute, apart from a silver ducat my uncle had pressed into my hand before he left. 'It is true I have no money of my own, but I am young and strong,' I replied. 'I will do what any unmarried woman must do if she has no family to support her, and find work to pay for my daily needs.'

'What do you propose to do?' she repeated.

'I must have some skill that could be put to good use here in the ghetto,' I replied.

'Are you learned in remedies, or experienced in delivering babies?'

I shook my head. 'I can do neither of those, but I can sew,' I replied.

Hadassah gave me a sceptical look. 'You don't sound very sure.'

'I can sew,' I repeated, with exaggerated confidence. 'My mother said...'

'Yes, well, that's good then,' Hadassah interrupted me quickly, before I could break down in tears at the memory of my mother. 'Tomorrow you can speak to Tamar, the seamstress. She employs several needleworkers. Perhaps she can use another pair of hands.' It was Hadassah's turn to sound doubtful.

Recalling how much better I had felt when a sailor set me to work on board the ship after we were attacked by pirates, I resolved to offer my services to Tamar, the seamstress, that same day. First I fortified myself with a hunk of bread accompanied by strips of goose skin, fried in their own fat over the open fire and served with crispy onions. With the confidence that comes from a full belly, I set off. Hadassah had told me the way but I had to ask several shopkeepers for directions before I found the workshop of the seamstress.

Tamar lived across the square from Hadassah, in a narrow street behind the synagogue. I was learning that the broad central piazza outside the synagogue was surrounded by a maze of streets and tiny courtyards which made up the ghetto. After taking several wrong turnings, I knocked on a low door which was opened by a girl younger than me.

'Is this the workshop of Tamar, the seamstress?' I asked.

Before I had finished speaking, the girl edged away to make room for a thin middle-aged woman with greying hair and a lined face. Her sharp nose and thin mouth gave her a mean appearance, but she smiled warmly enough at me.

'My dear,' she greeted me with an amiability belied by her

hard dark eyes. 'Have you brought some mending for my girls? Tell your mistress we will not disappoint her.'

'I am no one's servant,' I replied haughtily, 'and I have not brought any mending for you.'

Tamar's eyes narrowed suspiciously as she looked me up and down, assessing my travel-worn gown. 'If you have not brought me any work, you can have no business with me.'

'I am Abigail of Polotensk,' I replied quickly, before she could close the door. 'I was famed for my skill in needlework in my home town. Even wealthy Christian ladies would bring me garments to mend.'

That was an exaggeration. My mother used to give me old clothes to mend for my sisters, and she often praised my skill with a needle. Occasionally neighbours brought their mending to our house and paid me to alter and mend for them, and I had once altered a gown for a wealthy Christian woman who had praised my handiwork. I returned Tamar's gaze boldly, although I was quaking inwardly, ready to beg her to give me work.

The seamstress gave a little snort. 'If I had you as a saleswoman, perhaps my business would thrive better,' she said. 'Well, Abigail of Polotensk, you had better come in and show me what you can do. Hadassah has offered you lodging even though you are penniless. That must count as a recommendation of your character at least, if not of your skill, of which I alone shall be the judge. I will not tolerate inferior work. I have my reputation to maintain.'

'I have not come here looking for charity,' I replied.

She led me into a low-ceilinged apartment. One wall had been partly demolished to create a large chamber where five girls sat silently sewing. In one corner, a pile of neatly folded colourful articles of clothing lay on a bed where I guessed Tamar slept at night. The floor looked freshly scrubbed, and was covered in stray threads and scraps of fabric. One of the girls let out a yelp and put her finger in her mouth.

'That will be a week's pay, if you have any blood on that shirt,' Tamar snapped and the girl shook her head.

Tamar turned to me. 'I pay good wages, and that is why the best girls in the ghetto come to work for me. Yes, there are tailors who have their own seamstresses.' She snorted. 'Second rate at best. That is why everyone in the ghetto comes to me for their repairs. I brook no mistakes in here, no fumbling, no procrastinating, and no complaining.'

She turned to the offending girl who had already lowered her head over her work and did not see Tamar glaring at her.

'Now,' the seamstress said, 'show me what you can do.' She ushered me to a vacant stool and handed me a gown with a torn skirt, and a needle and thread. It was nerve-wracking sewing with her watching over me, and I was afraid I would not be able to mend the tear neatly enough to satisfy her, but after a moment, I relaxed into the familiar task, and my fingers flew over the fabric with a confidence of their own. Finishing, I broke the thread with my teeth and handed the gown to Tamar.

She took it with a grunt and stared at my work. 'Very well,' she conceded. 'You were right in saying you know how to sew. You start tomorrow at daybreak, and work until evening prayers, six days a week, for half what I pay my experienced girls. If your work is satisfactory, at the end of the month you will receive the same wages as the other girls. You will find the time passes quickly,' she added, seeing my disappointed expression.

I hesitated, uncertain whether to thank her or object to her terms, which struck me as unfair. Having acknowledged that my work was good, she should pay me a fair wage for it. But I dared not protest and left without a word and found my way back to my lodgings where Hadassah was waiting for me.

'Well?' she demanded, seeing my crestfallen face. 'How did you get on?'

'She has offered me work, but is only paying me half the usual wage for the first month.'

'So you will be earning money. Good for you.'

'But only half what the other girls earn for a month.'

'Then you must make sure you work hard and do not lose your job at the end of the month,' Hadassah said shrewdly. 'Tonight we will celebrate with a meat pie from the bakery, and lashings of griboli. Don't argue, I've already bought the strips of goose flesh and will fry them tonight. And from the end of the month I will double your rent,' she added with a grin.

13

Tamar was right when she said the time would pass quickly. Despite the oppressive heat in our sewing room, and our enforced silence whenever the seamstress was present, I enjoyed my work. It was the first time I had been independent, and I blessed my good fortune in being rid of my vicious husband. As for my family, I hoped to be reunited with them in the World to Come, when the Messiah resurrects the souls of the departed. My fear was that having slain a man, my soul would not be granted eternal life and I would never see my dear parents and sisters again. As a distraction from my gloomy fears, I threw myself into my work, and from time to time Tamar gave me an approving nod.

Every day I mended different garments, and enjoyed handling their vibrant colours and soft textures. It amazed me that there were ladies in the world grand and wealthy enough to wear such wonderful clothes. I would never be able to afford such luxury myself, but at least working for the seamstress I could stroke soft velvets and watch the colours of silks and satins ripple in the light. Some of the time we mended tears in drab brown and black garments of craftsmen and workers, or rough shirts the colour of raw dough, and that work was as dull as the fabrics. At other times servant girls brought mending from their grand mistresses, gowns in gorgeous shades of scarlet, blue, violet, green, and turquoise, and their masters' jackets of brocade decorated with intricate designs in gold thread, edged with pure white lace. When Tamar was out at the market, haggling over the price of thread or forcing a bargain for a pack of needles, we sometimes donned the magnificent gowns and jackets and paraded around the sewing room, admiring each other and strutting like the wives of rich patricians. Once, Tamar caught us, and we lost half our pay for that week.

'Imagine if you soiled one of those garments!' she scolded.

'Or tore it so it needed mending,' Sarai, one of my fellow needleworkers, added and we all giggled.

'Who said that?' Tamar demanded, her voice dangerously quiet.

For a moment, no one answered.

'It could have been any one of us,' I said boldly, because I liked Sarai and did not want to see her punished for a flippant remark. 'It was only a joke.'

Tamar's eyes narrowed as she glared at me.

'Abigail's right, any one of us could have said it,' another girl piped up and several others joined in, murmuring their agreement.

Tamar hesitated, but there was a large pile of mending to do that week, and she could not afford to antagonise all her needleworkers at once. 'Very well, girls, back to work, and don't let me catch you parading around in our customers' clothes again. Just imagine if someone had seen you. Our work depends on our reputation for care of the garments, and quality sewing. All of our wages rely on our customers' trust in us.'

She was almost pleading with us, and we understood that the danger of any one of us losing her job had passed.

As I walked back to my lodgings that evening, Sarai came part of the way with me. When she thanked me for saving her job, I dismissed her gratitude with a laugh. 'She wasn't going to lose you,' I replied. 'Your work is as good as anyone's, and that's all Tamar cares about.'

Sarai shook her head. 'She has thrown better needleworkers than me out for less,' she said. 'I am in your debt, Abigail of Polotensk. My mother is ailing and my father and brothers died of the fever last winter. Without my wages from Tamar, my mother and I would be paupers.'

'I am glad to have been of assistance,' I replied pompously, embarrassed by her protestations.

We reached Hadassah's door and I stopped. 'Well, this is where I live.'

Sarai looked surprised. 'You live here?' she asked.

'Yes. Hadassah is my landlady. So I'll say goodnight, Sarai.'

'You are neighbours with Daniel ben Elia,' she whispered, her eyes alight with excitement.

'Who is Daniel ben Elia?'

'You don't know Daniel ben Elia?'

I shook my head. 'Remember I have not been living here long. I don't know anyone in the ghetto apart from the girls who work for Tamar, and my landlady, Hadassah.'

Sarai giggled. 'Daniel ben Elia is only one of the best-looking men in the whole ghetto. You ask the other girls tomorrow. They'll tell you. He's a widower. His wife died oh, years ago, and he's been alone ever since.'

'Does he have no family?'

'Oh yes, he has a son and a daughter, twins. What I meant was that he has no wife. Guta, the matchmaker, has tried to persuade him to remarry many times. It must be over ten years since his first wife died, and they were only married for a couple of years, yet he refuses to look at another woman. That's so romantic, isn't it? He's remained loyal to his wife's memory all these years. Imagine inspiring such devotion in a man.' Sarai's eyes shone and she giggled again.

'He sounds a bit crazy,' I said.

'Oh no, he's not at all crazy. He's handsome and clever.'

'Is he a scholar?'

'No, he's a printer.' With that, Sarai turned and trotted off down the street towards her own home, where her ailing mother was waiting for her.

Sitting over supper with Hadassah, I wondered about my neighbour, the romantic printer who had loved one woman so deeply he refused to marry another. It was hard to imagine such a pure love between a man and a woman, but the idea of it stirred a strange yearning in me. Perhaps one day Hashem would send me such a man for a husband, so that my fingers would no longer smart from constant pricking of needles. Still, I comforted myself, whoever Hashem sent me could not be worse than my first husband. In the meantime, I was curious to meet a real printer, and ask him how he produced pages of text that were not written by a human hand. It seemed magical, and the mystery of the process had never ceased to fascinate me.

'What do you know about our neighbours?' I asked Hadassah as we sat companionably together after supper.

I had taken our bowls and knives to the fountain and washed them for the next day, and we were chatting before retiring to bed, as had become our habit now that we were accustomed to one another's company. I was content to have Hadassah as a friend, and counted myself blessed to have found a safe haven to rest in after the traumatic events in my home town of Polotensk. Now the summer was nearly over, and autumn winds shook the boughs of the tree in the Campo del Ghetto Nuovo. Watching leaves flutter to the ground, scarlet and golden, leaving the branches bare, I was beginning to feel unaccountably restless.

'Our neighbours?' she repeated. 'Which neighbours in particular are you referring to? There are many people living in this block. Far too many, if you ask me,' she added, with a sniff of disapproval.

Like the other residences in the Ghetto Nuovo, our apartment block had been modified from homes where Christians had lived in the days before the ghetto was established. With many Jews arriving from regions less tolerant than Venice, rooms had been divided, accommodating four or five Jewish families in spaces that had formerly housed a single Christian family. The building we lived in was never quiet, with constant disturbance from the cries of women in childbirth, babies yelling, and people cooking and cleaning, and arguing and calling out to each other, and running up and down the stairs.

'I was talking about the printer who lives in the apartment next door,' I said.

'Ah, you mean Daniel ben Elia, who lives in the apartment I manage next door? He is a righteous man, and a widower. But you have probably heard his mother is sick with a fever.'

I did not answer her, but decided to visit our neighbour with a bowl of soup for his mother the following evening after work. At the very least, it would be a good deed. It was a blessing to help the sick and the afflicted. At the same time, it was possible that I might actually get to meet a real printer and the idea filled me with excitement.

The next evening, with her permission, I took a bowl of Hadassah's soup and knocked on our neighbour's door. When it opened I was surprised to recognise the boy who had acted as our guide when my uncle and I had first arrived in Venice.

'Good evening, lady from Polotensk,' he greeted me politely.

'Good evening, swimmer from Venice.'

He grinned cheerfully, dropping the slightly pompous manner he had adopted. 'I am rather good at swimming, aren't I? The master says I have no further need of lessons. Are you here to see my grandmother? I'm afraid she's very sick.' His lips wobbled slightly.

'I am sorry to hear she is ailing, and have brought her some broth.'

'I'll give it to my sister,' he replied. 'She deals with things like that, cooking and stuff.'

As he was reaching for the bowl, a man appeared in the doorway behind him.

'Who is it, Elia?'

Daniel's voice was low and gentle, and his dark eyes looked kind. I was filled with a sudden fierce longing to feel his arms enfold me.

'It's the lady from Polotensk,' Elia replied.

'I live next door,' I stammered awkwardly, my face hot with shame at my hidden desire. 'I've brought some broth for your sick mother.'

My neighbour's eyes softened in a smile as he thanked me. Elia slipped away, leaving his father to take the soup. I handed the bowl to Daniel, and his fingers brushed mine. It was a fleeting touch, but he started at the contact and nearly let the bowl slip.

'It's nothing,' I stammered, 'nothing. It's just a bowl of soup. I didn't even make it myself. My landlady, Hadassah... Do you know Hadassah?'

Just then a girl appeared beside him. She was slender and dark-haired, with sallow skin and her father's almond-shaped eyes.

'This is my daughter,' Daniel said. 'Miriam, our new

neighbour has been kind enough to bring some broth for your grandmother.'

He handed the bowl carefully to his daughter, and I hurried away, wishing he had invited me in, yet fearing to linger. We had only spoken for a moment, and I longed to see him again.

14

The next morning I told Hadassah that I would make supper. At the end of the day, I hurried from the workshop without waiting for Sarai, who often walked with me part of the way. In place of nuts and acorns from the forest, I had vegetables, eggs, goose liver and fat. That evening, I fashioned parcels of egg pasta stuffed with liver and goose fat, flavoured with fried onions and salt. My mother had made these kreplach on festive occasions, when the ghetto in Polotensk had been especially generous in its donations to the poor. While I rolled out the egg pasta and cut it into squares for parcels, the onions sizzled in fat over the fire. Hadassah told me the aroma from my cooking was making her mouth water, and she could not wait to try it.

'I told you it smelled delicious,' Hadassah said, as we ate my kreplach in a simple vegetable soup. 'But tell me, where did you learn to cook like this? No, on second thoughts, don't tell me. I don't want to know, really I don't.' Hadassah knew that talking about my mother might reduce me to tears. 'Let us be cheerful tonight. After all, you don't cook for me every day.'

When we had finished eating, I took a pan of soup and

kreplach to our neighbours. This time Daniel came to the door himself. He smiled when he saw me, and I noticed how white his teeth were.

'You have been so kind, and I don't even know your name,' he said.

'Abigail.'

'Oh yes, of course, how stupid of me. I should have remembered. Abigail from Polotensk. Won't you come in? My daughter is here, and my mother is here in our apartment too, although she won't be seated with us at the table.'

'How is she?'

'She is recovering, thanks be to Hashem. I'm sure your soup will help her regain her strength more quickly.'

'I made it myself this time. I brought enough for all of you, at least I hope it will be enough. I imagine Elia has a healthy appetite.'

Daniel nodded, still smiling, and I turned to go, but he detained me. 'Won't you join us, please?'

It was time to walk away from my foolishness. A righteous man could feel no sympathy for a murderess like me. So although my neighbour's words were inviting, I shook my head. In any case, although a widow did not need to be as modest in her dealings with men as an unmarried woman, I did not want to sully my good name. Tamar would frown on a woman with a poor reputation, and Hadassah might turn me away.

'Abigail,' he said, and somehow on his lips my name sounded light and agreeable. 'Please come and share your food with my family. It would be a blessing. My daughter craves female company. It would be a kindness to her – and to me.' He hesitated before his next words, which seemed to tumble from him in a rush. 'It is a long time since I enjoyed the company of a beautiful woman at my table.'

I took a step back in alarm and he stammered an apology.

'Forgive me, my clumsy compliment was well intentioned. I did not wish to disconcert you. I spend so little time in company, I have forgotten how to conduct myself with women. But I know my daughter would be pleased if you joined us.' He paused. 'I hope you will be her friend as well as our neighbour, Abigail.'

Against all reason, I felt my resolve weaken. Something gentle in the way he uttered my name drew me to him. And besides, I had always been fascinated by the printing process, and wanted to hear about his work.

'Very well,' I replied. 'If your daughter is at home, I will join you at your table, and I thank you for your hospitality.'

'I should be thanking you,' he replied. 'Let me take that from you.'

He reached out and took the pan of soup from me. As he did so, his fingers brushed mine for a second time. It was the lightest of touches, and he turned away instantly, leaving me wondering if he too had noticed our brief contact. But perhaps he had merely wished to hide his hands that were blackened with ink. For my part, I hoped he had not noticed how red and raw my own fingers were from the constant pricking of needles.

'Let us go in and eat before the soup is cold,' he said.

Trembling at my own temerity, I followed him into his home.

Daniel's daughter, Miriam, was as serious as her twin brother was light-hearted. 'Elia has always been wild,' she told me earnestly. 'I am the responsible one. Are you betrothed?'

'No,' I replied.

'Why not?'

I shrugged. 'I cannot give you a reason.'

'But shouldn't you be betrothed at your age?' she persisted.

'Perhaps,' I replied, smiling at her childish candour.

'Haven't you spoken to the matchmaker?'

'No.'

'Why not?'

'Abigail is a widow,' Daniel told her severely, 'and your questions are impertinent. You are making our guest uncomfortable.'

Miriam looked crestfallen at the reprimand, and I quickly assured her that I was in no way vexed by her questions. 'It is natural to be curious about new neighbours,' I added.

Daniel looked relieved, and Miriam smiled. 'I am to be betrothed, aren't I, Father?' she said blithely. 'To a student of medicine. Father is arranging it, and we are to meet soon, aren't we, Father?' She babbled excitedly about the new dress she would have for this important meeting.

'And then you will see if you like the young man,' Daniel said gravely. 'Do not be blinded by his status, Miriam. To be the wife of a physician is a fine thing–'

'But it is more important that he does not make you unhappy,' I completed the thought, more fiercely than the words themselves warranted.

Daniel's eyes met mine across the table, his expression a mixture of curiosity and concern. I looked away, afraid I had revealed more about myself than was fitting. As though he perceived my confusion, Daniel began to praise my kreplach.

'This is my mother's recipe,' I said. It was the first time I had been able to speak of my mother without breaking down in tears. Perhaps it had something to do with my sense of ease at being seated with a family again.

'Your cooking's amazing,' Elia said with unrestrained enthusiasm. 'Are you coming back tomorrow?'

'Is Abigail's cooking as good as mine?' Miriam asked. 'Is mine better?' She turned to me. 'Abigail, please, please will you teach me how to make kreplach?'

'That would be brilliant,' Elia added. 'Then we could have them every night.'

'I'm not asking for your benefit,' his sister told him. 'Not everything is about you. I want to learn how to make them for my husband.'

'You haven't got a husband,' Elia said. 'You're only eleven.'

'I know that, silly. But I will have a husband one day, and you will have a wife.'

'I want to marry Abigail,' the boy said. 'Then I can eat kreplach every day.'

'She's far too old for you,' Miriam said decisively. 'She's much older than us and probably too old to find a husband.'

'Hardly,' Daniel said, smiling at me. 'I think Abigail will make some man very happy.'

Once again, he was paying me a compliment and I felt my face flush with embarrassment. I was not used to such kindness, especially from a man I scarcely knew.

Soon after that I took my leave, expressing my hope that Daniel's mother would recover speedily, and they thanked me again for the soup. 'Please do come back tomorrow,' Miriam said.

'You are always welcome at our table,' Daniel added. He accompanied me to the door. 'May I walk home with you?'

'I only live next door.' I laughed.

'I am glad you are so near,' he replied, adding quickly, 'because it means we may hope to eat more of your splendid kreplach.' He turned away, but when I opened Hadassah's door I noticed he had not closed his own door. May Hashem forgive me, but I was pleased that my kind neighbour had watched me walking home.

15

The following morning, Daniel was loitering in the street when I left my lodgings to go to work. I hardly dared hope he had been waiting for me. 'You are out early,' I said. 'It is not yet dawn.'

'I like to rise early and see the sky lighten after the darkness of the night. It's like a promise of renewed hope.'

When I enquired after his mother, he sighed. 'She grows weaker, and her fever shows no sign of abating, although my daughter, Miriam, is doing an excellent job of nursing her, and Elia has been up for an hour, flapping a stiff board by her bed to cool the air.'

'They must care for her very much.'

He nodded. 'She has been like a mother to them all their lives. I am going to the Rialto this morning to purchase bunches of sweet-smelling herbs to hang by her bed, and Miriam is keeping her closely swaddled in dry sheets to protect her from the poisons in the air. We are keeping the shutters at her casement closed so that no further pestilence can contaminate the air inside the apartment. We are doing everything we can but, despite all our efforts, the imbalance in her humours grows worse. The apothecary is coming to see her again this evening, and the Rabbi is joining us later to pray at my mother's bedside.'

'That is good. Hashem will surely heed the words of the Rabbi. And yours too, Daniel,' I added. 'You are a good man to look after your family so well. But what is it that ails your mother?'

'A sickness entered her body through the open pores of her skin and it has infected her blood. The only protection from further contagion is to keep her tightly wrapped against venomous miasmas in the air. Miriam is worried that the Rabbi may find the stench from my mother's bed offensive, but we cannot risk exposing her body to wash away her excretions while she is so weak.'

'The sick always reek,' I said. 'There is no help for it. The Rabbi must be accustomed to the smell. He will not even notice it.'

'That is what I told Miriam.' Daniel sighed again. 'I have assured my children she will recover, but I fear my mother is dying. How can I tell them? Was it not enough that Hashem took their mother?'

Without thinking, I reached out and placed my hand on his arm and he did not move away. 'Have you not always been a good father to your children? If your mother dies, Hashem will give you words to comfort them. In the meantime, while she lives let us not lose hope. Has a physician seen her?'

He shook his head. 'It's not easy. I have my daughter's dowry to think of, and physicians are expensive.'

That evening Hadassah and I went to the synagogue to attend prayers, after which I took hot soup to Daniel and his family.

'I know you are too busy caring for your grandmother to have time for cooking,' I told Miriam, who thanked me with tears in her eyes.

That evening, an apothecary came to see the ailing woman. With a thin face, long teeth, and small fingers curled at his chest, he looked like a rat as he scampered to the sick woman's bedside.

'There are several ways noxious fumes can enter the body,' the apothecary explained, when he had completed his examination of the patient and returned to the living room. 'The main infection routes are the mouth and nose, but we cannot block those orifices without stopping her breathing.' He gave an apologetic shrug, as though he regretted not being able to stifle the sick woman's breath altogether. 'In the meantime, you are doing the right thing wrapping her in sheets.' He bared his teeth in a smile at Miriam, who lowered her eyes. 'In a healthy body the skin itself creates a barrier to infection, but in her weak state sheets will help minimise the risk that further infection will enter through her pores. I would recommend wrapping her in clean sheets. Let them still be linen as it is particularly effective, acting like a sponge to draw perspiration from the skin into the weave of the cloth.'

'I'll go and buy some clean sheets right away,' Daniel said.

'Do so,' the apothecary replied. 'And I urge you to engage a skilled barber as soon as possible because fevers require bloodletting to maintain the right balance of bodily fluids. I will return tomorrow with a balm made of the finest grains of unicorn horn, mixed with ground phoenix liver, mermaid tongue and mandrake heart, distilled in sunbeams to restore youth and vigour.'

Daniel handed him his fee and hurried off to look for sheets before all the shops shut for the night. Feeling wretched, I returned to my own lodging. All next day at work I was distracted from the other girls' gossip, worrying about Miriam and Elia. And I thought of Daniel, his gentle voice and soft eyes, and the strength I had felt in his arm.

That evening when I took a pan of soup from the fire, Hadassah shook her head with a worried frown. 'Take care,' she warned me.

'There is nothing to worry about. I do not enter the sick woman's bedroom and am in no danger of catching her fever.'

'But you may catch a different sort of fever from Daniel's company.'

'That is foolish talk,' I replied. 'His daughter is always with us, and his mother could recover and join us at any time.'

'He is a good man, Abigail, but–' She hesitated.

'But what?'

She shook her head. 'May Hashem watch over you and preserve you from disappointment.'

I did not confess to Hadassah that, having taken a human life, I could never hope to marry a righteous man, so was in no danger of disappointment. In the meantime, I was lonely and he was worried, and our innocent friendship was a comfort to us both. There could be no harm in it.

The following morning, I did my best to conceal my delight when I saw Daniel waiting to walk to the seamstress with me again. Hadassah's warning rang in my ears, but I dismissed her fears with ease. Daniel would never be anything more than a friend to me, but it was pleasant to walk with him in the early morning as the mist rose from the waters and the air cleared around us. When we set out, the edges and corners of the grimy buildings were softened in a gentle haze, but by the time he left me at the corner of the street where Tamar had her workshop, it was possible to see the ugliness around us with perfect clarity.

'Tonight a physician is coming to see my mother,' Daniel told me. 'Jacob Mantino, the uncle of my wife, insists on attending her bedside. He refuses to accept a fee, since my children are his blood.'

It was not my place to point out that I had been impressed by the apothecary. Not every man can lay his hands on ground unicorn horn distilled in the beams of the sun. Its healing properties were well known. But Daniel seemed pleased to have secured the attention of a physician.

'Is he skilled in his work? A free service is not necessarily the best. It might be worth paying a better physician, if by doing so you help your mother to recover her health. I am thinking only of your mother, and your children,' I added quickly, afraid I might have offended him.

'I would not engage the services of an unskilled physician when my mother's life hangs in the balance,' he replied severely. 'Jacob ben Samuel Mantino of Tortosa is a renowned physician, and an eminent scholar. He acted as personal physician to the highest dignitaries at the court of Pope Clement VII. Now he lives in Venice, Hashem be praised, where he tends the French and English ambassadors, and the Papal Legate, and many wealthy patricians. That is why I could not afford his fees. If anyone can cure my mother of her fever, it is Jacob.'

'I shall pray for her speedy recovery,' I replied.

'And once the apothecary and the physician have done their work, and Miriam has nursed my mother back to health, Henriette will arrive with her trickery.' Daniel sniffed. 'That is when we will know my mother is recovered.'

'Who is Henriette?'

'Oh, you will find out as soon as my mother regains her strength.'

That evening, shortly after I took a hot barley stew to Miriam, the physician arrived. His cloak and hose were of black silk, and he wore a black velveteen cap in place of the yellow hat most Jews were required to wear. His forceful manner and arrogant bearing were those of a man accustomed to wielding authority, yet there was something comforting in his confidence. This was a man of knowledge who knew his own worth. The apothecary was already there, standing by the fireplace in the living room, mixing his costly concoction in a mortar.

'What is this you are making?' the physician enquired, with a disapproving frown.

The rat-faced healer started in dismay and yielded his place to the physician without demur, mumbling about the healing powers of his potion. Ignoring the fetid smell of sickness, Jacob turned to Miriam. 'Take me to her. We have no need of your cures here,' he added, with a dismissive nod at the apothecary.

The apothecary hastily stuffed bottles and jars back in his bulky pouch and took his leave, bowing his head and muttering about his fee. Daniel paced the room, as Jacob beckoned to Miriam and me to assist him. The sick woman lay in bed, her eyes closed and her mouth open. We watched Jacob take a small steel lancet from his bag, make a nick inside her elbow, and let a thin stream of blood trickle into a bowl. A long time seemed to elapse before he bound up her arm and grunted that it was well done, and we followed him back to the living room, where Daniel and Elia were waiting.

'Your mother has a fever,' Jacob said solemnly.

'What is the cause?' Daniel asked.

'Blood stagnates in the extremities when the humours cease to function in harmony. Women who no longer menstruate have no means by which to purge themselves of bad humours, and so this kind of sickness can fester in women after a certain age. But don't fret. When nature can no longer balance the humours, a physician, or even a skilled barber, can facilitate a return to health by bloodletting.' He nodded at Daniel. 'I consulted my charts before I came here, and today proved an auspicious day to treat your mother. She may yet recover her strength and return to health, but we must depend, as in all things, on the will of Hashem. You will have no further need of the apothecary and his quacksalver,' he added, wrinkling his nose as though he had just noticed the stench in the apartment. 'I have bled the patient and will return tomorrow to see if she has improved.' He wiped his hands on a rag, and looked serious. 'Watch her, and summon me if there is any sign of deterioration. Keep her shutters closed, day and night, and give her water to drink, one cup every four hours.'

'Is she going to die?' Elia asked, his face drawn with tension.

'The bloodletting will relieve her,' Jacob replied, 'but Hashem alone knows whether her name is written in the Book of Life. Watch her closely until I return.'

Daniel thanked him and he left, and we sat down to eat the stew I had brought. Even Elia did not eat more than one bowl of stew that evening and I returned to my lodgings with the pan still half full.

16

Daniel was outside waiting for me in the morning, and we walked to Tamar's workshop together. On the way, he told me his mother was much improved. She had sat up in bed that morning, demanding to be fed.

'To have an appetite is a sign of health,' I said. 'I am more pleased than words can say.'

'Well, I will make a prediction of my own,' he said. 'Tonight Henriette will appear at our table to give my mother a cure for her sickness.'

'But you said she is recovering?'

'Exactly.'

We arrived at the corner of Tamar's street and it was time for me to start work, sewing from dawn until dusk. As I entered the room and took my place at my bench, it struck me that I had lost my pretext for visiting Daniel's home every evening. No longer tending to her sick grandmother all day, Miriam would have time to cook for her family again. I walked back to my lodgings that evening and prepared a vegetable stew for Hadassah and myself. As I was stirring the pot over the fire, there was a knock at the door.

'There is a young man here asking for you,' my landlady told me, smiling warily as Elia walked in.

'Miriam would like to invite you both to eat with us tonight,' Elia said. 'We are very grateful for your help and want to thank you. And my father says I am not to let you refuse the invitation,' he added.

'That is kind, but we are already eating,' Hadassah said. 'Abigail has made us a vegetable stew.'

'Which will keep until tomorrow,' I said, rising to my feet. 'We will be pleased to accept your invitation.'

'Take care,' Hadassah murmured to me as we followed Elia next door.

'Of what?'

'Don't be a fool.'

'I don't know what you mean. We are accepting a kind invitation from Miriam.'

'The girl with a handsome widower for a father?' Hadassah muttered.

'We're visiting Miriam and her grandmother,' I replied firmly.

We passed an enjoyable evening with Daniel and his children. His mother was still too weak to join us at the table, but Miriam took her in a bowl of stew and she ate it all. We were in good spirits and the time went quickly.

'Your cooking is delicious,' I told Miriam when we had finished. 'Your betrothed will be a fortunate man.'

She smiled at the compliment.

'As will yours,' Daniel murmured so softly that I alone heard him.

I shifted uneasily in my seat.

'And then grandmother will cook for us again,' Elia remarked with a sour expression. He sighed. 'I don't understand why you're in such a hurry to leave us, Miriam.'

'A woman needs a husband,' she replied primly. 'How else are we to fulfil Hashem's commandment and bring children into the world? What would happen if we didn't? I have no choice, Elia. I can't stay here all my life, can I?'

'I don't see why not,' her brother said crossly. He turned to me. 'Maybe you will bring us supper when Miriam has abandoned us, until I am old enough to marry, or father takes a wife who knows how to cook.'

'That's enough,' Daniel said sternly.

'Abigail hasn't tasted Grandmother's cooking,' Elia mumbled, gazing miserably at his bowl.

The following day, Daniel was not waiting to accompany me to work. Disappointed, I hurried to the workshop alone. The mist had cleared early that morning, exposing the ugliness of the ghetto. Only the tree in the square was beautiful, reaching its leafy branches up towards the distant blue of the sky. One of the needleworkers was sick and the rest of us were expected to work harder than ever to fulfil Tamar's orders. She sat with us all that day, watching over us and exhorting us to work faster.

'If we sew too quickly, the threads break,' Sarai grumbled.

There was a momentary silence after her complaint, before Tamar's temper exploded. 'Do I pay you to break threads?' she demanded, standing in front of Sarai and glaring down at her.

'No, Tamar. You pay us to sew.'

One of the girls pricked her finger and let out an involuntary cry. Tamar spun round and turned the force of her glare on her. 'If I see a drop of blood on any of these garments you are working on, you will replace it out of your wages.'

It was an idle threat. Some of the silk and brocade gowns and jackets we handled would cost a lifetime's wages for poor needleworkers like us. The girl who had cried out lowered her head over her sewing and was silent. Yet for all her tantrums, Tamar was not an unreasonable employer. She paid us promptly at the end of every week, even when business was slack, and when business was brisk she treated us to cakes and wine before we went home to welcome the Sabbath. It could not have been easy for her to run her sewing shop with so many girls to watch over, and so many fussy customers to please. We all dreaded seeing certain servants who brought work to us, because we knew Tamar would be in a bad mood after their visit.

'The mending you sent last month was not neat enough for my master,' they might say, or 'The gown you made for mistress is not a good fit and must be altered before you are paid.'

'Perhaps your mistress has gained a little weight since we last measured her,' Tamar might reply, with an obsequious bow.

The haughty servant would rebuff any attempt to refute their criticism of our work. 'My mistress will not look kindly on your attempt to deny that your work is at fault.'

If the exchange threatened to become heated, the servant would invariably call Tamar 'Jew', reminding her of her inferior status to the servant of a patrician, and Tamar would be forced to capitulate or risk losing a customer. We all needed the work and there were other sewing shops that could make and patch and mend as we did.

'We have to be competitive,' Tamar would tell us. 'It's a crowded marketplace with more needleworkers than customers. We cannot afford to lose the goodwill of a single customer.'

'So we must accept their disparagement of our work, even when our sewing is perfect?' Sarai asked.

No one answered her. We all knew the only way out of needleworking was marriage to a man wealthy enough to support a wife and family. We discussed our prospects while Tamar was out at the market haggling for threads, and my thoughts would drift to Daniel. He was not wealthy, but he had a trade and he was kind and gentle.

Increasingly I lost myself in recollecting the time I had spent with him, remembering snatches of his conversation, and expressions that crossed his features when he looked at me. Sometimes he had a faraway look in his eyes and I wondered if he was thinking of his wife. It was foolish of me to feel jealous of a woman long dead, and I cursed myself for failing to heed Hadassah's warning. She had seen my feelings for Daniel while I had stubbornly denied them. I struggled to dismiss such foolish dreams from my mind, telling myself that Daniel had already been married, and was faithful to the memory of his wife. In any case, after what I had done, he could never be my husband. I prayed to be released from the spell he had cast on me, but Hashem abandoned me to my yearning. In some ways this torment was even worse than my guilt at having killed a man.

17

The following evening Elia again invited Hadassah and me to eat with his family. This time I insisted on bringing a pot of vegetables with me, so we could eat them with Miriam's bread and soup. As an independent woman earning my own wages, I was keen to reciprocate their generosity. Besides, I was eager not to appear beholden to Daniel, especially in front of Hadassah, whose warnings had begun to perturb me. We found Daniel, Miriam and Elia seated around their table with Daniel's mother, Debra, and another woman whom they introduced as Henriette. Wearing the long loose robe and woollen shawl of a Berber, Henriette had an exotic air about her. Even in middle age she was a beautiful woman, with thick glossy black hair, lustrous almond-shaped eyes, and graceful bearing. Daniel scowled as Debra told me Henriette was an alchemist and a seer who could see into the future.

'She told me I would recover and I have,' Debra cried out, with a triumphant glance at Daniel.

Henriette smiled and reeled off a list of exotic herbs and spices she had brought with her from Marrakesh: oil of the argan nut, lavender, eucalyptus, saffron, amber, musk, jasmine and sweetly scented rose water. She claimed each had its own special curative qualities.

'Whatever your ailment, Henriette has a cure,' Debra said. 'Her powers are unbelievable.'

'That at least is true,' Daniel muttered.

It was not long before Miriam returned to her favourite topic. 'Why did you never marry?' she asked Henriette.

Henriette told us that, as a young woman, she had indeed married. While her husband was away from their home in France, her children had died of the plague. Grieving for her beloved children, yet fearful of contracting the disease herself, she had fled the region. Afraid to return home while the pestilence raged, she had accepted a berth on a ship bound for the port of Casa Blanca, where she hoped she might find her husband. On her arrival in Morocco, the captain of the ship abandoned her, and she found herself alone in an alien land.

'What did you do then?' Miriam asked, wide-eyed.

Henriette shrugged her shoulders. She told us she had earned her living using the skills she had learned from her husband who, she claimed, was a famous prophet and astrologer. Eventually she had succeeded in saving enough money to make her way back to France, where she discovered her husband had remarried. Not wishing to cause him trouble, she had returned to Marrakesh where she had friends. Several years later she had been forced to flee from Morocco.

'Why was that?' Daniel asked.

Henriette looked sad and shook her head. 'Even to my best friend,' she smiled at Debra, 'there are experiences I cannot speak of.'

'I can imagine,' Daniel muttered.

When I enquired why she had come to Venice, she brushed off my question with a vague response about seeking sanctuary. Daniel looked sceptical, but Miriam was pursuing an agenda of her own. 'Why did you not find a husband here?' she persisted.

Henriette replied that she was already past the age of childbearing when she had arrived in Venice.

'I came to give you this,' she told Debra, handing her a small phial. 'Take one drop at night to make you sleep soundly. It will aid your recovery. And you,' she added, turning to me, 'do not deny the fate Hashem has decreed for you.'

After she had gone, Daniel vented his irritation. 'Why do you heed that woman's foolish talk?' he asked his mother.

Debra was indignant and refused to hear a word against her friend. 'You should be more charitable towards her, Daniel. She has had a hard life.'

'It certainly appears that the hard life of a solitary woman has turned her wits,' Daniel said. 'But she is cunning enough to befriend the women of the ghetto and spin her yarns about her rare revelations and mystical powers.' He turned to me. 'Young women pay her for love potions and tinctures to enhance their beauty while older women purchase her balms for aching bones and swollen ankles. Her customers are women, because few men are gullible enough to believe Hashem has chosen this wild woman as an instrument of His power.'

'Henriette sees truths that are hidden from the rest of us,' his mother said.

'The Rabbi himself dismisses her claims as the fantasies of a deluded woman, and exhorts us to beware of her,' Daniel replied. 'But women need something to believe in. Hashem has made you weak. Men know to trust only in what we know to be true.'

'She may have been unbalanced by her troubles, but Hashem has sent her here for sanctuary,' I pointed out. 'Her situation is no different to mine.'

'You earn your wages by honest work,' Daniel replied, 'not

by exploiting credulous women with false superstitions and foolishness.'

'She is a mystic who sees what we cannot,' Debra insisted.

'She is a leech, who preys on simple women. How can you defend her, Mother, when the Rabbi himself rejects her words as the ravings of a lunatic?'

'Well, you may scoff, Daniel, but I know Henriette's cordial will help me to sleep, and I am thankful she came to Venice.'

Hadassah and I fell into the habit of eating at Daniel's table in the evenings. When Henriette joined us again, she entertained us with descriptions of the exotic medina in Marrakesh, a city surrounded not by water, but by sand that stretched for miles in every direction until it reached the distant mountains. Elia's eyes grew round with wonder as he listened to her hypnotic voice that seemed to soothe away all stress.

'Distant hills glow crimson in the haze of heat rising from the ground, and nothing lives there but small prickly plants, and nomads who roam the dunes with hump-backed camels. The terracotta walls and minarets of Marrakesh rise above the sand like a floating island, an oasis of luxury in the vast desert.'

Henriette told us about the vast Jemaa el-Fna which, like the Piazza San Marco, was used both as a market and a place of execution. 'Jemaa el-Fna is always bustling with traders,' she said. 'You can find whatever you desire within the ancient red walls of the city: green and black olives, oils for the hair, spices and tagines, cures for every ailment, silks and herbs, teeth pullers and snake charmers, any kind of food and every colour apparel, while Berbers play their music and women dance for money.'

Henriette spoke of hammams where men and women immersed themselves in water and rubbed their skin with pungent health-giving oils.

'Do they get in the water together, naked?' Miriam giggled, and Elia pulled a face.

'No, Miriam,' Henriette replied gently. 'Men and women do not bathe together.'

'We shouldn't mock the customs of other cultures,' Debra scolded Miriam. 'What Henriette is describing is not so very different to our monthly immersion in the ritual bath.'

'It's not the same thing at all,' Miriam protested. 'Women go to the mikva seeking spiritual purity. It's nothing to do with physical health. Women don't go there with men, and we don't cover ourselves in smelly oils, grandmother.'

Daniel shook his head, muttering about wanton extravagance.

Unexpectedly, Henriette reached out and patted my hand. 'Here in the ghetto you will be safe,' she murmured.

'That is good to know,' I replied. 'The world outside is a dangerous place.'

No one disagreed with me.

18

I dared to believe Daniel enjoyed my company, because he often waited for me outside our apartment block so that we could walk together as far as the street where I worked.

'Surely this is out of your way?' I asked him once, but he replied that the exercise was good for him.

'It is healthy for a man to stretch his legs in walking,' he said. 'And when he can do so in pleasant company, it is so much the better for settling his humours.'

'Do you spend all day sitting, as I do?' I enquired, my eagerness to hear about his work at the print shop overcoming my embarrassment at the compliment.

He nodded solemnly. 'I am seated at a bench all day, setting the type.'

'What does that mean? Please, tell me all about it.'

He glanced regretfully at his ink-stained hands. 'It is dirty work, as you can see, and not very interesting, unless you are a printer.'

'On the contrary, I've always been intrigued to learn how it is done.'

When he expressed doubt, I launched into a description of

the prayer sheets we had used when I was a child, and how they had excited and mystified me. 'And it is not just prayer books that are printed, is it?' I added. 'There must be other things too. I cannot imagine what.'

He smiled. 'The first time I saw a printing press in use, it both terrified and thrilled me with its size and noise. The press stands higher than a man, and is as long as it is tall, and half as wide. Small metal blocks of type, each engraved with a letter, number or punctuation point, are arranged on a tray to form a page of text. Once they have been set out, ink is applied to them using balls of dog leather stuffed with sheep's wool, to make sure the ink is evenly applied. These are pressed onto damp paper held in place with pins, and a long handle moves a screw to exert pressure. The printing press was originally inspired by the grape press. But I am boring you.'

'No, not at all. Please continue.'

He glanced at me to see if I was genuinely interested. 'Oil-based ink lasts longer than a water-based variety,' he went on, 'and our type is made of a robust metal alloy.' He explained that his master possessed movable metal type in quantities large enough to print a complete page of text in one pressing.

'The only thing that holds us up, is having to wait for our paper to arrive,' he added.

'Why doesn't your master order enough paper so that you always have a stock of it to hand and never run out?'

'The paper manufacturer demands payment in advance,' Daniel replied, 'and the master doesn't want to part with his money any sooner than he has to. It is a massive outlay for him.'

'It's just the same with the seamstress,' I said. 'We are constantly running out of thread, because she will leave it to the last minute to purchase more. "If you were less careless and wasted fewer ends," she tells us, "we would not run out of thread so quickly. You should make it last longer." As though it is our fault when we do not have enough thread. As a result, we often struggle to complete our work in time, but we dare not hurry, because that is when mistakes are made.'

'It is the same problem exactly. Having to wait for paper holds us up, and makes us vulnerable,' Daniel grumbled. 'My master accuses us of wasting paper, but he speaks only in frustration. He knows we are careful and it is not our fault. Sometimes the wind is against us and the delivery of paper is delayed. And there is always the risk that pirates may intercept the ship carrying our supplies.'

'You think pirates steal your paper?' I laughed. 'I do not think that is the kind of loot they are after.' I told Daniel about my voyage from the port of Split to Venice, relating how the ship that transported us had been boarded by savage brigands who scoured the Adriatic from the Balkans to the coast of Northern Italy, plundering valuable merchandise, kidnapping wealthy Venetians, and disrupting commerce between Venice and her trading partners. 'They are only interested in profitable cargos like raw silk and spices from the East, and merchants rich enough to provide a significant ransom.'

Daniel's face grew pale as he listened. 'That is not an experience for a gentle soul like you,' he murmured.

'I have witnessed worse,' I replied quietly.

'At least your seamstress has only to go to the Rialto to replenish her stock,' he remarked. 'Our paper is sent from a manufacturer in Fabriano in the South, and reaches us by sea from the port at Ancona.'

'Why doesn't your master find a supplier closer to Venice?' I asked. Even with a following wind the boat from Ancona could take a week to reach Venice, apart from the risk that the ship might be lost at sea.

'The master purchases paper from Fabriano because his supplier uses water-powered stampers with multiple heads to pulp rags, which produces very high-quality paper. It's part of the reason why our printing shop is doing so well. The paper from Fabriano is coated in animal gelatine to produce a really smooth surface which takes ink well. I will bring you a slip of paper to examine so that you can feel how smooth it is.'

'Like silk as opposed to linen,' I suggested, and he nodded. 'Well, if you ask me, that's a shame. Nothing should be allowed to interrupt your work. It is too important.'

'No more important than making clothes.'

'You're wrong. Printing is more important than anything else.'

He laughed at my enthusiasm. 'What prompts that extravagant claim?'

'Because of printing, a day may come when the whole of humanity has access to books and we will see an end to ignorance. What could be more important?'

'I used to believe that literacy on a large scale would one day bring an end to mass ignorance, and eliminate prejudice and persecution. Man's inhumanity to his fellows would cease and the strong would no longer rule with superior might. In place of physical power, intelligence and understanding would become the driving force for an enlightened human race. Yes, Abigail, I used to believe that. When I was young, I thought that working in a print shop, my friends and I were not merely earning a living, we were helping to banish evil from the world by bringing about the end of ignorance. I believed, as you do, that one day every race would be reading books from other cultures and we would all come to understand one another and live in harmony. There would be peace throughout the world.'

'But if that happened, Jews would be assimilated into the wider community,' I replied, sensing a flaw in his vision. 'We would cease to exist as a people.'

'Do you not agree that would be a small sacrifice to pay for the greater good of all humanity?'

'But we are Hashem's chosen people, or do you not believe what the Rabbis tell us?' I did my best to conceal my dismay at his betrayal of our faith.

'Chosen for what?' he replied. 'Perhaps that is why we are a literate culture when others are not. We have been chosen to lead the rest of the world to knowledge and enlightenment.'

'Would you really place printing above the preservation of our religion?'

'Perhaps I would have done once,' he replied. 'But not any more. At the beginning of my career I was naive enough to appreciate the power of printing, without understanding how such power could be misused. The truth is that printing merely enables the powerful to strengthen their stranglehold on a gullible population. What could have been a force for enlightenment has become a propaganda tool for those in power, who have the means to censor what can be read.'

'You mean people can only read what their rulers allow them to read?' I asked.

'You follow my drift exactly,' he replied.

'The world is truly a terrible place,' I said.

He gazed at me. 'And yet it contains beauty and the possibility of great joy.' He hesitated as though there was more he would say to me, but we had arrived at Tamar's workshop and we parted. I hurried inside, my thoughts in turmoil.

The next morning Daniel was waiting to walk with me to work again. As we neared the sewing workshop, he stopped me, his eyes alight with a kind of mischief. 'I have brought you a book to read,' he said. 'You were right yesterday, when you said that printing is not only for prayer books. Have you heard of the great poet Dante?'

I shook my head.

'One day, when you are familiar with the Tuscan dialect in which he writes, I will show you his work.'

'I wish women could write words for other people to read,' I said.

'Of course they do,' he replied in surprise, and I looked at my feet, shamed by my ignorance. 'There have been many women who wrote great poetry. In fact, there's a Christian woman, Veronica Franco, living here in Venice, who came to see my master only this week to discuss printing her poems. When she does, perhaps we will read them together? But for now, I will lend you a book which is printed in Hebrew. I think you may like it.'

He told me the book had been written by a poet called Elia Levita, who had been living in Venice until his death sixteen years ago, not long after my own birth in Polotensk.

'I often saw his bowed white head in the synagogue,' Daniel told me, 'but we never spoke. He died in the year of my Bar Mitzvah. To me as a youth he was just another old man. It was only later that I discovered his writing.'

The idea of reading for enjoyment, rather than for the purpose of worshipping Hashem, was a novel one, and I accepted the book with a tremor of guilt. Sitting alone on a bench by the canal that evening, I opened the volume Daniel had thrust into my hand, and saw the title *Bovo Bukh*. Written in the Christian year 1508 and recently printed in Yiddish, it was the first non-religious book I had ever seen and I stared at it with a mixture of reverence and trepidation. As I began to read, the spellbinding narrative grabbed my attention and I read it every evening after work from beginning to end.

Levita related how Bovo's mother was married to the aged King of Ancona. My sympathy for the queen, forcibly tied to a man she loathed, vanished when I read how the queen arranged to have her husband killed. Horrified, I read how after the regicide she married the man who had murdered her husband. Afraid that her son, Bovo, would want to avenge his father when he reached manhood, the wicked queen attempted to poison her only son, but to my relief Bovo escaped. He was kidnapped and taken to Flanders where he became a servant to the King. Bovo was so handsome that the King's beautiful daughter, Druzane, fell in love with him as soon as she set eyes on him. The heathen Sultan of Babylonia marched on Flanders with an army of ten thousand soldiers, and demanded Druzane in marriage for his ugly son, Lucifer. When the request was refused the Sultan declared war on Flanders, and the King of Flanders was captured. At this point in the story Bovo appeared on a flying horse, wielding a magic sword. He defeated the Sultan's army, killed Lucifer, and freed the King of Flanders. As a reward Bovo was offered the hand of Druzane in marriage. Tears filled my eyes as I reached the end of the story where the two lovers were finally wed.

Holding the book in my hands, I pictured the hero, Bovo. In my imagination, he looked exactly like the printer, Daniel, who had lent me the enchanting book.

19

Summer was nearly at an end. Golden and red, the leaves on the tree in Campo del Ghetto Nuovo were ready to fall. Above us, a blue sky glowed in early morning light and the ghetto streets were quiet before the business of the day grew raucous with trading and lively gossip.

'The leaves are beautiful,' Daniel remarked, gazing up into the branches as we crossed the square. 'It is a pity we don't have more trees in the ghetto.'

'I suppose with all the waterways there is nowhere for them to grow. Where I grew up in Polotensk, we were surrounded by forest.'

I fell silent, remembering foraging in the forest with my sisters, and hiding there when the Streltsy came for us. As we drew near to the sewing shop, Daniel stopped and pulled a small package from his pouch.

'What is this?' I asked as he handed it to me.

'Open it, and you will see.'

Carefully I unfolded the paper. 'A thimble ring,' I cried out in surprise. 'Do you think I should use one?' With an involuntary gesture I covered my sore finger, embarrassed that he had noticed it.

'The thimble ring is a gift,' he replied, smiling.

'A gift?' I stammered, feeling my cheeks grow hot and my eyes fill with tears.

'Forgive me, but I could not help noticing your finger is pricked by needles, so I purchased this for you in the Rialto market. Have I offended you?' He added, with a strange urgency in his voice, when I did not respond.

Still I neither thanked him nor placed the thimble ring on my finger. Instead, I focused on hiding my tears, mortified that he should see me weeping when he had been so kind.

'What is the matter?' he asked, frowning in disappointment. 'I have offended you, haven't I? It was just... forgive me... it was well meant... from a friend who wishes you nothing but good fortune and freedom from pain...'

'You have not offended me,' I replied in a whisper, forcing myself to speak.

'Then tell me, Abigail, why are you weeping?'

'No one has ever given me a gift before.'

'But surely your husband–'

'My husband was a monster,' I hissed. 'He raised his hand to me many times, and would not allow me out of the house for fear the congregation would see my bruises. Not that they would have done anything about it,' I added bitterly. 'My parents could not even afford a dowry. We were paupers and I was lucky to have a husband at all.'

'Lucky? A husband who beat you,' he said, with a fury I had not seen in him before. 'If I ever get hold of that brute, he will crawl before you on his hands and knees, begging for your forgiveness. By the time I finish with him, he will be sorry he was ever born.'

I smiled through my tears. 'He is dead.'

'Praise be to Hashem.'

'That is a wicked thing to say about another human being, however evil he was,' I replied, wiping my eyes on my sleeve.

'I meant only that it means you are free to remarry, Abigail.'

'Not everyone who is free to marry chooses to do so,' I replied stiffly.

'What are you saying?'

'You have not accepted another match, have you? Your first wife died many years ago, yet you live alone. She must have been very happy with a husband who loved her so much.'

Daniel sighed. 'Poor Mira. We were both very young when we were betrothed, too young to know what marriage meant, barely old enough to know about the relations between a man and a woman. My wife was passionately attached to me, and yet for all her efforts to win my affection, I could not love her, not in the way she wanted to be loved. I tried to be a good husband to her, but she was not a wife I would have chosen, had we been free to decide for ourselves. Hashem forgive me, she had a wretched existence, married to a man who did not care for her.'

'But you treated her well? You did not beat her.'

'I never raised a hand to her and was as kind as I could be, but I was driven by pity, not love.'

'Perhaps she did not know how you truly felt. It is possible to hide one's feelings, even to those who should be closest to us.'

'That is true. I did my best to hide my coldness, but I think she always knew she did not arouse a deep and true affection in me. I have never spoken of this to another living soul,' he went on. 'What I have told you must never be repeated to my children. Poor Mira, all she wanted was to bear me a child. It was a year before she conceived, and during that year she prayed for a child every day, and lived in fear of my abandoning her. Truly she was my wife in name only. She thought if she bore me a son it would bind me to her, but all the birth of our twins did was take her from me. She was very young when she died, leaving my mother to raise my children. She has done her best, but I fear they have suffered from never knowing their mother.'

'Your son and daughter are fine, and you should be proud of them.' I told him how Elia had refused to accept a fee from my uncle, laughing when the swimming master had boxed his ears.

'Do you know how Elia responded to the swimming master's reprimand? He said it is a blessing to help others. That is what my parents taught me, and it is how all Jews should live.'

Daniel smiled. 'You are right, he is a righteous lad, honest and well meaning. Let us hope he grows out of his wild ways. But he must never hear of my feelings towards his mother. As far as my children know, we were a loving couple.' He sighed. 'She was a good woman.'

'If she had lived, you might have come to love her.'

'Had she lived, we would have found a path to contentment, but I want more than that.' He spoke with a fervour that scared me. 'Ever since poor Mira died, I have prayed for a wife I can love, a woman who will stand at my side, not walk always in my shadow. As the holy Torah teaches us, "It is not good for man to be alone." And so Hashem made Adam a helper suitable for him, to be a companion for him.' He paused. 'Mira and I were not companions. We could never have been friends. We never talked as openly as you and I have done, Abigail. She did not understand me as I believe you do.'

His words made me tremble. No man had ever spoken to me so tenderly before. 'I cannot be late for work,' I said hurriedly, turning away, flustered by his words.

'Will you come to our house this evening?' he asked.

'I think Hadassah is expecting me to spend the evening with her.'

'Then may I come to Tamar's after work and walk home with you?'

I knew it would be wise to resist his entreaty, but I was weak. 'Yes, I would like that.'

'And may I speak to Guta?' he added, suddenly grabbing my hand in his.

'Who is Guta?' I asked, agitated by the touch of his warm flesh.

'Guta, the matchmaker.'

'You are arranging Miriam's match?'

'No, no, Abigail, drop this pretence. I know you are not obtuse and I cannot believe you enjoy watching me suffer this agony of uncertainty. Have I not made my feelings clear to you? I wish to make a match for myself.'

I gasped, taken aback by his words. 'You are to be married?'

'If you will have me.'

I shook my head, stammering in confusion.

'Abigail, be my wife and make me the happiest of men.'

I should have refused, not knowingly sought to shackle the man I loved to a murderess. Instead, I heard myself speak. 'Nothing would make me happier than to be your wife, Daniel.'

And so it was agreed between us, a widow and a widower, speaking for ourselves without the need of a matchmaker's intermediation. Taking my seat at my bench in Tamar's workshop, I slipped my brass thimble ring on my finger but my hands were shaking so much that I could scarcely sew a stitch. I had agreed to be Daniel's wife without confessing my guilt to him. Once he learned what I had done, all my hopes of happiness would be over. I could only pray that my uncle would never return and reveal the truth about me. But I feared Hashem would not allow my secret to remain hidden forever.

20

Hadassah did not seem surprised by my wonderful news.

'I'm going to miss you,' she said, adding grudgingly, 'but I suppose I should be happy for you. There's no doubt you deserve your good fortune. And you can tell Daniel that if he ever mistreats you, I'll send a dybbuk to haunt his dreams and make his life a misery.'

We both made a spitting sound with our tongues behind our teeth, to ward off the evil spirits. It was not clever to mention them, even in jest. You never knew when they might be listening.

'Seriously, Abigail, it's good to see you looking so happy.'

'I pray that Hashem may send you a good man to lighten your load,' I replied. 'Someone who will bring you joy.'

'Me?' She laughed. 'I am too old and wise to be caught like that.'

'We have not yet announced our betrothal,' I told her, 'so please let it remain between us for now.'

She nodded. 'Do not fret. I am no gossip. It's no one else's business unless you choose to make it so. I am satisfied to enjoy your happiness in silence. You are like a sister to me.'

Her words made me weep, reminding me of my own sisters who had perished in the massacre at Polotensk.

Hadassah and I agreed to eat at Daniel's table that evening.

'You are always welcome under our roof,' he told Hadassah. 'We will not forget how you took Abigail in and gave her a home here in Venice.'

Elia arrived home late, after we had begun eating, and he accepted a berating from his father with a patience born of custom.

'Do not scold the boy,' Daniel's mother said, in a scene that had doubtless been played out many times before.

'I would not have reason to scold him if he arrived home in time for supper,' Daniel replied. 'Did you miss the curfew again, Elia?'

'No, father. But look what I have brought home with me.' He drew a letter out of his doublet with a flourish.

'Is it from my daughter, Ester?' Daniel's mother asked. News from Daniel's sister who lived in Ferrara was always a cause of excitement in their household.

But Elia shook his head. 'Unlikely,' he replied. 'Because it's addressed to Abigail. A travelling merchant sought me out on the waterfront at the Piazza San Marco and asked me if I could deliver it to the ghetto. "It is for Abigail of Polotensk," he said, "if you have heard of her." I assured him everyone in the Ghetto Nuovo knows Abigail.'

Smiling at me, Elia handed me the letter.

'It is from my uncle,' I cried out in sudden trepidation.

My dearest niece,
I have travelled far since leaving you in the ghetto of Venice, and I pray every day that you have found a home and pleasant company. All the residents of the ghetto I met seemed civilised and kind, and

their Rabbi is a righteous man. The ghetto is well established and feels as secure a place as any to stay while you await my return.

I have much to tell you, but have not time to write it all now. There is a travelling merchant about to leave for Venice, who has promised to see this letter safely delivered into your hand.

I plan to be in Venice in time to celebrate Chanukah with you this winter, and we can exchange our news then. I doubt you will have as much to say as I have, and trust you are in good health and living quietly.

Until the winter, with affection,
Uncle Abraham.

That evening Daniel and I walked to the Agudi Bridge where we stood discussing our plans. He put his arms around me and drew me close, and my intention to tell him the truth about my past shrivelled inside me. As long as my uncle kept silent, no one else need ever find out that I had killed a man in the forest outside Polotensk. Feeling Daniel's lips on mine, I resolved to throw myself on my uncle's mercy and hope that all would end well.

'I will love you as tenderly as a mother loves her child,' Daniel whispered. Hearing footsteps, we drew apart for fear of being seen. When Daniel expressed himself ready to marry me the very next day, I asked him to wait until my uncle's return. My uncle was bound to condemn me for hiding the truth from the man I was to marry. I had to persuade him to keep my secret, before I stood under the wedding canopy again.

'I understand you want him to be present,' he said, 'and I will respect your desire. But I wish we could have the wedding sooner.'

'He is my only living relative,' I replied.

'At least let us be betrothed in the synagogue before the week is over,' he said. 'It is such a long time to wait, and I cannot bear to think that anything could happen that might change your mind.'

I laughed at him. 'Nothing can possibly happen to change my mind, Daniel. As I love Hashem, I have given you my word and nothing will induce me to break it. I would sooner die than forego being your wife.'

'Abigail,' he said, 'I have waited so long to tell you how much I care for you, and will wait until Chanukah if that is what you wish, as long as I may one day call you my wife.'

'You may,' I replied, 'and you will.'

I prayed that my words would come true. As he bent to kiss me again, a woman opened a window to throw out her slops, and we parted before we could be seen together. We were considering approaching the Rabbi to bless our betrothal in the presence of the congregation, when Guta brought news that her match for Miriam was proceeding. The young man's father was agreeable, and the youth was visiting Venice from Padua where he was studying. Guta arrived at Daniel's home to arrange a meeting between the two young people.

'You will see your daughter wed to a physician, trained at the University of Padua, Hashem be praised,' Guta said, giving me an appraising glance as she spoke.

Like Jehudit of Polotensk, Guta was old and her back was bent, yet her eyes were shrewd and she spoke with a force that was hard to resist. 'This is an excellent match for Miriam,' she told us. 'He is a clever boy and she is no fool, that one. She has more sense than her father at any rate,' she added under her breath, no doubt referring to Daniel's refusal to remarry.

The young man in question was the son of Meir ben Eliezer, a quiet man who worked in the ghetto selling second-hand goods. Daniel was satisfied that he had a reputation as a righteous man.

'I will consult with my daughter,' Daniel told Guta, 'but she is hardly going to refuse a boy who is studying to become a physician.'

Miriam sat smiling and nodding her head.

'I should think not,' Guta replied, sounding indignant that Daniel could harbour any reservations about the match.

'Let them meet and if they like one another the betrothal can proceed and they can be promised to one another in the eyes of Hashem. There is no rush for them to marry. My daughter is not yet twelve.'

'That was my thinking exactly when Meir ben Eliezer came to me for a match. As long as the boy is studying at the University of Padua, Daniel will be happy for the marriage to wait, I told him. In the meantime, let us reach an agreement. Truly, only a Rabbi commands greater respect than a physician,' she added, 'and you can be sure David ben Meir will be able to keep your daughter in comfort. I warn you not to keep his father waiting,' Guta said. 'He expects an answer by tomorrow at the latest. Remember, this young man will put food on your daughter's table every day. If you turn him down, you will not receive another offer equal to this one. Do you want your daughter to end up married to lame old Adamo, the coffin maker?'

'She will be content with the son of Meir ben Eliezer,' Daniel said firmly, and Miriam nodded, her eyes shining with excitement.

'From your lips to the ears of Hashem,' Guta replied.

'Rest easy, Guta. She will be content,' Daniel repeated, and Miriam nodded eagerly again.

In view of Miriam's impending betrothal ceremony, Daniel and I decided to wait a while before announcing our own understanding. Two days later, Meir ben Eliezer's son arrived in the ghetto. Miriam's grandmother spent the day helping her to dress. Even so, my assistance was enlisted when I finished work.

'Look at my hair,' Miriam wailed. 'No self-respecting boy is going to want to marry a girl who looks like this.' She held out a strand of her unruly dark hair.

'Ribbons,' I said firmly. 'Sit still and I will tie some ribbons in your hair.'

The boy was barely a head taller than Miriam but, apart from his slight stature, he was a good-looking young man, with curly black hair and sharp dark eyes. Daniel had insisted the betrothal should not be announced until the young couple had met and confirmed they were satisfied with each other, and we all waited impatiently in the square while Guta sat with them in her apartment.

'My son is sixteen,' Meir told us nervously. 'He needs to be betrothed soon. He has never shown any interest in girls – or in anyone else for that matter,' he added quickly, as though afraid we might conclude that his son was a degenerate. 'He has only ever been interested in learning. It is good for a boy to study, and he is certainly blessed with intelligence, praise be to Hashem. He could have been a Rabbi, but he chose to be a physician. Truly it is a blessing for a man to save lives.' He sighed. 'But a man cannot devote himself to books alone. He must take a wife. Is it not written that we should go forth and multiply? Is this not the will of Hashem?' He paused. 'Miriam is a lovely girl. She is going to be a great beauty, like her mother.'

I was slightly surprised, having never heard Daniel's first wife described as a beautiful woman, but Daniel accepted Meir's words as the compliment he intended. Meir was usually a quiet man, but nerves made him babble, as they make some men taciturn.

'Do you believe all this talk of a war between the Turks and the Christians?' he asked Daniel.

'My brother-in-law in Ferrara seems to think it is inevitable,' Daniel replied.

'My cousin in Bologna tells me it is coming. Hashem protect us all,' Meir said, adding after a pause, 'all but the Officers of the Inquisition, that is.'

Daniel smiled grimly and the two fathers paced the square together, while I sat on the bench with Debra, waiting for the matchmaker to join us. At last she appeared. The young couple walked behind her, not looking at one another. For a moment we watched them in silence, but then I saw that Guta was beaming.

'It is agreed,' she said as she scurried over to join us.

'Thanks be to Hashem,' Meir cried out and he embraced Daniel.

Although the young couple never glanced at one another, Miriam looked pleased, and David ben Meir seemed satisfied. In the synagogue, Miriam sat upstairs between her grandmother and I, while David sat downstairs with his father and Daniel. When prayers were concluded, the Rabbi called the young couple up to stand before him on the raised bimah, where he blessed them for a long and happy life, while the congregation smiled in approbation.

'I hope this match doesn't mean you're going to give all your money away supporting Miriam's future husband in his studies,' Elia remarked, a trifle sourly over supper one evening after Miriam's intended had returned to his university.

'Don't fret, you stupid boy,' Miriam told him. 'You'll end up with a wealthy bride when your brother-in-law is an eminent physician.'

'He's not an eminent physician, he's a student,' Elia pointed out. 'He's only a boy.'

'Well, he will be a physician one day,' she replied, smiling. 'And he's not a boy, he's a man. He's sixteen.'

Even her brother's carping could not dampen Miriam's spirits. Her grandmother smiled complacently, and I was filled with joy at the pleasure on Daniel's face. A few weeks later, I caught a glimpse of a letter Miriam was writing to David. All I read was, 'But how can you be certain there are only four humours?' before she snatched up the paper and hid it. I smiled and thanked Hashem that she and David were well matched.

21

Chanukah was fast approaching and I had agreed to marry Daniel on the day after the festival ended, whether my uncle had arrived by then or not. Nothing I said could persuade Daniel to wait any longer. My uncle had not been in touch with me since the letter advising me of his plans to return to Venice for Chanukah. Daniel had tentatively pointed out that my uncle might be dead, in which case we might wait forever to celebrate our nuptials. If that was true, my dreadful secret would have gone with him to his grave. Although my uncle's death would relieve me of my fears, I desperately wanted him at my wedding. Without him, there would not be another living soul from Polotensk to witness the ceremony.

'I will be your family,' Daniel comforted me, when I lamented my situation. 'You are not alone now.'

On the last night of Chanukah I went home to my lodgings to be met at the door by the stout figure of my landlady blocking my way. Hadassah was never swayed by emotion, so I was surprised to see tears in her eyes.

'Oh my dear,' she whispered to me, 'something terrible has happened.'

'Is Daniel sick?'

She shook her head.

A coldness crept through me. 'Is he– dead?'

'No, nothing has happened to Daniel. But–' She hesitated before blurting out, 'You cannot marry him.'

'Why not? Hadassah, what are you talking about?'

A cold dread flooded through me as I understood that Daniel had discovered my terrible secret. Knowing me for a vile sinner, he had turned his back on me. Somehow I had to persuade him to reconsider. Without another word I pushed past her into our living room. For a second I did not recognise the old man seated at the table, resting his head on his hand. As soon as he looked up I sprang forward, joy overcoming my despair.

'Uncle! I am happy to see you.'

As we embraced, my mind raced. My uncle must have betrayed me to Hadassah for her to have spoken as she did, but he had not yet had time to reveal my dark secret to Daniel. Somehow I had to persuade him and Hadassah to remain silent. They both loved me. All hope was not yet lost. As I was thinking what to say, there was a loud grunt, and I noticed another man lying on my bed. Not troubling to lift his head, he raised a huge hand in greeting.

'Husband? Can it be you?' I stammered, recoiling in horror. 'I thought you were dead.'

'So you ran away and left me,' he snarled, heaving himself up onto one elbow and glaring at me, his fists clenched. 'Well? Are you not pleased to see me, wife?'

'I thought you were dead,' I repeated stupidly. 'I thought you were dead.'

His expression grew vicious and from across the room I could smell ale on his breath. 'What kind of a shit welcome is this, wife?' he growled, rising to his feet and scowling at me as I cowered away from him.

Swaying slightly, he turned his head to one side and spat on the floor.

'Please don't do that in here–' Hadassah began, and broke off as he turned to look at her.

'You can shut your face as well, woman,' he shouted, his voice slurred with drink, 'unless you want me to shut it for you.' He raised a fist, threatening to hit her. 'Abigail is my wife so you can mind your own business.' He waved his fist around the room. 'You can all mind your own business. Come here, wife, I'm sick of whores with their loose fannies. It's time to welcome your husband back as a wife should.'

'Abigail is my lodger–' Hadassah began helplessly.

'She's my wife,' he yelled.

Just then the door of the apartment flew open and Daniel burst in.

'And who is this pretty boy?' Reuven asked, looking round with a sneer. 'Have you come to watch how my wife welcomes me home? Come here, bitch, and open your legs, or do I have to force them open myself?'

My uncle fell on the chair and dropped his head in his hands, pleading with my husband to be civil. Daniel ran to my side and took my hand.

'What's this?' Reuven growled. 'Get your filthy hands off my wife, pretty boy.'

He swayed again on his feet, his eyes glazed from drinking. Had we been alone, I had no doubt he would have assaulted me by now, but the presence of strangers in the room made him pause.

'Surely you cannot intend to let your niece stay with a man like that,' Daniel said, dropping my hand and appealing to my uncle. 'She is your niece, your own blood. You must protect her from him.'

'They are married,' my uncle replied miserably. 'What can I do? The law is on his side. Not all husbands are kind to their wives.'

'He is not fit to be her husband,' Daniel said. 'You heard how he spoke to her.'

My uncle gave a helpless shrug. 'Reuven of Polotensk is her husband in the eyes of Hashem. Unless he agrees to give her a divorce, there is nothing any of us can do. The law is the law.'

'And according to the law, that bitch is my wife. Come here and lie with your husband, you with your big cow eyes. I'll give you more than a fuck.' He laughed. 'I'll make you smart for the cold welcome you gave me.' He swung his head, gazing belligerently around the room. 'What? Do you think I like her any less because she fights me when I fuck her? The more she pushes me away, the more I enjoy it. That's the kind of man I am.' In his drunken frenzy, he began boasting about his viciousness. 'She can't hold me off for long and then wham! I give it to her. Every time, right up her tight little fanny. Isn't that right, wife? You squeal when I fuck you, don't you? Squeal like a rabbit in a snare.' He threw his head back and roared with laughter.

'Abraham, please, you cannot leave her to suffer such violence at the hands of that brute,' Hadassah cried out angrily. 'We must have him taken before the tribunal.'

'On what grounds, you old hag?' Reuven demanded, glaring at her. 'For fucking my wife? Is a man not commanded to lie with his wife? I have come to take back what is lawfully mine. If a mincing fool tries to steal her away from me with his curly hair and his pretty face, whose side will the law come down on, do you suppose? Go on, pretty boy, do your worst. You may have bewitched her with your simpering lies, but she stood beside me beneath the wedding canopy, with her father's blessing, and married me before the Rabbi and the whole congregation of Polotensk. Do you deny it, wife?'

I shook my head, accepting this was my punishment for the sin of taking a man's life.

'Look at her, quivering like a frightened mouse. Where is the welcome for me, I'd like to know? Does no one here have a kind word to say to Reuven, who survived the massacre at Polotensk? No matter, Hashem loves me, even if my wife is a frigid bitch. Oh well, I see she has twisted your minds and turned you all against me with her sly ways.' He took a step towards Daniel. 'You can go, pretty boy. Fucking my wife will be all the sweeter, knowing you lust after her. You will have to be satisfied with pleasuring yourself, because after feeling my swollen cock, she will forget all about you. Now go. You are not welcome under my roof.'

'It is not your roof,' Hadassah said, trembling. 'This is my apartment and I want you to leave right now.'

'I am sleeping here tonight. This is my wife's bed, which makes it my bed.'

He flung himself down on my bed again and closed his eyes. Hadassah looked at me, horrified by my husband's behaviour, but we all knew he had the law on his side. Besides, I did not know what my uncle had told him about me while they were travelling together. If I challenged him, my husband would not hesitate to disclose my sin, careless of the consequences.

'Husband,' I hazarded, 'I am sorry I was not here to welcome you but my uncle did not send word you would be returning with him. I believed you had perished at the hand of the Streltsy, along with everyone else in our ghetto. I thought my uncle and I were the only ones who survived. It was an honest mistake. I am happy that you survived and wish you nothing but joy and continued good fortune for the rest of your days. But I have moved on in my life, in the belief that you were dead. I mourned for your death.' Hashem forgive my lie, but I was desperate to appease my husband. 'It is several years since we last set eyes on one another, and I have met another. We are betrothed, and I believe we will be happy. I beg of you, divorce me and let me marry Daniel, and I will bless your name in my prayers for as long as I live.'

In the silence that followed my speech, I prayed that my uncle and husband would go away and leave me in peace with Daniel.

My husband lay on the bed with his eyes closed. 'Do not speak your fancy man's name again,' he growled.

'Reuven, my husband, leave him alone. He is nothing to me,' I murmured.

I prayed that Hashem would forgive my lie, but my husband was not appeased.

He sat up suddenly, his face red with choler. 'Have you forgotten what follows if you dare to speak my name? I will deal with you later. I am going out for some air. This room stinks of Venetian vermin. See to it they are not here when I return.' He strode across the room, flung the door open and departed.

'I am afraid he has taken to excessive drinking,' my uncle muttered. 'I cannot help you, niece. Reuven is your husband in the sight of Hashem, I wish it were not so.' He drew in a shuddering breath. 'I cannot stay here any longer, watching his violent outbursts. At first light I will leave Venice and continue on my travels to spread the news about Polotensk. There is nothing else left for me. I will pray for you every day.'

Longing for him to stay, I stood mute as he embraced me, and left.

Daniel took a step towards me but I shook my head. 'My uncle is right. My situation is hopeless,' I said wretchedly. 'My husband will never grant me a divorce. Please, go. I cannot bear to look on your face, knowing that Hashem brought us together only to part us. How can I love Hashem, when he has taken from me the one person in the world that I care for most? Go, go, Daniel, leave me. Whatever happens, you must not be here when he returns.'

'I will stay here and protect you,' he replied.

'I am serious, Daniel, he will kill you and then he will flee, taking me with him, and then he will kill me too, on a deserted stretch of road where no one can see. You must see this cannot end well. There is no way you can rescue me from my lawful husband. At least give me the comfort of knowing you have saved yourself. You cannot save me. Now go. It will be worse for me if he finds you here when he returns.'

Daniel stared at me, distraught, and then he turned and left. I fell into Hadassah's arms, sobbing, and felt her trembling. There would be no hero on a flying horse to save me from my husband.

22

Early the following morning, my uncle announced he was setting off on his travels again. I beseeched him to stay, but he insisted that he wanted to continue spreading the word about the massacre at Polotensk. We both knew his precipitate departure was prompted by my husband's vicious behaviour. Miserably I watched him leave, not knowing whether we would ever see one another again. That evening, Hadassah and I were seated at the table eating bread and barley soup, with strips of goose flesh and crispy onions fried in fat, when my husband returned from the tavern, reeking of ale. Hadassah folded her thick arms across her chest and scowled at him. Taking no notice of either of us, he marched to the bed, lay down and barked at me to remove his boots.

'Is that any way to speak to your wife?' Hadassah snapped at him. 'Let her finish her supper. Come, join us,' she added grudgingly, 'while the soup is still hot.'

'I told you to remove my boots, cow eyes,' he repeated, sitting up and glowering at me, his face turning red with choler.

'It is all right,' I assured Hadassah. 'You finish your supper. I will see to my husband.'

As I crouched down to remove his filthy boots, he raised his leg abruptly to kick me under the chin so that I fell backwards. Accustomed to his violent moods, I returned to the task of removing his boots, for fear he would inflict even more harm on me if I resisted. Once I had placed his boots neatly by the bed he lay down again and closed his eyes.

'Now clean the shit off my boots,' he said.

'Yes, husband,' I replied meekly.

I turned and saw Hadassah frowning at me. 'Take them to the well,' she suggested, standing up. 'Come, I will help you.'

I gathered up my husband's boots and left, with Hadassah following me.

'I will not tolerate such behaviour under my roof,' she hissed at me when we were safely outside.

'What are you taking about?'

'That disgusting animal kicked you and you did not even remonstrate. He kicked you, Abigail. I saw it with my own eyes.'

Without a word, I pulled back one of my long sleeves and she gaped at the scars from my husband's brutality.

'Did he do that to you?'

I nodded. 'So you see, if I had not obeyed him just now, he would have done far worse than kick me.'

'Do you not fear for your safety?'

'I am past caring,' I replied, 'but now, let us be practical. It is clear to me that my husband and I must leave your lodgings. You are not happy with us being here, and there is a risk he may turn his anger on you one day. I am serious, Hadassah, you cannot imagine what he can do when the door is closed and no one else is here to see him.'

'Hashem sees everything,' she replied. 'And besides, he would not dare to touch me,' she replied. 'I would not stand for it.'

'He is violent and unpredictable, and extremely strong.

There is no knowing what he might do when he has been drinking. Listen to me. You must tell us that we have to leave your apartment. Invent what excuse you like. No, wait, say that your husband and son are returning from a journey, so my husband does not think you will be alone here. That way he will not dare to come back. But you must see that we cannot stay. If I can live alone with him, I may be able to exercise some control over his temper.'

'And he may kill you,' she said. 'No, it is not safe for you to be alone with him.'

'Hadassah, he is my husband. There is nothing you or I or anyone else can do to set me free. The law is clear on this, and I must endure the tribulations Hashem has sent me.'

'Then stay with me. If he assaults you again, I can summon help from our neighbours.'

'No, we will leave your apartment, and it must be soon. You have already provoked his wrath and I fear for your safety.'

'And what about your safety?' she insisted, her eyes glistening in the cold light of the moon.

Hashem forgive me, but I cursed my innocent uncle for bringing my husband back to me. Now that he knew where Daniel and Hadassah lived, I had no choice but to accede to his wishes. If I refused, I feared for the lives of my friends. 'I have been burdened with him since I stood at his side under the wedding canopy in Polotensk, and can never be free,' I told Hadassah. 'This is not your problem.'

I did not try to explain that my sin deserved this punishment. Quickly I cleaned my husband's boots and we returned to the apartment, Hadassah mumbling darkly under her breath. For my part, I hoped that he would be fast asleep, snoring as he always did when he was drunk. But when we walked back in, he was sitting at the table, eating the remains of our dinner. Hadassah scowled and I gave her a warning frown.

'That was our dinner,' she grumbled, too angry to hold her peace.

All he had left us was one hunk of bread.

'Not bad,' Reuven admitted, wiping his greasy mouth on his sleeve. 'Ah, my boots. About time, cow eyes.'

Distracted by Hadassah, I had not cleaned his boots thoroughly and trembled in case he inspected them, but he just grabbed them from me and slung them in the corner. Black bile overwhelmed my other humours with melancholy as I realised what that meant.

'Are you not going out, husband?' I enquired tentatively. 'We have no ale or wine in the apartment. I am only thinking of your comfort,' I added, doing my best to sound sincere.

He swore, flung himself down on my bed, rolled around, then suddenly sat up and held his feet out. I responded with alacrity, hurrying to put his boots on.

'Push harder!' he yelled, stamping on the floor as he stood up. Just in time I pulled my hand away, before my fingers were crushed under his boot. He pushed past me and left, seizing the remaining piece of bread and cramming it in his mouth on his way.

After he had gone, Hadassah and I stood side by side in silence for a few moments. When we were sure he had gone, she turned to me, her face contorted with fury. 'Abigail, how can you put up with him? Surely your submission to such a brute cannot be pleasing to Hashem.'

'Hashem has decreed my fate,' I replied. 'We are all in His hands.'

I had said everything I could in response to her question. Hadassah retired to bed and I did likewise, praying that my husband would not return later to molest me. Hashem heard my prayer that night because Reuven did not come back until the next morning, looking red faced and bloated. He flung himself on the bed and was soon snoring. I judged he would sleep for several hours.

Hadassah must have been mulling over what I had said, because she tackled us as soon as my husband woke. 'You have to find alternative accommodation,' she said, without any preamble. 'My husband and son have been away, travelling, but they have sent me word that they will be here tomorrow. I need you out of here today so that I can prepare the apartment for them.'

'That suits us well, does it not, wife?' my husband replied, flinging his arm around my shoulder and leaning his weight on me so that I stumbled. 'We were planning to leave this shithouse anyway. Do you think I want to live next door to my wife's fancy man? I might be tempted to wring his neck if I catch him sniffing around my cow-eyed wife. As for you–' He took a step towards Hadassah without releasing his hold on my neck, dragging me with him. 'You should have taken better care of my wife.'

'Hadassah took me in and gave me a bed,' I protested.

'And I say she pimped you out to her fancy neighbour!' he yelled suddenly. 'How else have you managed to survive, paying her rent and buying food? You have not been living on air, witch!'

'I found honest work with a seamstress,' I replied.

'As you would have known had you not been away from home or drunk ever since you arrived here,' Hadassah added.

'Do not contradict me, you filthy hag,' he growled at Hadassah before turning to me, his face choleric, his eyes glaring. 'No wife of mine goes out to work! Fetch your things. We are going.'

Hiding my misery as well as I could, I packed my few clothes and rags in a bed sheet Hadassah gave me along with a cooking pot, a couple of bowls and drinking vessels and a few cooking implements.

'Take them,' Hadassah urged me. 'He will be in a better temper when he is fed.'

She embraced me and I clung to her, overwhelmed by despair at having to leave the home where I had found happiness.

'Come, wife,' my husband said, and I followed him out onto the street.

23

My husband led me through the Campo del Ghetto Nuovo where a small boy and girl were crouching down rolling dice, while a couple of older boys took it in turns to throw sticks at a pebble. A few other children were running around the square playing tag, laughing and calling out to each other in shrill voices. Beneath the bare branches of the tree, a solitary boy shuffled through golden and brown leaves, kicking them up in the air and shrieking with glee as they seemed to float on the still air. My heart ached at the sight of such innocence.

When we reached the Agudi Bridge, it began to rain, a hard drizzle that fell steadily from a grey sky. My feet were soon wet and my cloak sodden, as I followed my husband over the bridge, where raindrops fell and vanished without trace into the dark water of the canal. We walked on through the Ghetto Vecchio, where the Sephardi Jews lived. The rain continued as we followed the twisting streets, and by the time we stopped in an alleyway at the far end of the Calle del Forno, I was shivering as with a fever. My husband knocked at a door and after a long time an ancient woman opened it and peered out at us.

'We have come for the room,' he said.

The old woman squinted at him suspiciously. 'I want no trouble and no profanity,' she mumbled through the toothless gums of one who has lived too long in this world. 'This is a respectable household.'

My husband seized my hand. 'This modest creature is my wife, bound to me under the holy wedding canopy in Polotensk. We live a righteous life.' He held out a coin. Muttering under her breath, the old woman snatched the money and showed us into a room with barely space for a narrow bed, a small table and a stool. High above the bed there was a tiny window, letting in a thin shaft of light.

'I will need a chair,' my husband said, looking around.

The old woman leered at us. 'I have a proper room, with a larger bed, but it will cost you more.'

'This bed is fine,' he replied. 'My wife sleeps on the floor.'

There was hardly enough room for me to lie curled up beside the table but I dared not protest, and if our landlady was surprised by his words, she was shrewd enough to conceal it.

Reuven nodded. 'We will take the room. And you will bring me a chair.'

My husband brought vegetables home for me to cook on our small fire, so that I had no need to go to the shops along the Calle del Ghetto Vecchio and there was no call for him to give me any money. Now that I was no longer going to Tamar's, I did not have so much as a soldo of my own. Reuven claimed he wanted to save me the trouble, but we both knew the real reason for his parsimony: he did not want me stepping foot outside our room for fear I would run away. Somehow he sensed I was no longer the scared girl he had married, but a survivor who knew what it was to live an independent life, with friends across the bridge in the Ghetto Nuovo.

Yet we had been married in the sight of Hashem under the

holy wedding canopy, and I had no choice. To disobey my husband would mean incurring divine wrath, and risk exposing my dark past. And besides all of those reasons, visceral fear of his fists kept me trapped, like a fly in a spider's web. I could not escape from him without endangering the lives of the people I loved in the Ghetto Nuovo. Before long, the power he exerted over my spirit so cowed me again, that the mere thought of him robbed me of my strength.

Since I never knew when he would be home, I kept food permanently simmering on the fire. If he came home hungry and nothing was prepared, he would fall into a rage. He only brought home food enough for himself, which meant I ate only on the days he did not return home. Fortunately that happened often. Even so, I frequently lay down on the floor hungry at the end of a dreary day. Yet for all that he was miserly with me, my husband boasted of his profligacy at the tavern in the ghetto, and his generosity to the whores in the city. So I drifted into a kind of weary death-in-life, with my husband acting as my jailor, and hunger and fear my constant companions. The memory of my life in the Ghetto Nuovo faded like a half-forgotten dream until I struggled to recall Daniel's face.

We passed a harsh winter in our cell, but at least I was able to keep the fire burning, day and night. Every morning, a water carrier delivered buckets from door to door. Before long, my husband fell out with the young man, accusing him of extortion.

'Do you think I'm a wealthy man?' he roared, raising his huge fist.

'Fine,' the water carrier answered, starting back in alarm. 'You can fetch your own water from now on.' Grumbling insults, he scuttled away.

I was grateful for the opportunity to step out of our apartment once a day to fetch water from the well. Blinking in sunlight to which my eyes had grown unaccustomed, I carried an empty bucket to the well. On the way back, I would stop off at our ancient landlady's home to fill her ewer with water. With its solitary well, the Ghetto Vecchio was not as comfortably served as the Ghetto Nuovo on the other side of the Agudi Bridge, which had four public wells. As a result, I often had to wait in line to fill my bucket. This suited me, as I overheard snatches of local gossip, a reminder that there was life outside the four walls where I had been incarcerated for months. As the spring advanced, instead of hurrying home with my bucket, I took to loitering by the well. For a few moments each day, I remembered that life could be beautiful.

Gradually I learned to recognise the women who came regularly for water. We greeted one another with silent nods. It was company of a sort. After a few weeks, my daily trips to the well gave me an opportunity to pay a different kind of visit while I was out of the house. My husband had only to look for me at the well, and my subterfuge would be discovered, but my condition had made me desperate enough to take that chance. What I was about to do was a terrible sin, but I had made enquiries at the well, and knew of a woman who might help me. With the empty water bucket over my arm, I hurried on my way, driven by a desperate determination.

My first visit was to Hadassah. There was no time to waste. I had to be back in our lodgings in the Ghetto Vecchio soon, with a full bucket of water. If Hadassah was not home, my plan would fail. Rapping loudly at her door, I waited. Probably no more than a moment passed before I heard her footsteps, but the waiting felt interminable.

'Who is it–?' Her voice petered out as she saw me, and her expression changed from annoyance to astonishment.

'Abigail? Can it really be you? You look like a wraith.' She drew back and studied me, muttering a prayer to ward off evil spirits.

'It is me,' I replied. 'Hashem be praised that I can look on your beloved face again.'

'Seriously, my dear, your cheeks have fallen in and your eyes are bloodshot. What ails you? But forgive me. Come in, come in at once and sit down.'

May Hashem bless her for her kindness, she did not shut her door against me.

'I am not sick,' I reassured her, 'my health is good, Hashem be praised. But I am in desperate need of your help. I have come to beg you to lend me money.'

She neither flinched nor hesitated, but immediately asked me how much I needed and hurried inside to fetch it. Taking the money with tears of gratitude, I assured her that I could not stay. Every moment away from my home increased my danger.

'He still lives, then?' she asked shortly.

'Yes.'

'Then may Hashem protect you,' she said. 'And may He forgive me, but I hoped you had escaped and needed money to flee from Venice. It is not too late. I will help you.'

I shook my head. 'There is no getting away from him. Wherever I go he will find me. This is the fate Hashem has willed for me and I must submit.'

I did not add that were I to flee, her life would be in danger. We embraced and I left, the empty bucket on my arm and Hadassah's ducats in my pocket. No one recognised me as I hurried along the streets with my face half concealed by my shawl, turning away whenever I saw a familiar face.

Henriette lived near the Agudi Bridge, in an alley off a street bustling with traders selling all manner of second-hand goods and garments, vegetables and grain, fish and squawking fowl, and firewood. Her neighbours must have been accustomed to women visiting her discreetly at all hours, and no one took any notice of me as I stole into the alley and tapped at her door.

Once again Hashem smiled on my plan because Henriette was at home and alone. She ushered me inside and gazed earnestly into my eyes when I removed my shawl.

'You are sick,' she said, and then shook her head. 'My poor girl. You are with child.'

Holding out the ducats Hadassah had given me, I begged her to help me.

'You must eat, even if you have no appetite,' she said, taking the coins which disappeared in her voluminous skirts. 'I will give you a tincture of herbs to stop the sickness. Look at you, skin and bones with no flesh or fat. A woman carrying a child needs nourishment. But first you must take a balm I am going to make, especially for you, that will make you feel stronger–'

'No, no,' I interrupted her. 'Listen to me–'

'Hush. There is no need to worry about anything. The money you have paid me is more than sufficient for–'

'No, please listen to me,' I interrupted her again, my voice growing shrill with panic. 'There is not much time. He will be home soon and must not find me gone. Listen to me, Henriette, I cannot allow this baby to live. My condition has to end now, before he sees it, and you must help me. There is no one else.'

A frown creased Henriette's brow and she drew back, gazing at me in consternation. 'Abigail, my child, you do not know what you are asking of me.'

'Don't ask me to explain. Just help me, I beg of you. Hashem will forgive us both, I know it. And please hurry. I cannot stay long.'

Henriette stood perfectly still, gazing at me with such a severe expression, I feared she was going to launch into a homily about how none but Hashem can give or take a life. She would have been right to berate me for wishing to commit the terrible sin of killing my own unborn child. But she must have seen the terrified resolution in my eyes, because she inclined her head.

'Are you sure there is no other way?' she asked.

'There is no other way. But, Henriette, you must swear to me on all you hold sacred, that you will never tell another living soul about this.'

'Very well,' she said. 'If you are sure this is what you want. But I must warn you that you may die in the attempt.'

'I am prepared to take that risk. My own death would be preferable to bringing an innocent child into my home.'

'Very well. I will prepare a physic for you that will do what you ask, and a balm to soothe your pains if you survive.'

'Will it hurt very much? No,' I added, seeing her hesitate. 'Don't think for one moment the fear of pain can deter me. I suffer daily from his vile assaults on my body and am inured to physical suffering.'

'You will experience excruciating cramps in your belly until you bleed. And then it will be over.' She stared closely at me and nodded, as though reading my wretched history in my face. 'There may be a lot of blood, so you will need plenty of rags and fresh bed linen. Are you sure, Abigail? Remember, you may die if you do this.'

Seeing my fixed expression, she turned and rummaged in her chest and handed me some bed linen, stained with use. 'It has been washed,' she said. 'There is no need to return it to me. You can tear some of it into strips and use the rest to cover your bed when the need arises.'

'How long after I take the physic will I bleed?'

She shook her head. 'It varies. You are very slender, so you will not have to wait long. Drink it as soon as you are able to sit down, as it could work quickly and once it takes effect you will not be able to stand.'

I took the linen from her gratefully, mumbling my thanks, reluctant to confess that I had given her all my money, and could not even afford to purchase a few old rags.

'Do you have a woman to take care of you and nurse you through your travail?'

'There is one who will watch over me.'

Hashem forgive me for telling another lie. Henriette must have realised I had no servant, but she did not know I was completely friendless in the Ghetto Vecchio. The only women I could turn to for help lived in the Ghetto Nuovo and my husband would beat me severely were he to learn that I had returned there. Henriette handed me a vial of evil smelling liquid that would end my confinement, together with a flask of strange green balm, and I hurriedly took my leave of her. The thought that my husband might discover my absence made me tremble.

'Hashem be with you,' Henriette whispered to me on her doorstep, thrusting a ducat in my hand. 'May He have mercy on your poor soul, and may my services be for a blessing and not a curse.' She spat on the ground to ward off evil spirits.

We both had tears in our eyes as I turned away.

24

Hashem protected me, because my husband was asleep when I returned home carrying my bundle under one arm, a bucket full of water over the other. On the bed beside him lay his dagger, with which he so often threatened me. Once he had traced a line down my body with the point of the blade, drawing blood. He had watched the drops gather and slide down my belly with a horrible fascination while I had stood before him, trembling, in fear of my life. And now the dagger had slipped out of his belt and was lying on the bed beside him.

Recalling the stranger I had killed in the forest, my hands trembled, and my soul fought against the urge to thrust the point of the blade into my husband's foul heart. As though I was watching the scene from outside my own body, I pictured myself seizing the dagger and slashing at him as he lay snoring on the bed. Yet even while he slept he cowed my spirit, and terror overpowered me. The dybbuk that had possessed me in the forest outside Polotensk was far away, and could not help me now. Alone, I lacked the strength to take hold of the blade and strike my husband as he lay sprawled out on the bed.

As I struggled against a temptation surely sent by an evil

spirit, Hashem moved my husband to grasp his dagger in his sleep. I tried to feel relieved at being thwarted. Hashem had saved me from killing a second man, but now I had a worse sin to commit. Putting my bundle down softly in a corner, I unwrapped the vial of dark liquid Henriette had given me. Its bitterness made me gag, but I forced myself to swallow it all. Then I lay down on the pile of rags Henriette had given me, and closed my eyes. Before long my whole body began to convulse. The summer was over and the nights were chilly, but I felt as though my belly was on fire. Slowly my mind grew numb and I lost consciousness.

Roused by a sharp jabbing in my back, I woke to discover my husband was kicking me. 'Get up, you lazy piece of piss. There's no food on the table, and nothing on the fire. Stir yourself and prepare something. I haven't eaten all day.'

I hauled myself to my feet but sank to my knees again at once. The pile of rags broke my fall.

'I told you to shift your lazy arse.'

'Husband, I am sick.'

'I said get up.'

'Husband, can you not see I am too ill to stand?' As I remonstrated, the cramps started and I knew that the bleeding would begin soon. Shaking uncontrollably and crying in agony, I barely noticed my husband yelling at me. His voice reached me through a fog of pain. I saw his arms waving in the air, leaving trails of light in their wake, and then he was gone, leaving me howling in grief at the loss of my baby. But how could I have brought an innocent child into a house of such violence?

'Hashem forgive me,' I repeated, over and over, before I passed out again.

When I awoke, I was lying on a pile of linen, with a clean sheet covering me. Across the room I saw flames flickering brightly. Despite the fire, I could not stop shivering.

'Where am I?' I whispered, raising myself and leaning on one elbow.

'Do not try to move yet,' a hoarse voice croaked.

The old woman who collected our rent was seated on the bed, watching me with her sharp eyes.

'That is my husband's bed,' I told her.

'Yes, well he's not here now,' she replied. 'He buggered off and left you bleeding. You could have frozen to death if I hadn't taken pity on you and come to light your fire.'

When I stammered my thanks, she shook her grey head. 'Someone had to come and stop your racket,' she replied. 'You were shrieking as though a thousand dybbuks were competing to possess your soul.'

She shuffled over to me and held a cup to my lips. As the water slid down my parched throat, I recalled the bitter taste of the physic Henriette had given me and was sick. Frantically I scrabbled through the linen, searching for the empty vial. The old woman pressed her lips together as she held it up.

'Is this what you are looking for?'

'I– I took it for the sickness.'

'Best I take it away so your husband doesn't see it,' she replied with a knowing look, and I sobbed with relief. 'Hashem sees into our hearts and knows our deepest hopes and fears,' she said gently. 'He understands the choices we make and although He does not condone sin, yet He forgives the sinner.'

'Do you really think so?'

'We have to believe that, when our lives are filled with tribulations that force us to take such desperate remedies.'

Overcome with weakness and sorrow, I lay back, and the old woman sat silently watching me.

'There is another bottle,' I said when I was strong enough to speak again. 'A balm to help with the cramps.'

The old woman took the bottle of green liquid from her apron and held it out to me.

'May it soothe your pain,' she said. 'And may the witch who sold you these potions burn for all eternity,' she added.

'You have saved my life,' I told her. 'Hashem will reward you.'

'He has already rewarded me by stopping your screaming. You would have kept the whole of the ghetto awake if you had continued through the night.' She stood up. 'Now you are settled, I must leave before he returns. See to it that your husband keeps the fire burning tonight. You will need the warmth.'

I wanted her to stay with me, but she hobbled to the door and vanished, leaving me alone with my regrets and my guilt. My husband did not return for three days, but the old woman came in every evening to bring me soup and tend to the fire, and on the third day I was strong enough to stand up and walk around. My limbs were stiff from lying still for so long, and a dull ache in my belly plagued me, a constant reminder of my transgression.

On the third day, my husband returned and it was not long before he gave me reason to remember why I had taken physic to end my confinement.

'You plague me worse than a rotten tooth,' he snarled.

'Why will you not divorce me, if you hate me so much?' I wailed, clutching my bruised arms.

He answered me with his fists, cursing me for being unclean.

Gradually the pain in my belly faded and life continued. My daily trip to fetch water was my only respite. As I visited the well one morning, I overheard two women talking about Henriette. Instantly alert, I listened closely to their conversation.

'I'm telling you they took her,' the first woman said. She was plump and rosy cheeked, and her hands were raw from immersion in water. 'The Duke's guards seized her by her arms and dragged her away. And when Debra tried to stop them, they threw the old woman to the floor.'

'Debra?' I repeated, interrupting her. 'Debra, the mother of Daniel, the printer?'

'Yes, the same,' the plump woman replied.

'Did you say the guards pushed her over?'

'If my brothers had been there, they would have sent those guards packing,' the other woman said fiercely.

'It was as well they were not there to attempt anything so stupid,' I said. 'An unarmed man does not serve the will of Hashem by throwing his life away in combat against armed guards.'

The two women both nodded, acknowledging the justice of my comment.

'Who did you say was arrested?' I asked.

'Her name is Henriette,' the plump woman replied. 'She is a seer and a healer. She has brought many cures to Venice from her travels in France and Morocco. She is a mystic who can see into the future–'

The other woman interrupted her with a grunt. 'She didn't see the guards coming for her.'

Struggling to breathe, I could barely speak, but I had to know the answer to my next question. 'Was anyone else there when they took Henriette?'

The plump woman shook her head. 'All I know is that they arrested Henriette and threw Debra to the ground when she tried to stop them.'

The guards' treatment of Debra was disturbing, yet that was nothing compared to the fate that now awaited Henriette.

'What will they do to her?' the second woman asked.

'Who can say?' the plump woman replied. 'My guess is that she will be tried as a witch. If they find her guilty, they will surely burn her.'

We stared at one another, struck dumb with the horror of Henriette's plight. The witch craze was spreading throughout Europe and there seemed to be no stopping it. Misfits and unmarried women like Henriette were being accused every day. In such a volatile climate, no woman was safe.

I turned to the plump woman. 'We must pray for Henriette.'

'And for all poor souls in torment,' she replied, gazing pityingly at me.

I wondered how much my neighbours knew about my marriage to a man who had driven me to commit a terrible sin.

25

My husband was not home when I went out to fill our empty water bucket. As usual I went to visit our landlady on my way back.

'I have brought you water,' I told her.

'Help me,' she wheezed, waving a gnarled hand in the air.

'What would you have me do?' I asked, putting down my bucket.

'I am too weak to break bread with my gums,' she replied, 'and it is too hard for me to slice. Help me.'

A loaf stood on her small wooden table, beside a bread knife. I cut the bread into thin slices, which she could manage to tear with her toothless gums. Seeing that the old woman was lying on her straw mattress with her eyes closed, without thinking I concealed the sharp knife in my skirt. I left quickly, before she could notice what had happened.

Back in my own lodging, I hid the knife beneath the bundle of rags that served as my bed. It seemed Hashem had given me the means to free myself from my bondage, but if my husband discovered the knife, he would surely guess its intended purpose, and use it on me. Somehow I had to find the strength to take his life before he ended mine. The knowledge that Henriette had been abandoned by Hashem seemed to confirm that my soul was lost, since my guilt was surely worse than hers. Now that no sin of mine could damn me further, before I died I determined to have the satisfaction of killing my tormentor. After that, I would spend the rest of my life making what penance I could. Perhaps one day I would find salvation in good works and prayer.

Mumbling a prayer that he would not come back until the morning, I covered my face with a veil and set off for the synagogue in the Ghetto Nuovo, pleading with Hashem for His protection. Should my husband discover I had defied his command and left the house, he could hardly treat me worse than he did already, and if he killed me, it would be a welcome release from my daily torment. I often struggled against the sin of hoping for death to release me, and there were times when I was tempted to end my life by my own hand. Had my husband not taken to spending his nights elsewhere, I might have succumbed to the enticement of the evil spirits who whispered such thoughts in my ears at night.

Meanwhile, a miracle had furnished me with the means to kill my husband. All I needed now was an opportunity to stab him in his filthy heart while he slept. Arriving unnoticed at the synagogue, I took a seat at the back of the women's gallery, near the door, hoping to escape attention, and prepared to pray for the strength to save myself from my husband. No one turned and spoke to me as I sat in the familiar gallery, musing at how low I had sunk since my last visit to the Ghetto Nuovo. All of my suffering stemmed from my ill-fated marriage, and even as I sat in the synagogue, that most holy of places, I cursed the name of Reuven ben Yitzhak. Truly my soul was lost to the powers of darkness. Yet I felt no remorse for my plan, only a bitter conviction that my husband deserved to die.

The other women were engrossed in conversation as they waited for the service to begin, and gradually I began listening to them.

'And you heard what happened to Debra?' I heard one woman say. 'The Duke's guards assaulted her, poor woman.'

'It could have happened to any one of us, if the guards had come for Henriette while we were visiting her.'

'The Catholics persecute women living alone as though they are an abomination sent by the devil.'

'Perhaps women living alone are an abomination sent by the devil. Is it not a sin for a woman not to bear children? Doesn't the Bible instruct us to be fruitful and multiply? What kind of woman defies the will of Hashem? Do they not deserve to be punished?'

'That is an uncharitable thought. Some women cannot bear children. They want to, and they try, and they are virtuous women, but they are not blessed.'

'Nonsense. Hashem blesses all righteous women with children. That is His purpose for them. Women who refuse to fulfil their sacred destiny deserve to be cast out.'

I wondered miserably what these women would say if they knew what I had done. Worse than a barren woman was one who ended the life of her own child before the birth. I would have liked to ask the Rabbi whether Hashem saved the souls of unborn children, but dared not speak of such things to anyone. Meanwhile, most of the women agreed that it is no sin to be barren, but a great misfortune, while a few insisted that women who were not blessed with children could not possibly be righteous. Examples were cited from the Bible, and the argument was growing heated, when Miriam arrived and the women fell silent.

'How is your grandmother?' the Rabbi's wife enquired gently.

'She has worn herself out with weeping and is asleep. I am worried about her fragile state of mind. She keeps calling me "mother" and she mistakes my father for her husband. My father is greatly distressed by her wandering thoughts. Henriette used to give her salves for her pains and cures to stop her mind from straying. Have you heard what happened to her?'

'We were just talking about Henriette,' one of the women said.

'Is there nothing we can do to save her?' Miriam asked, breaking down in tears.

I longed to comfort her, but dared not reveal myself for fear my husband would hear of my visit to the synagogue.

'We must pray that the authorities will be merciful,' the Rabbi's wife replied softly. 'Not all who are arrested and tried are condemned. Other than that, you must try to put her out of your mind, and focus on looking after your grandmother. There is nothing we can do for Henriette but pray to Hashem to soften the hearts of her judges here on earth.'

'How can I put her out of my mind when we know she is being interrogated by the Inquisitors?' Miriam replied. 'We all know how they torture their prisoners. Henriette is a good woman who has used her skills and knowledge to help others less fortunate than herself. She lost her babies to the plague, and her husband to another woman. And now Venice, which should have offered her sanctuary in her declining years, has turned against her.' She wept as she spoke.

'We must pray with all our might that Hashem in his mercy will take pity on her and end this persecution of her and all who are accused of witchcraft.'

'Henriette is no witch,' Miriam said. 'I know her. She learned her skills from her husband, who was an adviser to the King of France himself. How can such a man be a sinner, or his words be false? Would a king not have enough wisdom to expose the lies of a charlatan?'

'Kings are no wiser than other men,' the Rabbi's wife replied, 'and they are more likely to be set on by mountebanks who wish to cheat them for a share of their wealth.'

The Rabbi began evening prayers and the discussion ended. A few of the women threw me curious glances as they settled to their prayers. Before the last line of the concluding prayer ended, I slipped away and hurried home, clutching my shawl around me and trembling in case my husband had discovered my absence. Hashem took pity on me that night, and I returned to an empty home.

The following day, my husband came back in an unusually cheerful mood.

'That whore does the trick,' he told me, exposing his flaccid member and shaking it at me with a laugh. 'You are safe, at least until tonight.'

I lowered my eyes, afraid of provoking him by speaking what was in my mind.

'You'd like to take a knife and chop it right off, wouldn't you, you frigid cow?' He laughed again. 'Oh well, it looks as though we'll see a witch from the ghetto burned in the Piazza San Marco before the week is out.'

'What do you mean?' I asked, although I knew the answer to my question. 'My husband, what have you heard?'

'Oh, it's the talk of the whorehouse. They're all scared it will be their turn next. First the witches, then the Jews, and finally the degenerate women. The Catholics have their agenda for purging the world of sin.' He spat on the floor.

'What have you heard?' I asked again.

'You may have met the witch from the Ghetto Nuovo, the one they call Henriette?'

I nodded cautiously.

'Well, she has been arrested. The woman has been living in the ghetto claiming to be the wife of a Frenchman. Last night, in the tavern, I met a merchant who said her lies have been exposed. So she will be condemned to burn, and we will have a spectacle!' He chuckled in anticipation.

'What lies did she tell?'

'The witch claims a famous astrologer in France for her husband, but he already has a wife, so her lies have caught her out.'

'Henriette fled from the plague in France. Is it not possible her husband took a second wife, believing her dead?'

'No, no, the astrologer's first wife died of the plague, and Henriette is an imposter.'

'How can anyone be sure his first wife died in the plague?' I persisted. 'The pits received many unidentified bodies, and no one can say for certain whether any one individual died or fled the area and survived.'

'Well, both her children died in the epidemic, so it's safe to assume their mother was also a victim,' he replied cheerfully. 'Certainly her husband mourned for her, according to the account I heard. She is reported to have been a great beauty. But all women lose their looks if they live long enough.'

I was silent, considering the implications of her husband's second marriage, if Henriette had indeed been the Frenchman's first wife. 'If a husband takes a second wife, in the belief that his first wife is dead, would he still be guilty of bigamy?' I asked.

'A man may not marry a second wife while the first wife lives,' Reuven replied, 'unless they were divorced, which was never going to happen. The Catholic Church does not allow divorce, unlike our more enlightened religion.'

If Judaism had granted the power of divorce to women, I would have put in a request to the Rabbi at once, but only men were allowed that privilege and my husband had steadfastly refused to release me.

'I would rather kill you than divorce you,' he snapped suddenly, seeing the hopeful expression on my face.

There was no point in arguing with him. We both knew how any disagreement between us would end.

26

The following day, my husband rose in good spirits and announced that he was going to the city to witness Henriette's trial.

'We shall see the witch burned before the day is out,' he told me cheerfully.

Concealing my face in my cloak, I followed him at a distance, fearful of losing myself in the streets of the city. I need not have worried about him observing me, as I was soon lost in a throng of people walking in the same direction. An atmosphere of festivity enlivened the crowd, who jostled one another good-naturedly as they chattered about the witch trial.

'Let's hope they burn her,' a woman called out and a chorus of voices cheered.

Worried that my husband might spot me, I had decided against wearing the yellow shawl which was obligatory for Jewish women. If the authorities discovered my identity I would be thrown in prison, yet I was more afraid of my husband than of the guards who patrolled the courtroom in the grand palace of the Duke. There are punishments worse than prison. At some distance away, a cluster of women in yellow shawls were standing beside a group of men in yellow hats. With so many people packed together the air grew warm, although the chamber was spacious and the ceiling high. Surrounded by strangers who smelt of tallow candles, incense and strange spices, I kept my hood up and my cloak wrapped around me.

As the temperature in the room rose, the impatient crowd began taunting the Jews, and a scuffle broke out. The guards rushed over, shouting abuse at the Jews and taking the opportunity to beat some of them over the head with their pikes. I scanned the men's faces, searching for Daniel, but could not see him, and my momentary disappointment was tempered by relief that he had not been injured in the fracas. The disturbance ceased as abruptly as it had begun, and everyone turned to watch the judges take their seats.

Glancing back at the Jews gathered in the opposite corner to me, I drew in a sharp breath and the room seemed to spin around me as I caught sight of Daniel bending over a man whose head was bleeding. Even though I knew we could never be together, it was a thrill to look at him. All at once, he raised his head and looked in my direction, as though searching for someone. Before he noticed me, I turned away. No doubt he had forgotten about me, and was betrothed to another woman. I tried to feel pleased that someone else might bring him the happiness I had once hoped to give him, but it was hard not to feel bereft.

A moment later Henriette was led in from the dungeons. Her hair was matted, and she glared wildly around the room, her eyes seeming to gaze through her surroundings as though she could indeed see spirits hidden from the rest of us. Before her sat a jury of three. Approaching his eightieth year, Doge Girolamo Priuli had been in office for many years. Above his full grey beard and sunken cheeks, his eyes looked kind as he peered at the accused woman. His rule over Venice had been a peaceful one, and he was well respected. Confident that such a man would be reasonable in his judgement, I felt a flicker of hope for Henriette.

The second judge was an elderly patrician whom I did not recognise. Tottering to his seat, he looked as though a breath of wind would blow him over. Ready to meet his maker, I hoped he might be merciful.

The third judge was a different kind of man altogether. Stocky and in his prime, he had a long face with a neatly trimmed dark beard and moustache, heavy eyebrows, and red cheeks that suggested a choleric disposition. He fixed the defendant with a hard stare that seemed to brook no equivocation. His severe expression made me tremble for Henriette.

The Duke spoke so softly, I had to strain to hear him. 'You all know the noble patrician seated on my right hand.' The elderly man bowed his head. Next, the Duke gestured towards the youngest of the three judges. 'Cardinal Alessandrino is passing through our Most Serene Republic of Venice on business of His Holiness the Pope of Rome. We pray daily for the success of his mission.'

Many of the onlookers nudged one another and smiled on hearing the name of the third judge, but the Jews listened in shocked silence. Everyone had heard of Cardinal Alessandrino. More significant than the Legate's illustrious career was his reputation as a fanatical persecutor of heretics.

Finally the Duke turned to the accused. 'Woman, state your full name.'

Henriette was shaking, but her voice rang out, loud and steady. 'I was born Henriette d'Encausse, daughter of Roger d'Encausse and Bonnefemme de Thebes, sister of the Holy Canon Pierre Raymond d'Encausse.'

'Woman, you are accused before God of dealing with the

devil and practising witchcraft,' the Cardinal cried out in ringing tones.

A faint sigh whispered through the watching crowd at his words.

'Burn the witch,' someone called out, and the cry was taken up by other voices, 'Burn the witch! Burn the witch!'

Aware of the risk I faced standing in the Duke's palace without a yellow shawl, I kept silent. If the authorities did not apprehend me, my husband might see me. I shrank further into a shadowy corner of the chamber.

'I am no witch!' Henriette cried out, the wildness in her eyes serving to denounce her more effectively than the words of her accuser. 'I am the daughter of Roger d'Encausse. I learned my skills in healing and astrology from my husband, and we are God-fearing Catholics. My husband, Michel de Nostredame, was chosen by Catherine de' Medici, wife of Henry II of France, to serve as counsellor and physician to King Charles IX of France himself. My husband travelled widely in different lands and discovered the powers of many herbs. From him I learned to use plants created by the Lord himself so that men may be healed of sickness. My visions of the future and my knowledge of astrology are well known, but these powers are not heresy, as you well know, as long as they are not coupled with magic. On the immortal souls of my beloved children, I vow before God that I have never used magic in my healing or my visions.'

The Cardinal pounced. 'So you confess to having visions?'

The crowd resumed chanting. 'Burn the witch! Burn the witch!'

'Do you want to offend the King of France by condemning me, an innocent, wife of the great Michel de Nostredame, known to the Pope himself as Nostradamus?' Henriette screeched. 'My husband reads the stars for royalty. He has many powerful allies who will wreak vengeance on you if you take my life.'

The jury of three conferred and appeared to be arguing.

'Very well,' the Duke announced at last, in his quiet voice, and the crowd fell silent to hear his judgement. 'We will send to France for corroboration of your claim. If it is refuted, you will be burned at the stake.'

The crowd who had gathered in expectation of a burning yelled in frustration as Henriette was led back to her cell, and I stole away unseen. Nothing would now be decided until word had been sent to France, and a reply received. But Henriette's fate was sealed. Even if her story was true, her husband would have to deny her, or be accused of breaking the law in taking a second wife. I hurried home, fearing my husband's return. Cheated of a burning, he was almost certain to be in a violent mood. But he must have found a whore to vent his anger on, because he arrived home several hours later and fell asleep almost at once. Relieved, I curled up on the floor and closed my eyes, trying to block out the memory of the terror on Henriette's face. If this was her punishment for assisting me in ending the life of my unborn child, I trembled to think what further torments might be visited on me.

27

A couple of weeks later my husband burst into our lodgings in great excitement, to tell me that Henriette was to be sentenced that afternoon. Seizing me with both hands he held me at arm's length, studying my face and my neck closely before announcing that I was to attend the trial with him. Surprised, I drew my yellow shawl around my head and shoulders.

'You can't go out in that disgusting rag,' he said. 'Where is your red gown?'

I had mended the dress, sewing my precious thimble ring from Daniel inside the bodice, close to my heart. I wore it on the rare occasions my husband allowed me to accompany him to the synagogue. Quickly I pulled on the gown before he could change his mind.

'I am ready, my husband.'

He scowled and strode out of our apartment with me trotting at his heels like a servant. We entered the courtroom and stood at the back, with the other Jews. Gazing around, I caught sight of Daniel standing beside Miriam, their faces taut with apprehension. I yearned to run to him with words of comfort, but the chasm between us seemed as wide as the ocean I had crossed to reach Venice, and as deep. Yet I had crossed that ocean. Gazing at Daniel from a distance, I forced myself to suppress a flicker of hope. Even if my husband were to die, I would never be free of my sin.

The judges took their seats and the crowd fell silent, waiting to hear the sentence.

'We have received a reply,' the Duke said gently, gazing at Henriette with his sorrowful eyes. He nodded at the Pope's Legate, who rose to his feet and unrolled a parchment with a satisfied air that did not augur well for the accused woman.

'This is the testimony of Michel de Nostredame, Counsellor and Physician-in-Ordinary to King Charles IX of France,' the Cardinal read aloud. 'It is God's truth I had a wife named Henriette. May the good Lord rest her soul and save her from the eternal flames of hell. While I was abroad, travelling to Morocco, for the purchase of such herbs as my work required, the plague struck my home town of Agen in the year of our Lord 1536, carrying off my beloved son and daughter. By the time I returned home, my wife's body lay with our children in the plague pit. Her name was not included in the blessings recited for their souls, as she had taken her own life when our children perished. I pray for her salvation, and may the Lord have mercy on her and on all Christian souls.'

'He has abandoned me again!' Henriette cried out.

It was not clear whether she was talking about her husband or her God. Either way, she was doomed. The Duke rose to his feet. His gold cap pointed towards heaven but his sad eyes remained fixed on the figure trembling before him. 'I sentence the accused, Henriette,' he stammered in his weak voice. 'She is condemned for practising witchcraft and will accordingly be put to death by fire–'

The rest of his mumbling was drowned by the eager clamour of the mob. My husband was shouting with them. As I followed the yelling crowd from the chamber, I wondered if Henriette had been telling the truth about Michel de Nostredame, or whether that had been another of her tales. Although I had no desire to stay and witness the burning, it was impossible to force my way through the crowd.

'What's this?' I imagined one of the onlookers shout, seeing me stealing away from the scene. 'Here's someone who doesn't want to watch the witch burn. How's that, then? What's wrong with her?'

'She's a filthy Jew,' another voice might take up the cry.

'The devil sent her, that's why she can't watch the witch burn!'

'Burn her and save our children from the servant of the devil!'

'Burn her! Burn her!'

I could not risk drawing attention to myself, surrounded by a crowd whose bloodlust was roused. Difficult though it was to watch Henriette led to the stake, in some ways looking around at the faces of the crowd was even worse. Surrounded by so many expressions of hatred, I felt dizzy with fear. Not one face showed any sign of compassion. Admittedly, the spectators were convinced the victim was a witch, sent by the devil to lure them to damnation. All the same, it was a frightening experience, standing in that crowd and feeling the hostility surrounding me. At any moment they might turn on me, a sinner in their midst.

Peering between the heads of the people in front of me, I watched Henriette being dragged to the stake, her hair blown about in a lively breeze. As the fire was lit and flames began to lick at her skirt, her mouth opened in a scream of terror inaudible above the jeers and chanting of the mob. I shifted so that my view was obscured. My ears could not hear her shrieks, nor could my eyes see the flames catch at her clothes and consume her flesh, but my imagination gave me no such respite.

A suffocating aroma of garlic and onions mingled with the odour of perspiration and piss, until both were engulfed by acrid smoke that billowed across the heads of the crowd. Those closest to the stake drew back as the flames flickered wildly, forcing the onlookers to sway and shuffle, while the smoke became infused with the stench of burning flesh. When, at last, the rabble began to disperse, I followed my husband without looking back at the smouldering fire. So, although I was present at the burning, I did not witness Henriette's death.

That evening, my husband ordered me to accompany him to the synagogue in the Ghetto Nuovo. I walked with difficulty, having suffered one of his violent assaults on my body when we returned home from the burning. Clambering painfully up to the women's gallery, I found them talking in hushed tones about what had happened to Henriette. Many of them had regarded her as a friend, and almost all of them were weeping.

'They say she was a Jewess, although her family were conversos,' someone said.

'But do we know if her mother was Jewish?' the Rabbi's wife asked. 'Or was it only her father who was born into a family of conversos?'

'Who cares?' Miriam asked, a trifle curtly.

'It matters,' the Rabbi's wife asserted. 'If her mother was not a Jewess, then according to the law–'

'The law, the law,' Miriam snapped. 'She was a human being, a woman who lived among us, and the Christian law sentenced her to death. What difference whether she was a Jew or not? Are we not all the children of Hashem, whatever path we follow in this life?'

'If they are burning witches today, you can be sure they will be burning Jews tomorrow,' someone else said bitterly.

It was time for the prayers to begin and the women stopped talking.

'Let us forget our own troubles and pray for the soul of the poor woman who lived among us for such a short time. May Hashem grant her soul peace,' the Rabbi said. 'Truly this craze for burning witches is growing at an alarming pace,' he added. 'Is it really possible so many women have been recruited to the service of the devil?'

'Women are weak, Rabbi,' one of the men reminded him.

The Rabbi answered gently, 'When did weakness become a sign of evil? Are the strong always righteous?'

28

In the spring my husband stayed away from me for longer than usual. Destitute and exhausted, I dared to hope he had been killed in a brawl. I cared little what would become of me if he stopped bringing home food. Using the ducat Henriette had given me, I trembled in case he returned and caught me purchasing vegetables and firewood for myself. I would claim I had prepared the food not for myself, but for him. And then I vowed I would kill him. Alone, I felt for the comfort of the knife concealed in my rags, no longer heeding the consequences for my immortal soul. After all, I had killed a man before. My soul was already lost. Every time my husband was away, I summoned up the courage to kill him, but as soon as he returned, my courage drained away.

After a few days had passed, there was a knock at my door. Wearily I hauled myself to my feet and went to see who it was. The knocking was too vigorous for my ancient landlady, and I wondered if the water carrier had come to enquire if we wanted him to resume his deliveries. My astonishment on seeing my visitor was so extreme that for a moment I could not speak.

'Daniel,' I gasped at length, 'you cannot visit me. If my husband returns and discovers you here, he will kill us both.'

'He will not return,' Daniel said solemnly. 'I came to let you know that he has been arrested for brawling in a Christian tavern.'

'My husband? Arrested? In a Christian tavern?' I repeated stupidly. 'Are you sure?'

'As sure as a man can be of something he saw with his own eyes.'

'You saw... What happened? Tell me, Daniel!' In a fervour of impatience, I reached out and grasped him by the arm.

'Let me come in, and I will tell you everything.'

I hesitated before standing back to allow him to enter. He glanced around our sparse apartment, taking in the narrow bed and my pile of straw bedding, which rippled with lice crawling among the stalks. There was no point in trying to shake the creatures off. I had tried repeatedly, but the vermin always returned. Daniel wanted me to sit on the one chair, but I insisted he take it, while I sat on edge of the bed.

'I was on my way home from work yesterday evening when I heard a slurred voice calling to me: "Daniel, my neighbour, where are you off to in such a hurry? Come and drink with me!"'

'An arm fell on my shoulder, and an unpleasant smell assailed me. It was your husband, reeking of ale and swaying on his feet.

'"A man does not like to drink alone," he went on, leaning heavily on me. "Come to the tavern with me. All my other drinking companions are gone. They all drowned. Every last one of them swallowed up in the waters of the Dvina River. But we are alive, and can drink to their memory. Come, have a drink with me."

'You can believe that your husband was the last person I

wanted to consort with but I dared not refuse him, fearing that he might become violent if he returned home to you with his choler aroused.'

I murmured my thanks for Daniel's consideration.

'The only way I could protect you, at least for an evening, was by keeping him company so that he left you in peace for a few hours. Besides, it is not unusual for a drunkard to stumble and fall into a canal. If your husband were to slip, I would not have gone out of my way to rescue him from drowning. In fact, I was tempted to risk my own salvation to deliver you from further harm.'

I trembled, hearing Daniel's declaration, but before I could remonstrate, he continued with his narrative.

'When I pointed out to your drunken brute of a husband that we were going the wrong way, he fell to cursing the landlord of the tavern in the ghetto. "That bloody fool," he fumed. "He refused to serve me. Yes, me, Reuven ben Yitzhak, one of his best customers."

'Curiosity overcame my scruples and I asked him why the landlord would turn away a regular customer.

'"Because he's a swindler who can't read his own tally sticks," Reuven replied. "He claims I owe him money, the filthy cheat."

'It struck me that the landlord of the tavern was probably in the right. "If he had your tally stick as evidence of debt–" I began, but Reuven turned on me.'

Daniel paused and I held my breath, afraid to hear what he was going to say next, yet unable to stop listening. No one knew better than I the danger of arguing with my husband, especially when he had been drinking.

'Your husband's face reddened with choler. "Are you calling me a liar too?" he demanded. "Is everyone in this damned ghetto going to accuse me of lying?"

'I did not answer. We reached the Agudi Bridge and he clung to the railing as we walked across. "Best to hold on," he warned me. "What happened in Polotensk has given me a terror of drowning. Let's go for a drink, but we'll avoid walking too close to any canals."

'He shuddered as we crossed the bridge, and I muttered a silent curse as we reached the Calle del Ghetto Vecchio without him falling into the canal, and then prayed for forgiveness for my unworthy thoughts. Reuven clapped me on the back, seemingly oblivious to the fact that I wished him nothing but harm. He appeared to have forgotten I had good reason to be his enemy.'

I nodded, drawn by the intensity of Daniel's gaze, and so caught up in his story that I started when the bed creaked beneath me.

'"A man needs a friend," he told me as he stumbled along, clinging to my neck and nearly choking me. "Everywhere we are beset by enemies. They surround us on all sides. Daniel, do you ever feel that Hashem has abandoned you? No, you wouldn't. You are a righteous man living a righteous life in your safe corner of a tempestuous world. Hashem has rewarded you for your devotion. But tell me, were all the inhabitants of Polotensk wicked? All but me and a handful of others?" His voice shook with emotion. "Better men than I perished that day. Better men than you. What had I ever done that I deserved to be saved when they were all slaughtered?"

'I tell you, Abigail,' said Daniel, 'in that moment I almost felt the stirrings of pity for the brute. He rambled some more, talking about his wives, but I could barely understand what he was saying, and I was distracted by thinking of how I might escape his company.'

I trembled but was silent, and Daniel continued. 'He fell

silent as we stepped through the gate of the ghetto into the world outside. We had about an hour before the curfew, and I told him we needed to return to the ghetto, but he shook his head vehemently, as though the movement could toss his thoughts aside.

'"Where shall we go for a drink?" he asked. "Take me to the nearest tavern."'

Daniel looked troubled at the memory. 'My apprehension increased on hearing what he was saying. The taverns outside the ghetto walls do not welcome Jews. But he would not listen to reason.

'"Curse you, Daniel. My ducats are as good as any man's. Lead on."

'I reminded him that the ale in the taverns outside the ghetto was not kosher, but he interrupted my protest impatiently. "Ale is ale," he said. "That sweet kosher wine in the ghetto makes me sick. I need a real drink. Do you think I travelled halfway around the world drinking only kosher wine? Even you cannot be such a damn fool, Daniel."

'He flung his arm around my shoulders again, leaning against me for support. There is a tavern near the Fondamenta Delle Pescaria which I pass every morning on my way to work, and again every evening on my way home. It is not a place that welcomes Jews, and I had never crossed the threshold. Hashem is my witness, in that moment I was more afraid of Reuven than of the drinkers in the tavern.'

Hearing that, I reached out and placed my hand on Daniel's. I understood only too well what he meant.

'I led him to the tavern, and warned him that we would not be allowed inside. For answer, he removed his yellow hat and stuffed it in his pocket. As a printer, you know I am permitted to walk around the city without wearing a yellow hat. So, tucking the ends of our prayer shawls into our hose, we entered the tavern without anything to identify us as Jews.'

I gasped on hearing that my husband had led Daniel into a forbidden tavern but, before I could speak, he continued with his story.

'A wall of voices greeted us, and the place stank of sour bodies and ale. Everywhere I looked men were seated or standing in small groups, all talking and gesticulating. A few were dallying with prostitutes. An old whore raised her filthy skirts and the landlord ran over to her, waving his arms and shouting at her that it was a respectable tavern. A group of men seated nearby called out, jeering. It was not clear if they were mocking the landlord or the prostitute, but she continued to display her wares, showing her backside to the landlord who retreated, still swearing at her. Clearly his outrage was merely for show. Reuven muttered to me to wait for him, before he disappeared into the crowd of men thronging the bar where drinking horns and glass cups were being filled.

'No one even glanced at me perched on a stool near the door, with my head lowered, doing my best to avoid attracting attention. I did not witness the start of the altercation, but suddenly voices were raised in anger. The men standing near the bar parted and I saw Reuven arguing with a Christian. It had not taken your husband long to find trouble.

'"He's a stinking Jew!" a tall man shouted. "Get out of here before I chop off your stunted cock!"

'Gathering the drift of the argument, I rose to my feet and edged towards the door. There was nothing I could do to help Reuven, who was swaying on his feet, his face purple with rage. From across the room, the black mole on his nose looked like a malevolent third eye.'

I nodded, and tightened my grip on Daniel's hand in my excitement. 'What happened then?' I asked.

'Yelling foul insults at his adversary, your husband whipped out a knife and brandished it in the air, but he was too drunk to pose a serious threat. "Armed as well as stinking?" one of the Christians shouted out.

'Before I reached the doorway, three men set on Reuven. They quickly disarmed him and forced him to the floor, pressing his face into the dirt, while the landlord shouted for someone to summon the guards.

'"We've caught a filthy Jew, and he's carrying a knife. Let's see what the authorities have to say about that." He looked around and nodded cheerfully before kicking Reuven, who yelped and cursed. "You know cockroaches like you are forbidden to carry weapons," the landlord crowed, grinning and kicking him again.

'One of the onlookers cried out that Reuven had not entered the tavern alone, but had arrived with a drinking companion.'

Hearing that, I held my breath, even though Daniel was seated beside me, apparently unharmed.

'The landlord grabbed Reuven's hair and raised his head from the floor so he could speak. Blood was streaming from Reuven's nose, and his face was smeared with dirt. "Where's your friend, Jew?" the landlord demanded roughly.

'"I have no friends," Reuven replied. "No one wants to drink with me. Even my wife is unwilling to fuck me."

'The men surrounding Reuven burst out laughing on hearing that. Without waiting to hear more, I slipped out of the tavern and hurried along the street and back to the safety of the ghetto. As soon as I returned, I came straight here to tell you what happened.'

Daniel fell silent and we sat together for a while, gazing at the ashes of the dead fire, while tears spilled from my eyes. Hashem had seen my resolve and had saved me from killing again.

'Do not weep,' Daniel said gently. 'It is over.'

I felt the warmth of his body as he sat beside me on the bed and put his arms around me to comfort me. His lips found mine and for once I felt no regret for my sin, only a desperate joy, and fear that my husband might return.

29

Putting on my best red gown, I wrapped my yellow shawl around me and set off once more for the court, this time to witness my husband's trial. Having been there twice before, I knew the way, and hurried along the streets of the city keeping my head lowered, hoping not to attract attention. Where Henriette's hearing had offered the chance of witnessing a witch being burnt, the trial of a Jew was of little interest to the citizens of Venice, and only a small crowd attended the proceedings.

The idea of my husband facing justice in this world gave me great satisfaction. I hoped the judge would show no mercy. Without witnesses, Reuven might have escaped with a fine, but there were many Christians who could attest he had been armed when he had assaulted one of their number in the tavern. With luck they would all come forward to condemn him, and he would serve a prison sentence, the longer the better. By the time he was released, I hoped he would be too old and frail to raise his hand against me, and I would never have to use the knife that remained hidden where I slept.

The atmosphere among the Christian spectators in the courtroom seemed cheerful, with men and women calling out greetings to each other. A small number of Jews stood huddled together in their accustomed corner, and I joined them. Hadassah spotted me lurking at the back of the group and made her way over to me. We embraced, and she gazed at me curiously.

'You look no better than you did the last time I saw you, in fact you look skinnier than ever.' She looked sceptical at my assurance that I was just tired. 'I am not sorry about your husband being arrested,' she added under her breath.

'Nor me,' I replied. 'If they hang him it will be more than he deserves. Burning at the stake would be too good for him.'

Hadassah drew back, shaking her head. 'You cannot seriously wish that on anyone.'

'You are right. But tell me, how are you keeping?'

Hadassah told me she was fine. She had found a lodger to share her rooms, but added quickly that she still missed me and wished I would return to the Ghetto Nuovo. As she was speaking, I caught sight of the back of Daniel's head and lowered my gaze.

'He says he will wait for you all his life,' Hadassah murmured.

A court official called for silence, preventing me from questioning her further, and the trial began. My husband's trial was heard by one judge, an elderly man with a portly figure and a serious demeanour. 'The accused man is wicked, even for a Jew,' the judge began in a sonorous voice. 'He is said to regularly visit Christian whores in the city.' He glared at my husband from beneath bushy grey eyebrows.

'Where are the witnesses to your lies?' Reuven called out, facing the judge with surprising bravado. 'Show me a whore who will testify to that.'

'You know they will not,' the judge replied coldly. 'They would be arrested for fornicating with a Jew.' The judge spat out the last word as though it stung his lips, and I felt hopeful my husband would serve a long prison sentence.

'You cannot accuse a man without evidence,' Reuven complained. 'That is not justice, but a licence to persecute the innocent.'

Reuven had a point, but the judge snapped at him to hold his tongue. My husband's face reddened with choler, and a string of witnesses were summoned to testify. The first to speak was a huge man, with a mane of ginger hair, a pale face and huge hands. He identified himself as the landlord of the tavern where the brawl had broken out.

'There was a scuffle,' he said. 'I did not see how it began–'

'It was not my fault,' Reuven shouted out, and the judge reprimanded him, reminding him that he must remain silent until questioned.

'It took three strong men to restrain the accused, he was so violent, completely out of control, raging with drink,' the landlord continued with his account. 'He had not yet had a drink in my tavern. I do not serve ale to drunks, or to Jews. He and his companion had only just walked in, and must have drunk excessively before they arrived. Three stalwart Christian men pulled the scoundrel away from his victim and together they wrestled him to the floor. A knife fell from the Jew's grasp as he went down, and I seized it as evidence of his transgression.'

He held up a dagger which I recognised as belonging to my husband.

'That's not mine!' Reuven raged. 'I never saw it before in my life!'

I wanted to shout out that he was lying, but there was nothing I could do but watch and pray. The next witness was a feeble-looking man who claimed to have been attacked by Reuven. 'He tried to push past me and my friends,' he whined.

'He was impatient to purchase a jug of ale, and shouted at us to shift out of his way. He was pissed, his breath stank of ale and he could not stand upright but lurched at us, trying to barge past. I boldly barred his path and told him to wait his turn, and that was when he took out his knife and waved it at me in a threatening manner, yelling at me to move aside. Before he could stab me, my friends grabbed his arms and pushed him to the floor.'

Several more witnesses came forward and confirmed the victim's story. Three of them claimed to have restrained the Jew, to prevent him from injuring their friend.

'A Jew who carries a weapon in the city is breaking the law,' the judge said.

'That knife was for protection,' Reuven protested. 'I have been attacked many times on the streets for being a Jew, and so I carry a knife. A man has a right to defend himself.'

'You just told us you had never seen that knife before,' the judge reminded him.

'Yes, well, I haven't,' Reuven blustered, but he could see that he was beaten. 'They're all lying when they say no one provoked me. That tavern is a den of anti-Semites. I could tell that from the moment I set foot inside the place.'

'Yet you still decided to drink there,' the judge pointed out.

'Oh fuck you,' Reuven retorted. 'You weren't even there. Ask Daniel, he'll tell you what really happened.'

'Who is Daniel?' the judge enquired in a frosty voice. 'Are you appealing to another lying Jew to back up your own deceit?'

'Daniel was there,' Reuven insisted. 'Ask him, he'll tell you what happened and how I was set upon in that wretched tavern. Daniel ben Elia. He's here in the courtroom.'

'Very well,' the judge said, 'summon Daniel ben Elia and let us get the matter settled. This Jew has already taken up too much of the court's time.'

There was a faint disturbance in front of me as Daniel stepped forward. 'I am Daniel ben Elia,' he said.

Hearing his familiar voice I quaked, for fear my husband might drag Daniel into trouble with the authorities. They needed no encouragement to punish two Jews instead of one.

The judge beckoned to him. 'Come closer, Jew, so we can hear you. Tell the court what happened last night, when you went to the tavern with the Jew who assaulted an honest Christian.'

'I didn't assault anyone!' Reuven cried out. 'This is a conspiracy!'

'Reuven approached me in the ghetto,' Daniel said. 'He asked me to go for a drink with him.'

'And what was your reply?'

'I could see he had been drinking.'

'Excessively?' the judge asked.

'Yes, I would say so.'

'What is this?' Reuven roared. 'Tell them I didn't start the argument, damn you.'

'Silence,' the judge barked, raising his hand.

'The accused man was already intoxicated, yet he wished to leave the ghetto and visit a tavern to continue drinking.'

'Why did you not go to the tavern in the ghetto, where Jews are welcome?' the judge asked.

'He told me the tavern keeper in the ghetto would no longer serve him until he paid for what he had already drunk there.'

'Lies, lies!' Reuven shouted.

'You can ask the tavern keeper in the ghetto if you doubt my word,' Daniel replied evenly, addressing the judge.

'It was a disagreement,' Reuven said. 'The bastard tried to overcharge me. He's a fucking crook.'

Raising his hand at my husband to silence him, the judge asked Daniel to continue his account.

'I accompanied Reuven with the intention of persuading him to return to the ghetto before the gate was closed for the night. I was afraid he was too drunk to realise the time, and would fail to observe the curfew. I remonstrated with him, telling him he had already drunk too much and needed to go home and sleep it off. He refused to listen to me and led me to the tavern just past the Fondamenta Delle Pescaria, a place where Jews are forbidden to enter. I am a law-abiding man. Ask anyone in the ghetto, or you can speak to my master, an Italian nobleman called Marco Antonio Giustiniani who has a printing shop on the Calle dei Cinque. He is a respected Christian printer here in Venice, and he will vouch for my good character.'

The judge inclined his head. 'Continue with your account of the events leading up to the arrest of the Jew.'

'I was afraid of what might happen to us if we went in the tavern,' Daniel resumed. 'I didn't want any trouble. But Reuven insisted on going there. He is a powerful man, and I could not restrain him once he had made up his mind. He was too intoxicated to listen to reason and insisted on going to the tavern.'

'What happened then?' the judge prompted him.

'Then I went home,' Daniel said.

At the back of the room, I breathed a sigh of relief that Daniel was not prepared to be implicated in my husband's troubles. Predictably, my husband flew into a rage, cursing those who had testified that he had attacked a Christian while drunk, and crying out that Daniel had betrayed him. The judge questioned several of the Christian witnesses, all of whom confirmed that my husband had entered the tavern alone.

'He told us no one wants to drink with him,' the landlord attested.

'He said he has no friends,' another witness added.

'Daniel is lying!' my husband raged. 'He wants to see me

locked up so he can fuck my wife! This is not justice. He is lying to serve his own ends. Do not believe him. He is a lecher! The word of such a man is not to be trusted.'

'You yourself insisted we hear his testimony,' the judge reminded him.

Still yelling, Reuven was dragged from the courtroom by two guards, and did not hear the judge pass sentence.

'The Jew's attack on an innocent Christian is compounded by the fact that he was drinking in a tavern where Jews are prohibited. For entering the tavern he is fined five ducats. His assault on a Christian increases the fine by another fifteen ducats, together with a term in prison. The most serious of his transgressions is that he was caught carrying a knife with which he attacked a Christian. Had other good Christian men not been on hand to end the fray, who knows what harm might have been inflicted by this drunken Jew? There is a reason why Jews are forbidden to carry weapons in the city. It is my solemn duty to uphold our laws and protect law abiding citizens of the Republic. If this crime goes unpunished, what is to stop every other Jew from arming himself? No Christian would be safe on the streets of Venice, and the lives of our women and children would be endangered. As a punishment for that threatened violence, and to protect our Christian community from the savage heathen, I have no choice but to sentence the accused to the galleys for fifteen years. He will be chained on the next ship to leave the harbour, whatever its destination. If he fails to pay the fine of twenty ducats, it will be supplied twofold from the coffers of the ghetto.'

With that, the judge rose to his feet and strode from the chamber. Forty ducats from the communal funds to be rid of my husband for fifteen years was the best bargain I had ever heard. Had I the means, I would gladly have paid the fine myself, and turned the key that chained him to his oar as well.

30

I stumbled back onto the street in a daze, scarcely able to believe what had just happened. While I stood amazed, Hadassah ran over to me.

'It is done and he is gone, praise be to Hashem. Now, you must return to the Ghetto Nuovo with me and live among your friends again. My current tenant will leave today and we will be as we were, and,' she smiled anxiously at me, 'I am going to feed you griboli and kreplach, and goose fat and onions, until you are plump and healthy again. No,' she added, seeing me shake my head, 'this is not a matter for debate, Abigail. I will not take no for an answer. You are coming back to live with me and that is final.'

'Let us wait and see,' I replied, still reeling from my respite both from my husband, and from my own murderous scheming. 'I can't come and live with you without paying rent. Do you think I am a parasite, who would take advantage of your generosity?'

'Very well, go and speak to Tamar. I will be waiting for you with a pot of tsimmes on the fire.'

We walked back to the ghetto where we embraced before I

hurried off to speak to the seamstress. Tamar's eyes widened in amazement when she saw me standing in her doorway, but I thought she looked cautiously pleased.

'I have come back,' I announced. 'Please, Tamar, may I work for you as before?'

She grunted as her eyes travelled to my feet and back to my face. 'You will have to start on half pay for a month,' she said.

'I am content.'

'Tomorrow then, at dawn. I need to see that you are strong enough for the work.' She shook her head. 'Right now you look too weak to hold a needle.'

Before returning to Hadassah, I went back to my miserable room in the Ghetto Vecchio to collect my few possessions and thank the ancient crone who had been my only friend there. She took a long time to open her door.

'What do you want?'

'I came to tell you I am leaving the Ghetto Vecchio.'

She squinted up at me. 'Leaving that fiend? Make sure he does not follow you, and do not tell me where you are going because he will beat it out of me. Go now, before he comes back and sees you talking to me.'

'Have no fear, my husband will not return here. He has been sentenced to the galleys for fifteen years for drunken brawling. He attacked a Christian with a dagger!'

The old woman's eyes grew round, and she cackled as I related my husband's crimes. 'Well, well, praise be to Hashem, he will not be bothering you again. Fifteen years is enough for me and for your sake I pray he dies in the bowels of a stinking ship and his bones are tossed in the sea without a prayer to mark his passing. You can stay here, if you wish,' she added, her moist eyes pleading. 'You can pay your way by helping me. I will not ask for rent.'

I felt guilty for refusing, after she had saved my life. 'I will come back and visit you often,' I promised, and she smiled sadly at me.

'Go and live,' she replied. 'I am old and will soon be dead. You have no need of me.'

'I will not forget how you saved my life,' I replied. 'Rest assured, I will come and see you, and I will cook for you and tend to your fire, as you did for me.'

True to her word, Hadassah found alternative accommodation for her tenant who left, grumbling at having to move.

'It hardly seems fair on her,' I said, as I placed my bundle of linen and cooking pots on the bed in our living room and began to unpack them. 'You gave her very little notice.'

'Oh, she was fine with it,' Hadassah assured me. 'She just enjoys complaining. Believe me, I made it clear to her when she moved in that if you were ever to return, she would have to move out. She accepted the bed on those conditions, so it is not true to say she had no warning.' She broke off to scowl at my bundle of stained rags. 'Now that you are working for Tamar again, you can discard those filthy rags.' She peered more closely at them. 'Abigail,' she added severely, 'they are crawling with vermin. I beg you, throw them on the fire.'

Later I learned that Hadassah had paid her other tenant's rent for the first week in her new accommodation as an inducement to her to leave promptly.

So my life settled back into its former routine, almost as though Reuven had never survived the massacre at Polotensk and followed me to Venice. Every day I gave thanks to Hashem for releasing me from my husband, and prayed that he would never return. The chances of his surviving many years at the oars were slim. Galley slaves were not expected to live long, and the navy was in constant need of replacements. All the time I had been living with my husband in the Ghetto Vecchio, my thimble ring had been hidden in the bodice of my red gown. Now I retrieved it. Although I could never lie with Daniel again, at least I could wear his gift. The thimble ring comforted me during the day, and at night I slept with it under my pillow.

Sleeping in a bed again felt strange, and at night I fell prey to sinful thoughts which my prayers could not banish. The memory of Daniel's sinewy arms around me, and the smell of his body, haunted my dreams, nor could I forget how our bodies had moved together. Yet the recollection of our transient intimacy brought me some comfort despite my guilt, and thanks to Hadassah I went to bed warm and well fed every night.

Twice a week I called on my ancient landlady in the Ghetto Vecchio, taking her a supply of fresh water, a bundle of sticks for her fire, and a trencher of food: soft fatty goose meat, or a dish of carrot and barley soup which I heated over the fire for her. She gobbled the provisions noisily and embraced me in her frail arms with tears in her eyes, blessing me for showing kindness to an old woman.

'You were kind to me,' I reminded her. 'You took pity on me when you could have turned your back on my suffering. The difference between us is that I am doing this to pay a debt of gratitude, because you saved my life. You helped me for no reason other than that you are a righteous woman. Hashem will reward you in the next life.'

'Go in peace, Abigail of Polotensk.'

'I will come and see you again soon. I am Abigail of Venice now,' I reminded her, and she smiled.

She did not know that the woman she was thanking had murdered a stranger, and would have killed her husband had he not paralysed her spirit. I was in need of many virtuous deeds if my sins were to be forgiven.

One morning, Tamar announced that she needed one of us to deliver a gown to a wealthy customer called Veronica Franco.

This was the third time in as many days that one of us had been summoned to carry a parcel to this particular customer's house. I had heard Daniel mention Veronica Franco's name as a Christian woman who wrote poetry, so at each opportunity I had volunteered eagerly, curious to see her. This time, to my delight, Tamar gave the commission to me.

'I would prefer to send a slower needleworker,' Tamar grumbled, 'but the customer insists a different girl deliver her mending each time, and with Rahab lame I am running out of options. The wealthy can afford to be capricious, not caring that it costs me valuable sewing time. And of course she cannot spare one of her own servants to fetch her precious garments, but must insist on one of my girls running around for her.'

A young boy had been sent to guide me to the house and I hurried after him, alert to the danger from anti-Semites once we were outside the ghetto walls. If my yellow shawl attracted attention, my youthful escort was hardly going to protect me against a crowd gathered to bait me. He would be more likely to join in. Passing through the Campo del San Samuele, I averted my eyes from the abject prostitutes loitering in the square in the shadow of the church and its ancient stone campanile. The fallen women flashed past in a jumble of painted faces, coloured skirts and bare flesh. With the jeering of whores ringing in my ears, and my heart pounding from my exertion, I arrived outside a tall, elegant house beside the Canale Grande. Gondolas and barges glided on the open stretch of water, without having to jostle for space. This was very different to the packed waterways and narrow streets to which I had grown accustomed. Even the air smelt fresher here.

A beady-eyed little girl opened the front door and my guide darted away, his errand completed. Clearly my safe return to the ghetto was not his concern. The girl gazed out at me with a wary expression.

'I am here to deliver a parcel to Veronica Franco,' I announced.

'A parcel?' the child lisped. 'What parcel?'

For answer I held up my package, which was wrapped in fine linen and tied with a crimson ribbon.

'What's in it?' the girl asked, reaching to take it from me.

Impulsively I took a step back, withdrawing the package out of her reach, suddenly resolved to hand my parcel to no one but the poet herself.

'Is your name Veronica?' I asked, reading out the name on the parcel.

The little girl burst out laughing. 'Of course not! Don't you know who she is?' Her brows lowered in renewed suspicion. 'Who are you, anyway? Where are you from? You are no lady's maid.'

Before I could reply, an imperious voice called out from inside the house, 'Go and see who is at the door.'

A moment later, I was astonished to see Domitilla appear in the doorway. I recognised her instantly, although she had changed in the four years since we first met on board a ship sailing from Split. She had grown sleek and plump, but her dark eyes and mischievous smile remained the same. Her hair was caught back tightly in a net ornamented with tiny seed pearls, a gift perhaps from her mistress, and her gown was of fine linen.

'Domitilla,' I said. 'I hardly recognised you. It is wonderful to see life is treating you so well.'

She gave me a warning frown and shook her head almost imperceptibly. 'Why would you recognise me?' she enquired. 'Have you been here before?'

'From the ship,' I said. 'We travelled to Venice together from Split. Surely you haven't forgotten how we were attacked by pirates?'

Domitilla looked flustered. 'You are mistaken. I have never

set eyes on you before.' She spoke firmly, but her expression was troubled, and I knew she recognised me. Perhaps she was angry that I had deceived her on our journey to Venice, although I had never denied my religion to her; or her antagonism might have been caused by fear that I would reveal something about her past that she wished to conceal. I could not imagine what that might be.

Turning to the young girl at her side, she ordered her to go to the kitchen and help the cook. The child scampered away, but before I could ask Domitilla the reason for her hostility, a woman appeared in the hallway. Not much older than me, she gazed levelly at me with heavy lidded dark eyes. Her light brown hair was tied back off her face, only a few stray wisps escaping to curl delicately around her ears. Her round cheeks were tinged with pink, and her lips were full and painted bright red. Lustrous pearls hung from her ears and around her neck. Her dress was of pale yellow satin ornamented with silver and gold inlay, and her crimson bodice was cut low to reveal the mounds of her white breasts. Seeing my eyes linger on her gown, she acknowledged my admiration with a faint nod. There was no reserve about her, yet she bore herself with dignity, unlike the brazen whores in the Campo del San Samuele. She was simply a beautiful woman accustomed to attracting the gaze of men and women.

As she approached, with her hands outstretched, I held out my parcel. 'My mistress, Tamar the seamstress, sent me,' I said quickly, before this glorious apparition closed the door on me.

On hearing my mistress's name, the lady lowered her hands and the jewels on her white fingers flashed and sparkled as she moved. 'Oh, you have brought me my gown.' She sounded disappointed. 'I thought you were delivering my new books.'

'Books?' I repeated in surprise. 'So it's true you can read?'

'My mistress writes books,' Domitilla announced haughtily.

'Not exactly,' Veronica smiled, 'at least not yet. But I am a poet, and I hope my work will be printed before long.'

'If you could read, you would know that her name is Veronica Franco,' Domitilla snapped, glaring at my yellow shawl, the badge of the Jewish ghetto.

'I can read as well as any man,' I replied, stung by her words.

'Wait,' Veronica said. She reached into her bosom and held out a silver ducat. 'This is for your trouble.'

'It is no trouble to serve you, madam. I am merely doing my mistress's bidding. But I would like to read your poems,' I added.

Veronica stared at me and smiled. 'Please, come in and take a glass of spiced wine. Domitilla,' she turned to her maid, 'tell Agnese to prepare my supper.'

Reluctant to tell her that I could neither eat nor drink at her house, I hesitated.

'Come, come,' she insisted.

'The mistress is inviting you to enter her house,' Domitilla told me sharply.

Stammering my thanks, I followed Veronica into a spacious hallway. A wide staircase with an ornate stone balustrade led upstairs. On a gilt table facing the front door someone had filled a jug of blue glass with white lilac blooms. Above it on the wall hung a portrait of Veronica in a gown of rich russet and blue, her hair held back from her face by a string of pearls. The artist had not merely copied her features closely, but he had captured a quality of life in his painting so that his subject's face appeared slightly flushed, and a smile seemed to hover on her warm lips. Her figure gave an illusion of movement, as though she had just paused for a second with her skirt swirling around her legs.

'I see you are admiring my portrait,' Veronica said. 'It was painted by Tiziano Vecellio.' She announced the artist's name proudly. 'You must know him,' she added, seeing my unresponsive expression. 'He is sometimes known by his family name, di Cadore. Or maybe you've heard him referred to simply as Titian? He is possessed of a prodigious talent as you can see. They call him "The Sun Amidst Small Stars". You recognise the reference?'

I did not like to admit that I had no idea what she was talking about, and was relieved when she continued without waiting for a response.

'He painted it for me as a gift. It's very valuable. Because of the artist, Titian, of course, not on account of his subject,' she added with a teasing smile.

'It's an amazing likeness,' I said.

With a pang of envy for the man who had created so beautiful an artefact, I wondered why Hashem would grant any man the power to create something so sublime, if it was truly a sin for man to create an image of his own form. But all I said was that it must be wonderful to paint like that, with such a subtle combination of soft tones and vivid colours. Veronica smiled, accepting my praise of the artist's skill as though it were a compliment intended for her. As she moved away, I noticed that she smelt not of bodily odours, but of flowers and herbs, light and fragrant. Closing my eyes, I savoured her scent, fresh and enticing, trying to commit it to memory.

'You smell lovely,' I stammered.

'It's Waters of Hungary.'

'Waters of Hungary?' I repeated. 'Where in Hungary does the water smell so sweet?'

Veronica burst out laughing. 'That's just the name they give it, because it is a perfume created for the Queen of Hungary. Everyone's wearing it these days.'

No one of my acquaintance was so delicately perfumed. I hung back, hoping she would not notice my own scent. Living and working so close to other people, beside fetid waters, I had grown accustomed to the smell of the ghetto. Now I felt ashamed of the pungent odour which clung to my clothes and seemed to penetrate my skin. Beckoning to me to follow her, my hostess glided gracefully into another room, her skirts rustling as she moved.

As soon as she was out of sight, Domitilla darted forward. 'Do not mention how we met,' she whispered to me.

'We have never seen one another before today,' I replied. 'But I am glad you have found employment in the house of so noble a lady.'

'Noble?' Domitilla whispered. 'Veronica Franco is a cortigiana onesta, you poor innocent.'

'I don't understand.'

'She is what is known as an honest courtesan. It's an honourable profession.'

'Prostitution is not honourable.'

'Veronica Franco is no common whore. She earns her keep entertaining patricians with her mental agility, in addition to her physical attractions.'

Understanding the reason for Veronica's immodest dress and bold eyes, I told Domitilla that I was sorry for my mistake.

'Oh, don't be. She is cultured and intelligent, and truly the most generous of charitable mistresses.'

'Well, you can rely on my discretion about your journey here,' I assured her.

We nodded at one another, before I followed Veronica into an imposing chamber. If Domitilla had confidences she wished to keep from her mistress, that was her business. Her secret could not be as shameful as mine.

31

Never having visited the house of a wealthy woman before, I expected to see a blazing fire and perhaps several geese in a basket, with clean straw on the floor, if not a woven rug. But the room Veronica led me into was magnificent beyond my most extravagant imaginings. It appeared to me wantonly opulent, rather than elegant like its mistress. Perhaps because I knew its resident was a courtesan, the grandiose decor had an air of decadence. Veronica stretched out on a cushioned couch, its bronze legs inlaid with tortoiseshell and ivory. The rug beneath our feet was softer than fresh grass. On the wall hung another full-length portrait of Veronica. In this one she wore a beaded green dress edged with lace that exposed half of her voluptuous bosom, with pearls and green stones glittering at her throat.

Veronica gestured gracefully at a chair upholstered in rich crimson velvet. A Jew from the ghetto, filthy and stinking of perspiration and foul water, a poor woman who worked with her fingers to earn a meagre living, I sat down on the plush armchair as though I were a high-born lady, while Domitilla served us a silver platter of marzipan, preserved fruits and sugared almonds, along with two goblets of spiced wine. Neither the sweetmeats nor the wine were kosher, but having travelled far from my home in Polotensk, and sailed with a foreign crew across the Adriatic Sea to Venice, I was not ignorant of the world outside the ghetto. During our travels, my uncle and I had not adhered strictly to the rules laid down by our holy books.

'Starving ourselves to death is a worse transgression than eating forbidden food,' my uncle told me. 'Hashem has seen fit to save our pitiful lives and we must submit to His will.'

Although I was not now starving, nevertheless it was hard to resist the sweetmeats Domitilla placed before us. Besides, I had already committed a sin far worse by accepting the hospitality of a Christian. Intrigued by this educated Christian woman who had fearlessly invited me into her home, I guzzled tiny coloured cakes of marzipan, along with sugared almonds and dried raisins, washing them down with rich wine sweetened with honey, until a surfeit of sweetness made me feel queasy, while Veronica read her poetry to me. In return, I related the story of Bovo and his love for the Princess Druzane.

'I imagined you would read only your Hebrew prayers,' she said, gazing at me with genuine interest. 'How wrong we are to judge others without first taking the trouble to converse with them.'

'That is certainly true. It is easy to jump to conclusions,' I agreed. 'But you were not entirely wrong in your supposition, because access to secular books is limited in the Jewish ghetto. An enlightened friend lent me the *Bovo Bukh*, or I would never have come across it. It was written nearly seventy years ago by a Jew living in the ghetto. Other books must have been written since then, but I have not seen them.'

'Many books have been written over the past seventy years,' she replied, with a smile. 'If you like, I will lend you some books of poetry.'

My face flushed hotly with pleasure and I stammered my

thanks for her generosity, too overwhelmed to admit that I struggled to read Italian.

'So, what do you think of all this?' she asked, waving her jewelled fingers to indicate her room, moving our conversation on from her benevolence.

'Your room is beautiful,' I replied, 'but I admire you more.'

She laughed. 'I am a courtesan,' she said, glancing at me from under lowered eyelids to watch my reaction. 'Naturally, I am accustomed to receiving praise from all manner of men, but many women despise what I do. Tell me, do you admire nothing in me but my beauty, for which I am not responsible?'

It was a direct question of a personal nature, but the wine and sweetmeats had emboldened me, and I answered without hesitation. 'You are undeniably beautiful, but I admire your superior learning and wisdom more than I admire your physical attractions. Of course you may argue that you were born with your intellect, just as you were born with your beauty, but I applaud how you have chosen to apply it, which is to say I admire your education, your wisdom, and your strength of character.'

'Are not all women strong?' Veronica replied. 'How many men could endure as we do? Do women not have hands and hearts, as men do? They see us as delicate and soft, yet men who are delicate can also be strong, while others, coarse and harsh, are cowards.' She raised herself on her couch and her eyes glowed brightly with the force of her conviction as she continued. 'A day will come when women realise that if we were only armed and trained, as men are, we would be able to fight them until death, and we would win.'

'Is it not wrong to kill?' I asked her.

'It cannot be wrong to defend yourself should the need arise,' she replied, staring at me as though she could read my mind as well as she read her books.

For the first time, I questioned whether murdering a stranger in the forest had been a heinous sin, after all, or rather the act of a courageous woman. It seemed that Veronica would have commended me for my strength and valour in saving my uncle's life. When I considered my action in that light, a weight seemed to lift from my shoulders. Probably no one other than this remarkable courtesan would condone my sin, but her understanding was enough to change me. If only one other person were able to excuse my sin, surely Hashem would too. I felt as though a darkness had been purged from my soul. Astonished, I glimpsed myself not as a victim of a sinful frailty, but as a strong and valiant woman.

'Tell me, who is your favourite poet?' she asked.

Desperate though I was to impress her with a learned opinion, I had no answer. 'Forgive me, but I have not read any of the poets,' I replied, expressing bitter regret at my ignorance.

'That is easily remedied,' she said, gazing at me shrewdly. 'There is a sadness about you that runs deeper than your desire to read poetry. You may unburden yourself to me.'

'There is no greater sorrow than to recall happiness in times of misery,' I replied softly, repeating words Daniel had once recited to me.

'A Jew who tells me she has read no poetry but quotes Dante Alighieri!' Veronica replied, laughing, and clapping her hands. 'But the poet Sappho wrote that there is no place for grief in a house which serves the Muse.'

'Sadly the Muses have not blessed me. My talents lie elsewhere.' I held up my hands and wiggled my fingers. 'I earn my living sewing. Yours is a far nobler calling.'

Veronica laughed again. 'Not many women would say that to a courtesan.'

'What you do with your physical body does not alone define who you are,' I replied. 'When I listen to your poetry, I am touched by something more sublime than sewing, although I am only a humble needleworker.'

Veronica read some more of her poems aloud. Sipping wine sweetened with honey, we discussed her verses. It may have been the effect of the wine, and the excess of sugar, but Veronica's poems seemed to me the most wonderful words I had ever come across.

'Do you still admire me, having heard my verses?' she asked.

Fervently I told her how inspiring it was for a poor Jewess to discover such learning in a good Christian woman.

'But I am not a good Christian woman,' she replied, laughing. 'Many in the church would consider me beyond redemption, although our Lord himself did not turn his back on a fallen woman.'

I tried to explain that her example seemed to me proof that through literacy the world could indeed become enlightened, and the key to this change lay in the invention of printing.

'If your poetry was printed, think how it would enlighten all who read it. Most men believe women are inferior to them. You are living proof they are mistaken. Don't you see? If everyone could read your words, no man would ever again regard women as inferior.'

'You really think printing can bring about such a change in men's minds?'

'The written word is the only way elevated thought and learning can be shared, and education on a wide scale must surely lead to an enlightened population. So yes, I believe printing can help bring about a better world. As long as it is not exploited by those in power,' I added, remembering Daniel's scepticism.

'Well, I will think on what you have said, and thank you for your approval of my poor literary efforts.'

'It was my honest opinion.'

'You must know that I too am honest, an honest courtesan.' She half sat up and leaned forward, exposing more of her bosom. 'The rulers of La Serenissima tolerate courtesans because we keep the young men of the city out of trouble. Your people also carry out a necessary function, fending off unrest among the profligate citizens, with your loan banks. In our different ways we both prevent civil disorder.'

'That is true,' I agreed. 'And let us not forget the exorbitant taxes we both pay into our rulers' coffers.'

'Indeed,' she agreed. 'How would the government of Venice manage its finances without our contributions? They depend on us for their survival, although they decry us in public.'

'Yet despite that, we Jews live in fear of expulsion from Venice.'

'Oh, pshaw. They are never going to send your people away. They cannot afford to lose you any more than they can live without us. Admittedly, they issue idle threats, popular with ignorant citizens, but they are never going to banish the people who preserve the stability of the Republic.'

'Even though they hate and despise us.'

Veronica nodded solemnly. 'You must take care, Abigail. You have done nothing to provoke enmity, yet you are hated because you are a Jew. The Catholics wish to annihilate your people, and although your literacy does you credit, it makes you vulnerable. The ignorant persist in the belief that the written word is possessed of magic powers, and women who can read are suspected of witchcraft.'

'Then you too must take care.'

'I have powerful friends to protect me. Who do you have?'

'I trust in my God,' I told her, smiling.

'And how has that faith served your people so far? But I did not invite you into my house to challenge your religious beliefs,' she added quickly, as my smile faded. She rose and crossed the room to close the door. Seated once again on her couch, she leaned towards me and continued, in a low voice, 'Nor did I ask you to enter my house to discuss poetry, enjoyable though our discourse has been. That was a genuine pleasure, but I had a less agreeable reason for wishing to talk to you. You must have wondered why I sent my servant to escort you here, when he could have simply collected my parcel from Tamar himself, and why I requested a different needleworker come to my house each day. I was hoping to find a woman wise enough to heed my words, and strong enough to act on them. I will be honest with you, Abigail, I was beginning to despair of finding such a woman among Tamar's needleworkers.'

'You think of me as wise and strong?' I stammered. I wanted to assure her that she was mistaken. I had never considered myself as anything but foolish and feeble. Staring at me with fierce intensity, Veronica ignored my question and continued speaking. Her voice was soft, yet there was a note of urgency in her tone that compelled my attention.

'Abigail,' she said, 'I invited Tamar to send a needleworker from the ghetto to my house, so that I could pass on a warning. Listen to me, Abigail. One of the patricians who visits me regularly is a member of the Council of Ten. He told me the Executors Against Blasphemy are reconvening. They are planning to burn your holy books when the Papal Legate returns in two months' time.'

Everyone in the ghetto knew about the atrocity of 5313, corresponding to the Christian year 1553, when all the holy books in the ghetto were seized by the Duke's guards and burned in the Piazza San Marco. The Church of Rome thought we would cease to exist as Jews once the word of our God had been consumed by fire, yet the ghetto had survived and our prayers had continued uninterrupted. But it seemed that our prayers had not been answered.

'I am telling you this so you can warn your community,' she said. 'Your people understand the value of the printed word, and the Inquisitors are my enemy as they are yours. We are not so very different, you and I.'

Remembering my sins, I trembled at her words.

32

Quickly I made my way back along the Canale Grande, and across the Campo del San Samuele, ignoring the mocking calls of prostitutes loitering on the shady side of the piazza. As a Jew, and a woman, I was doubly at risk, and wished I had thought to bring my knife with me. Even now, Hadassah was probably using it to slice carrots. As the cries of the fallen women faded behind me, I heard another voice calling my name and paused. Looking back, I saw Domitilla scuttling after me.

'Lord above, are you deaf?' she panted as she drew level with me. 'Did you not hear me shouting?'

Her face was red from her exertion and she stopped for a moment to catch her breath. 'You walk very fast for one who looks so sickly,' she added, squinting at me. 'Have you been ill?'

'Yes, my friend, I was sick, but I am recovered now.' I lowered my voice. 'My husband found me, and my life was hard. Before he returned, believing him dead, I had just become betrothed to another–'

'A more deserving man, I hope.'

I nodded. 'The most deserving man alive.'

Domitilla nodded knowingly, her dark eyes softened with sympathy. 'Don't tell me your husband returned from the dead, more's the pity. I hope you stuck a skewer in his black heart.'

She spoke lightly, but her words made me shudder as I recalled my intention to do just that. I wanted to ask if her suggestion was serious, and whether she could ever be moved to kill a violent husband, but I dared not speak of such dark matters. Instead, I told her that my husband had been sentenced to the galleys for brawling, and she grinned.

'May he die at sea and rot while his soul suffers the eternal torments of hell. But tell me, how are you managing? I have a comfortable life with my mistress, as you can see.' She patted her hair and smoothed down her elegant skirt with a satisfied air. 'She believes I was a fallen woman, like many other unfortunates she helps. If she knew I had been a respectable married woman, I would probably lose my job.'

Laughing, I promised not to betray the secret of her virtue, and told her about my job with the seamstress. 'It is dull work, but honest, and the girls in the sewing workshop are company during the long hours. I am fortunate that my landlady is a good woman and a true friend to me and I am not unhappy with my life. I pray you are happy in yours.'

'Veronica Franco is a great lady, and many eminent patricians visit her,' Domitilla replied, as though she was proud of her mistress's profession.

A woman like Veronica Franco would dismiss my scruples about lying with Daniel, but the more I thought about my situation, the more hopeless it seemed. It was true that my life was not unhappy. I was safe, and free from hunger and pain. But that was not the same as being happy. The words of the poet Dante Alighieri repeated themselves in my mind on my way back to the ghetto: 'There is no greater sorrow than to recall happiness in times of misery.' The poet was right. It would have been better for me had I never met Daniel and glimpsed unattainable happiness.

In the meantime, there were troubles more pressing than my own selfish concerns. That evening, after work, I went to Daniel's lodgings and told him I wished to address the leaders of the congregation.

'Why do you wish to speak to them?' he asked me, staring at me in surprise. 'It is somewhat irregular.'

'For myself, I have no desire to speak to any man,' I replied with unnecessary cruelty, annoyed that he saw fit to challenge my request. 'But on this occasion, believe me, Daniel, I have no choice. I have received a warning that must be passed on to the leaders of our congregation, and they must be forced to heed it.'

I could have shared Veronica's message with Hadassah and Tamar, and all my fellow needleworkers, and no doubt the message would have spread quickly through the community. Yet unsubstantiated rumours are easy to overlook, especially when they are unwelcome. The responsibility for ensuring attention was paid to the warning rested with me.

The following evening, Daniel invited me to accompany him to the synagogue, where the Rabbi and all the leaders of the congregation were waiting to hear why he had asked to see them. He had not confessed the summons came from me. Many leaders of the congregation were scholars. Others were influential residents of the ghetto, prosperous enough to pay a significant contribution to communal funds. I struggled to control my nerves, wondering how these important men could be persuaded to listen to a poor woman.

Yet, by the grace of Hashem, I had tackled and overcome a man who would have killed my uncle and ravished me. It was true I was a woman, but I was beginning to understand that my sex did not make me weak. Men might perceive me as frail and helpless, but Veronica had described me as wise and strong. 'A day will come,' she had said, 'when women will understand that if we were armed and trained, we would be able to fight as well as men.' So I kept my nerve and gazed calmly at the leaders of the congregation who had unknowingly gathered to hear my words. Clearing my throat, I launched into an account of my visit to Veronica. Several of the men began to mutter to one another when I mentioned her name.

'The Council have not issued any warnings to us,' the stout baker remarked when I finished speaking. 'This is nonsense. Why would they confide in a common whore before speaking to us?'

'She is a courtesan,' I protested, 'not a whore.'

'What is the difference?' one of the men sneered.

'A courtesan is an educated woman,' I told them. 'Veronica Franco reads and writes, and is a charitable woman. Why will you not listen to me?'

'We are listening to you, child,' the Rabbi said, although clearly Veronica's warning was falling on deaf ears.

A woman had issued us with a warning. Now the congregation were refusing to heed it because it was being delivered by another woman.

'Do not be put off by her profession,' I urged them, frustrated that they were not taking me seriously. 'She is well read and informed and can engage in intelligent conversation, and that is why patricians confide in her. They visit her and discuss their concerns, and share their secrets with her. It was a member of the Council of Ten himself who told her that the Executors Against Blasphemy are preparing to burn our holy books. You have not heard about it because they are making their plans behind closed doors, and few are privy to the secret workings of the Council of Ten. Veronica was told in confidence.'

'It is possible. They have done it before,' the stout baker

admitted. 'But I, for one, have many distinguished customers among the patricians. I cannot believe we would not have been told.'

'You are being told now,' I said, raising myself to my full height and affecting a confidence I did not feel.

Other members of the congregation were equally cynical.

'This is the chatter of prattling women,' a pawnbroker said.

'We cannot pay heed to every piece of tittle-tattle,' someone else agreed.

'Our lives are precarious enough,' the butcher said. 'We don't need more hysterical rumours flying around, upsetting our women.'

'I am not hysterical,' I protested through gritted teeth, struggling to control tears of frustration that threatened to undermine my protestation.

'This is mere scaremongering,' another voice said dismissively.

'Abigail is an honest woman,' Daniel interrupted their muttering.

'No one doubts that,' the pawnbroker replied, 'but like all women she is gullible. Are we really going to trust the word of a common whore, on the evidence of a naive young woman?'

'Why would we not believe her?' Daniel countered. 'She may be a woman, but she is not a fool.'

My face grew hot and I felt dizzy, hearing his praise.

'What makes you so sure this courtesan is telling the truth?' the Rabbi asked me gently.

'We cannot trust the word of a licentious Christian woman,' the baker said. 'Let that be the end of it.'

'You ask me why I believe she was telling the truth,' I said, looking at the Rabbi. 'Let me ask you, all of you,' I turned to gaze at each of the men in turn, 'what possible reason could she have for lying to me? What can she hope to gain from warning us that we must save our books? She only repeated what she was told. Why would she tell me, unless she was concerned for the safety of our holy books?'

'What does a Christian whore care about our holy books?' the pawnbroker asked.

'She cares about our books because she is a poet who loves learning. I had the same reaction as you, so I asked her why she wanted to help us and she replied that it is because we understand the value of the printed word, and because the Inquisitors are her enemy as well as ours. She may not believe in our religion, but she neither fears nor hates us. She fears and hates the Inquisitors, as we do.'

A furious debate ensued and I listened in helpless silence as they argued with each other.

'So now we make friends with whores and Christians?'

'It is true that she too is hated by the Inquisition.'

'We cannot trust the word of a licentious woman.'

'A whore is not to be trusted.'

'She is an educated woman who has the ear of the Council of Ten.'

'One member of the Council of Ten.'

'Still, a member of the Council of Ten.'

The row continued for a while until one of the men appealed to the Rabbi for his opinion.

'Surely we are better informed about affairs of the Republic than this young woman can possibly be,' the baker said, with a faint sneer.

'Beware the sin of pride,' the Rabbi replied mildly.

'But we are the leaders of our congregation, and we have heard nothing about it,' the baker insisted.

'You are hearing about it now,' I cried out.

The Rabbi bowed his head. 'That is true, my child. If Hashem has seen fit to use a courtesan and a needleworker as

His instruments, who are we to question His will? We must heed the warning, whatever the source, and make our preparations.'

Trembling, I turned to leave, my mission accomplished. As I reached the Campo del Ghetto Nuovo, Daniel caught up with me. 'May I walk with you to the seamstress in the morning, as I used to?'

'No, it cannot be. Daniel, I beg you, do not ask me again.'

The following morning, I was both relieved and disappointed when Daniel did not appear and try to walk with me to Tamar's workshop, but as I was returning from work, he again fell into step beside me in the Campo del Ghetto Nuovo. This time he spoke with an urgency impossible to ignore. 'I have been waiting for you,' he murmured. 'I must speak with you.'

I tried to remain calm, but he must surely have heard the pounding of my blood as it coursed through my body.

'Your husband has been sentenced to fifteen years in the galleys,' he continued in a low voice.

'My husband has not led a happy life,' I replied shortly, refusing to meet his eye. 'We must pray for his safe return.'

'I will not pray for his return,' he replied in a fierce whisper, 'and I know you will not. I pray for news that he is dead, and I know you wish for that too, whatever you say.'

I turned to walk away from him.

'Wait,' he called out softly. 'Will you at least come to supper with us so that I may see your face sometimes, and have the joy of conversing with you?'

'I cannot.'

'Why not? Abigail, what is wrong? How have I offended you?'

'Daniel, you must not talk to me like that.'

'How should I talk to you then? Tell me. I do not know what I can do to please you. I only know that I cannot bear this separation.'

Gazing into his glistening eyes, I responded with unshed tears of my own as I answered. 'I can never eat at your table again, Daniel. We cannot return to how we were. I am a married woman. Even if my husband dies in slavery in the galleys, I will never hear of it. Never. Do you understand what I am saying? No one will ever bring me news that I am at liberty to take another husband. Hashem has saved me from living with a violent man, but I will never be released from my marriage vows, because I will never know my husband's fate. Slaves die in the galleys every day and are tossed into the sea, and no one hears of them again. I can never have another husband, and am destined to die childless. That is the fate Hashem has decreed for me.'

'Then I am destined never to marry again,' he said.

I walked away from him with tears streaming down my cheeks, and this time he did not try to stop me.

33

One evening there was an urgent knocking at our door just as Hadassah and I were preparing to retire for the night. We found Daniel standing outside, in the company of a stranger.

'Can you help this visitor?' Daniel asked us. 'He is a stranger here in the ghetto and he has a cut on his face. I would take him home with me, but my mother will fuss, and she is still weak and needs to rest, and Miriam will not know what to do.'

'Who is he?' I enquired cautiously as Daniel led his companion into our apartment.

With an effort, I drew my eyes away from Daniel and observed the stranger more closely. He had a neat moustache and pointed beard, and his eyes were merry, despite his current difficulty. He was dressed in a dark travelling cloak and breeches, with a cap on his head, and his high white collar was edged with lace and stained with blood from a wound on his cheek.

'My name is John, madam,' he replied, with a bow, speaking in a coarse foreign accent.

'How did you come by your wound?' I asked, surprised that

he would show so much respect to a poor Jew. From his dress it was clear the stranger was a foreigner, and I wondered if he was even aware that we were Jews.

'Madam, I was set on by a ruffian who threatened me at knife point. If your neighbour here had not come to my defence and tripped the scoundrel up, I would have lost my purse.' He clapped Daniel on the back. 'This brave fellow sent the thief packing, with a few bruises for his pains.'

Daniel shook his head, muttering that it was no more than anyone else might have done in the same situation.

'You should not have intervened,' I scolded him. 'You could have been arrested.'

'Arrested?' John repeated in surprise. 'Your friend did nothing wrong. I witnessed the whole incident myself.'

I did not explain to the stranger that as a Jew, Daniel could have been fined or imprisoned for brawling on the street. Few Christian judges would condemn a Christian thief when a Jew was present to act as scapegoat.

John winked at Daniel. 'I see the lady has a soft spot for you.'

Daniel gazed at me with an intensity I could not bear. I looked away. It seemed that however hard I strived to avoid him, Daniel returned to torment me.

'Sir, you are welcome in our home,' Hadassah said. 'We will tend to your injuries. You are bleeding from a wound on your face that may cause you some problems if it is not cleaned.'

The stranger touched his cheek with a gloved hand and frowned.

'Now you have blood on your glove,' I said, unable to refrain from reproaching him for his carelessness.

He shrugged. 'It is no matter. I have a roomful of gloves at home.'

'You must be a wealthy man,' I replied.

'Or I make and sell gloves.' He smiled. 'Never make assumptions about strangers, my child.'

'Where are you from?' I asked, warming to the foreigner in spite of my reservations.

'Is it obvious I am not Venetian?'

'Well, your voice, sir... and your attire...'

He laughed and winced as the movement in his face disturbed his wound. 'I am from England, madam,' he told me, with another bow.

I hesitated. Here in Venice, no Christian addressed a Jewish woman with respect, nor would he ever bow his head to us. It seemed the stranger still had not realised who we were.

'I accept your offer of help with gratitude,' he added.

Curiosity overcame my caution. 'Well, you had best sit down and let me tend the cut on your face,' I said. 'It should be covered before any pestilential vapours enter your blood. Besides, if you bleed any more you will ruin your fine jacket.'

He took a seat at the table while Hadassah lit tallow candles, heedless of the expense. She was in cheerful spirits that day, and insisted our guest take a seat while she bound his head after I had cleaned it.

'You must stay too,' she said to Daniel.

'No,' I said, before he could reply. 'Daniel must get home to his family.' I turned my back on him and a moment later he took his leave.

'Tell me,' John said when his wound was bound and he had eaten, 'what is this place?'

'You are in the Jewish ghetto of Venice,' Hadassah told him.

John started, and gazed at us in astonishment. 'You are Jews?'

'Yes, we are Jews, and so is Daniel who brought you to our door,' Hadassah replied.

'He is a valiant Jew,' our visitor murmured in surprise.

'Now, sir, if you remove your collar, Abigail will wash it for you at the well, and dry it by the fire.'

'Are you sure you don't mind?' he asked. 'You know this mark is blood?'

'Why would I mind?' I replied. 'It is just from a cut on your face, and the blood will stain if left too long. You may be a Christian, but are you not a living breathing person as we are, and is your blood not red, as ours is? The knife that injured you would have cut me had it struck my face. Do we not all bleed and heal in the same way?'

John inclined his head and unpinned his collar, thanking me. It was growing dark by the time we had finished, and the gate to the ghetto was about to close.

'It would be safer for you to stay here in the ghetto until morning,' Hadassah told our guest.

He frowned. 'I am no infidel. I am a good Christian, whatever that means these days,' he added almost under his breath. 'Catholics, Protestants, we are all at one another's throats. We should have stuck with the one true religion and have done with it. All the rest is hogwash, and–'

'I am not ashamed of my faith,' I interrupted him fiercely.

'Forgive me, madam, I was not talking about your religion. I was referring to my fellow Christians, who are all at loggerheads since the Reformers began their challenge to the Catholics. Take it from me, this dissent will not end well. Many will die before it is all over.'

'And the sword will fall heaviest on the Jews,' Hadassah said.

'That would be a pity. I can see you are both virtuous women, and Daniel saved my life, as well as my purse. He is a good man.'

The traveller from England talked to us until late and our candles burnt low.

'To tell you the truth,' he confessed, 'you are the first Jews I have ever spoken to like this, and you are nothing like I imagined you would be.'

I smiled uneasily. 'What did you think Jews were like?'

'Well, you certainly do not strike me as an abomination, either of you. Our priest tells us you keep a store of fresh blood from good Christians, to anoint your Jewish dead with, before you bury them. Of course, I never believed that,' he added, seeing our dismay.

Hadassah inclined her head. 'We thank you for that.'

'Oh, it is not that I think Jews are any better than the rest of us, I just do not believe there are enough good Christians to provide enough fresh blood to make that possible.' He laughed. 'Although I have to admit the priest was right about one thing: your ghetto does not exactly smell sweet. It reminds me of my youngest boy when he has eaten too many plums.' He laughed again.

'How many sons do you have?' I asked.

'I have two lads at home. The younger one never does what he is told, although I swear the rascal understands everything.' He smiled affectionately. 'As for my older boy, all he ever wants is for his mother to tell him stories. But I count my blessings that they survived. My first two died.'

'You will have a few stories of your own to tell your older boy when you get home from your travels,' I said.

'I guess I will.' He smiled. 'He will be intrigued to hear about the Jews of Venice.'

'You never told us what you are doing here,' Hadassah said.

'I am on my way home from Genoa, and I stopped off here to see the famed beauty of Venice for myself.'

'What were you doing in Genoa?' I asked.

'There is a supplier of velvet in Genoa who can beat anyone in Flanders on price. And,' he put his finger on his lips, 'in Genoa you can purchase silk fabric woven with silver and gold threads. But that is just between us. The fewer people who know about my dealings, the better. I have already been accused of dealing illegally in wool and cannot afford to face similar allegations again.'

Hadassah nodded. 'You are right to be discreet about your affairs. The world is full of busybodies who cause a lot of trouble.'

After a hearty breakfast, our visitor set off mid-morning, when the gateway to the ghetto was busy and no one was likely to notice him leaving. I accompanied him as far as the ghetto wall, warning him to avoid placing his weight on the fractured balustrade of the Agudi Bridge, and we parted at the gate.

'If you ever find yourself in England,' he said, 'make your way to the city of Stratford on the River Avon, and ask for Henley Street. Should I be away from home, tell my good wife, Mary, who you are, and she will gladly repay your hospitality. And you can tell my lad, Will, a story. He is a good boy, for all that he has a lively imagination. But travel the highways of my country with caution,' he added in a low voice. 'Jews are not welcome in England.'

'My people are not welcome anywhere,' I replied.

34

Assiduous as I was in avoiding meeting Daniel, I could not help looking out for him whenever I entered or left the synagogue. On the rare occasion that I had a glimpse of him, I tried to watch him for as long as possible without being spotted, careful to turn away before he noticed me. Perhaps he was doing the same, because once or twice I caught him gazing at me. I was always the first to look away. I had a feeling he continued staring at me, but I dared not look round to see. Seated upstairs in the women's gallery, I had no such qualms about talking to Miriam. To be fair, we spoke very little about Daniel because she was too preoccupied with plans for her forthcoming wedding.

'Father said I may have a new dress.'

'How lovely. Why do you not visit Tamar's workshop? I will persuade her to give you a good price, and I will work on your dress myself to make sure it is a perfect fit.'

Privately I resolved to make her dress in my own time at home in the evenings. There was little enough I could do for the girl I had once hoped to embrace as my daughter. The next morning, I spoke to Tamar and arranged that if Miriam came to her, she would only charge for the fabric and thread to make the wedding gown.

'I cannot afford to do favours,' Tamar said.

I assured her she would not be out of pocket by so much as a soldo. It was as well I had spoken to Tamar, because that very afternoon Miriam turned up, and I saw Tamar glance at her timepiece as I took Miriam's measurements and showed her a selection of fabrics. Every minute she spent poring over swatches and comparing colours was costing me money, but I refused to curtail her pleasure. Miriam might only experience one wedding day in her life, and I wanted her to enjoy it to the full. At last she declared herself satisfied and, in a fit of generosity, Tamar threw in a length of matching satin ribbon for her hair.

'You are marrying a fine young man,' she said. 'We must make sure you look beautiful.'

'Tamar has her eye on Miriam as a future customer. As the wife of a physician, she will have money to spend on gowns,' Sarai whispered in my ear, giving voice to my own thought.

Tamar lent me a two-bladed spring cutting tool, and I spent the evening working on the length of fabric Miriam had selected, until Hadassah told me she was snuffing out the tallow candle, after which it was too dark to continue. I was up early and resumed my work so that I would be finished in time to take the cutting tool back to the seamstress that day. For an instant, Tamar looked impressed that I had returned the tool so quickly, then she pursed her lips disapprovingly.

'I hope you were not working on Miriam's dress all night,' she said. 'Do not think I will not notice if you are too tired to work hard today.'

I assured her that Hadassah had snuffed out my candle when she retired to sleep, after which it had been too dark for me to continue my work.

'Well, I hope you did not rush the cutting,' she replied sourly. 'Miriam is a valued customer, and her wedding gown must be perfect.'

For the next few weeks, I spent every evening working on Miriam's wedding gown, and by the time she returned to the sewing shop, it was finished. Even Tamar did not immediately hector me to get back to work, but paused to compliment Miriam on her new gown, which fitted her perfectly. Her pleasure gave me some consolation.

The whole congregation attended the wedding, which was a joyful affair, as such occasions should be, but I had to force myself to smile, remembering that this was Miriam's celebration.

'Come, sit with us,' Hadassah called out to Debra.

'You look well in that gown,' the Rabbi's wife told me as she walked past.

I thanked her, and she moved on to the next table where we heard her telling someone else she looked well in her gown. Hadassah chuckled.

'Don't laugh,' I scolded her quietly. 'She's trying to be kind.'

'And she's right,' Debra added, 'you do look well, Abigail. When I recall how ill you looked when you returned to us from the Ghetto Vecchio, I give thanks to Hashem you have recovered your strength. You look lovely in that dress.'

'I will have to let it out if I keep eating Hadassah's griboli.' I grinned.

Several times I noticed Daniel staring wistfully at me, and I looked away. It was excruciating to be in the same room as him, yet unable to speak to him or touch him. I dared not look at him, for fear he would see through my pretended indifference.

When I went to fetch a glass of sweetened wine for Debra, he came over and thanked me.

'What for?' I asked, without raising my eyes.

'For Miriam's wedding gown.' He leaned closer to me and

lowered his voice. 'Did you think I would not find out what you did for her, sewing every night at home to save on the cost?' He spoke even more softly than before. 'Every time I look at my daughter's wedding gown, I see your fingers delicately stitching the threads and smoothing the fabric. I think of you all the time, Abigail. Your voice calls to me in my dreams, and the memory of you torments me when I wake.'

'It was my pleasure to work on Miriam's wedding gown,' I said, before hurrying away.

Seeing him looking crestfallen, I longed to run to him with words of comfort, but such happiness was out of reach for us. Shortly after our exchange, a fiddler struck up a lively tune, accompanied by a taborer who beat out a rapid tattoo. Elia and another young man lifted the bridegroom on a chair which they spun around at shoulder height, while men danced in a circle around them. Entertainers danced with bottles balanced on top of their hats, while others somersaulted and tumbled in front of the guests. I laughed at the antics of a juggler. Distracted by the spectacle, I did not notice that Daniel had come to stand behind my chair.

'It does me good to hear you laugh,' he said.

'I am glad it pleases you.'

Having answered him politely, I rose to my feet and walked away, before he could say anything else. He did not approach me again but sat by his mother and watched his daughter, like a dutiful father. But he smiled only when Miriam was looking at him, and it saddened me to know that I had caused him pain.

The day after her wedding, Miriam left Venice for Padua, where her new husband had decided to start his practice as a physician. She was excited to leave Venice for an apartment of her own, with a husband who was well respected and had every prospect of thriving. As though she had been waiting to see her granddaughter married, a week after Miriam's wedding Debra was struck down by a sudden apoplexy and was taken in the night. Word was sent to Miriam, but Padua was over a day's journey away and the burial could not be delayed long enough for her to attend. Miriam arrived in Venice on the second day of the week of ritual mourning, filled with remorse at having missed the funeral.

'Do not distress yourself,' I said. 'You could not possibly have returned to Venice in time. You came as soon as you could.'

'I should have been with her,' she wept. 'She was like a mother to me, and I wasn't even here to say goodbye.'

'You are here now, and that is what matters,' I consoled her. 'Debra knew how much you loved her. Did you not care for her when she was sick?'

Miriam nodded tearfully. 'I blame myself,' she said. 'My grandmother was never the same after the apothecary attended to her deafness. He may have improved her hearing, but she became confused afterwards, and it was all my fault. If I had not nagged her, she never would have gone to the apothecary to have hot candles put on her ears to draw the obstruction out. I believe he removed more than just wax from her ears. His candling upset the balance of her humours so severely that she died of it. If I hadn't insisted she consult the apothecary, she would still be alive now.'

'You cannot take the blame for her growing older,' I said.

'I just feel so guilty that I was not here when she died.'

'You came as quickly as you could,' I repeated.

I longed to be able to offer her the support that only a mother or a stepmother could give.

'We can only do what we can do,' Elia said. 'And what must be will be.'

Miriam smiled through her tears. 'Since when did you become a philosopher, brother?'

35

By now rumours were rife throughout the ghetto that the Executors Against Blasphemy were preparing to seize our holy books. Nothing had yet been done to protect our holy scroll, but with the Papal Legate due to return to Venice in a week, the leaders of the community were taking the threat seriously.

'They cannot burn our books,' Sarai protested. 'Hashem would never allow such sacrilege here in Venice.'

'It has happened before,' Tamar replied. 'What makes you so sure it will not happen again?'

If the other girls had been alive during the previous atrocity, they would have been infants, although a couple of them claimed to remember the panic, and the outpouring of grief in the piazza as the congregation gathered to watch the fire.

Tamar must have remembered it clearly, but when we asked her about it, she shook her head and refused to describe the terrible scene. 'The old baker, may his soul rest in peace, hid one of our Holy Scrolls inside a large challah,' she said. 'Otherwise we would have lost both scrolls of the law.'

'Moishe, the baker, could do what his father did,' Sarai asked.

'It was done on the night the guards marched into the ghetto to seize our books,' Tamar replied. 'If Moishe were to hide a scroll in a challah today, the bread would go stale and the guards might become suspicious.'

'You cannot see when a loaf of bread is stale,' one of the girls pointed out.

'But it might turn green with mildew,' I said, remembering the rations we had been forced to eat on our sea voyage from Split to Venice. 'And that might damage the scroll inside it.'

We fell silent for a moment, horrified by the idea of defacing the word of the living God.

'In any case, the authorities will have heard rumours about the hiding of the scroll last time. The bakery will be the first place they will search.'

'There must be another way to hide our holy Torah,' Sarai said. 'There must.'

Destroying printed books would be a wickedness, but prayer books could be reprinted. A holy Torah scroll, handwritten on parchment, took years to complete and was the most sacred of our possessions, the foundation of our faith, giving us the words of Hashem Himself. We all agreed we would defend it with our lives.

'Such talk is easy,' Tamar interrupted our fervent protestations, 'especially on the lips of foolish young women. Now, you are here to work, not to sit chattering about how you would save our Torah. We must leave that to the leaders of the congregation in their wisdom.'

Tamar spoke sternly, but she looked worried. Inspired by the words of a Christian poet, and the strength I had gained from my own survival, I did not agree that the solution to our difficulty could only be decided on by men. I stayed silent, but as we sat sewing, a plan began to form in my mind. The needleworkers were young and eager to gossip. I could not rely on their discretion. Tamar might agree to my idea but if she raised objections, as seemed likely, given her caution and her parsimony, then my plan would founder before it even had a chance to succeed.

That night, I lay awake puzzling over how to realise my plan. Time was running out, if Veronica's warning was accurate. It had been impossible to smuggle many books out, as guards had been posted at the gate for a few weeks, searching anyone leaving the ghetto. Some people had already decided where they were going to hide their books, while others argued that they could not be confident their hiding places would not be discovered, and anyone caught attempting to conceal books would face the wrath of the Executors Against Blasphemy.

Hashem had sent me an idea, but He had left it to me to see it through. If I was to escape attention, I could not implement my strategy alone. Miriam would have helped me, but she had left Venice. Besides, she might have insisted on confiding in her husband, who was bound to object to his wife becoming involved in so dangerous a plan. Hadassah was my only possible ally. She could be relied on not to divulge my plan to another living soul, and she had enough money to make it practicable. The next morning, I explained my idea to her.

'You want me to give you back your rent money for an entire month so you can make yourself a gown?' she repeated in surprise. 'What is this? Has sewing for wealthy women turned your wits? I have never bought a new gown for myself, not even for my own wedding. No one has ever made a gown especially for me. What is wrong with second-hand garments, that you need to make a gown for yourself?' She glanced at my threadbare brown dress, and sighed.

Carefully I explained my plan to her.

'And if the guards come and seize our books, you think you alone can escape their attention?'

'It's possible,' I replied firmly. 'At the very least, I will have a new gown,' I added, smiling uneasily.

If my plan failed, we both knew I would not live to wear my new gown for long.

'Very well,' she said, frowning at me. 'I will think about it. But I make no promises.'

When I returned home that evening, Hadassah held out the money I had requested. 'May Hashem protect you,' she said.

Rather than be late for work, I trusted Hadassah to purchase the fabric for me the next day, since I had decided against telling Tamar what I was doing.

'Repeat what I told you,' I said.

'A packet of needles,' she replied, 'a cutting tool, and twice my own height in brown fabric, not too thick so it is easy to work, and nothing fancy. It must not attract attention.'

'And brown thread,' I said. 'Don't forget the thread.'

Hadassah nodded. 'Very well. That's four items to remember. Needles, thread, fabric and cutters. Don't worry. I'll get everything you need. I pray that I am doing the right thing.'

All that day as I sat sewing one garment in Tamar's workshop, I was thinking about another. That evening, Hadassah greeted me with all that I had asked for, along with a brand-new tinder box, and four tallow candles which would allow me to sew after sunset.

'Do not sit up too late,' she fussed. 'You do not want to fall sick from exhaustion.'

Her concern made me laugh. 'No one ever fell sick from sewing.'

'But many succumb to the pestilence when lack of sleep overwhelms the balance of their humours.'

While Hadassah prepared our supper of barley soup,

accompanied by the fried goose skin to which she was partial, I unrolled my new brown fabric, laid it out on the table, and began to cut my gown. The light faded soon after we had eaten, and I lit one of the candles that Hadassah had purchased for me.

After watching me in silence for a while, she stood up. 'I'm going to bed. Don't stay up too late.'

That night I worked on my gown, until I could no longer force my eyes to stay open. The next day I waited impatiently to finish at the workshop, before hurrying home to continue with my clandestine project. So I continued for a week, sewing in the seamstress's workshop during the day and working on my own gown at night. Hadassah complained several times that I looked worn out, but she never challenged my plan. So I worked on, until at last my gown was finished. It fitted me well, since I had made it to my own measurements.

Hadassah admired my new gown. 'It's a perfect fit. It's a strong fabric, and well made. It should last for years. And the skirt is full,' she added approvingly.

'Which will allow me to continue eating your fried griboli,' I smiled, patting my belly which was no longer as flat as when I had returned from the Ghetto Vecchio.

'You look healthy,' she replied, with a broad grin.

The next day, I wore my new gown. The colour of the fabric was similar to that of my old gown, so it was unlikely to attract attention, but I had not counted on Tamar's sharp eyes. As soon as I entered the workshop, she scrutinised me with a shrewd eye.

'You have a new gown?' she challenged me.

'It belonged to Hadassah.'

There was a grain of truth in what I told Tamar, as Hadassah had purchased the fabric for me.

'She barely wore it and now it no longer fits her,' I added.

'She could have brought it here to be altered,' Tamar replied tartly, as though I had cheated her out of a job.

'She chose to give it to me instead.'

Tamar stared at me. 'It fits as perfectly as though it was made for you,' she said at last.

'I made a few alterations,' I murmured.

'Not with my thread, I hope.'

'No, indeed. Hadassah purchased thread for me in the market. I am no thief.'

Picking up the doublet I had begun mending the day before, I bent my head over my sewing. As I had expected, the seamstress did not want to interrupt me in my work. After that, my new gown was not remarked on again, and I felt a surge of satisfaction at having completed the first stage of my plan.

As it turned out, there was no time to test my idea. The morning after my gown was finished, we heard a loud outcry as we sat working quietly in the sewing shop. Voices bellowed, and footsteps pounded along the street. Tamar stepped outside to enquire what the source of the disturbance was, and returned looking pale. Her thin lips trembled visibly and her voice, usually so sharp, shook so that she could scarcely frame the words to tell us the news. Her dark eyes filled with tears. No longer a fierce taskmaster, she was a frightened woman.

'It is happening,' she said. 'They have come.'

'Is it the Day of Judgement?' one of the young girls stammered.

'It is worse than that,' Tamar replied. 'What is happening now is not the will of Hashem. The Duke's guards are coming to seize our holy books.'

As she spoke, a woman burst into the sewing room, her face wet with tears. 'Hide your books and risk imprisonment,' she cried out, 'or surrender your books and save your lives!'

With that, she dashed out again. Without saying a word, I put down my sewing and left. Everyone around me was panicking, but I had a clear idea of what I must do, and Hashem guided my steps to the synagogue.

In the entrance, Daniel stopped me. 'Where are you going?' he asked. 'There is no sanctuary here. This is the first place the guards will come. Go home, Abigail, and stay out of sight.'

Quickly I confided my plan to him.

Daniel shook his head. 'You cannot do that,' he replied fiercely. 'It is too dangerous. Abigail, you will not risk your life. I cannot allow it.'

'My life is not yours that you can dictate what I may or may not do with it,' I reminded him gently. 'In any case, what is so important about the life of one poor woman?'

'Your life is more important to me than anything else in the whole world,' he replied wildly, grabbing my arms and clinging to me. 'Anything.'

'Hush,' I told him. 'We are all flustered by what is happening. Let me go and, if you value my life, do not repeat what I have told you to a living soul.' Wrenching myself from his grasp, I hurried into the synagogue and he followed me, still remonstrating.

36

Traditionally the domain of men alone, the prayer hall downstairs was packed with men, women and children, all talking at once. Many were weeping. The elders of the congregation were gathered in a disorderly assembly around the Rabbi.

'I never thought it would come to this,' the stout baker was saying.

'We must think calmly,' the Rabbi said, his voice quavering with age, not fear.

'We were warned,' Salomone, the pawnbroker, cried out, catching sight of me.

'The time we were given to make our preparations, we wasted in arguments,' the baker replied, beating his chest.

'Rabbi, what can we do?' the butcher asked.

'We must trust in Hashem that He will show us a way to protect His holy words,' the Rabbi replied.

'Your era of great enlightenment seems to have been cancelled,' one of the younger men said to Daniel. 'What is the point of printing books only to see them burned?'

'It has merely been postponed. It will happen,' Daniel replied heavily. 'I still believe in it.'

'Wanting to believe is not the same as believing,' his companion said.

Whatever happened to the Holy Scrolls, everyone understood that discretion was paramount. In Rome, financial rewards had been paid for information leading to the discovery of holy books. A similar bounty was no doubt being offered to informers by the Executors Against Blasphemy in Venice. We did not know who might succumb to temptation, or terror, and betray us all. The Rabbi sent most of the congregation home to gather together as many books as they could, on the grounds that we must give the impression of co-operating fully with the authorities. If they suspected we were hiding anything from them, the leading figures in the ghetto would almost certainly be sentenced to death. This warning sent many of the men scurrying for the door.

'The fewer of us who know what happens to the Torah scroll, the better,' the Rabbi said. 'Our enemies have eyes and ears everywhere, even among our own people.'

As the number of men who remained behind in the synagogue dwindled, I was dismayed to see how fear of our enemy had made us distrust one another. In some ways that was the most pernicious outcome of the persecution.

'There is a space behind my oven,' the baker said, his face running with sweat.

'They are bound to search there,' Daniel objected. 'Remember the last time they came for our books, and your father, may his soul rest in peace, concealed a scroll in a large challah and so saved it. If they have learned of his trick, they will search every cranny of the bakery.'

'The Rabbi can wrap the scrolls in a shroud and we can

smuggle them out to the cemetery in a child's coffin,' the pawnbroker suggested.

'The guards might find them,' someone else objected.

'Surely the guards will not search inside a coffin,' Salomone replied. 'We can say it contains the body of a child who died of a contagious disease. Even if the guards have instructions to search everywhere, they are going to overlook their orders rather than risk falling ill. I will say I am the chief mourner, and carry the scroll to the cemetery. They will not look for it there. The Rabbi can cut the parchment from its wooden handles and roll it up and carry it to the undertaker where it could be wrapped in a white shroud, like a dead child, and taken to the cemetery.'

'We would need a physician to write out a false death certificate to make sure they believe you. Where is Jacob Mantino?' someone asked.

'He is tending to a sick patrician, and may not be back in time,' the baker replied.

'No, no, with or without a death certificate, the idea is too dangerous,' the Rabbi said. 'They are searching everyone who leaves the ghetto. They will be expecting us to attempt to smuggle the scrolls out. If the scrolls are discovered, they will be destroyed, along with you and your family.'

The Rabbi spoke with uncharacteristic caution, but there was no doubt the Executors Against Blasphemy would be merciless in their determination to discover the whereabouts of the Holy Scrolls.

'So they will search anyone who passes through the gate, and they will search everywhere in the ghetto,' Salomone said miserably. 'What are we to do, Rabbi?'

Several voices spoke up, each putting forward a different suggestion.

'We could unroll the scroll and stick the parchment against the wall in the passage between the synagogues.'

'It will show. It has been rolled up and will not lie flat.'

'Besides, how are we going to attach it to the wall without damaging it?'

'We could bury it.'

'And where would we do that?'

'If we could wrap it in something that is proof against water, we could lower it off the side of the Agudi Bridge.'

'A leather bag might protect it.'

'Are you seriously proposing we let the filthy water of the canal seep in through the seams to pollute the holy writing?'

'The scroll would wind only once about the baker's wide girth. He could carry it out concealed on his person,' a young man joked.

'They would find it.'

'If anyone was brave enough to search him,' the joker chuckled.

'This is no laughing matter,' the butcher scolded him.

'If we had time, we could hollow out the crutch carried by Abe, the cripple, and hide the scroll inside it,' someone suggested.

'It would never fit,' the baker replied, 'and besides, we could not entrust the sacred task to such a simpleton. He would blab and be thrown on the fire along with the scroll.'

'Let us pray to Hashem that He will write us all in His book for a long life,' the Rabbi said, with a sigh.

Moving closer to Daniel, I appealed to him for help. 'You know that Hashem has shown me a place where we can hide the Torah. Keep the others talking while I explain my idea to the Rabbi. My life may depend on their ignorance.'

Daniel nodded with a worried frown, and turned to address the small crowd of men left standing in the synagogue, the leaders of our congregation. As he did so, I whispered frantically to the Rabbi, outlining my plan.

'This is what we must do,' I heard Daniel say loudly. 'Each of you must take your own prayer book home with you, and hide it if you can. But if necessary, you must surrender it to the guards. Do not risk your lives, my friends. Remember Hashem loves us, and our lives are more precious to Him than they are to us.'

'Should we not stay together, here in the synagogue?' one of the men asked.

'No,' Daniel replied quickly. 'We stand a better chance of saving as many of our holy books as possible if they are spread around in different hiding places. Each of you take a book and hide it if you can, but do not risk your lives to save the books. Go now! The guards are already at the gate.'

The Rabbi looked at me uncertainly. 'If Hashem has guided you in this path, my child...' He sighed. 'We must all do what we can and who is to say that a woman cannot be an instrument of His will? Did not a woman save Moses from the water, and–'

He broke off as one of the men interrupted his musing. 'Rabbi, we need to make a decision.'

'What are we to do?' another man called out. 'We cannot debate endlessly. Time is running out. The guards will be here at any moment.'

The Rabbi turned to me. 'Tell no one,' he whispered urgently. 'We are beset by spies.'

Surreptitiously I slipped behind the bimah and lingered there out of sight, shocked that the Rabbi did not trust the most senior members of the congregation. But he was right. The fewer people who knew about my plan the better. The Inquisitors had their means of extracting information from the most strong willed of people, and no one can say for certain how they will respond under torture.

'Do as Daniel says,' the Rabbi urged the congregation, 'and

remember, do nothing to risk your own lives, or the lives of your families.'

'But Rabbi, what about the Torah?' someone asked. 'Who will protect the Holy Scrolls?'

'The Holy Scrolls will remain here with me,' the Rabbi replied quietly. 'We will pray for a miracle. Only Hashem can protect them now.'

'Where will you hide the Torah, Rabbi?'

'Do not ask any more questions, but go,' the Rabbi replied, his voice growing firmer with his conviction. 'No one else will know where the scroll is to be hidden.'

'So you do not trust us to hold our tongues,' one of the men growled.

'As the leaders of the congregation, we have the right to reach a decision together,' the baker objected.

He had a fair point. The Rabbi was our religious leader, but the leading members of the congregation all had a voice in important decisions that affected everyone in the ghetto.

'Hashem has shown me a way we may preserve his holy writings,' the old man replied. 'In all matters pertaining to religion you defer to me, as your spiritual leader, and what is more sacred than our Holy Scrolls?'

'Only a man intending to share information would want to know of it,' Daniel called out. 'I am doing as the Rabbi asked, and going home to hide my books.'

The men dispersed with a buzz of discontent. All were curious, but no one wished to be accused of intending to betray the Rabbi's hiding place. Certainly none could have suspected where the Rabbi was planning to conceal the scrolls.

'The Rabbi has something up his sleeve,' one of the men muttered as Daniel ushered them all towards the door.

'Now, Abigail,' the Rabbi said to me when they had all gone. 'It is time.' Fetching a knife, he detached one of the scrolls from the wooden dowels around which it was wound and handed it to me. 'Here, and may Hashem guard your steps and keep you safe.'

'I can only stow one of the scrolls in my gown,' I said.

He nodded sadly, gazing at the other scroll of law that lay on the bench in front of us.

'We must sacrifice one to save the other, as we did fourteen years ago,' he said. 'If they do not take at least one scroll of law from us they will not leave without burning down the whole ghetto. We have to convince them they have what they came for.'

'How do we do that?' I asked, forcing myself to remain steadfast in my resolve.

'That is for me to do,' he replied as calmly as if we were discussing the weather. 'You must leave it to me to convince the guards to be satisfied with one scroll. The task Hashem has given you is to conceal the other. Go now, before the guards arrive and seize them both.'

The street was nearly empty as I hurried home. Only a few people passed me, scurrying purposefully on business of their own, most of them clutching books. In the early evening the air was still mild, but the atmosphere was heavy with the threat of violence. Distant shouting echoed along the streets as I skulked in the shadows, making my way to my lodgings. Hearing a disturbance close by, I dodged out of sight to watch a group of guards tearing holy books out of people's hands, shoving men, women and children out of the way in their zeal. I had nearly reached my own building, when two of the Duke's guards appeared along the street, marching towards me. Hardly daring to breathe, I kept walking.

37

To my horror, the guards stopped outside my door. Trembling, I forced my legs to keep moving. It was imperative that I did not arouse their suspicion. More than my life was at stake. My visible terror was understandable, given the sight of so many of the Duke's guards in the ghetto. If I walked past my door, I would doubtless encounter more guards who might stop me and demand to know where I was going. It was better to continue on my way home as though I was doing nothing unusual. As I was dithering, Daniel emerged from the building, clutching a handful of books.

'I have gathered up all the books from this block,' he shouted angrily.

He did not once look at me, but I sensed he was aware of my presence. He must have been watching for my approach, ready to cause a distraction if necessary.

A guard seized the books from him, and spat in his face. 'Do you think we are going to trust the word of a Jew? What other books are you hiding from us?'

He nodded at his companion who ran forward and shoved Daniel roughly against the wall. Terrified, I slipped indoors and told Hadassah I would make the soup for that evening. There was no time to explain that it was more comfortable for me to stand and stir the broth. Sitting, my skirts fell awkwardly. Raising no objection when I ousted her from her place at the fire, she stood aside in grim silence. As I grabbed the stirring spoon from her, our door flew open and the guard who had assaulted Daniel came in, his partner at his heels. Restraining myself from rushing outside to see if Daniel was injured, I resolutely attended to the soup. It was surely the most vigorously stirred soup our fire had ever warmed.

'Where are your books?' the first guard demanded roughly.

'We have no books here,' I replied.

My voice shook, yet I had the presence of mind to raise my eyebrows ever so slightly as I turned to him, as though perplexed by the question.

'You can see for yourself we are just two poor widows,' I went on. 'We scratch out a living mending torn clothes, and are preparing our daily soup of vegetables to eat with stale bread which the baker gives us, because we cannot afford to buy a fresh loaf every day. Do you think we have money to purchase books, even if we wanted to? Or do you suppose–'

'You talk a lot,' the guard interrupted me. 'And you,' he turned to Hadassah. 'Do you have no tongue? Speak, Jew, or I will remove your tongue for you, since you seem to have no use for it.'

'We have no books here,' she mumbled, trembling. 'We are poor widows.'

The guard approached and I drew away from him. With a grunt, he kicked the cooking pot which clattered to the floor, spilling the soup, while his companion pulled the linen from our beds and knocked our table and chairs over. Then they marched out, without a backward glance.

'Nothing but two hags, too ugly even to fuck,' one of them snarled as they left.

'Charming,' Hadassah muttered under her breath, when she was sure they had gone.

Shaking, I sat on the bed, resting my palm on the rolled up scroll resting in a hidden pocket of my gown, thankful the soup had not splashed my skirt. Hadassah fetched some rags and began mopping up the spilled soup. Once I had sewn the pocket in my skirt closed, I helped her, wiping the wet floor with more rags. All the while, from outside, we heard sounds of crashing doors, shouting and screaming. I wanted to go and see if Daniel was hurt, but Hadassah persuaded me to stay inside, out of sight. With the scroll hidden in my gown, I could not afford to take any unnecessary risk. For a long time the racket continued, but eventually the ghetto quietened down and only the muffled sounds of weeping and wailing reached us.

'It sounds as though the guards have gone,' Hadassah said. 'Shall I go out and see what is happening?'

I nodded. 'Hadassah,' I whispered, 'will you see that Daniel is unharmed?'

She scowled at me. 'At a time like this, you think only of him,' she muttered.

Before I could respond, she went out, closing the door gently behind her. Sitting on my bed, I waited, my hand still resting on the precious load hidden in a secret pocket in my gown. Hadassah was gone for so long, I feared she was reluctant to return because her news was too terrible to share with me. By the time she walked in, I was nearly fainting with fear.

'Daniel is dead, isn't he?' I blurted out, bursting into tears. 'My life is over.'

'You can see for yourself he is not,' a familiar voice replied.

Looking up, I saw he had entered the room behind Hadassah.

'I thought you were dead,' I cried out, smiling through my tears.

Daniel gazed at me. 'And that made you weep and say your life was over?'

'She is weeping with the rest of us for the loss of our holy prayer books, so rudely snatched away,' Hadassah replied sharply.

'And now they are to be burned,' he said. 'The congregation are going to watch the atrocity. Are you not coming?'

I hesitated. 'I may stay here,' I replied, still sitting with my hand on the scroll concealed in my skirts.

'It would be best if you come with us,' Daniel said. 'You must not draw attention to yourself. Even if the guards do not notice your absence, there are those in the ghetto who may, and the Inquisition has spies everywhere.'

Hadassah agreed with Daniel.

'Are you sure it is safely stowed?' he asked me as I stood up.

I nodded. 'It will not fall out. I have sewn it safely in. Does it show?'

I walked to the door, turning around several times. My face felt hot as I observed Daniel's eyes following me across the room.

'It does not show,' Hadassah said, and Daniel agreed I had done a good job with my new gown.

'Hashem guided my hand,' I said.

Together the three of us joined the throng of Jews walking across the Campo del Ghetto Nuovo, over the narrow Agudi Bridge, along the Calle del Ghetto Vecchio, and out of the gate. Leading us all, the elderly Rabbi shuffled with bowed head, weeping and beating his frail chest. We filed past the stinking Fondamenta Delle Pescaria, through the Rialto market and across the bridge to the Piazza San Marco where a fire was blazing, a fire whose warmth would bring only despair to the inhabitants of the ghetto.

The aged Duke was standing on the steps of his magnificent palace, dressed in golden robes and a splendid white fur cape, with a golden cap on his head, flanked on either side by officials in their formal regalia. In a thin reedy voice, the Duke introduced one of his companions as a Papal Legate, representative of the Pope of Rome. The Legate's eyes blazed with fanatical fervour as he addressed the jostling spectators. Everyone fell silent to hear him.

'Once again,' he declaimed in loud ringing tones, 'the Executors Against Blasphemy are rooting out the evil that dwells among us. We will burn the heathens' books and put an end to their blasphemy!'

The crowd cheered, drowning out our weeping, as guards began to throw handfuls of books onto the fire. Their pages caught quickly, and the flames burned brightly. Our entire congregation fell silent, watching as our holy scroll was held up in triumph.

'Where is the other scroll of law from the Ghetto Nuovo?' the Papal Legate called out.

In the flickering firelight, Daniel clasped my hand. I did not draw away from his strong grasp.

'My guards found only one scroll in the Ghetto Nuovo,' the Duke replied. 'They scoured the place, looking everywhere. No other scroll was found.'

'Where is the leader of this Jewish rabble?' the Legate demanded, turning to where our congregation was standing, trembling and sobbing.

The Rabbi stepped forward. 'My name is Isaac ben Zadich,' he said in a soft voice that carried on the breeze. 'I am the Rabbi of the Ghetto Nuovo.'

'Rabbi,' the Legate addressed him, and on his lips the

highest term of respect sounded like an insult. 'Where are the rest of your scrolls?'

'As Hashem is my witness, we possess only one,' the Rabbi replied, truthfully enough, since one had been taken from us. 'Your Holiness knows, our beloved scroll was destroyed fourteen years ago. The Duke's guards seized its replacement today.'

He did not add that one of our original scrolls had been saved by a miracle from the previous book burning, nor that a second scroll had arrived from Krakow two years later.

'Two scrolls have been seen in your synagogue!' the Legate roared.

'We have only one,' the Rabbi insisted sorrowfully.

'You thought to hide your scrolls from us once before,' the Legate replied, 'but the arm of the Inquisition is long and we can be patient. Today you will witness the destruction of your blasphemy, and you will kneel before the might of the Pope of Rome.'

The wailing of the ghetto dwellers rose to a crescendo, drowning out the Rabbi's reply as he fell to his knees, weeping.

The Legate's lips curled in a gratified smile. 'See how the heathens kneel before the might of the Pope of Rome. Burn the scroll!' he commanded.

The crowd took up the cry, chanting, 'Burn the scroll! Burn the scroll!'

Had they known what was hidden in my gown, they would have hurled me on the blazing fire, along with the one precious scroll concealed in my skirt. Standing among people weeping and shaking with terror and shock, my own fear went unnoticed, and my courage, or recklessness, was known only to the Rabbi, Hadassah and Daniel, and Hashem who sees all. A light wind swept across the piazza, fanning the flames, and rustling my skirt. The flames gave off a heat so fierce that onlookers at the front of the crowd fell back for fear of being scorched. It was hard to believe such an atrocity could take place before the sublime architecture of the palace and the cathedral, testament to man's power to create a beautiful world on this earth.

Watching flames consume the parchment of one holy scroll, I was aware of the other swinging almost imperceptibly beneath my skirt, and felt a sudden fierce joy amid the outpouring of grief surrounding me. This was the reason why Hashem had brought me safely out of the massacre of Polotensk, and had protected me from the dangers I had faced. Feeling the heat from the flames on my face, I knew that Hashem had chosen me to fulfil His sacred purpose and I wept in awe of His loving kindness towards me, even as the congregation around me wept at the destruction of our sacred writings.

38

A few days after the burning, the Rabbi came to see me one evening, strong in resolution, despite his advanced age and physical frailty.

'The Papal Legate is back in Rome, receiving false blessings from the Pope, and it is time for you to return the Torah,' he told me. 'Hashem will sanctify your name for rescuing His teachings, and He will bless you for your courage, my child, as I do every day.'

His words comforted me, and I dared hope that Hashem would heed the Rabbi's prayers and forgive me my sins.

'We should have a celebration in the synagogue, in honour of Abigail's bravery,' Hadassah chipped in, beaming.

The Rabbi shook his head. 'No, no, the scroll must be returned to the synagogue as discreetly as possible. No one must know it escaped the flames. We must ensure the Officers of the Inquisition never discover that it has been returned to the synagogue.'

'Surely they are bound to discover the truth,' Hadassah said. 'The whole congregation will witness its return, and you know how people talk.'

'The congregation will talk of how Hashem performed a miracle in our ghetto, or perhaps the rumour will spread that the congregation in Krakow came to our rescue once again. But that is all they will discover, and all they ever need to know. Now the Papal Legate has returned to Rome, the rulers of Venice will feel less inclined to pursue their policy of burning our books. By the time rumours of the new Torah reach the Council of Ten, they will be preoccupied with their war against the Ottomans and we will no longer be the focus of their enmity.'

Thanking the Rabbi, I retrieved the Torah from its hiding place. It had remained in the secret pocket of my new gown, which I had not worn since the night the books were burned. Carefully I handed over the scroll, and the old man accepted it reverently, reciting a prayer as he stowed it beneath his cloak. Still mumbling prayers, he shuffled out of our apartment.

'That was a task well accomplished,' Hadassah grinned at me. 'To think that my tenant was chosen by Hashem to save His holy words from the fires of the Inquisition. I declare, I am quite overcome.' She sat down and began to sob hysterically.

I sat beside her and patted her chapped hands, making soothing noises as one might to a crying baby. I was not sure what else to do. Hadassah was usually so composed and practical, I was bewildered by her emotional outburst.

After a while she calmed down and began to laugh. 'I am a fool,' she said, 'crying tears of happiness at the success of your plan. May your name be remembered for a blessing among the righteous, Abigail of Polotensk.'

'I am Abigail of Venice now,' I reminded her.

The summer passed without further disturbance, and slowly replacement books were smuggled in by merchants travelling from Poland and Russia and the Ottoman Empire, as well as from other Venetian territories.

A few days before our Jewish New Year, on a mild day in

September, we were sitting quietly sewing when once again we heard a disturbance outside the shop. Going out into the street to see what was happening, we saw several members of the ghetto shouting and running towards the gate, waving and gesticulating wildly.

'What has happened?' I asked one of my neighbours who was charging past the sewing shop.

'Fire at the Arsenale!' she shouted.

'The Arsenale is on fire!' a man called out as he ran past. 'The whole place is going up in flames!'

If true, this would be a serious blow for the Republic of Venice. Ship building at the Arsenale safeguarded Venice's military supremacy on the seas. Surrounded as it was by water, the city not only depended on its galleys and warships for protection, it relied on them for trade. If the Arsenale was damaged, the Republic could suffer serious consequences, both mercantile and military.

'We are going to watch from a distance,' a woman told me. 'Some of the men from the ghetto have gone to see for themselves.'

My spirits were overcome with dread on hearing this. Tamar summoned us all back to the sewing shop and we worked on in uneasy silence until sunset. That evening, just after the curfew, Hadassah and I heard a knock at our door and opened it to see our neighbour, Elia. His face and clothes were covered in soot, as were his hands, and his shoes left black marks on the floor. Hadassah began to scold him for bringing so much filthy soot into our apartment. I was about to question him when Daniel joined us, in the company of a tall man in a dark hooded cloak. Their faces were also blackened from proximity to the fire, but I would have recognised Daniel's eyes anywhere.

Despite his covering of soot and ash, it was obvious that the stranger was no ordinary visitor to the ghetto. It could not escape the eyes of a needleworker that his cloak was costly, and his boots were of fine leather. As the man flung off his hood, Elia introduced our guest as Joseph Nasi.

'Now that Elia has stupidly blurted out the truth, there is no point in claiming our visitor is an ordinary travelling merchant.' Daniel sighed. 'This is indeed Joseph Nasi, but his presence here in Venice must be kept secret for all our sakes. If the Inquisitors discover we are harbouring an enemy of the Republic, we will all be tortured and killed.'

'Hadassah and Abigail can be trusted,' Elia said with youthful confidence. 'You don't need to worry about them. They will be silent as the grave.'

'Let us hope your indiscretion will not send them straight there,' Daniel muttered, giving Elia a light cuff on the head.

'We are honoured that you wish to grace us with your presence,' Hadassah said, gazing in awe at our exalted visitor. 'You could have found accommodation somewhere far grander than my lowly lodgings.'

'More grand perhaps, but not as discreet,' Joseph replied. He spoke softly, yet his voice was deep and powerful.

Hadassah insisted they eat with us, and the three men went to the well to clean themselves as thoroughly as they could, before they joined us at our table.

'You know Joseph Nasi's reputation?' Hadassah hissed at me when they had gone.

'Every Jew has heard of Joseph Nasi,' I whispered back. 'I know he is an enemy of the Inquisition, and that is good enough for me.'

'He is not just any enemy. He is a favourite of the Sultan of Turkey, who has made him a prince. They say he wields great influence in Constantinople and is the most powerful man at the Ottoman court. What he is doing here while Venice is at war with the Ottomans is anyone's guess, but if you ask me, it is no coincidence that he has turned up here just when there is a fire at the Arsenale.'

'I think you are jumping to conclusions,' I replied.

If Hadassah's speculation was right, Daniel and Elia would be risking their lives by consorting with Joseph Nasi.

'Much as he hates Spain and Rome, they say he hates Venice more, because his mother was once imprisoned here. The Senate banished him for attacking them, and that is why his presence here must be kept secret.'

'I have heard the same rumours as you,' I told her. 'And that is all they are, rumours. Daniel would not have brought him here if his presence would endanger our lives.'

Before we could continue our whispered conversation, Daniel and Elia returned with Joseph and we took our places at the table and recited the prayer before food.

'Were you not banished from Venice?' I asked Joseph, while Hadassah was serving vegetable and barley broth.

The visitor put his finger to his lips and smiled, but did not answer.

'So when did you become friendly with my neighbour?' I continued.

'Daniel is a brave man,' Joseph replied.

'A foolhardy one,' I retorted.

'You are a fine one to talk,' Daniel said, and he told Joseph Nasi about how I had hidden the Torah scroll from the Executors Against Blasphemy. 'Do not worry,' Daniel added, turning to me, 'Joseph is to be trusted above all men. One day he is going to lead our people to great victory.'

I frowned, worried at hearing such intemperate words from Daniel. 'What kind of victory are you talking about?' I asked.

'Hashem alone can save us from our enemies. We must leave our future in His hands.'

'Hashem is waiting to grant us victory, it is true,' Joseph replied, 'but we have to play our part. Were you not instrumental in saving the Torah from the flames? Hashem could not have done that without your help.'

I gaped at such blasphemous talk, but Joseph had not finished. 'We will never achieve true independence until we have a land of our own,' he said.

'A land of our own?' Hadassah repeated, as startled as I was.

'What fantasy is this?' I asked. 'Where are we going to find a land of own?'

Daniel shook his head at us. 'With the help of Hashem, nothing is impossible. Joseph has already tried to re-establish Jewish communities in the towns of Tiberias and Safed.'

'That was more than ten years ago,' Joseph added with a sigh.

'But the important point is that the attempt was made,' Daniel said. 'You must see the significance of it. Joseph is the first person in centuries to come up with a practical plan to settle Jews in the cities of Southern Syria. Thanks be to Hashem, he enlisted the support of the Sultan and rebuilt the walls around the town of Tiberias.'

Joseph nodded. 'We planted mulberry trees and encouraged craftsmen to move there and set up a silk industry.'

'He was making arrangements for Jews to move to Tiberias from the Papal States, where they were being persecuted, and the plan very nearly worked,' Daniel went on. 'It was only because war broke out between the Ottomans and the Republic of Venice that the project had to be abandoned. Now that a peace treaty has been signed, there is nothing to stop us from picking up where we left off.'

'A plan that failed once may fail again,' I replied.

'It has happened once, and it will happen again, if we only have faith in Hashem,' Daniel insisted.

'We are His chosen people,' Joseph said, 'chosen to fulfil His purpose. We cannot sit around waiting for the Messiah to save us. Hashem expects us to take action. This day, He has delivered a blow against the Catholics from which they will not recover in a hurry.'

Listening to them crow about what had happened, I could not help wondering about the people who had been harmed in the fire. When I asked about the casualties, there was a pause. 'How many of them were there?' I repeated. 'Tell me.'

'Maybe a couple of thousand,' Joseph answered lightly.

'Two thousand people injured?' I echoed, aghast.

'That's right,' Daniel said. 'That's what they're saying, two thousand Venetian ship builders and officials lost in the fire.'

'Lost? What do you mean, lost?'

'What I said,' Daniel replied.

'Tell me they didn't all perish?'

Joseph shrugged. 'Abigail, we are fighting a war. What do you expect? Surely you understand this is a significant victory?'

His composure made me shudder.

'Those men were not soldiers,' I said.

'We are all soldiers now,' Joseph replied sternly. 'Every man – and woman – must decide which side he is on.'

'I am a Jewess of the ghetto,' I protested, almost reduced to tears of anger and frustration. 'There is no place for a woman like me in a war between Christendom and the Ottoman Empire. We must leave these matters to Hashem. I have seen a whole community slaughtered before my own eyes, three thousand men, women and children, all killed. We should not add a single soul to their number.'

As I spoke, I realised I could never have stabbed my husband as he slept. Admittedly I had once killed a man, but that had been in self-defence. To kill a man was always a sin in the sight of Hashem and man.

'We have to consider the bigger picture,' Joseph was saying. 'Think how many ships that fire cost the Venetian navy, warships that would have taken many more lives. If we do not resist the might of our enemies, they will destroy us. Can we sit idly by and watch the Catholics systematically eliminate every living Jew, men, women and children, until our people have vanished from the face of the earth?'

'Two thousand innocent men were burned alive at the Arsenale,' I said.

'No man is innocent,' Joseph replied.

'Abigail, there are many casualties in a war,' Daniel added gently. 'Has Venice been so kind to us that you are keen for them to build a strong navy? The Turks are waging war against the Pope, whose Inquisition is determined to kill or convert every Jew, and wipe us out. So, Abigail, which side are you going to choose?'

'Nothing justifies burning even one man alive, let alone two thousand,' I answered wretchedly. 'Those ship builders were not attacking us. Their deaths did not save anyone.'

'It was an act of self-defence,' Daniel insisted, but he looked uncomfortable. 'One race defending itself against another.'

'It was an act of war,' Joseph said. 'We Jews are too few in number to have a substantial army of our own, so we must fight in other ways, whenever and however we can.'

'This was not an act of war,' I replied. 'Those ship builders were peaceful men going about their business.'

'Don't be naive,' Joseph told me. 'Their business was constructing galleasses for the coming war. Why do you suppose the Venetians have been so busy building ships? They were expanding their military power at sea, but we have smashed their plans. Wars are not only fought on the battlefield. Believe me, Abigail, I share your desire for peace, but we cannot continue to suffer persecution without ever daring to raise a hand in our own defence. You are fortunate indeed that you have never felt the necessity to take up arms just to survive.'

I lowered my gaze for fear he might see a demon blazing in my eyes at the memory of a cudgel swinging in my grasp. With an effort I dismissed the memory of a stranger lying in the forest outside Polotensk, his head smashed to a bloody pulp.

'Leave matters of war to those who understand what is at stake,' Joseph concluded, smiling kindly at me.

'Perhaps it would be best if you left the ghetto mid-morning, when the streets are at their busiest,' I suggested, uneasy with memories the conversation had provoked. 'If you leave at sunrise, there will not be so many people around, and you are more likely to attract the attention of the guards.'

'They will certainly be looking for him,' Elia agreed earnestly. 'He will have to leave in disguise.' He turned to Joseph. 'I have brought you a costume from Avrom's second-hand clothes store. It's a pity you're so tall. We wanted to dress you as a woman, but that might attract more notice than if you wore no disguise at all.'

Opening his bundle, Elia produced a light brown wig and an outfit more suited to a vagabond than a prince. 'Walk a bit hunched to hide your height, and no one will recognise you,' he said.

Elia was right. In a faded brown doublet and a ragged black jacket, with scuffed boots and wearing a light brown wig, a transformed Joseph stood before us. It was strange to think that a prince had eaten Hadassah's barley broth, and was departing in the guise of a vagrant. As he was leaving our lodgings, Joseph detained me on the doorstep. I was afraid he was going to berate me for my opinions, but instead he thrust a leather pouch into my hand and was gone before I could remonstrate. When I opened the purse, I found it contained a handful of gold ducats. Having counted them, I took half the sum which I concealed beneath my mattress. The rest I left for Hadassah to find in the morning.

39

The next day in the sewing shop we discussed whether the fire had been started deliberately. The debate continued after prayers in the synagogue on the Sabbath.

'The authorities are claiming Joseph Nasi was responsible,' one of the women said.

'They blame everything on Joseph Nasi,' Tamar replied. 'So now he's an arsonist on top of everything else.'

'It's absurd to blame Joseph Nasi,' the Rabbi's wife said. 'He wasn't even in Venice when the fire started. He was banished from the Republic years ago and has been living at the court of the Turkish Sultan ever since. But he's a Jew, which makes him a convenient scapegoat.'

'Whoever started that fire wreaked havoc on the Venetian navy,' one of the women said.

'Let us be thankful for that,' the Rabbi's wife replied.

Silently I prayed to Hashem that our troubles in Venice were over, but as the days grew shorter with the arrival of autumn winds, not one but five banks in the Most Serene Republic of Venice failed. It was not the fault of the Jewish bankers that the authorities had made excessive demands on their funds.

'But we all know who will be blamed,' the Rabbi's wife said sourly.

Hadassah and I walked home together, but our supper that night did little to raise my spirits.

'Where is the Friday night challah?' I asked, taking my seat at the table. 'What is this?' I pointed at half a loaf on the plate between us.

'It's all I could get today,' Hadassah replied.

'Half a challah? Where is the other half?'

'Our neighbour, the tailor's widow, has it.'

Irritation momentarily overcame my charity. 'So you cut our challah in half because our neighbour cannot afford to buy one? Hadassah, you know we already share our food with others.'

I visited my former landlady in the Ghetto Vecchio every week with a portion of challah, candles and a flagon of wine. Without that, she would have nothing for the Sabbath. Charity was a blessing for the giver, but between the old crone in the Ghetto Vecchio and our impoverished neighbour in the Ghetto Nuovo, there was barely enough leftover for us. 'Surely you could have told our neighbour that we could not afford to give her any more for her family?'

Hadassah shook her head. 'It was not like that.'

'What was it like then?'

'She shared her challah with us. I could not buy one today.'

'What are you talking about? Was the bakery closed when you got there?'

'I had not taken enough money with me, and they are refusing to give credit,' she muttered.

'Why did you not take enough money with you? You know how much a challah costs.'

'How was I to know they were going to put the price up so much?' she replied crossly.

'So they are charging more. Why did you not tell them you

would pay the extra after the Sabbath? Moishe knows you would pay your debt.'

'It was not just me. They are refusing credit to everyone.'

She scowled as she described the scene at the bakery, with women at the back of the queue clamouring to be served, while those at the front complained about the extortionate price of a challah. In the end Moishe, the baker, had shouted at the women, telling them he too had a family to feed. According to Hadassah, his words had done little to appease the angry women.

'He kept insisting there was nothing he could do, and it was not his fault if the price of flour had more than doubled. It was all due to a shortage of wheat.'

'But why did you not go back with more money?' I asked.

'There was no point. They had already almost run out. But that is not all. It was not just challahs. There was no bread in the shop at all, and Moishe told us there is no possibility things will improve before next year.'

'People will starve,' I said.

'People will starve,' she echoed wretchedly.

The following week the shortage of bread did not improve, but we all cheered up when a holiday was held in honour of a visiting prince and Tamar sent us all home at midday. We understood that we would not be paid for our afternoon off, but we still left the workshop in high spirits. The weather was fine and my friend, Sarai, wanted to show me a bridge fight, so I walked with her to join the throng that had gathered by the Ponte dei Pugni to watch a battle between rival factions in the city. Sarai had told me these ferocious martial festivals were hugely popular, and before the fight began I saw what she meant. All manner of pedlars and tinkers, street vendors and food hawkers, had gathered by the bridge where the combatants were due to meet. In an atmosphere of such festivity, it was hard to believe there was a threatened shortage of food in the city.

'It is pointless scattering sawdust on the bridge to prevent the contestants from slipping and injuring themselves, when they are all trying to kill one another,' Sarai said.

The water below the bridge had been cleared of rubbish, and by the time the fight began, the canal was crammed with barges and gondolas and other small vessels, all packed with spectators cheering on the fighters, along with the rest of the watching crowds. Four champions took their positions at the four corners of the bridge while behind them, hundreds of commoners jostled one another, eager for the fray. They formed a motley army, clutching shields of leather or wood, and wearing wooden helmets or padded iron breastplates. The Duke himself sat on a raised dais beside the visiting prince, who was surrounded by guards.

At a signal from the capos who were in charge, the champions dashed forward and their followers attacked each other, in a chaotic melee of flailing arms.

Their lethal weapons were objects routinely carried on the city streets: pointed sticks hardened by soaking in boiling oil, stilettos, spiked boat poles, and handfuls of iron balls and stones to hurl at the opposition. Many injuries were inflicted, ranging from scratches and sprains and bloodied noses to broken jaws, gouged out eyes, smashed ribs, and crippled legs. It sickened me to think that all of this was being enacted for sport. Yet, despite the harrowing injuries, it was hard to resist the enthusiasm of the crowd who watched the spectacle with noisy cheering, whistling, and waving.

Sarai told me that sometimes soldiers were summoned to break up the fighting, when a mob lost control. Venetian commoners were far more likely to join in a fight than assist in breaking it up and, excited by wine, they now began throwing roof tiles from nearby balconies. As the crowd grew increasingly riotous, Sarai and I slipped away. Women were not safe in such unruly company, especially wearing the yellow shawls of the Jewish ghetto. As we made our way towards the Rialto, I became separated from my friend in the crowd. The way back was now familiar to me, but I hurried all the same, nervous about walking alone in the city.

Without warning, a hand was clapped over my mouth, and I was lifted off my feet, my arms pinned to my sides. I kicked out as hard as I could, doing my best to yell, but my captor only held me more tightly as he dragged me into a deserted walkway alongside a narrow canal. The fury that had seized me in the forest when my uncle was attacked filled me once again, and I twisted round and kneed my assailant in the groin as hard as I could. With a cry, he loosened his hold on me.

Dashing along the wet cobbles, I nearly slipped over. As I scrambled to regain my balance, I glanced back and saw my assailant pull out a knife. It occurred to me that my body might never be recovered and buried in the sanctified cemetery at the Lido. In my despair I called out for help and, miraculously, Hashem heard my cry.

A gondola pulled up beside me and a voice invited me aboard. 'Hurry, my friend,' my saviour added, 'or I may be too late to help you.'

A strong hand gripped my arm to steady me as the craft bobbed in the water when I clambered aboard. Before I had time to find a seat, our boatman pushed away from the side, and we sped away over the water. Trembling, I sat down and turned to thank my rescuer.

'I did not take you for a troublemaker,' Joseph Nasi said, peering at me from inside his hood. 'Daniel warned me that there is more to you than your meekness suggests.' His haughty features softened in a smile.

'You saved my life,' I stammered, 'thanks be to Hashem.'

He inclined his head. 'Daniel risked his life to shield me from discovery by the Officers of the Inquisition. Thanks to you, my debt to him has been repaid. I know of his affection for you. But there is no need to tell him what happened today. I did not save you to win any man's gratitude, but because it was the right thing to do. Let virtue be its own reward.'

'Hashem sees all. May He reward you for your good deeds,' I replied politely, and he inclined his head.

'You are a strong woman,' he said. 'Our long-suffering people need courage like yours. If you ever want to help our cause, ask for me at the court of the Sultan in Constantinople. There will always be a place there for Abigail of Venice. And now, where can we take you?'

'I don't want to take you out of your way. You have already helped me enough.'

Joseph nodded at his boatman and instructed him to take us to the gate of the ghetto, where I disembarked. Walking back to my lodgings, I pondered what Joseph had said. It seemed that everyone knew about Daniel's feelings for me. I resolved to speak to him severely, and convince him that he would be a fool to wait for me. It was right that I should be punished for my sins, and I had learned to accept my fate. But I wondered what terrible deeds Daniel had committed that he too should suffer this painful separation, knowing that I would never be free.

40

The following day, Daniel met me after work and asked to walk home with me.

'Daniel, you must stop this,' I told him firmly. 'You know I can never marry you.'

'But I thought–' he stammered.

'What did you presume to think? I have said nothing to suggest I have changed my mind.'

'I thought–' he repeated, staring at me so intensely his dark eyes seemed to bore a hole in my head. 'At the burning of the books, when you held on to my hand, I thought we had come to an understanding. Abigail, I cannot stay silent. I beg you to have pity on me. I cannot live without you. In the day my eyes search everywhere for you, and at night I cannot bear that you are not by my side. I cannot bear it, Abigail.'

'Daniel, whatever our feelings for one another may be, you must know I cannot marry you.'

'So what is there left for us?'

'I know you to be a righteous man and I am trying to be a virtuous woman. We must accept that we can never be together. Hashem has willed it so. You must take another wife–'

He turned from me with a cry so heartfelt that I almost ran after him. But I stood my ground, muttering a prayer to Hashem to save me from the sinful longing that drew me to this man. A moment later, he had disappeared from view, and I made my way miserably back to my lodgings.

The burning of books had an impact on us all, and the Christian printers of Venice suffered with us. One by one their presses ceased to print, and they were forced to move to more tolerant territories, until I feared for Daniel's position.

'It is not as if what happened last year was the first time,' Hadassah said. 'After the book burning fifteen years ago, the printing shops managed to start up again. But look at them now! Fifteen years' work gone up in smoke. They cannot stay here. They have a living to make.'

Despite the warnings, I was surprised when Daniel knocked at our door shortly before dawn one morning.

'I have come to say goodbye,' he announced, looking only at me.

'What do you mean?' I stammered.

'I am taking my son to visit my sister in Ferrara,' he replied.

Ever practical, Hadassah asked him whether he would like her to keep an eye on his apartment for him in his absence.

'You may find another tenant to live there while we are away, for all I care,' he told her.

'Very well. When are you leaving?' she enquired.

'We are going now.'

'Now?' I repeated, unable to conceal my dismay.

'Yes, now. That is why I have come to say goodbye to you.'

There was a brief pause. 'And when do you expect to return?' I asked.

He shook his head, his eyes blazing with suppressed emotion. 'I do not know whether we will ever return.'

Standing in the doorway, I watched Daniel and his son stride away, out of my sight and out of my life. If he had once glanced over his shoulder at me, I would probably have run after him and begged him to take me with him, but he never looked back.

'Why are you standing there like a graven image?' Hadassah asked me roughly. 'Are you expecting the Messiah to arrive in the ghetto?'

'I think he just left,' I replied and burst into tears.

'Come indoors, Abigail, and stop being ridiculous. You are making a spectacle of yourself. What if someone were to see you?'

She chivvied me back inside and sat me down at the table where she served me a cup of thin broth. 'Drink this, and it will warm your cold spirits. Listen to me, Abigail, we were both fond of our neighbour, but people come and go and we must pray to Hashem to watch over Daniel and Elia on their journey to join his sister. May they both find happiness in Ferrara. I hear it is an enlightened place to live. And who knows?' she added, as I continued weeping, 'Daniel may return to Venice one day and then you will see him again. In the meantime, dry your eyes. It is time for you to go to work. You do not want to be late for Tamar. See, there is more to life than the whim of one man.'

I shook my head. 'No,' I said with sudden conviction, 'I am not going back to the sewing shop.'

'What are you talking about? Have you lost your wits over this man? You know you could never marry Daniel. That is the reason he has left the ghetto. Hashem has willed it so, and you must accept your fate.'

She was right. Daniel and I could not have continued living next door to one another, seeing each other, yet unable to live together without sin. It was better he left and found a new life for himself. And there was nothing to stop me from doing the same. By the time I recovered my composure and dried my eyes, I had resolved to travel back to Polotensk. Not only my uncle and I, but also my husband, had survived the massacre. It was possible others might have hidden in the forest and escaped the Streltsy. My uncle had been alerted to the soldiers' arrival. Perhaps he had not been the only one to receive a warning. My sisters knew about the gap in the ghetto wall. It was possible my family had not all died in the massacre. Besides, I was sure I had not seen my parents or my sisters among the victims who had been driven into the river. Nothing I had seen or heard had confirmed they were dead.

When I explained my plan to Hadassah, she did her best to dissuade me from leaving, but my mind was made up.

'And once you have travelled all the way to Polotensk, what then? Will you return to Venice?'

'I hope so. But I do not know what I may discover on my travels, and cannot make any decisions about my future until I know more.'

'I am truly sorry that you are leaving,' Hadassah said, and there were tears in her eyes as we embraced. 'First Daniel and Elia went away, and now you are deserting me,' she muttered. 'I will be all alone in the building soon.'

I shook my head, too upset to speak, but we both knew she would easily find other tenants to take the place of those of us who had left. Wearing my new gown, I packed a bundle of rags and a few utensils, and prepared to leave.

'Wait,' Hadassah said.

'Hadassah, I am leaving. There is no point in attempting to persuade me to stay.'

She handed me a parcel. 'Here is some bread and griboli for your journey, and a flagon for water. And take this.' She held out her own fine cloak. 'It will keep you warm until the cold months pass, yet it is not too warm in summer. It is a good cloak for travelling. After the friendship we have shared, do not refuse me this one last request.'

With Hadassah's cloak around my shoulders, and clutching the food parcel she had packed for me, I set off with my ducats from Joseph Nasi hidden in my pouch. By the time I reached the gate of the ghetto I had already begun to regret my rash decision, but I pressed on, resolved to adhere to my plan, however difficult the path ahead of me might prove.

With Daniel gone, there was nothing to keep me in Venice, apart from my friendship with Hadassah. Perhaps that should have been enough, but I was angry with Daniel. Even though I had rejected him, I felt as though he had abandoned me. If he thought better of his decision to desert me, I did not want him to return and find me waiting for him. Choler upset the balance of my humours, until I hoped he would come back and suffer in finding me gone. That would make him sorry for leaving me. My love for him had soured in bitter disappointment at his departure. Unable to punish him, I turned my bile upon myself and left the shelter of Hadassah's home, determined to endure whatever hardship my journey entailed.

At the waterfront of the Piazza San Marco I found a passage on a ship bound for Split, and set off to retrace my steps back to Polotensk. The thought of seeing my old home filled me with dread at what I might find, and more than once on that sea voyage I regretted my rashness in leaving the safety of Venice. At least this ship was not assailed by brigands. The merchant galley had deposited her cargo successfully in Venice and was riding high on the waves, a sure sign that she was carrying little or no cargo, and the pirates, if they noticed our vessel at all, left us alone.

'They will be looking out for us on our way back. We'll be safe enough on the way there,' an old sailor told me and the handful of travellers who had taken passage to Split. 'Unless we are hit by a storm,' he added cheerfully.

There were no other women travelling alone on the ship, but

I attached myself to a family group of three sisters, two of whom were accompanied by their husbands. The other sister, I learned, was a widow, as I claimed to be. For all I knew, it was the truth. Together there were six of us, a sizeable enough company for a journey. They were on their way to a village near Vilna in Lithuania to visit relatives. I had the impression they were pleased of my company, which enabled them to talk to me rather than to one another. On the ship I had overheard a few raised voices and heated discussions between the sisters that ceased the moment I joined them. For my part, I was grateful to them for allowing me to travel with them as far as Vilna, from where it was only a few days journey on foot to Polotensk.

After a long and arduous journey, we arrived in their village. They invited me to stay with them for a while, but having travelled this far, I was eager to return to the place of my birth. So we parted, with many promises to visit one another again should the opportunity arise.

A few days later, weary and footsore, I limped into the town of Polotensk. Summer was half over. Even the sun seemed weary of its own heat as it beat down remorselessly on the roofs of the buildings. As a child I had only stepped outside the walls of the ghetto to forage in the forest, and I did not recognise the bustling market or winding streets of the town, or the houses bunched together in the shadows of high church spires. Slowly I made my way to the river, and followed it until the ghetto came into view. Furtively I skirted the high wall and reached the gate which hung open, with no one to guard it. There was no sign of life, other than a mangy cat that wandered past, its tail in the air. The instant I stepped through the gate a wave of sickness gripped me, and I seemed to see the ghosts of the congregation fleeing once more before the guns of the Streltsy in their hateful uniforms. A vision flashed in front of me: laughing men in red coats and black hats, armed with muskets and pikes, pursuing my family. Too shocked to pray, I leaned against the warm stone of the wall and vomited on the dry ground.

After a while I regained control of my shaking legs and followed a familiar path to my old home. Hurrying past the hovel where I had lived with my husband, I made my way to my parents' house. Peering through the open door, I gazed at a few sticks of smashed furniture coated in dusty cobwebs. Venturing inside, I disturbed a horde of insects that scuttled across the floor to disappear in the shadows. There was no other sign of life in a place that stank of dereliction and despair. The walls of the ghetto had begun to crumble. Stunned at the rapidity with which my childhood home was disintegrating, I turned to leave and noticed a scrap of yellow fabric lying in the rubble, torn from the shawl worn by my mother or one of my sisters when the Streltsy came for them. With tears sliding down my cheeks, I retrieved the filthy remnant and murmured a prayer of mourning for my family, and for all who had perished in the massacre of Polotensk. After that, I stood in that derelict place for a long time, howling my grief into the emptiness that had once been home to so many living souls.

41

Stupefied, I wandered around the deserted streets of the ghetto, my hopes of seeing another living soul dashed. It had been a foolish dream to think there might be any survivors lingering in this dead place. Apart from insects that buzzed and flitted around me, the only signs of life were the occasional beating of wings as a bird flew past overhead, or the sound of scuttling feet and a glimpse of a tail as a wild rodent fled at my approach. Wrapping Hadassah's cloak tightly around me I walked on, afraid of summoning the ghosts who roamed the hushed streets seeking ritual burial, without which their souls would never find peace. My feet carried me to the house where my friend, Jael, had grown up. The door to this building was closed. I tapped softly, terrified of disturbing spirits from the world of the dead. A cloud of dust flew up, making me cough as I stood, waiting, but no one answered my knock. I tried again, even more gently this time, but still no one came to the door.

Defeated, I made my way towards the synagogue. No doubt the scrolls had been destroyed years ago, along with their custodians, but I wanted to see if any relic of the holy writing had survived the atrocity. Reaching the building where we had once worshipped, I fell to the ground and sobbed uncontrollably in the dirt, my tears forming a tiny patch of damp in the dust. As soon as I stopped weeping, the moisture vanished, ephemeral as the life of man. My grief spent, I clambered to my feet. My head throbbed, my eyes were sore, and my throat was raw from weeping.

'Who's there?' a hoarse voice croaked suddenly, startling me so much that I dropped my bundle.

I spun around to see an old man leaning on a staff. He appeared to be studying me, but the eyes in his withered face were vacant and did not react when I stooped down to retrieve my bundle.

'Who is there? What do you want?' he challenged me again. 'My soul is not ready to depart. My penance is not yet done.' He looked as though he would fall over at the slightest touch, yet he terrified me.

'Are you a ghost, or a fiend sent by the forces of evil?' I whispered, clutching Hadassah's cloak around me and murmuring a prayer to Hashem.

For answer, the old man raised his skinny hand and sketched out the shape of a cross in the air. 'Who are you?' he croaked, muttering under his breath.

I guessed he was reciting a prayer of his own to ward off evil spirits. 'Old man, I mean you no harm,' I said, taking a step closer to him. 'I came here on a foolish errand. There is nothing left for me in this empty place.'

'Yet you are here,' he said. 'Tell me, who are you and whom do you seek?'

'No, no, I'm sorry to have disturbed you,' I answered awkwardly. 'I should not have come.'

'Sit a while, my child,' the old man said, hobbling towards a stone bench outside the synagogue and feeling for it with his stick. 'Tell me what has brought you to this place of death.'

'I am a Jew and I grew up here in the ghetto here in Polotensk, before the Streltsy came and destroyed the community.'

'I had a friend among the Jews of the ghetto,' the old man told me, his voice dry as withered grass. 'We used to play chess together.' He broke off and gazed around with unseeing eyes. 'But the Streltsy came, and my friend perished in the massacre, along with thousands of other poor souls. The blood of our Jewish neighbours stained the waters of the Dvina. They have gone, leaving us to bear the guilt.'

'I know only too well how the Streltsy came and slaughtered the inhabitants of the ghetto,' I told him. 'I am a living witness to what happened here.'

'It happens often that Jews are persecuted,' the old man said, reaching out and feeling for my hand. 'The Catholics are your sworn enemies, my child. But there are some who do not share the common hatred.' He sighed and gripped my hand tightly in his.

'What are you doing here, old man?' I asked. 'Do you have no family to take care of you?'

'I sit here, day after day, waiting for survivors to return,' he said. 'It is all I can do to mitigate my terrible guilt. I sit here waiting for the Jews to return.'

'They will never come back here, old man,' I told him sadly. 'They are all dead.'

He shook his head impatiently. 'A few have come back, as you have done, searching for news of other survivors. I pass on their messages when I can, but very few return... too few... too few...' The old man mumbled under his breath, and I guessed he was reciting a prayer for the departed souls, while tears coursed down his shrivelled cheeks and his lips moved silently.

'Forgive me,' I said, extricating my hand from his grasp. 'I

277

will disturb your solitude no longer. I will leave you to your prayers. There is nothing here for me.'

'Yet you have returned,' he said. 'There is nothing left, only you and me and the ghosts of our memories. Listen,' he went on with a curious urgency, as though anything could matter in that desolate place. 'I tried to save my friend, but my warning came too late. Few survived the Streltsy. Few, too few.'

A thought struck me. 'Were you a beadle in the town?' I asked, recalling what my uncle had told me, while we were escaping from the Streltsy.

The old man nodded his withered head, and his sightless eyes searched the empty air.

'Who are you?' he asked, clutching my hand again.

'My name is Abigail, daughter of Rebeka,' I replied. 'My father was Saul ben Menachem, and Abraham ben Tedeschi is my uncle, my mother's brother.' I paused, overwhelmed with the enormity of speaking my parents' names aloud in that desolate place.

'Abraham,' the old man repeated softly. 'Abraham ben Tedeschi. I did not think to hear his name again on this cursed earth.'

My next words were painful to utter. 'My parents and my sisters were slaughtered in the massacre.'

'Your uncle was my friend,' he said. 'May God have mercy on his soul, he was good to me, even though he was a Jew.'

'Do not pray for his departed soul yet. My uncle did not die in the massacre. We escaped to the forest together and travelled far from here.'

The old man looked at me with his unseeing eyes. 'Abraham survived?' he whispered.

'Yes. He is travelling, spreading news of the massacre that destroyed the ghetto of Polotensk.'

A smile flitted across the old man's face, ephemeral as a ripple on water.

'I pass on messages of hope to other survivors who come here searching for news of loved ones lost in the attack,' he murmured. 'Perhaps God has forgiven me, because He sent you here with news of my friend, Abraham. My heart is bowed down with sorrow, but your words have lightened my burden. When you see Abraham ben Tedeschi, tell him I mourned for him, and prayed that he would find eternal salvation at the right hand of God, even though he was a Jew.'

'What was there to forgive?' I asked, removing my hand from his grasp.

'My cowardice.' A sigh shook his frail shoulders. 'I should have warned Abraham sooner. Together we could have saved many souls, but I was frightened of the Streltsy.'

'With good reason.'

'For two whole days I knew of the impending attack on the ghetto but kept silent. Only at the very last moment did I run to warn my friend. I should have spoken out sooner, but I was afraid. If the Jews had fled the ghetto before the attack, the Muscovites would have realised they had been betrayed. Since my friendship with a Jew was no secret, suspicion was bound to fall on me. So instead of protecting a rabble of Jews, I held my tongue to save myself, and thousands of lives were lost.'

'You were wise to be cautious,' I reassured him. 'The Streltsy would have killed you if they had learned about your friendship with my uncle.'

'But so many dead... so many dead... their bloated bodies packed together in the Dvina... contaminated water that will never again be clean.'

As he mumbled to himself, lost in his memories, I began reciting a prayer for each member of my lost family: Saul ben

Menachem, my mother, Rebeka, and my four sisters, Keturah, Bekah, Jecoliah and Hannah. All at once, the old beadle stirred at my side, and interrupted my prayers to tell me he had a message for me. He seemed curiously excited, and his words grew wild.

'I don't understand what you mean,' I replied. 'What message can you possibly have for me?'

'Your name is Abigail, daughter of Saul ben Menachem, is it not?'

'Yes, I just told you that.'

'And you had a sister, Keturah.'

'I did, may her innocent soul rest in peace.'

I listened in amazement as the old man told me that Keturah had escaped the Streltsy by hiding under a covering of sacks. When night fell, she had slipped away through a gap in the ghetto wall and had gone to find her friend, Shiphrah, who was visiting relatives in the town of Buda on the Danube River. It was true that Keturah had been friends with a girl called Shiphrah. The beadle could not have known that. In addition, his description of my sister's escape through a gap in the ghetto wall was enough to convince me to believe his account. His news threw me into a turmoil so violent, I was scarcely able to speak. My voice shook as I asked him how he knew about Keturah's flight from Polotensk.

'A travelling Jewish merchant came here one day, just as you have done. He was looking for any trace of your sister's lost family, and left word of her whereabouts with me, in case anyone should come looking for her.'

The old man enquired where I now lived, in case any other survivor returned after I had gone. I hesitated before telling him I had settled in Venice, and did not add that I might never return there. When he enquired where Abraham was now, I could not tell him, but promised to pass on his message if I ever saw my uncle again. Given that my uncle and I were both itinerant, it was unlikely our paths would cross again, but I gave the old beadle my word and he seemed content. As for me, my whole body was trembling at the thought that my beloved sister, Keturah, might still be alive. My impatience to seek her out possessed me like a hurricane, driving me away from the ghetto of dead souls and back to the world of the living.

42

Leaving the ghetto and returning to the town centre, I found the marketplace thronged with traders, and fell into conversation with the wife of a merchant. She was a comfortable, well-dressed woman, whose husband was clearly thriving. My own clothes were dusty from travelling but she peered at my cloak, which was of good quality, and said she would help me if she could.

'Does your husband happen to know of anyone who is travelling to Buda?' I asked her. 'I wish to go there and visit my sister, but I do not know the way and am seeking a travelling companion to escort me there in safety. I have money,' I added cautiously.

At the mention of money, the woman nodded briskly. 'I will ask.'

The merchant's wife disappeared and I sat down by the roadside to wait, watching as customers jostled each other to make their purchases. A stout woman in a dirty white apron marched past carrying a squawking chicken, a girl sauntered by eating an apple, and a gaggle of shrieking young boys chased each other through the stalls. The busy life of the market carried on around me, with its bartering, squabbles, and petty triumphs, much as it had done for hundreds of years, and as it had probably done on the day the Streltsy had marched through the town on their way to the ghetto.

At last my new acquaintance reappeared, smiling. 'I found my husband in the tavern. One of his companions there told me of a troupe of musicians who are leaving tomorrow, bound for Tunis, and they will be stopping at Buda on their way.'

She smiled eagerly, and I handed her half a ducat. Her eyes widened at my generosity.

'Where can I find the musicians?' I asked her.

'For that you must use your ears.'

Disappointed, I wandered around the market, fearing I had just lost half a ducat for nothing, when I heard pipes accompanied by a tabor. Following the sound of the music, I found three musicians playing a fiddle and a pipe, and beating a rapid rhythm on a tabor. When they finished, I was reassured to see a woman join them, carrying a cap in which she had been collecting coins from people who had gathered to listen to the music. She had long fair hair tied back off her face with a red kerchief. Approaching her, I repeated my request, assuring her that I would contribute a gold ducat to their takings if they would allow me to travel with them as far as Buda. At the mention of a ducat, she readily agreed, and the three men greeted me respectfully.

'My Elena will be pleased of your company,' the fiddler said, slapping the fair-haired woman on the backside.

Early next morning I set off for Buda in the company of Elena and her husband, Kende, and the other musicians. When they were not playing their instruments, they were a sober group, talking little and walking so fast I had to trot to keep up with them. But they were friendly towards me, sharing their food with me, and talking amiably to one another. Despite their rapid pace, we made slow progress, since they stopped to entertain people in every hamlet and village we passed through. The sun beat down on us as we journeyed, wearying our spirits and further slowing our pace. Finally the heat abated, and the leaves around us turned brown and golden, reminding me of the tree in the Campo del Ghetto Nuovo in Venice. I was homesick, not for Polotensk, but for the ghetto of Venice.

At night I lay down in the fields with Hadassah's cloak to protect me from the damp that rose from the ground and creatures that crawled on the earth. Gazing up at the stars, I wondered what my former landlady was doing, and who was now sleeping in my bed at her lodgings. I did my best not to think about Daniel living with his son in Ferrara, in the house of his sister and her family. He would never return to Venice. If my beloved sister was not living in Buda, I would find my way back to the Ghetto Nuovo and live out my days in Hadassah's apartment, sewing for Tamar. Polotensk had vanished and I had no other home. With such thoughts in my head, I slept uneasily, too tired to dream, and woke with aching legs and a weariness in my soul.

After many days' walk the weather grew cold, and I shivered even with Hadassah's cloak to protect me. The ground was hard with frost, slowing our progress. At last Kende pointed to a distant castle that stood on the crest of a high hill.

'There it is,' he said. 'The Castle of Buda, home of kings.'

My destination was far away but eventually we reached the lower slopes of the hill. Several times I stumbled as we climbed. The first time Elena caught my elbow. After that she held her husband's arm, leaving me to struggle on alone. The incline grew steeper as we ascended towards the vast castle which loomed above us, overlooking a wide river.

'That is the Duna River,' Kende told me, seeing me looking back.

Recalling my last view of the Dvina, I trembled. By the time we reached the outer walls of the town, my legs were shaking with the effort of climbing. The ground levelled off as we skirted the castle, walking along cobbled streets that led past many fine houses. Our road wound around a broad square. We walked on, and at length reached a smaller square where Kende stopped.

'Here we are,' he said, nodding at me.

I gazed around a cobbled marketplace dominated by a church with a very high tower, a pyramid at its distant apex.

'But where is the ghetto?' I stammered in dismay.

Kende shrugged. 'We are in Buda, and I have brought you to Szombathely Square, where the Jews live.'

Shocked that my companions were abandoning me in this alien place, I was about to remonstrate, when a woman in a familiar yellow shawl passed us on the far side of the square. I paid Kende the sum we had agreed and he led his troupe away, back towards the castle. There was nothing I could do now but trust in Hashem. The woman in the shawl had vanished into one of the buildings on the square, but as I stood hesitating, another woman in a yellow shawl appeared.

'Forgive me,' I called out, approaching her. 'I am a stranger here. Where is the ghetto?'

'The ghetto?' she repeated, frowning. 'What ghetto?'

'The ghetto where the Jews live.'

The woman shook head. 'There is no ghetto here.' She started to walk away but I detained her and explained I was looking for Keturah, daughter of Rebeka.

'You mean Keturah from Polotensk?' she replied.

I flung my arms around her, so great was my relief on discovering she knew my sister's name. Even better, she offered to guide me to Keturah's lodgings. Standing in front of the house where my sister lived, I trembled so violently my legs almost gave way. Muttering a prayer to Hashem, I knocked on the door. The woman who opened the door resembled my mother so closely, I let out a cry of astonishment. Even though I had been expecting to see my sister, I could not believe it was really her. Meanwhile Keturah stood as though turned to stone.

'Keturah, my sister,' I stammered, as tears slid down my face.

'Abigail? Is it really you? Are you alive? I don't believe it! How can this be? How have you been living? Where are you living? How did you escape?'

Laughing and crying as she fired questions at me, I followed her inside the house and we fell into one another's arms. We drank a glass of sweetened wine to celebrate our reunion, and I told her all about my journey with our Uncle Abraham – all but the murder in the forest – and how I had settled in Venice with a landlady who was kind to me, and how I had learned of her survival. I did not mention Daniel, nor that Reuven had returned. He had gone, and I hoped never to look on his face again. In her turn, Keturah told me how she had reached Buda only to discover that the friend she had gone to visit had died of a fever. Her friend's aunt had taken her in, and in time a match had been arranged for her.

'Are you happy here?' I asked her.

'My husband is a lot older than me,' she said, 'but he is a good man, and he is kind to me. And besides,' she added with a sly grin, 'he is a travelling merchant so he is away most of the year and does not bother me much.'

We both laughed, and I hid my sadness that she had not found true happiness in her marriage; life can treat a woman far worse than to give her a kind husband.

'It is better this way,' she added gently, perceiving the disappointment I had failed to conceal. 'I am content, my sister, and count myself truly blessed. We are safe. I have many friends among the women of the congregation here. And I have a child.'

As if on cue, a baby began to cry, and I noticed something stir in an open wooden crate in the corner of the room. Keturah jumped up and lifted the bawling bundle in her arms, soothing the baby and cradling it against her breast. As soon as the baby began to feed, the crying stopped. I watched my sister, a contented mother with a baby at her breast. She had been a child of ten when we had last set eyes on one another. Seeing her now, my happiness was complete. But such moments do not last.

'I am glad you have found a home,' I said.

'You must stay with us,' she replied, speaking softly so not to disturb the infant who was dozing in her arms, her tiny lips still making a sucking motion as she slept.

'Thank you, my sister, but I am settled in the ghetto in Venice.'

'You have no family there. Abigail, stay with us. We have a good life here.'

'Surely it would be best if you returned to Venice with me,' I replied. 'In the ghetto of Venice Jews live in safety, protected by the Christian rulers of the Republic.'

Keturah was silent for a moment, and I knew what she was thinking. We had believed we were safe in the ghetto of Polotensk. When she spoke again, she reassured me that the Jews in Buda lived under the protection of the King.

'How can you be safe, having no ghetto walls?' I protested.

'We walk around the town freely among the Christians. It did feel strange at first,' Keturah admitted. 'But you soon get used to it, and after that it is not so very different, really.'

'Are you not scared at night without the protection of the ghetto walls?'

Keturah shook her head. 'I thought I would be, but we are safer here than we were in the ghetto where we both grew up.'

'We are safe within the ghetto in Venice,' I insisted. 'What protection do you have? I do not like to think of you and your child being exposed to danger.'

'We are safer living freely here in Buda than we would be in any ghetto,' she replied firmly. 'There is no escape if a ghetto is attacked. I could not return to that, and live in constant fear. In Buda, if there were any trouble, at least we would have a chance to slip away and escape down the hill. But the important thing is, no one threatens us here. We have the protection of the King himself, and the Christians regard us as their neighbours, not strangers, so they do not attack us like they do in other Christian territories. Believe me, my sister, it is better this way. The Christians are not all bad people.'

I thought of the old beadle in Polotensk, and Veronica Franco, and all the Christians who had assisted me on my travels.

'As long as your child is not influenced by Christian ways,' I muttered.

'No one causes us any trouble here,' my sister insisted. 'We live in peace with our neighbours and that is why many Jews have moved to Hungary, because we are safe here. It is a good life. Jews are treated well. The men work and are allowed to own shops, and we have a synagogue. Even the small Sephardi congregation have their own prayer room. You must stay here with me, Abigail, and we will find you a good match.'

'I can never marry again,' I told her firmly.

'Of course you must be wed. You are still young enough to bear many children and–'

'No,' I interrupted her. 'You do not understand, sister. My husband may still be alive.'

'Abigail, very few of us escaped the attack on our ghetto in

Polotensk,' she told me gravely. 'Believe me, there is no one left. My husband travelled through the town, on business, and he went to the ghetto to see who had returned there. He found no one, Abigail, no one. You saw for yourself the buildings are falling down and only vermin and crawling creatures inhabit the streets where we played as children. Your husband must have drowned or been shot along with everyone else in the ghetto. You can neither hope nor fear for his return. It was only by a miracle that you and Uncle Abraham escaped, and had you not been close to the gap in the wall when the Streltsy marched in, you too would have perished.'

'My husband survived,' I told her flatly.

She gazed at me in horror as I recounted how Reuven had returned to me, only to be arrested for brawling and sentenced to fifteen years as a galley slave.

'That was two years ago,' I said. 'So in thirteen years' time he may return.'

'Do not go back to Venice,' she said, putting her hand on my arm as though to restrain me from leaving. 'He was not good to you. Please, my sister, do not let him find you again.'

'Keturah, wherever I go he will find me,' I replied sadly. 'He followed me to Venice, do you not think he can track me down here, living with my sister?'

We were silent for a moment. Gazing at her sleeping infant, I recalled the noxious potion Henriette had given me to end my own pregnancy, and wondered if I would ever have a child of my own. By the time Reuven was freed, I would be thirty-five, an age at which most women were already grandmothers. But even if he did not return, I would never know whether I was a wife or a widow.

'You have a beautiful baby,' I said.

Keturah smiled down at the infant nestling at her bosom. 'She is called Rebeka, in memory of our mother, may her dear soul rest in peace.' She patted her belly and I saw that it was swollen. 'We were going to call my next daughter Abigail. Thanks be to Hashem, we will have to think of a different name if I have another girl.'

We were silent. Like me, she was probably remembering our other three sisters. We did not speak their names.

43

As we were waiting for the evening service to begin in the synagogue one evening, I overheard someone mention the Republic of Venice, and was seized with nostalgia on hearing the name of the only place I had found true happiness as a grown woman. Contented though I was to live with my beloved sister, my affection for Hadassah had not waned, and nor had my feelings for Daniel. My thoughts dwelled on him during the day as I watched over my infant niece. Sometimes I made believe the child was mine and Daniel's, pretending that he would soon walk into the room and embrace me. It was sinful of me, but such thoughts tormented me and visited me nightly in my dreams. I prayed to be released from the enchantment the printer of Venice had cast over me, but in vain. After prayers finished and the women gathered to gossip before returning home, I approached the woman who had spoken of Venice, and introduced myself.

'Ah yes, Abigail from Polotensk,' she replied. 'I heard you were living here with Keturah. I wish you long life.'

Introducing herself as Leah, daughter of Elkanah, she told me she was the wife of a travelling merchant who had recently returned home with news from Venice. 'But tell me, why are you interested in Venice? Do you have family there?' she asked.

'I lived there for several years, after I fled from Polotensk, and I have many friends in the ghetto in Venice.'

'Not any more,' she replied, her face twisted with sympathy.

Her words shocked me so that I could barely stammer a word. Memories of the massacre in Polotensk came flooding back, and I feared for the lives of people I had grown to care about.

'What do you mean? Tell me, quickly,' I blurted out when my power of speech returned.

'I am sorry to be the bearer of bad news, but if what my husband has heard is true, the ghetto in Venice will soon close its gates for the last time. Come and eat with us tonight, and you can hear about it directly from my husband. He was there just a few weeks ago, and can give you the latest news himself.'

I followed Leah from the synagogue along the street to her home, impatient to hear what her husband had to say. She was a very short plump woman, with a round pink face and small brown eyes that almost closed when she smiled. Her husband, Jakov, was tall and thin. They looked an oddly matched couple, walking side by side, but they seemed content in one another's company.

Once we were seated at the table and the prayer before the meal concluded, Jakov told me that he had been visiting Venice when the decree was announced.

'What decree?' I asked, struggling to control my agitation.

'You may have heard rumours of a threatened expulsion? Well, one afternoon the whole congregation gathered in the Campo del Ghetto Nuovo to hear a decree announced. I chanced to be there and heard it for myself.'

I nodded. 'The Senate are always issuing decrees,' I muttered. 'It probably means nothing.'

'It was a cold day in December,' Jakov continued. 'We hid our hands inside our winter cloaks and stamped our feet as we stood waiting. At last a trumpeter blew a few notes to command our attention, and a herald thanked the false God of the Roman Catholic Church for the Republic's victory against their enemies. Then he announced in the name of the Holy Ghost and for the honour of God, and so on and so forth, that at the expiration of the current condotta granting them right of residence, the Jews must leave Venice. In conclusion, he said the alternatives were conversion or death.'

It was hard to comprehend such shocking news. For nearly a century, Venice had offered a safe haven for the Jews inside the ghetto. And now this.

'Not again,' Leah said. 'What harm have we Jews ever done? All we ask is that we be left alone to live our lives in peace. Will this madness never end?'

'With the burgeoning threat from the new Protestant faith, the paranoia of the Pope of Rome has grown beyond all reason,' Jakov replied. 'The Inquisition is set on converting or eliminating anyone they see as a threat to the power of Rome, and that means anyone who is not a Catholic.'

'How can Jews threaten the power of the Catholic Church?' I asked angrily. 'We are few in number and we keep to ourselves. The Catholics should concentrate on their real enemies. Muslims are trying to destroy them, and Christian Reformers want to cast off the yoke of the Pope in Rome. Jews pose no threat to the survival of the Catholic Church.'

'The Catholics are misguided in turning on us, but who among us has never vented his feelings against the wrong person?' Jakov replied mildly.

'So once again Jews are the scapegoat,' his wife snapped.

The news of the expulsion order threw my thoughts into turmoil. I had to reach Venice before the expiration of the condotta that decreed the duration of our permitted residence there, or it might no longer be safe to return, and I might never again find Daniel or Hadassah, or any other members of the congregation of the Ghetto Nuovo. With a darkness in my heart, I took my leave of Keturah.

'I cannot bear another long separation, and will not rest until you return,' she said, as she clung to me. 'May Hashem guard you on your journey, and may you find peace and happiness, as I have done here in Buda. Promise me you will come back and see me again, sister. You must give me your word, as you love Hashem.'

'I will do my best,' I assured her.

We both knew the fulfilment of my promise depended not on my wishes, but on the will of Hashem. Kissing her infant on the head, I took my leave. Once again, I pursued the arduous journey overland back to Split. My travelling companions were merchants and peddlers, and together we trudged to the coast. At the harbour in Split, I secured a passage on a ship bound for Venice. There was no comfort or privacy on that wretched sea voyage, but at least we were not troubled by storms or brigands. Grown accustomed to the movement of a vessel on the water, I was thankful not to be sick. Finally we reached the familiar lagoon of the Most Serene Republic of Venice and dropped anchor, and I gave thanks to Hashem for once again delivering me from the hazards of a long journey.

The winter was far advanced by the time I disembarked in Venice. Shivering in Hadassah's cloak, I made my way along icy streets until, nearly frozen and sick with relief, I reached the entrance to the ghetto. I slithered over the Agudi Bridge, and knocked at the door of my former apartment.

Overjoyed to see me again, Hadassah held me close as though she would never let me go. 'Come in, come in, sit by the fire and I'll heat up some broth,' she said when she finally released me from her embrace. 'You look half frozen.'

'More than half,' I replied. My teeth were chattering so hard it was difficult to speak.

It was wonderful to see my friend again. The lodger who had replaced me had recently left, unsettled by the expulsion order, and Hadassah had not yet found another tenant. As I sat sipping hot soup, feeling its warmth spread through my body, Hadassah told me that many people had already packed up and gone. Others had decided to stay until the expiration of the condotta that gave us permission to reside in Venice. Hadassah had been watching a steady stream of Jews leave the ghetto to take their chances elsewhere in the Republic or further afield.

Some of my neighbours were leaving the ghetto when I went out the next day. They traipsed over the Agudi Bridge, taking care not to lean on the cracked balustrade, before disappearing along the Calle del Ghetto Vecchio that led to the gate to the outside world. The wealthier pushed hand carts in front of them, while their wives and children trotted miserably behind them. Others were laden with heavy bundles. Many of them had relatives in other lands and were hoping to establish lives far away from Venice, in Hungary or Morocco, the Netherlands or Poland.

'Sarai, I didn't know you were leaving,' I called out, recognising my friend from Tamar's workshop in the procession of people leaving the ghetto.

'We cannot stay here much longer, so we thought we might as well go at once and not prolong the misery,' Sarai replied, smiling sadly. 'Since Tamar left there have been no jobs for needleworkers in the ghetto and, to be honest, I am not sorry to be moving on. Ever since Tamar left, it has been hard to find any work at all. I have been doing a bit of mending here and there, and living on the charity of my neighbours. But I am surprised to see you again. Hadassah told me she heard from a travelling merchant that you were living with your sister in Buda.'

Another neighbour told me that she and her family were going to relatives in Krakow. 'My cousin has offered us lodging until we find a place of our own, and he says he can find work for my husband when we get there. We are lucky to have somewhere to go.' She hurried after her children, calling out to them to be careful on the Agudi Bridge.

Many of the affluent Jews left without delay, but some struggled to convert their possessions into wealth that they could carry with them on their travels. The majority of our congregation procrastinated, dithering over when they should leave, and where they could go, while other members of the community were too frail to contemplate a long journey. So the summer passed in parting from our friends, people who had been our neighbours for many years. Hadassah had known them all her life. Those who had already been thinking of leaving went at once, along with those who had family offering them homes elsewhere, but after the first tranche of the congregation had packed up and gone, the situation settled down and there was no longer a steady stream of departures. By the following spring, when the initial shock of hearing about the expulsion had worn off, those of us left in the ghetto discussed our options and future prospects with growing resignation. Some managed to remain optimistic about the possibility of staying in our homes, although it was hard to see how we could remain for much longer.

Hadassah decided she would not leave until she was forced to go. For my part, I was keen to stay as long as possible. My uncle had sent me word via an itinerant visitor to the ghetto, to say that he was on his way back to Venice, so I wanted to wait for him. Besides, secretly I hoped that Daniel might return to Venice before the ghetto closed. Even though we could never marry, we might at least see each again, and I yearned to look on his beloved face and hear his voice at least once more in this earthly life. Meanwhile, we struggled to make ends meet. I found employment where I could, doing alterations and mending garments. The work was sporadic and poorly paid, and although Hadassah did not charge me rent, I barely earned enough to feed us both.

One morning a neighbour brought me a torn gown. 'I would do it myself and save the money,' she said, 'but my sewing is so uneven. If you mend it for me, Abigail, I know the gown will last longer than if I try to patch it up myself.'

Taking the gown from her, I studied the tear. Hadassah and I were using our candles sparingly, so the mending would have to be done in the daylight, which meant I would have to work fast.

'I can have this done for you by tomorrow evening,' I told her.

We agreed a price. It was not much, but my neighbour was no better off than I was.

'So, your husband has returned to you, praise be to Hashem,' she said, as she turned to leave.

The torn gown fell from my hand and I bent down to retrieve it, hiding my confusion as well as I could. 'My husband? You are mistaken,' I murmured. 'My husband is away, serving his time on the galleys.'

'Well, either someone paid a ransom for his release or he escaped, because I saw him going into the tavern in the ghetto, just this morning,' she replied. 'I recognised him at once. I am surprised he has not been to see you yet.'

She gave me a shrewd look. With an effort I returned her gaze steadily, too distraught to speak. In waiting for Daniel, I had allowed my husband to find me. Hashem had abandoned me once again.

44

That evening, Hadassah and I were seated at the table with a pot of vegetable stew she had made for our supper. It was an excellent meal, and well-seasoned, but neither of us ate much. The news of my husband's return had taken away our appetites. Mentally, I struggled to prepare myself for a return to his violent abuse, and determined to greet him with quiet dignity. Reminding myself that he had been enslaved below the deck of a ship, chained in filth and compelled to strain his muscles, I tried to feel pity for him. However violently he had abused me, he was still a man, and Hashem's creature. I dared hope his own suffering might have transformed him and led him to the path of virtue. His sister had told me that Reuven's heart had been broken by the death of his first wife, a woman he had loved with a fierce passion. I knew what it was to love another to the exclusion of all else. Even after all the suffering my husband had caused me, I was prepared to forgive him.

As I was lost in musing, the door of the apartment flew open and he swaggered in.

'So?' he bellowed, glaring at me as he kicked the door shut behind him. 'Are you surprised to see me, wife? Hashem willed it that I be released along with the other galley slaves. The Christians freed us from our fetters so we could join in the glorious battle against the Turks, and I was not slow in showing my gratitude.' With a triumphant laugh, he pulled a dagger from his belt and waved it in the air. 'The deck was awash with the dead and dying. The air rang with their cries and the sea around us turned red with blood.'

His hair had grown long, and reached below his shoulders, his clothes were ingrained with dirt, and he approached the table, stinking of excrement and sweat and swaying with the effect of the ale he had been drinking. Overcome with disgust, I nodded my head.

He yanked my stool from under me, causing me to fall to the floor. 'Do you not stand and offer your seat to your husband?' he shouted, glaring at me. 'Well? Why the long face? Are you not overjoyed that Hashem has restored your husband to you, or do you have no womanly feelings at all?'

Having raised his voice, he now raised his hand. Perhaps he intended to embrace me, but I instinctively cowered away. My craven response enraged him. 'What is this?' he yelled, his expression dark with choler. 'Does a virtuous wife not run to greet her husband after such a long absence?'

Not long enough, I thought, but dared not speak aloud.

No sooner had I clambered to my feet than his grimy palm slapped the side of my head. 'I will show you how to treat your husband with respect,' he roared. 'I will teach you how to behave, you little witch.'

As I grabbed at the edge of the table to keep my balance, a clear voice rang out behind me, a voice raised in anger.

'Abigail is no witch,' Hadassah shrieked in a passion of fear. 'You take your hands off her, you animal, and treat her with the respect she deserves, or you will be sorry.'

Grinning, Reuven turned to her. 'And what are you going to do to make me sorry, you old hag?'

Hadassah was beside herself with fury. 'Everyone will learn how you treat your wife. Leave her alone, or I will see you hounded out of the ghetto!'

He threw his head back and laughed. 'You think a man can be cowed by the squawking of a woman? I am not one of your pretty boys who runs away at the first hint of a fight.'

Behind his back, I scrambled to my feet. As I did so, he started towards Hadassah, roaring like a wild beast.

Alarmed, Hadassah ran around the table so that it stood between her and Reuven. 'Get out!' she screeched. 'Get out of here! Get out of my apartment!'

Reuven spat on the floor, leaned forward and chased her round the table, staggering and laughing. She raced ahead of him until she reached me and threw herself into my arms. We clung together, trembling, and Reuven smirked at our terror.

'That filthy harridan is my wife,' he said, his quiet threat more menacing than his rage. 'I will not leave, and if I do, my wife comes with me.'

'Why?' I demanded, finding my voice at last. 'You do not want me. You never wanted me.'

'You are mine, by law,' he replied. 'There will be no more discussion.'

Hadassah pulled away from me and ran to her room. As my husband moved around the table to reach me, she emerged carrying a pouch which she heaved onto the table, dropping it with a loud thump.

'Take this,' she said, glaring at him. 'Take it and go.'

Surprised, I watched her tip a pile of coins onto the table. They glowed and sparkled in the flickering candlelight.

'This is the money you gave me,' she said. 'I have been saving it for just such an exigency. I can think of no better way to spend it.'

This was the money Joseph Nasi had given to me, that I had shared with Hadassah.

'You can have all of this,' she said to my husband, speaking very slowly and carefully, 'if you agree to leave her alone. Abigail does not want to live with you, and you cannot keep up this pretence that you want her.' She scooped up all the coins and stuffed them back in the pouch which she heaved across the table towards him. 'It is not too heavy for a strong man like you to carry.'

While I was stammering that she could not possibly hand all her savings over to my husband, he lunged forwards. Seizing the pouch, he checked inside it before grabbing hold of it and weighing it in his huge hand. Then he turned to me.

'Put on your cloak,' he told me.

'Where are we going?'

Hadassah stared at me. 'What is going on? What are you doing?'

'We are leaving,' he replied shortly.

'How can we leave in the middle of the night? Where are we going?' I babbled.

'What about the money I gave you?' Hadassah protested. 'You have to leave her alone. That was the agreement.'

Reuven turned to her, growling like an animal. 'What is it with all these questions? How is it any of your business what I do with my wife? Is she your property? No, she is mine. So you had best shut up, if you do not want me to smash your face in. I thank you for the money, which will come in handy. A man cannot be too wealthy. But my wife comes with me. The law is on my side.'

There was nothing more Hadassah could do to help me. She

sank to her knees, weeping with indignation, but my eyes remained dry. My despair was too dark to express.

We set off in the direction of the Ghetto Vecchio, my husband lurching unsteadily across the square while I followed him. Every few minutes he spun round to glare at me in the moonlight. Several times he nearly lost his footing, unbalanced by the drink, and the weight of Hadassah's coins in his pocket. I was tempted to turn and flee, but he was bound to find me hiding in the ghetto and would bribe the guard to stop me leaving, confident the law would allow him to protect his rights. The only sensible course of action was to be patient, and retrieve Hadassah's pouch while he was asleep during the day when the gate was open. With so much money, I could at least attempt an escape. But first I would return half of the ducats to Hadassah. So I stumbled behind him, away from my friend and the home where I had found happiness.

Reuven's staggering gait led him up onto the bridge, where he grabbed hold of the rail to help him balance. Everyone in the ghetto was aware that the rail was unsafe, but in his drunken state he had forgotten to take care. Before I could call out to warn him, there was a loud crack, and a section of the rail keeled over beneath his weight. With a terrible roar, he toppled head first into the black water. The splash was so tumultuous I thought the whole ghetto would turn out to see what had happened, but no one emerged from the shadows around us. Hurrying onto the bridge, I peered over the edge and saw my husband's eyes and mouth gaping at me, before he sank below the surface. Rigid with shock, I stared down at a violent disturbance in the water. It was not long before the turbulence subsided. A moment later, there was no trace of my husband. He had been too drunk, or too avaricious, to divest himself of Hadassah's money, and the weight of the coins had dragged him down beneath the surface.

I do not know how long I remained on the bridge, transfixed with horror. At last I turned and hurried to tell Hadassah what had happened.

'I cannot think of a better use for the money I have been saving for so long,' she said, when my tale was done. 'I offered to pay that brute to leave you alone, and Hashem saw to it that the bargain was honoured.' She grinned. 'Well, that's that. Praise be the name of the Lord, for releasing you from bondage. You have waited long enough to be free of that monster.'

We agreed to tell no one what had happened to my husband, for fear I might be accused of having helped him on his way. The next time I saw my neighbour who had spotted Reuven in the ghetto, I persuaded her she had been mistaken in believing my husband had returned to Venice. Anchored in the depths of the canal by his misbegotten gold, his body would never surface to reveal the truth. I was not sorry that I could not tear my garments as a wife should, when she mourns the death of her husband. Reuven had survived slavery on the ocean, only to drown in the canals of Venice. Yet every night, he pursued me in my dreams. Sometimes he rose from the canal with a hundred tentacles, like a vast sea monster, and dragged me down under the water with him. In other dreams, he raised his fist and beat me until I woke, screaming with terror. Hadassah wearied of hearing his spirit haunting me in my sleep.

'Even when I am awake, I am afraid,' I told her.

At last, after some months, she tired of my complaints.

'Forgive me,' I begged her. 'I have no one else to talk to.'

'Then you must pray,' she replied. 'My patience has run out. I will hear the name Reuven ben Yitzhak no more.'

I took her advice, and prayed to be free of the memory of my husband. Gradually my nightmares ceased, and I no longer dreamed of Reuven returning from the dead to torment me.

45

The last leaves had fallen from the tree in the Campo del Ghetto Nuovo, and for a few weeks I had been busy altering warm gowns and doublets, as we prepared for the coming of winter. One chilly morning I was crossing the Campo del Ghetto Nuovo when someone called my name. Recognising the voice at once, I spun round and felt my breath catch in my throat.

'Daniel? Is it really you, returned at last from Ferrara?'

'I travelled further than Ferrara,' he replied solemnly.

'Where have you been?'

'If you will allow me to accompany you to your lodgings, I will tell you all my adventures. But be warned, it is a long story.' He paused. 'It may take a while.'

'Where is Elia?' I asked.

He sighed. 'That is part of my story.'

He looked travel worn, his clothes in tatters, his face burned by the sun, his hair grey with a dusting of salt from the sea. But his eyes had not lost their intense longing as he gazed at me, and I had to fight against a desire to put my arms around him and whisper words of comfort. I had news of my own to impart, but first I wanted to hear what he had been doing. Before I told him about my husband's death, I wanted to know whether Daniel had taken a wife in Ferrara. We walked to Hadassah's lodgings and she was astonished to see us together. Seated at the table, with a cup of hot wine to warm him, Daniel told us how he had been on his way back to Venice when his ship had been diverted to Messina to fight in the Battle of Lepanto, where the Christian Holy Alliance had defeated the Turks.

'So the Catholic stranglehold continues,' he concluded, frowning.

'What about Elia?' I asked, hardly daring to hope he too had survived the battle.

'After the Christian victory, tens of thousands of men were dead, yet Elia and I were still alive, and I began to hope that Hashem might bring us safely out of the slaughter,' Daniel told us. 'As we stood together, marvelling that we had both survived the battle, the ship rocked violently, and an icy wall of water washed us both overboard. All around me in the churning water limbs thrashed, faces appeared and vanished, eyes glared wildly, and mouths gaped in voiceless screams. Salt water stung my eyes and filled my mouth and nose, burning my throat. Kicking as strongly as I could, and fighting for every breath, I was tossed around like a splinter of wood.

'The current was pulling me downwards, when an arm grabbed me and held my head above the water. Vainly I struggled to free myself. In the din and clamour of the dying, it took me a few seconds to register the words being yelled in my ear. "Father, stop struggling, or you'll drown us both!"

'I felt myself being dragged through the water, away from the melee of men fighting to swim through the ranks of bloody corpses. Finally we reached the side of a ship. Elia forced a rope between my numb fingers and I was dragged from the water, shivering and barely conscious, all the humours in my body nearly frozen from my immersion in the sea. But when I looked down at the water, Elia had gone.'

Daniel's eyes seemed to look inward at the darkness of his memories.

'May Hashem have mercy on his soul. He sacrificed his life to save you,' I whispered tearfully. *As I would have done*, I thought, but dared not say.

'My story is not over yet,' Daniel said, smiling faintly. 'Pour me another glass of that good sweet wine, Hadassah, and I will finish my tale. Convinced that my son had drowned, I gazed out over the water. Among drifting dead bodies, and floundering victims still alive, I saw one man swimming purposefully, making his way between the high sides of the ships. Did you know that my son can swim?'

On my arrival in Venice, when Elia had hauled himself from the water to guide me and my uncle to the ghetto, he had boasted that he was a really strong swimmer.

I nodded, and Daniel resumed speaking. 'Elia turned and raised a hand in farewell, and I understood then that my son was not returning to the ghetto in Venice with me. He has chosen to travel far away, seeking a home where he can be free from the long shadow of the Inquisition. He probably intends to make his way to the court of the Sultan, where Joseph Nasi will offer him shelter. I raised my hand in response, and with a final wave of his hand he turned away and continued swimming towards the distant shore. My son has chosen a different path, but the Ghetto Nuovo is the only home I know, a place where everyone believes in Hashem, and battles are fought in words, not blood. The ship that had rescued me was sailing to Venice, so I resolved to see the ghetto once more before returning to my sister in Ferrara.'

In my turn, I described how I had gone to Polotensk, and

found my sister in Buda. Daniel was surprised that I had not stayed with Keturah.

'She returned to Venice to wait for you,' Hadassah said.

Daniel gazed at me. 'If I am honest, you are the reason I returned here. Even though we cannot marry, I wished to look on your face once more.'

I smiled and shook my head. 'There is more to tell you.'

He listened, rapt, as I told him about Reuven's death. When I finished my tale, Daniel sat staring at me, shaking his head in disbelief.

'If he had not made off with my money, he might have remained afloat until someone came along and rescued him,' Hadassah pointed out with obvious satisfaction, as though she herself had personally arranged for my husband to drown.

'So your husband is truly dead?' Daniel asked at last.

I nodded, and for a moment neither of us spoke. After that, we talked until after sunset, careless that we were missing prayers in the synagogue.

'I suppose I had better feed you,' Hadassah said, with a broad smile.

As we ate, she told us she had rented Daniel's apartment to a succession of travellers, none of whom had stayed long in the ghetto. Daniel, she said, was welcome to stay there as long as he liked, and if he could not pay his rent straight away, she offered to cover it for him until he found a job.

It was not long before Daniel approached me with the words I both longed and dreaded to hear. Although I desired to be Daniel's wife more than anything else, I knew we could never marry. My uncle had seen me kill a stranger in the forest outside Polotensk. I could not wed Daniel, while I deliberately kept him in ignorance of my sin. Knowing my uncle would soon be with us, once again I used his approaching visit as an excuse to delay our wedding plans.

'I have waited this long,' Daniel replied. 'I will be patient a while longer, if that is truly what you want.'

So I put off the evil hour when Daniel would learn the truth about me. It was selfish of me, but I could not willingly forfeit my last few days of happiness, basking in the good opinion of the man I loved. And all the time, I fought against the wicked hope that my uncle would meet with an accident on the way, and be silenced forever. That did not happen, and one day he arrived in Venice, in high spirits. We had endured a lot together, and were both pleased to meet again in the relative safety of the ghetto in Venice, but my joy was tainted by the knowledge that he had witnessed me beat a man to death.

'I also returned to Polotensk,' my uncle told me when he had heard about my travels. 'You will hear all about my visit later, when we have more time. It is not an account that can be rushed.'

Before he could say any more, Daniel joined us, and I had to wait for another time to hear my uncle's story.

After supper at Hadassah's table, my uncle looked around with a solemn expression. 'Now, I have something to tell you all, something that concerns Abigail.'

My spirits were overcome with dread. The time had come when Daniel would learn the truth about me.

46

Before my uncle could say any more, I pushed my chair back with sudden resolution and stood up. 'Daniel,' I said. 'Let us take a walk outside. I would like some fresh air before we hear what my uncle has to say.'

We went out to the Campo del Ghetto Nuovo and sat on the bench, side by side, for the last time. In a few moments, he would recoil from me in horror and I would never look on his beloved face again.

'Abigail, now that you are free, I intend to ask you one more time. If you refuse me again, I will leave Venice and return to my sister in Ferrara and never trouble you again.' He hesitated. 'You told me once that nothing would make you happier than to be my wife.' He paused again, fidgeting with the tassel of his prayer shawl, a habit he had when nervous.

'Daniel,' I replied and bit my lip, searching for the right words. 'There is something I need to confess to you.'

'You are not going to tell me there is another husband I did not know about?' he joked, but he was frowning.

'Before I met you, before I came to Venice, I...'

It was so hard to speak, knowing he would despise me, but I

had no choice. I had to tell him the truth or deliberately allow him to commit himself to a murderess. Haltingly, I confessed that I had killed a man.

'Abigail, I don't understand,' Daniel stammered.

With difficulty, I related what had happened in the forest when my uncle and I were attacked by robbers. I expected Daniel to draw back from me aghast, and was amazed when he took my hand and raised it to his lips.

I stared at him in disbelief. 'Are you not horrified by what I did? Do I not disgust you?'

'When I heard what troubles you had suffered and overcome, I understood that Hashem had sent you here to Venice to find sanctuary from hardship and danger. And when I saw your face, I prayed that I might be the one chosen to shield and protect you for the rest of your life.'

'But I killed a man,' I protested. 'A rage possessed me and I beat him to death with a stick.'

'Would you hate me if Hashem had willed it that I killed your husband? Given the chance, believe me, I would not have hesitated. Abigail, listen to me, but tell no one what I am about to say. I went to fight in the Battle of Lepanto, knowing your husband was a galley slave on a Venetian ship. I went there to search for your husband, but could not find him in the melee. Had I seen that fiend in the battle, I would have cut him down in the midst of the slaughter, or died in the attempt, knowing that if I succeeded, the murder would go unnoticed. Is such an intention so different to the deed? I would have done it, Abigail. I prayed to Hashem that I could be the instrument of your freedom. I prayed to Hashem to let me murder him. By your own logic, you should hate me.'

'My husband was an evil man,' I muttered.

'As was the man who attacked your uncle in the forest. What do you suppose he intended, if not to rob and kill your uncle and violate you? You saved your uncle's life, Abigail, and no doubt your own as well. In that way you were surely the instrument of Hashem. Now, please let me ask you–'

'The answer is yes, Daniel,' I replied, without even allowing him time to finish the question. 'The answer has always been yes. From the first moment I saw you and heard your voice, my feelings have remained constant. You are right to remember what I told you once before, that nothing would make me happier than to be your wife.'

We realised we would need to make it known I was a widow, but I prevaricated. It would be impossible to reveal the truth about Reuven's death after so long a silence, without provoking gossip and suspicion. Daniel told me that during the battle at Lepanto, he had witnessed a group of galley slaves set free to fight alongside the Catholics.

'I will claim that, in the heat of battle, I caught sight of Reuven. Although injured, he was bravely fighting a Turk. Before I had time to cross the deck and go to his aid, the Turk's scimitar found its mark, and Reuven fell to the deck, struck down by a fierce blow. He never rose again but lay on the deck, one of many corpses slain in battle that day.'

'You would bear false witness to protect my good name?' I asked.

'I would gladly have killed that brute to protect you. Hashem forgive me, but I would have done so joyfully. Hashem led us to each other, and we must bear the consequences of our love. I would kill for you, Abigail. Do you think it would pain me to lie for you? Hashem has willed it that we love one another. Let us seize this chance of happiness while we can. I cannot lose you again.'

Neither of us spoke for a moment after that, because he swept me up in his arms, holding me so close that I could feel the pounding of his heart. Or perhaps it was my own heart I felt beating.

'What was it you wanted to tell me, Uncle?' I asked when we went back indoors to share our news.

'I believe I may speak freely in front of Hadassah,' my uncle replied slowly.

'Of course,' I replied at once. 'Hadassah is like a sister to me.'

'And Daniel is as good as family,' my uncle added, with a smile. 'There is no reason why he should not hear this. After all this time, he can hardly be accused of marrying you for your money.'

I laughed. 'My only money is what I can earn, and there is little enough of that.'

'No, niece, that is not the case as you will shortly hear. After Reuven and I discovered we had both escaped the massacre at Polotensk, we spent many months travelling together on our way back to Venice to rejoin you. I told him about our journey from Polotensk, and he told me how he managed to escape the Streltsy by killing two of them with his bare hands. I cannot say either of us shed any tears over his victims. One night, in drunken cordiality, he confided his circumstances to me.'

'What circumstances are you talking about?' I asked.

'Reuven lived like a pauper, but he came from a wealthy family,' my uncle replied. 'His father owned a chain of taverns in Russia, and Reuven inherited a fortune, much good it did him. One night he confided to me that he had buried his earthly inheritance beneath his house in Polotensk. To be honest, I was not sure whether to believe his story. When I heard of his sentence, I immediately set off for Polotensk to discover whether the treasure he talked of really existed, so that I might be able to pay a ransom for him and restore his freedom. It took me some time to find it, but find it I did.'

My uncle paused to take a gulp of wine.

'What did you find?' Hadassah demanded eagerly. 'What did you find? Do not keep us in suspense, Abraham.'

'Buried beneath his hearth in a filthy hovel by the ghetto wall was a chest filled with gold coins. I packed as many as I could carry into a large bag, and returned the rest to their hiding place. My intention was to free him, but my help was not needed. He had already been released from his bonds. Now that he is dead, your husband's entire fortune is yours by right, Abigail. You are a very wealthy woman.' He held up his hand as I began to protest. 'You can do with it what you will, hoard it, spend it, give it all to the poor, toss it in the canal and let it sink. But I am honour bound to give you what is yours.'

'I want nothing to do with my first husband's wealth,' I said bitterly. 'You should have left it buried.'

'I cannot believe you would have paid a ransom for that brute,' Hadassah burst out in fury. 'Have your travels turned your wits? He would have resumed his abuse of your niece, your own flesh and blood. Your concern should have been to protect her, not hasten her death.'

'Hadassah,' my uncle remonstrated with her, 'please do not be hasty. A wise person does not speak in anger.' He turned to me. 'Is this not divine justice? Does your first husband not owe you recompense for the suffering he caused you?'

'This is not money that Reuven earned for himself, but his family's wealth,' Hadassah added. 'So it is yours as much as it was his. You deserve this, Abigail. Do not be a fool.'

'What you are saying makes no sense,' I told her crossly.

Meanwhile, my uncle fetched his large leather satchel and hoisted it up onto the table, where he emptied out a heap of golden coins. At my side I heard Hadassah gasp and we sat transfixed. More gold than I had ever seen before lay shimmering and glinting on the rough wooden table.

'And this is only a small portion of the treasure I found buried beneath Reuven's house,' my uncle said.

'Daniel and I will discuss what to do about this once we are married,' I said stiffly. 'I dare say he will be as reluctant as I am to have anything to do this gold.'

But Daniel looked thoughtful. 'There is enough here to set up a print shop of my own,' he murmured. One look at the hungry expression on Daniel's face was enough to weaken my resolve to have nothing to do with Reuven's wealth.

'First let us marry,' I said, 'and then we will decide what to do.'

Daniel and I slept in our own beds that night, and for several nights afterwards, content in the expectation of sharing a marriage bed before the year was over.

47

On a chilly winter day, when a light dusting of snow had fallen in the night, the sun rose on a day I had never dared hope to see. The Rabbi recited the seven marriage blessings as I walked around the bridegroom seven times, and stood at his side beneath the wedding canopy. Daniel wore his Sabbath clothes, and I the gown in which the holy Torah had been successfully hidden from the Officers of the Inquisition. Apart from Hashem who sees all, no one but the Rabbi, my husband, and Hadassah knew about the panel in my gown which had been blessed by the touch of the holy scroll.

Miriam and her family travelled to Venice for the ceremony. At four, her first son, Uri, was robust, with a square face and broad shoulders, while her second son, three-year-old Ya'akov, was wiry, and ran as fast as his older brother.

'I cannot believe how quickly my grandsons have grown,' Daniel said.

'It must be three years since you last saw Uri,' Miriam replied. 'You should make the effort to visit us, Father, and not wait for us to come to you.'

Daniel and I had agreed to have a small quiet ceremony,

since it was a second marriage for us both. As we were preparing to return home, there was a sudden hubbub and a band of musicians joined us in the synagogue.

I turned to Daniel, surprised that he had arranged this entertainment without consulting me first. 'I thought we agreed not to have a party.'

'Believe me, my wife,' he replied, his face breaking into a smile as he addressed me, 'this is a surprise to me too. It is not of my making. We can leave right now and go home, if that is what you would like to do.'

I shook my head, reluctant to appear churlish. 'But who booked the musicians, if not you?'

It did not take us long to discover that my husband's colleagues from the print shop had ignored our wishes and organised a party. Hadassah had been involved in the secret preparations.

'Abigail,' Hadassah said severely. 'We are entitled to a party, even if you are not. How many years have I spent watching you yearn for Daniel? Now, at last, I can find myself a tenant who is not lovesick, and I can spend my evenings in cheerful company.'

Daniel's colleagues agreed. 'We have spent years at work seeing our friend Daniel pining for you,' one of them said.

'We wish to celebrate his good fortune and happiness in marrying the woman he has loved for so long,' another of his friends said.

'Yes, we deserve to celebrate, because at last we will not have to watch him moping all day, struck down with a lover's melancholy,' the first man added.

'My husband and I are fortunate in our friends,' I said.

'He is indeed fortunate,' agreed one of the printers, clapping my husband on the back. 'Your patient fidelity has been rewarded, and we all rejoice.'

'It is good fortune he well deserves,' another added.

Daniel seized my hand and kissed it. 'You have made me the happiest man alive.'

After that, we had little opportunity to talk to one another, as the celebrations grew increasingly riotous.

'I never thought I could be happy again,' I confessed to Daniel that night, as we lay in bed, talking as contented couples do at the end of the day. 'When Reuven returned, as if risen from the dead, I longed to die. Only the hope of seeing you again kept me alive.'

He leaned over and kissed me. 'You are so beautiful,' he replied. 'May Hashem write us both in the Book of Life, so that we may find joy in one another's company for many years to come.'

Some months after our wedding, a peace treaty was signed between The Republic of Venice and the Ottoman Empire. Venice was forced to cede Cyprus to the Turks. In spite of their ignoble defeat at Lepanto, in the end the Muslims seemed to have benefited from the conflict more than the Catholics did.

'It seems my son and I fought for the winning side after all, although we did not know it at the time,' Daniel remarked drily.

Rumours that the expulsion might be revoked had been spreading for a while, and the exodus from the ghetto had virtually halted as we waited to learn our fate. Not long after the peace treaty was signed, heralds again traversed the city. In itself this was nothing unusual since the Senate were constantly issuing decrees, mostly relating to minor misdemeanours. But the import of this particular announcement spread through the ghetto in advance: the decree to expel the Jews from Venice had been rescinded. A herald arrived in the Campo del Ghetto Nuovo, and near enough the entire population of the ghetto gathered to listen to the announcement. Daniel and I waited with our neighbours and friends in an atmosphere of muted excitement.

'In the name of the Holy Ghost and for the honour of God, and in the public and private interest,' the herald proclaimed in a booming voice, 'the Senate has decreed that a new condotta be agreed with the Jews living within the walls of the ghetto.'

The herald went on to say that Jews were granted the privilege of remaining in the city on the same conditions as before: we were required to live inside the ghetto walls and observe the curfew. Failure to comply would incur a severe penalty. Every man had to wear a yellow hat outside the gate, unless he had been granted dispensation to wear another head covering, and women were to wear yellow shawls whenever they set foot outside the ghetto walls. Having completed his proclamation, the herald departed with all due pomp and solemnity, leaving us relieved and elated.

Many of our congregation had already departed. Some returned, but others had settled elsewhere, while newcomers arrived, fleeing persecution in other lands as the Inquisition raged on. Daniel and I decided to remain in Venice, where we still had many friends. Everyone in the ghetto was confident the condotta would again be renewed after five years, as had happened so often before. Even when the government announced the Jews would be banished from Venice, they dared not carry out their threat. Veronica Franco was right. The government of the Republic might despise us, but they could not survive without our taxes, and our loan banks which prevented an uprising of insolvent young patricians. Our future in Venice secure, we agreed to risk investing my inheritance in a business of our own.

As it turned out, opening a print shop cost significantly less than Daniel had estimated. With many other printers having closed, necessary equipment and supplies of paper and ink were readily available at reduced prices, and Daniel's former colleagues were happy to join him in his endeavour. Employing experienced printers accustomed to operating as a team, Daniel quickly gained a reputation for running the most reliable print shop in Venice, while my mending was in constant demand.

With sufficient income to rent spacious lodgings, we moved to a larger apartment two doors away from Hadassah. The old woman from the Ghetto Vecchio came to live with Hadassah, who cared for her for the rest of her life.

'Nothing is too good for a woman who saved Abigail's life,' Hadassah replied, whenever the old crone protested that she did not deserve her good fortune.

My uncle's travelling days were over, and he came to live with us. Hadassah did not want to move from her own apartment, but she joined us at our table every evening, and gradually came to spend more time cooking for my family than I did. She chopped and seasoned and stirred, while I sewed, and we chatted companionably together.

'What on earth do you two find to talk about every day?' my uncle asked us one evening as we all sat together around the table.

'There is no shortage of gossip in the ghetto,' Daniel replied.

'We do not waste our time in idle gossip,' Hadassah retorted indignantly. 'Intelligent women like myself and Abigail have loftier matters to discuss.'

In truth, we talked mostly about our neighbours' affairs, but I did not contradict Hadassah. It had not escaped my attention that she seemed keen to impress my uncle, even though she denied the suggestion hotly when I questioned her.

With more than enough money for our modest needs, we never made the journey back to Polotensk to recover the rest of Reuven's money. When my sister visited us, I told her about the treasure hidden beneath the house in Polotensk where I had been so unhappy. I do not know if she ever went to find it. In addition to supporting the poor of our community, we made an anonymous donation to a charity set up by Veronica Franco, to support fallen women. But we were careful to put a substantial amount of Reuven's money aside, aware that our future security would always rely on the protection of our capricious Christian rulers.

Two years later, Hashem blessed our union with a healthy son. Daniel had already raised a son and a daughter, but Saul was my first child and he brought me a joy I had not felt before. Every day I thanked Hashem for guiding my steps to Daniel. Truly I had done nothing to deserve such good fortune. Yet my happiness was tainted by a sadness I sometimes sensed in my husband. One evening I challenged him about it, but he merely shook his head and, forcing a smile, refused to share his sorrow. At last, he confessed the reason for his occasional melancholy. As he witnessed our little boy develop and grow, he could not help recalling the other son he had raised, a son he would never set eyes on again. With the passing seasons, the chance of our seeing Elia again grew ever more remote.

'He could be long dead. Such uncertainty is harder to bear than a painful truth. If I knew he was dead, I could recite the prayers of mourning for him and know his soul was at peace.'

'We must pray for him,' I replied, grieving that I could offer my husband no other words of comfort.

For now our lives were settled, and Daniel was pleased by the success of his business. He told me he would never abandon his print shop, or our home in the Ghetto Nuovo, but I suspected the real reason we stayed in Venice was that he still clung to the hope that Elia would return. If we left Venice, his son might never find us again.

48

One day, while Daniel was working at the print shop, I heard a knock at our door and opened it to find a well-built stranger standing outside. He put down his bag and greeted me by name, as though we were acquainted.

'It is good to see you looking so well, Abigail. But is this not the lodging of Daniel ben Elia?'

'It is my lodging too,' I replied, puzzled by his question. 'Daniel and I have been married for nearly five years.'

The stranger's expression of joy on hearing about our marriage took me by surprise. Even though I did not recognise him, there was a familiarity about him that bewildered me. He must surely have visited the ghetto before, because he seemed to know me. Gazing at him, I was embarrassed to admit that I could not recall who he was. His face was burnt by a distant sun which had bleached the colour from his long hair, his leathery cheeks bore the scars of many battles, and his nose had clearly been broken more than once. As I was wondering who this stranger could be, Saul toddled over to us. Before I could stop him, the stranger swept my son up in his brawny arms.

'Is this little man yours?' he asked, studying the child closely.

'He is.'

'And tell me, is he Daniel's son?'

'Of course he is Daniel's son,' I replied testily. 'Did I not just tell you we have been married for nearly five years? How old do you suppose my son is?'

Seemingly oblivious to my irritation, the man swung Saul high in the air. Usually shy with strangers, my son gurgled with pleasure and kicked his chubby little legs in glee. They both laughed, as though they shared a secret.

'Do you mind?' the man asked me, holding Saul close to his chest. 'May I take him to the Campo del Ghetto Nuovo to play?'

As I hesitated, Saul flung his arms around the stranger's neck and I was reluctant to tear him away.

'Very well, but be careful with him,' I said. 'He never walks, but runs everywhere, and has fallen more than once.'

'What is your name, little man?'

'His name is Saul, in memory of my father,' I replied.

'So, Saul ben Daniel, shall we go and play?'

We walked to the Campo del Ghetto Nuovo where the stranger began to throw Saul in the air, making silly noises to entertain him, exactly as Daniel might do. My little boy laughed uproariously, and I could not help smiling at their antics. I had not yet discovered the name of my son's new friend, when Daniel arrived home from work. Seeing the man playing with Saul, Daniel started and gaped, as though he was looking at a dybbuk. I felt a frisson of fear, although it was hard to believe that the laughing stranger was possessed by an evil spirit.

'Are you a blessed spirit sent from Hashem, or a fiend come to tempt me to evil?' Daniel whispered. 'Hashem preserve us from this spectre of my long dead father. What do you want with my son?'

'So you fail to recognise me, Father,' the stranger replied, his smile broadening. He placed Saul gently on the ground, and the little boy ran to me and clung to my skirt, watching.

'Father?' Daniel echoed, seeming perplexed, although the truth was clear. So warm and exuberant an apparition could not be a dead spirit, yet his unexpected return was almost too astonishing to believe.

'Yes, it is me, your long-lost son, Elia.' He laughed. 'I have come back. Have you forgotten me already, Father, or do you have no use for me now that this little fellow has taken my place at your table?' He leaned down and ruffled Saul's hair. 'I had no idea I had a brother.'

'Bruvver,' the little boy echoed, gazing up in awe at the stranger who had been playing with him.

More than five years had passed since Daniel last saw Elia, and in all that time he had sent his father no message. And now, incredibly, he was standing before us in the ghetto, laughing at our confusion.

Wordlessly Daniel stumbled forward and embraced him. 'Perhaps you are finally ready to settle down, my son,' he said in a voice that shook with emotion.

Elia gave a carefree shrug. 'Perhaps.'

'There is a job for a strong young man at my print shop,' Daniel said.

'Your master will not employ an unskilled worker,' Elia replied, with a shake of his head.

'He will,' Daniel replied, smiling. 'Trust me, he will.'

Elia crouched down, distracted by Saul, and did not hear Daniel murmur, 'You have my word on that, my son. I will not only offer you paid work, but I will train you to become a master printer, so that one day I can pass my business on to you. Not that you deserve it, you rascal,' he added, raising his voice. 'How could you stay away so long without a word to your father?'

'You look at me as though I am returned from the dead,' Elia said, straightening up. 'Did I not tell you I would come back one day?' He smiled. 'I suppose I was too busy swimming for my life to mention that, when we took leave of one another after the battle.'

'You know, your father never tore his garments to mark your death,' I said.

'Miriam would not allow us to mourn for you,' Daniel added. 'She insisted that, being your twin, she would have known if you were dead. Hashem be praised, you have returned to us, my beloved son. Blessed be the name of the Lord. Now come inside, sit, and after we have eaten, we will pray, and then we will talk.'

'Always with the prayers, Father,' Elia said.

'Is it not the power of prayer that has brought you home?'

'Was it your prayers, or my own two legs that carried me here?' Elia replied, laughing.

'I see we have much to talk about,' Daniel replied.

'And I have many tales to tell you, Father.'

His dark eyes glistening with tears of joy, Daniel led his two sons into the house. I had prepared dinner myself that day, a barley soup, and soft goose meat fried with onions, a favourite with Daniel, but hardly a morsel touched his lips. I did not mind that he barely touched the supper I had so lovingly prepared. Seated at my husband's side, one hand resting on my belly swollen again with child, I was content.

'Thanks be to Hashem, all my prayers have been answered,' Daniel said, as he gazed around the table.

And so had mine.

THE END

ACKNOWLEDGEMENTS

I am grateful to Jeremy Leigh, of the Hebrew Union College in Jerusalem, whose Jewish Journey to Venice inspired this story.

I would like to thank my publisher, Betsy Freeman Reavley, for her faith in Abigail's story; my agent, Bill Goodall, for his constant support and guidance; my editor, Clare Law for her advice; Tara Lyons for her kindness and patience with my technological incompetence; Shirley, Maria and everyone at Bloodhound Books.

My thanks also go to Sir Simon Shama for his kind permission to quote him on the title pages.

A NOTE FROM THE PUBLISHER

Thank you for reading this book. If you enjoyed it please do consider leaving a review on Amazon to help others find it too.

We hate typos. All of our books have been rigorously edited and proofread, but sometimes mistakes do slip through. If you have spotted a typo, please do let us know and we can get it amended within hours.

info@bloodhoundbooks.com

BIBLIOGRAPHY

BOOKS

Non-Fiction

A History of the Jews in Venice – Cecil Roth (Schocken Books 1975)

The Ghetto of Venice – Riccardo Calimani (Mondadori 2005)

Venice and its Jews – Donatella Calabi (Officina Libraria 2017)

Marking the Jews in Renaissance Italy – Flora Cassen (Cambridge University Press 2017)

The Jews of Early Modern Venice – Robert C Davis (John Hopkins University Press 2001)

The Jews of Europe and the Inquisition of Venice 1550-1670 – Brian Pullan (I.B. Taurus 1997)

A Feast of History – Chaim Raphael (Weidenfeld and Nicolson 1972)

Belonging, The Story of the Jews 1492-1900 – Simon Scharma (Vintage 2018)

The Jew in the Medieval World – Jacob R Marcus (Hebrew Union College Press 1999)

The Jewish People – Max Wurmbrand and Cecil Roth (Adama Books 1986)

A History of Judaism – Martin Goodman (Penguin 2019)

Jewish Journeys – Jeremy Leigh (Armchair Travellers at the BookHaus 2006)

100 Most Popular Jewish Communities – wikipedia contributors (Focus On 2018)

Venice and Environs Jewish Itineraries – ed Francesca Brandes (Marsilio Regione de Veneto 1996)

History of the World Map by Map – Peter Snow (Penguin 2018)

Background of Shylock – Cecil Roth (Review of English Studies, Oxford University Press 1933)

The Merchant – Arnold Wesker (Methuen 1983)

The Uskoks of Senji – Catherine Wendy Bracewell (Cornell University Press 2001)

Battle of Lepanto: Armada of the Cross (The New American 2003)

Galleys at Lepanto – Jack Beeching (Scribner 1985)

Best Guns – Michael McIntosh (Missoula Down East Books 1989)

Letters that Changed the World – Simon Sebag Montefiore (Orion 2018)

Women and Men in Renaissance Venice – Stanley Chojnacki (John Hopkins University Press 2000)

Women, Sex and Marriage in Early Modern Venice – Daniela Hacke (Routledge 2004)

Civic Ritual in Renaissance Venice – Edward Muir (Princeton University Press 1981)

Monte Di Pieta in Modern Scholarship – Renaissance and Reformation (Vol. 40, No. 4, 2019).

Scholastic Analysis of Usury – John Thomas Noonan (Catholic University of America Press 1957)

Rich and Poor in Renaissance Venice – Brian Pullen (Harvard University Press 1971)

The Sixteenth Century Italian Duel – Frederick R Bryson (University of Chicago Press 1938)

Diplomatic Gifts on Henri III's Visit to Venice in 1574 – Evelyn Korsch (Rhode Island UP 2007)

Cosimo de Medici and the Monte Di Pietro – Carol Bresnahan Menning (paper, Chicago UP 1989)

Religion and the Decline of Magic – Keith Thomas (Penguin 1991)

Physicians and Surgeons in sixteenth century Venice – Richard Palmer (Cambridge Journals 1979)

The Silk Roads – Peter Frankopan (Bloomsbury 2015)

The Diary of Samuel Pepys -

Cervantes in Algiers – Maria Antonia Garces (Vanderbilt University Press 2005)

Medieval Children – Nicholas Orme (Yale University Press 2001)

History of Thimbles – Edwin F Holmes (Cornwall Books 1985)

Encyclopedia of Historical Archaeology – editor Charles E. Orser Jr (Routledge 2002)

The Curious Cures of Old England – Nigel Cawthorne (Little, Brown 2005)

Elizabethan Treasures – Catharine MacLeod (National Portrait Gallery 2019)

Jewish Musical Traditions – Amnon Shiloh (Wayne State University Press 1992)

The Recorder – David Lasocki and Richard Grissom (Routledge 1989)

Sufism, Music and Society in Turkey and the Middle East – Anders Hamarlund (Routledge 2004)

Art Culture and Cuisine – Phyllis Bober (University of Chicago Press 1991)

Eat and be Satisfied, A Social History of Jewish Food – John Cooper – (Jason Aronson 1993)

Copyright in the Renaissance – Christopher LCE Witcombe (Brill 2004)

The Complete Costume History – Auguste Racinet (Taschen 2003)

A Pictorial History of Costume – Wolfgang Bruhn (A Zwemmer 1955)

Costume and Fashion – James Laver (Thomas and Hudson World of Art 2012)

Costumes du Marco – Jean Besancenot (Edition's la Croisee des Chemins 2000)

The Talmud – Arsene Darmesteter (Leopoldo Classic Library 2015)

King James Bible (Collins 2011)

Forms of Prayer for Jewish Worship, Days of Awe – Reform Synagogue of Great Britain

Holy Men and Hunger Artists – Eliezer Diamond (OUP 2003)

Climatic Variability in Sixteenth Century Europe – Christian Pfister & Rudolf Brazil (Springer 1999)

Nostradamus devant l'Inquisition en 1538 – Patrice Guinard (Books on Demand 2015)

The Honest Courtesan: Veronica Franco – Margaret F Rosenthal (Chicago University Press 2012)

Works of fiction

The Gondola Maker – Laura Morelli (Laura Morelli 2014)

The Midwife of Venice – Roberta Rich (Ebury Press 2012)

The Second Duchess – Elizabeth Loupas (Random House 2013)

Eliza Rose – Lucy Worsley (Bloomsbury 2016)

The Turquoise Ring – Grace Tiffany (Berkley Books, Penguin Group 2006)

IMAGES
"Children's Games" By Pieter Brueghel the Elder. Oil on
Panel 1560

WEBSITES
https://www.haaretz.com/jewish/1547-jewish-villagers-
massacred-in-italy-1.5424292
https://en.m.wikipedia.org/wiki/Pope_Julius_III
https://en.m.wikipedia.org/wiki/Leon_of_Modena
http://edizionicafoscari.unive.it/media/pdf/book/978-88-6969-
138-6/978-88-6969-138-6.pdf
https://www.jstor.org/stable/41166866?
seq=1#page_scan_tab_contents
https://www.kedem/manuscript-on-parchment-concerning-
rights-of-jews-in-ferrara-1550-31511/
https://dbs.bh.org.il/place/ferrara
https://www.encyclopedia.com/almanacs-transcripts-and-maps/
del-banco-anselmo
https://books.google.co.uk/books
http://www.open.edu/openlearn/medical-knowledge-and-
beliefs-renaissance-italy
http://www.open.edu/openlearn/the-italian-patient-health-care-
renaissance-italy
https://www.jstor.org/stable/pdf/43059382.pdf
http://borzykowski.users.ch/EnglYidDance.htm
https://stores.renstore.com/childrens-lives-in-the-middle-ages-
and-the-renaissance
http://www.renfesthq.com/renaissance-games/introduction-to-
renaissance-games/
https://stores.renstore.com/history-and-traditions/16th-century-
pirates-terrorized-the-adriatic
http://www.balkanhistory.com/uskoks_of_senj.htm
https://www.jstor.org/stable/

Bibliography

http://www.crystalinks.com/hair.history.html
http://www.vinetowinecircle.com/en/history/the-late-middle-ages-and-the-renaissance/
https://en.m.wikipedia.org/wiki/
History_of_French_wine#Influences_on_the_French_wine_indu
stry
http://www.slate.com/articles/arts/design/
2012/06/the_history_of_the_fork
https://wepa.unima.org/en/italy/
https://www.theaterseatstore.com/history-of-puppetry
http://www.hist-chron.com/MA/judentum-EncJud_judenfleck-u-judenhut-im-MA-ENGL.html
https://en.m.wikipedia.org/wiki/Turkish_bath#Morocco
https://en.m.wikipedia.org/wiki/Baldassare_Castiglione
https://en.m.wikipedia.org/wiki/Conquest_of_Tunis_(1574)